IGNITING EMBERS

IGNITING EMBERS

a novel by

KIRSTEN OLSON

Igniting Embers © Kirsten Olson, 2021

978-0-578-90200-5 (printed)
978-0-578-90201-2 (E-book)
978-0-578-90202-9 (audio book)

All rights reserved. No part of this publication may be reproduced, distributed, or transmitted in any form or by any means, including photocopy, recording, or other electronic or mechanical methods, without the prior written permission of the author, except in the case of brief quotations embodied in critical reviews and certain other noncommercial uses permitted by copyright law.

This is a work of fiction. Names, characters, businesses, events, and incidents are the products of the author's imagination. Any resemblance to actual events or persons, living or dead, is entirely coincidental.

Edited by
Jenny Watz
www.writeambitions.com

Published with
Manda and Friends LLC
www.mandafriends.com

Book cover and interior design by
HR Hegnauer
www.hrhegnauer.com

Thank you to all the individuals that have already read my story and have given me encouraging feedback. To name a few; Ayla Secor, Cameron Olson, Sydney Lyon, Lyndsi Leon, Naomi Aguirre, Cassie Horner, Jennifer Coody, and Cat Urso. Without your input and insights, I would never have been able to make my tale as clean and crisp as it is.

*Dedicated to my brother, Cameron Olson,
for his' inspirations and creative collaborations.*

NATASHA

It had been another long, taxing day on the unit. After working seven straight twelve-hour shifts, my body was starting to feel the toll it had taken. Although legends and stories fantasize my kind as never growing tired or weak, they are vastly inaccurate in their presumptions. Along with exhaustion, I started feeling the sharp, throbbing pain forming right in the center of the back of my skull, radiating all the way down my spine to my fingertips and toes. I hadn't had my needed fix in a few days, and I was starting to feel the effects wearing on my body. I hadn't had time to go hunting, and my supplier had been out of town for a few days.

I had been so preoccupied with the piercing pain in my skull that I didn't hear Tracy come up behind me. The short, bubbly girl with long, dirty-blond hair, and bright blue eyes, always had a cheerful smile on her face. It was pleasant, having such a happy, soft presence around during drudging days like today.

"Are you feeling OK?" she asked me with a concerned look.

"Yeah, I'm fine. Just a small headache," I said, trying to hide my grimace.

"I have some Advil in my purse if you want some."

With a grateful smile in her direction, I dismissed her offer. Advil wouldn't curb this penetrating pain.

Tracy was the only nurse in the unit who would make an effort to interact with me at work. It wasn't that any of the others knew what I was, but they all seemed to be intimidated or skeptical of me because I was new to the area and not homegrown. It didn't bother me. My kind typically avoided people altogether. The only reason I got a job amongst these people was that they fascinated me. Their obsession with time intrigued me. Unlike the standard romanticized versions of my kind, we were not immortal, although we could live for centuries. Time was never usually a concern for us. Humans, however, always wanted to make the best of the little time they had on this planet. They were always rushing through activities, not worrying about the consequences, trying to get to the top of a career as fast as they could, and doing dangerous, outlandish activities that landed a lot of those people in my unit. Working amongst them gave me a different outlook on life. It helped me remember not to take life for granted, as so many of my kind did.

Finally, it was six-thirty, and my relief arrived on time for once. Julie was a Black, short, lumpy, seasoned nurse who never smiled unless she was interacting with patients. I gave my quick handoff report to her without getting so much as a look in my direction.

As I started walking to the elevator, I felt the joyful energy radiating off Tracy before she even came skipping into view. "I'm so excited! I have seven days off, and Todd and I are going to spend a well-earned week's vacation together."

I wasn't much of a fan for small talk, but Tracy's constant enthusiastic energy was so palpable that I was always willing to lend an ear her way. Plus, she was the closest thing I had to a human friend. I liked spending time with her and talking with her. "And what do you and Todd have planned?" I asked with genuine curiosity.

She continued skipping. "A short getaway to a cabin in Mellville on the river. It's supposed to be beautiful!"

Her spirit made the corners of my lips curve into a smile. "If you are going into the woods, make sure you two are careful. I don't want to come into work one day and find either of you in one of the rooms." I playfully nudged her with my shoulder.

Although Mellville was a small town not far from here with little troubles, there were always the dangers of wild animals attacking people. "We will be safe. Todd is bringing his .45, and my dad gave me enough bear spray to scare away a pack of them."

With a low, soft laugh, I replied, "I'm pretty sure a group of bears is called a sleuth."

She rolled her eyes at me and smirked. "How do you know so many random useless facts?"

Because I have been alive for centuries and have had time to learn so many facts, I wanted to say, but unfortunately, it wasn't my place to tell her about my true nature, so I just smiled at her as we walked into the elevator.

After riding the elevator down together and hearing more of her planned vacation, I walked her to her car and then parted ways after giving her another speech about being careful up in the woods. Although Trendberge was a smaller city, it was still a bit of a dangerous place downtown around the hospital, especially for a young woman walking alone. When I could, I would always walk her to her car so no threats would ever jeopardize her well-being.

I made my way to my little gold crossover, and started it up. Once I got on the highway, I started a book on tape. My home was about a thirty-five-minute drive from the hospital, and I loved listening to a good story—especially the fantasy science fiction ones. Although I was living a somewhat mythical life myself, it was nice to get lost in an imaginary world after a long day at work.

My house was located out in the middle of nowhere far off the main road. It had a mile-long gravel driveway surrounded by forest on either side. I turned onto the long path leading to the house, feeling relief in knowing I was finally home. After I passed the tree line, I came into the clearing that surrounded my home and spotted a figure standing on the porch, arms crossed, leaning against one of the columns. Max was a tall, muscular, fair-skinned man. He had the typical amber eyes of my kind, and black hair styled in a crew cut. He was also a nurse who worked in the outpatient clinic on the first floor of the same hospital where I worked.

When I got out of the car, he jumped off the porch, skipping the stairs altogether, and started my way. "What took you so long? I have been waiting forever, and your sister already left," he said, giving me a toothy grin. He was constantly in a playful mood and was always trying to provoke me. Usually I was eager to dish out comebacks, but I wasn't in a mood for it right then.

I replied with a growl. "It must be nice working in a clinic where nothing happens, and you work a laidback nine- to-five day."

He laughed and gave my back a hard slap that made the splitting headache feel like lightning running through my body.

"Come on, lighten up. It can't be too bad up on the unit."

I turned and glared at him with every ounce of spite I could muster. "I can't deal with you right now. I need my fix, or I'm going to end up literally killing you."

At my threat, he backed off a little and put both hands in the air in an exaggerated surrender. "OK fine, fine. Let's go," he said, still smiling.

As I let the splitting sensation envelop my body, I instantly felt the empowering energy flow through me. It was second nature to me now—controlled, quick, fluid, and almost painless. When I was younger and less skillful, the change was almost intoxicating, as I let the wild, primitive side out, feeling all my muscles, bones, and tissue on fire all at once, almost losing control as the pain and pleasure hit me simultaneously. I was stronger and faster with better senses than humans in my typical day-to-day life form, but when I let my predatory side takeover, I was a completely different beast.

JAMIE

The sun hadn't yet peaked over the horizon as I pulled up to the station. There was a pink tinge to the clouds, turning the sky into a beautiful scene, almost like looking at a watercolor painting. My dad had told me when I was little about the old sailor's saying, "Red sky at night, sailors' delight. Red sky at morning, sailors take warning." I guessed it was an omen that a storm was on the horizon. I laughed to myself. What a silly notion to base the outcome of a day off of the color of the sky.

I sat in my car for a few minutes, mentally preparing for the day before I got out. I was one of the sheriff's deputies in our county. Most of my family had served in the military, either active duty or the reserves. When I was growing up, I had no desire to sign my life away and get shipped off to someplace I had no intention of living or visiting. I did, however, want to protect the people I loved and cared about. The next best thing in my eyes was working with the sheriff's department, fighting crime at home and having a direct connection to keeping my town safe. So far in my three-year career, I hadn't had to handle any abysmal crimes. Mostly just DUIs, the occasional teenager breaking in and entering, and some bar scuffles, but mostly the sheriff had me doing paperwork at the office. It was a pretty quiet town. Not much ever happened in Mellville.

I got out of my car and grabbed my coffee cup. As I walked to the front of the building, my cell phone rang. I looked at the screen and saw it was the sheriff calling. *What the hell was he doing calling me so early?* He usually wasn't even awake yet.

I pushed the button to answer the call, but before I could even say a word, he blurted out, "Jamie, where are you?" His voice was frantic and brisk. He was always so composed, collected, and in control of his emotions. I had never seen him falter from his normal unyielding persona before, so his tone made the hair on the back of my neck stand up. I felt the instant adrenaline surge through my body, my heart pounding so hard and fast that I could hear it in my ears.

Before I could answer his questions, I heard him speak again. "I need you to get to the cabins on the river now!" His voice was rapid. I couldn't even get a response in before he hung up. Instinct took over me. I pivoted on my heels and sprinted to the cruiser in the parking lot, flung open the door, and threw myself in. After the car's engine roared to life, my foot pushed the acceleration pedal to the floor, and I peeled out as fast as the car would allow.

The park where the cabins were located was only a ten-minute drive, but it was just enough time for a feeling of gut-wrenching dread to set in. Something terrible must have happened to get under the sheriff's skin like that. The entire ride there, my fear and unease grew, not knowing what I was about to face at the cabin.

As I drove up to the park, I realized the sheriff hadn't given me a cabin number, so I drove down the main back road till I got a small glimpse of his '89 grey Ford pickup truck. I turned and parked by his vehicle. The cabin was surrounded by trees that cast long, dark shadows over the building in the twilight of the early hour. No lights in the cabin were on, and I couldn't see the sheriff anywhere. I took three long, deep breaths before jarring the cruiser door open and getting out.

Once I got out, I drew my issued 9mm. Usually having a weapon of any kind in my hand put my mind at ease, even just a little. But now it didn't calm my nerves at all. It was way too quiet for me. I took long, swift strides to the front door that was already wide open. I was on high alert. I could feel the small tremble in my hands as my adrenaline spiked and the knot in my stomach grew.

As I got closer to the cabin, I could see through the open door that it was almost pitch black inside the front room, so I pulled out my flashlight. Right when I took my first prudent step across the threshold, a thick, putrid smell hit my nostrils like a physical entity. It was so strong that it took my breath away.

I knew the smell of blood from the many times I went hunting with my dad, having to field-dress a deer or elk out on the mountains and carry it back. It never really bothered me then, probably because of the open space and natural breezes that carried the scent away. However, this was in a confined space and had a musty, spoiled, decaying stench along with the signature metallic smell of blood.

It took a second for me to recover from the initial odor, but when I was ready, I started breathing through my mouth. I got back into my defensive position with my 9mm at the ready and the flashlight pointing in front of me. As I scanned the room, within seconds, the beam of light landed on the source of the stench.

I felt the color drain from my face. Dizziness took over, and a cold sweat instantly lined my brow. I lost all composure of my body, going weak in my legs. I felt the wretch start to make its way up as I fell to my knees. Not having eaten breakfast or getting any of my coffee down, my retching came up as a loud, dry heave. I was light-headed and felt like I was going to hyperventilate and faint. Out of the corner of my eye, I saw a rapid beam of light coming out from the bedroom. All of a sudden, a large, strong hand grabbed around my right bicep and hoisted me to my feet.

The next thing I knew, Sheriff Davis was in front of me. "I know it is a lot to take in, but we don't have time for queasy feelings right now. Take a couple of deep breaths and follow me." Then he was gone again, back into the bedroom.

I did what he said and took two or three long, deep breaths to center myself and regain control. I headed in his direction. The body I had initially seen in the front room appeared to be male from what I could tell at first glance. The body was completely mangled, and its limbs contorted in so many ways that bones jutted out in more places than I could count. The left arm hung loosely at the body's side as if something had ripped it off, the torso completely disemboweled with the inners strewn all over the body and the ground. There was a vast concave area in the neck like something had taken a bite out of it. The face was swollen and bruised like it had taken a beating before the more gruesome events took place. And there was an immense amount of blood surrounding the body.

I put that image in the back of my mind as I walked through the door to the bedroom. I saw the sheriff kneeling on the floor and heard him whispering, almost cooing. I slowly made my way around the bed to see what he was doing. In front of him, a young blond woman lay on her back. She looked to be in horrific condition. The sheriff held a towel over her left side above her hip and another over the spot that connected her neck and shoulder. There was a lot of blood on the floor, and the woman's clothes were blood-soaked. I couldn't tell if there were any other injuries. At the site the woman was in, I started to feel sick again. I stood there for a moment, afraid to move.

When the sheriff heard me next to him, he motioned me down with his head. I instantly took over, applying pressure on her side as it freed up his other hand to put more on her neck area.

His voice sounded low and exhausted. "She is still alive, but barely. I got a call early that someone heard loud screaming and gunshots coming from here, so I drove over to check it out. When I got here, I saw three shadows run off into the woods. I couldn't tell if they were animals or people."

I was shocked. "People?! What kind of person could have done this?"

The sheriff just shook his head slowly. "I don't know. I have to keep every option open. It doesn't look like forced entry, and as far as I know, most predatory animals can't just open doors." He took a long, tired breath in. "Life Flight should be here any minute. They are taking her to the hospital in Trendberge. I want you to meet them there and get all the information you can."

My brain was still trying to catch up with the conversation. The fact that a person could do this made my mind swirl and try to come up with a different explanation. "But what about here? The scene? Don't you need help with securing the scene and collecting evidence? Plus, what if those things come back?" Then I heard the faint sound of helicopter blades splitting the air in the distance.

"Chance is on his way. I need you to go to the hospital," he said in his usual definitive tone when questioned. I nodded at his order. I had so many things going on in my head about what had happened here. There hadn't been an animal attack this bad in years. Then there were the gunshots. Usually, that loud of a sound would scare off an animal. There hadn't even been an intentional murder in this town as far as I was aware. I felt a feeling of unease take over me. Can we protect our home from something this malevolent?

I looked out the window and saw the helicopter touch down. In seconds the medics were in the room taking over the first-responder duties. My job there was done, so I turned and walked out of the cabin without another word. When I saw the helicopter take off, I made my way to the cruiser to start driving to meet the young woman at the hospital.

NATASHA

It had been a relaxing couple of days off. But after working the seven straight twelve hours, two days didn't seem long enough. It did, however, give me the chance to replenish my supply so that I wouldn't get the extreme aching craving at work for a while. As I was driving to work, I saw the Life Flight helicopter flying up north. I was hoping they weren't going to pick someone up to bring to the unit today.

When I pulled up to the employee parking lot, I sat in my car and finished my coffee. Caffeine didn't have a physiological effect on my body, but I had grown to love the taste, and it had become part of my morning ritual. After I drained the cup, I got out of my car and grabbed my backpack and lunch cooler, then headed in the direction of the hospital.

When I got through the doors, I swiped my employee badge and headed to the elevator. I hit the button to my floor, and with a lurch, the elevator ascended. After the doors opened, I walked through and headed down the hall. My manager was at the other end and, when she saw me, she hastily made her way in my direction, waving me down. *Great,* I thought. Talking to this woman this early in the morning was not the way I wanted today to start. Delilah was a middle-aged woman. She was tall and thin from all the triathlons she did. She had beady little black eyes and a high-pitched voice that reminded me of a raptor scream from the dinosaur movies Max had taken an interest in recently.

As she got close to me, she said, "We have a patient coming in on Life Flight from Mellville. It looks as though some type of wild animal attacked her. We don't have much information. Just she lost a lot of blood with multiple severe lacerations. I want you to do one-on-one with her today. Set up room one and get ready." Without even giving me a chance to ask questions, she whirled around and left me standing there. I stood for a second and looked back at the elevator, debating if I should leave and never come back, but something in the back of my mind told me I needed to stay.

I went to the supply room and gathered all the equipment I needed and took it to room one, then set everything up and headed back out to the nursing station to wait for a phone report. It probably would be a while till I got a call, considering what time I saw the helicopter flying to Mellville. Once they picked the patient up, they would take her to the ER till she was stable enough to transport up here to ICU.

I texted Max and told him how amazing my day had started and was going to go. After about five minutes, he texted back. *You know you could always quit. It's not like you need the money.*

I huffed to myself because I knew he was right. If I did quit, I would always be set for life, but I liked working here regardless of the repulsive working circumstances sometimes. I sent him a GIF of a man sticking his middle finger up. He sent back a kissy-face emoji then texted back. *Well I hear the helicopter coming in. Good luck!* I laughed a little and shook my head. I needed all the luck I could get.

Knowing Life Flight had arrived, I went to the phone to wait for the call. It took about thirty minutes before the phone rang. I answered. "ICU, this is Natasha."

A familiar voice replied on the other end. "Nat, this is Gabe." Gabe was another nurse who worked in the ER. He was good friends with Tracy, so I had more than a few pleasant run-ins with the man. He was usually just as friendly and kind to me as well.

The tone of his voice set me on high alert. "What do you have for me, Gabe?"

I heard the pain in his voice, and the struggle to get out the next words. "It's Tracy. It's Tracy that Life Flight flew in." He finally was able to get the words out with a slight sob.

I was in shock. I didn't know if I could believe what Gabe was saying. "What do you mean, it's Tracy?" I asked, a little louder than I planned.

I heard him take a couple of deep breaths on the phone to try and gain his composure. "You know she and Todd went to the cabin for their vacation. I guess some kind of animal attacked them. She's in bad shape, Nat. She lost a lot of blood. They had to code her on the flight over here. Right now, she is tachycardic and hypotensive, but she is hanging on by a thread. We gave her two units of blood, and we have bolus normal saline going. She might need another unit or two, A positive, and has IV access in her right hand and forearm. She has two massive lacerations. One on her left abdomen and one on her left neck area. We are bringing her up now."

I was at such a loss for words that all I could get out was, "OK. I will be ready." I hung up the phone, but I was fixed in the seat. My head started swimming, and I started feeling the sharp pain in the back of my skull. I closed my eyes and grabbed the back of my neck. *Could this be happening?* My one true human friend that I had on this planet. The only person at my job who was compassionate toward me. I had never really been emotional, especially when it came to the lives of humans. This was a strange feeling, a sense of dread and fear. I hadn't felt those feelings in a long time. When you are at the top of the food chain, that rarely happens. But I was feeling it, feeling it not for myself but for a human. *How could this be happening?* Then a sense of determination washed over me. I was going to do everything in my power to save my friend's life. I pushed the fear away, as well as the now splitting pain in my head. I called the blood bank and ordered A+ blood to be delivered to the ICU STAT. After that, I ran to the elevator to wait for Tracy.

The elevator doors opened to reveal the dismal sight. Tracy was on the stretcher, already intubated. She looked even smaller than she really was. Her face was snow white. There was blood everywhere. I saw two large wound dressings, one on her neck area and one on her left side. They were already saturated in blood. There were other smaller lacerations all over her body, but her neck and abdomen were far worse. Her long blond hair was soaked in blood, and her clothes were askew. I could see the already forming bruises from where the nurse or paramedics had performed CPR in the helicopter.

When I got closer, I closed my eyes and took a deep breath in through my nose. Instantly I knew that no wild animal was responsible for this gruesome act. Although faint, the smell still lingered on Tracy. I knew without a doubt what had done this, and it set my teeth on edge and sent a crack of lightning through my body. I felt instantly overcome by my predatory instinct. It started to wash over me, and I felt myself beginning to lose the battle with control, fighting with myself—a struggle I knew I would lose in the end. I hadn't lost control in decades.

As it started to flood over me, I felt my muscles unwillingly become tight and ridged. I felt my conscious slowly giving way, and my heart started beating fast: I was losing grasp of my own body and mind. Reality became a blur because I was fighting so hard to keep in control. I was losing though, and I knew it. But then I was suddenly jerked by the back of my neck and thrown against the wall with such force that it jostled me back to consciousness. No one on the floor noticed, since they were too preoccupied with getting Tracy to the room.

Two strong hands grabbed both of my shoulders, and I knew it was Max. He shook me hard. "Fight it!" he said, as I focused on re-taking over my body. He violently shook me again. "Fight it! If you lose control, you could jeopardize us all. And think of the people you could kill," he hissed through a whisper.

As he talked me down, I felt myself regain control and I was back, but the pain in my skull felt like it was splitting my head in half. Tracy was dying, and all I could do at the moment was lean against the wall and clutch the back of my head. I grit my teeth, unable to move.

Then Max shoved a bottle into my hand. He whispered in a softer tone. "I heard it was your friend they brought in, and I thought maybe you could use some support."

I gulped down the entire contents of the blacked-out bottle and felt better within seconds. "Thanks for that."

Feeling the splitting pain dissipate, I stood up, wiped my mouth, and started following Tracy's caravan to the room I had set up earlier, with Max at my heels. As we walked, I didn't know if I should tell Max about my newly discovered information about what attacked Tracy. I knew he would ask later what was so unnerving that it would drive me to go on the verge of losing control. I trusted Max though, so I decided it would be best for him to know.

"It wasn't a wild animal, Max. It was one of our kind. I have never smelled whoever it was before." He grabbed me again to stop me and looked at me with wide eyes. Before he could say anything, I said, "We will talk about it later. Be on your guard! I need to help Tracy and maybe find out more about what happened." He looked at me, perplexed, as I turned and ran to the room.

We were able to get Tracy a little more stable. Even though we treated every patient with the best care we could provide, everyone in the unit was working at their best because Tracy was one of our own. After we got three units of blood in her, we started seeing a little positive progress. Even though her vital signs were still not within limits, they had improved since she had come in. Her labs had slightly improved as well. I hadn't left her room since she was brought in. One of the reasons I was so worried was because her status could deteriorate rapidly with the amount of trauma she had sustained. The other reason had me a little more on edge. I observed her for signs of a change in her humanity. A bite from my kind could change a human, but it had to be a meaningful and purposeful bite with the intent of changing someone. Usually, it was excruciating pain for both parties. So far, it looked like it was just a vicious senseless attack. It made me angry, but I didn't have the energy or time to let those emotions boil over to the surface. I had to make sure I could do my best to help Tracy.

I pulled my chair to the head of Tracy's bed, and continually checked her statuses. After the initial panicked frenzy I was in earlier trying to get Tracy stable, all my senses were focused on her. I was in a kind of tunnel vision state of mind. When I was younger, I was taught never to let one thing distract all my senses at one time. It left you open and vulnerable to your environment. I have only gotten that way a couple of times in my life, where I would tune everything out and focus solely on one thing. I had cursed myself when I let this happen before. Earlier today, I didn't care that my environment was an invisible field to my senses. I was intent on saving my friend. Now that things had calmed down, I was able to extend my senses and observe my environment from afar as I usually did. Over the loud sounds of the machines working to keep Tracy alive, I was able to hear two sets of footsteps heading toward room one from my manager's office.

As they approached, a scent filled my nose so pleasant I thought maybe I had dozed off and was dreaming, considering the smells in a hospital were never enjoyable. I knew they were at the door before there was even a knock. The overwhelming scent emanated from one of them. I turned at the rap on the door, and standing there next to my manager was a woman, one of the most beautiful women I had ever seen in my life.

All I could do was sit and stare in an awestruck stupor. I saw my manager's mouth moving but purposefully blocked out every single word she was saying. I wanted to take in everything about this new person. She had my full attention. Even though she had her uniform trousers on, they fit tight, and I could tell her legs were firm and muscular. Her hips curved out and back in at the perfect rounded angle, meeting with her petite waist. I had never found any type of officer uniform flattering in the slightest, but she filled out the top perfectly. I could see her breasts pressed tight against the blouse, but not so much as to be unprofessional. I could see her pulse jumping along her slender neck. Her arms were folded across her stomach in a protective gesture. I could sense fear, uneasiness, and exhaustion radiating off her in waves, and, at that moment, for some reason, every impulse in me wanted to grab her in a protective embrace.

Her pink lips pursed together, and the corners slightly turned down. Her dark brown hair was slicked back into a work bun. Her face was pale, and when her light brown, almost golden, soft eyes met mine, I felt a sudden penetrating jolt in my chest that made me catch my breath. When I focused more on her eyes, I could see all the distress and weight she was carrying. I could see her fear. She had been through something extremely traumatizing very recently.

I immediately stood, now trying to focus on the sounds my manager was making with her mouth. "Did you hear me, Natasha?" I glanced at her and saw the annoyance in her face. "This is Deputy Jamie Stone. She has some questions for you about Tracy." And without another word, she turned and quickly walked back to her office. I glared at her, hoping she could feel the piercing daggers my eyes were sending in her back.

Finally, I looked back at Deputy Stone. There was another smell under her intoxicating aroma. I took another silent sniff and realized it was Tracy's blood I smelled on her. That made me tense a little. How did she have the scent on her? Our eyes met again, and that same sensation hit my chest like a bolt of electricity. She was something to behold. I had never experienced this sensation before. It was as though I was hypnotized or under a trance. I couldn't help but stare even when she looked away uncomfortably.

She was the one to break the silence. She cleared her throat apprehensively and asked, "Could I ask you a few questions?"

I shook my head as to break the daze I had been trapped in. "Yes. Of course. What can I help you with?"

"Well, like your manager said, my name is Deputy Stone. I work up in Mellville. I was one of the first people on the scene of Miss Young's attack and was told you are her nurse today, and that you were close to her." She looked a little unsettled at my staring.

That's how she got Tracy's blood on her. I wonder if she saw anything unusual at the scene. Without waiting for her to say anything more, I asked, "What exactly happened? She was going away for a few days with her boyfriend…" I trailed off, remembering that Todd should have been with her. "What happened to Todd? Is he OK?" I blurted out without thinking. She looked away, grabbing her arm with her other hand and holding it close to her body. She bit her lip nervously, which accented a deep dimple on her cheek that made my heart flutter a little.

What was wrong with me? My friend was barely hanging on to life, and her boyfriend was MIA, and here I am, getting the butterflies over this human girl, no less, and I didn't even know her. I started to get frustrated with myself. I never lost control of my emotions, and it had happened too many times today. In a frustrated huff, I asked, "Where is Todd? He would never leave Tracy alone."

She exhaled a shaky breath and looked down at her deputy-issued boots. It was clear she had never had to do something like this before. Finally, she took a deep breath in and brought her eyes back up to meet mine. "I'm sorry, but the case is ongoing, and I can't share those kinds of details." She did this with uncertainty as if she didn't know she was giving me the right information. Her eyes quickly darted away again.

I raised one of my eyebrows in surprise at how bold she was to deny me as she had. I let out a little frustrated huff and said, "Well then, Deputy Stone, if you can't let me know the status of a friend, I know nothing about my patient's personal life or the events that have come to pass, and this will be the end of our conversation."

At my response, her eyebrows furrowed in confusion as if I said something in a foreign language. My frustration kept growing, so I decided I needed to take myself out of the situation before things escalated.

As I turned to take my seat, I caught sight of the deputy's hand reaching for mine. "Wait! I'm sorry." Her hand lightly grasped my wrist to stop me from turning away. It was the softest, warmest touch I had ever felt. It sent heat radiating through my arm to my chest.

I turned around and looked into her pleading eyes. "I'm a little new to this and don't know protocols very well. This is my first assignment so far from home. I'm a little frightened at what I saw this morning. Please forgive me." Her soft, trembling voice and defeated look took me off high alert, and all my frustration melted away, replaced with guilt. I had been an ass and taken out my frustration on her. I felt sympathy for what she must have seen. I hadn't even considered that she had never witnessed something this gruesome before.

I pulled up another chair and gestured for her to take a seat. When she did, she dropped in the chair with a slump, and I saw all the tension and exhaustion flood out onto her face. She set her notepad on the ground under her chair, and without looking at me, she brought both hands up to her face and started rubbing her eyes, and then bowed her head down a little like she was trying to erase something horrifying she had seen. "Todd didn't make it. He was gone when I arrived at the scene," she said in a quiet, fragile voice.

When she removed her hands from her face, her eyes seemed to glisten a little as if she were holding back tears. It took everything in me to not jump up to comfort her, but I held fast.

"Do you have any idea what happened?" I asked with a sympathetic tone.

She let her hands fall to her thighs and let out a long, exaggerated breath. "We think it was an animal attack. But there is evidence that humans could have been responsible. We are trying to figure out what or who we need to be looking for."

I could tell this was taxing on her. She seemed emotionally drained, and I felt the same way. I decided to give her as much information about Tracy's status that I could. "Well, you won't get much from Tracy for a while. She will be kept sedated until she becomes more stable, but I guarantee that no one had it out for her. She was caring toward everyone and had no enemies."

Before I even knew it, my hand was moving on its own in her direction. My heart started to flutter, and when I gently set my hand on hers, the warmth and softness made my heart feel as though it would jump out of my throat. I couldn't believe I just did that. "We can talk more tomorrow if you would like. After you have gotten some rest and processed the events of this morning." Instead of pulling away like I expected her to do, she looked at me, and I saw a thankful gleam in her eyes. She gave me a small smile, the first smile I had seen from her, and it was captivating. It highlighted the dimple even more, and I had every intention of taking this woman right there for my own. But I knew I had to restrain myself. She was a human, after all; one I had just met.

"Thank you. I will come back tomorrow to check on Tracy and see if I can get more information. Here is my number if you can think of anything else." She pulled out a smaller notepad, scribbled her name and number on a page, and ripped it out. When she handed it to me, she sheepishly said, "I'm sorry I don't have any cards. I'm just one of the deputies."

I gave a low, soft laugh. "It's no problem at all. I will call with any updates." With that, she gave one last smile and exited the room.

JAMIE

I clutched my hand to my chest; the warmth of her touch still lingered there. It was a small comfort from the events that had transpired earlier in the morning. Natasha had a mysterious aura that surrounded her. She had a very powerful, almost commanding persona, but also had a softer, gentler charisma. When her eyes were transfixed on me, it felt as though she was reaching inside my very being, unfolding my actuality layer by layer, like she could perceive what I was feeling and thinking. I didn't know how it made me feel—unnerving yet reassuring at the same time. Her piercing, dark honey-colored amber eyes with flakes of red, a color I had never seen before, glowed almost as if the sun was reflecting off petrified tree sap. They scanned over me like they were trying to find some explanation to an unanswered question.

I was slightly taller than the average woman, but she stood an entire head taller than me. Her well-defined, chiseled arms, I imagined, matched a well-sculpted body underneath her loose-fitting scrubs. Her dirty blond hair was pulled back into a ponytail, but I could see that it was thick and wavy as it ran down to the small of her back. There was no sign that any blemish had ever invaded her face. Her eyes, nose, cheekbones, and mouth were in perfect symmetry as if Michelangelo himself had molded her. It felt like I had been graced with the presence of a Greek goddess, or maybe it was just my exhaustion playing tricks on my mind.

Although I was captivated by this new woman I had just encountered, I was feeling the entirety of the day weighing heavy on my shoulders. My muscles were aching, and the anticipated crash from my adrenaline rush was starting to catch up with me. I trudged to the elevator and got inside, hit the button for the first floor, and waited as the elevator descended.

I walked out of the hospital, still with so many unanswered questions about what had happened earlier. Tracy was barely alive, so I knew we wouldn't get any answers soon. I was so lost in my thoughts that I didn't initially notice the figure lingering near my car. I was on the opposite side of the street, but when I looked up, I saw a man taking a particular interest in my cruiser. He looked up and saw me staring at him, and I froze, initially wondering what the man was doing. I was about to run across the street to question his intentions when the loud horn of a bus stopped me. I was so startled I almost fell backward on the ground. After the bus passed, I looked back in the direction of the cruiser, but the figure had disappeared.

I crossed the street and cautiously approached my car. I circled the cruiser, looking for any signs of foul play. I looked in the back seat to see if there were any stowaways, but it was empty. Then I knelt to one knee on the asphalt to look below the undercarriage. As I poked my head down to start my scan, I felt a light hand touch down on my deltoid. The unexpectedness caused such a fright within me that my entire chest felt like it had collapsed from the tightness. I acted out of pure instinct. I grabbed my gun from its snug holster and turned around so fast it made me a little dizzy. I saw Natasha jump back with cat-like reflexes and throw her hands in the air as if she had just touched a hot stovetop. There was no sign of fear in her face, just concern directed toward me.

She looked at me with those burning amber eyes. Although it was overcast right now, the natural light made it look as though her irises were a dancing flame as she scanned my face with worry. "Whoa, deputy! I'm sorry I scared you. I didn't mean to sneak up on you. You just left your notebook in the unit, and I was trying to catch you before you left. I didn't know if you needed it for homework tonight or not."

I let out a loud sigh of relief and dropped my hands to my side. I clicked the safety on my gun and holstered it. As I did this, Natasha lowered her arms and reached out to give me my notebook. When I grabbed it, my fingers brushed against hers. I saw the faintest flush of her cheeks. *Did she just blush when I touched her hand?* At that thought, I felt my cheeks starting to become warm, so before I was full-on blushing, I broke the silence. "I didn't mean to pull my gun on you. I'm sorry. I saw someone when I was coming out of the hospital taking a particular interest in my car. But by the time I got here... it's like he just vanished. I thought maybe you were him."

A look of puzzlement spread across her face. Her body became rigid. Her perfectly shaped lips pressed together in a hard line. A crease formed between her eyebrows, and she started scanning the parking lot. It almost looked like she was smelling for something, or maybe she was taking deep breaths to calm herself from having a gun pointed at her. I couldn't tell, though. "What did the guy look like?" she asked, still intently scanning the area.

"I don't know. I only saw the guy briefly because I was on the other side of the street. White hoodie, baseball hat, and aviator sunglasses. That's all I could make out." I was staring at her inquisitively, wondering why she was interested in the man.

Her eyes finally became level with mine again. Her features finally relaxed. "I'm sure everything is fine. Probably just some thug curious about what a sheriff's cruiser was doing here. But still, be safe on your drive back home." She smiled at me.

"I will be. It's not too far of a drive, and the roads aren't bad at this time." I smiled at her in return. It was comforting that she was worried about my well-being. There was an awkward moment of silence between us. I didn't know how to part ways with her. The internal side of me did the most natural movement I felt at the time. I stood on my toes and wrapped my arms around her neck in a quick hug. I always gave people hugs, and even though she was a total stranger, she had given me comfort and a little bit of stability on one of the worst days of my life. I felt her entire body tense up at my sudden embrace. Alarms started going off in my head like I had done something wrong. It took a few moments until I felt her body relax slightly and wrap her arms around my waist cautiously. I released my embrace after a few seconds. Instead of drawing this moment out and making her feel more uncomfortable than I had already made her, I gave her a parting smile.

"Thank you again. I will see you tomorrow." I opened the door and plopped myself in the driver's seat. She gave me one last look and headed back toward the hospital. I hope I hadn't just made a fool out of myself in front of her. I was always doing awkward things in front of pretty girls.

Before I started the car, I decided to call Sheriff Davis and give him what little intel I had received. When he answered, I could hear the weariness in his voice. It had been a long day for everyone. "How is the girl? Did you find out anything useful?"

I couldn't hide the fatigue in my own voice when I replied. "Her name is Tracy Young. She works as a nurse at the hospital." The sheriff let me finish my report without interrupting once. "She went into cardiac arrest on the helicopter ride, but they were able to revive her. After she was taken to the ICU, they were able to stabilize her a little. She is sedated, so I wasn't able to get any information from her. She looks in rough shape. I was told she has no enemies and that no one would ever consider hurting her. She was nice to everyone." I finished my report, trying to remember as many details as I could.

"Alright. We may have found some evidence at the scene. Head to the station, and I will go over it with you. It shouldn't take long," he said with a course gruff. Then I heard the line go dead.

With a long exhale, I lowered my head to the steering wheel and grumbled to myself. The last thing I wanted to do was go to the station and relive the gruesome morning I had. Why couldn't this wait until the morning when I was fresh? With a slow unwillingness, I put the cruiser in drive and pulled out onto the road.

It was too quiet in the car, which gave my mind the capability to wonder over all the day's events that had transpired, and I didn't want to be thinking right then. I rolled down the window to let the cool, late afternoon breeze flow over my face. I turned the radio on and the volume up. I needed to clear my mind, and that was working. The drive seemed too short. I was lost in my own world, away from all the troubles and strife that had occurred that day.

I pulled into the station's parking lot, and the only cars that I could see were the sheriff's grey truck and my Bronco. I parked the cruiser in the closest spot to the door and got out. Slowly I willed my legs to move toward the station. When I got to the front door, I forced my arm to pull the door open, wanting to be anywhere but here. The sheriff wasn't in the main office, so I walked back to his office. His door was shut, so I gave it a soft knock. He beckoned me in with a low, grumbled voice.

I quietly opened the door, and cautiously made my way to his desk. His body was leaning over his dark brown, heavy oak desk with the heels of his hands pressed to the surface, holding himself up. There were pictures scattered all over the desktop. I had to avert my eyes when I glimpsed the distorted body of Todd.

Without even lifting his head to look in my direction, the sheriff started giving me his brief, almost sounding like he was talking to himself. "I don't think it was a wild animal attack. Like I said earlier, there were no signs of forced entry. An animal that could do this kind of damage wouldn't be able to open a door. Around the back of the cabin, I found tracks that look like human shoe prints. We found three bullet casings but couldn't find the bullets anywhere. Maybe the guy hit whoever or whatever attacked them. I put out a BOLO to all nearby medical facilities to report any recent gunshot wounds to us. The medical examiner says the bruises on the deceased's face were sustained before death. It looks like he had been tortured. Maybe when I drove up, I scared them off before they could finish the girl off. Forensics collected fingerprints and fibers from the scene. They said not to hold our breaths though, because so many people use those cabins." He then plopped down in his chair and ran his large, calloused hand through his short, peppered hair.

As he talked, I tried to absorb all the new information. I couldn't believe a person could do this. Dread spilled into every pore of my being. The sheriff must have seen the dismay on my face. He looked at me with a hard expression. "We can't falter right now. I know it's a little chilling knowing there is someone out there that would do this to another human being, but that means we have to put on our game face. We have to do our job and find out who did this, so it doesn't happen again. You signed up for this kind of thing, Stone."

I closed my eyes and felt my brows furrow together. My fists clenched at my sides, and I took a deep breath to try and center myself and push the fear away. Before I opened my eyes, I heard the sheriff speak again; this time his tone was a little lighter. "By the way Stone, you look like crap. Go home and get some sleep."

I still had blood on my uniform and parts of my body from helping Tracy this morning. I could tell he was trying to lighten the mood. So I threw up an exaggerated salute. "Yes, sir."

He shook his head with a slight smile. "Out with you, then."

With his approving dismissal, I headed out of the office. By the time I got outside, the sun had nearly disappeared over the horizon, with just a little sliver still admitting some light. On most days, I loved watching the awe-inspiring sunsets, but today the thought of impending darkness, brought on by night, sent a shiver down my spine. I quickly walked up to my Bronco and jumped in. I wanted to get to the safety of my house before darkness blanketed Mellville.

My home was only fifteen minutes from the station, so it didn't take me long to reach my familiar neighborhood. I pulled into my driveway as dusk transformed into the blackness of night. I quickly got out of my Bronco and raced to my front door, fumbled for my house key, then unlocked the door. I practically fell through the door when it opened, then slammed it shut behind me. I clicked both the deadbolt and door handle into the locked position. When I turned around, I slumped my back against the front door and let the weight of my body slide me to the floor. My head fell back against the door, and my eyes closed. I could have drifted off to sleep right there. I was so tired. Suddenly from the back room, I heard the unmistakable noise of plastic and metal thrashing together and then the sound of nails clicking hastily on the hardwood floor. I smiled and braced myself for the expected impact. I cracked one eye open and saw a big black mass fumbling down the hall.

Walter was my four-year-old black Lab I had rescued from the local Humane Society. When I first bought my house and moved in, I always felt lonely, especially at night. I wanted to share my home with another. Considering I wasn't dating anyone because my career took precedence over everything, I decided to get a dog. Plus, my mother thought it would be safer to have a dog around to guard me. Not that Walt had an ounce of malice in him. He would probably walk right up to an intruder, rope in mouth, asking for a game of tug of war. But that was OK. He was my boy, and I loved him.

When I went to the Humane Society to look for a companion, he was sitting in the corner of the kennel with his head bowed down, shivering. His ears were drooped down so low, and you could see his ribs and spine. He wouldn't even acknowledge anyone who spoke to him. When I asked the worker about him, they informed me his owner had abandoned him there. He was meant to be a hunting dog but would rather play fetch and roll in the mud than listen to commands. They also informed me that there were signs of neglect and that he had been abused. It was obvious by the appearance of this precious creature. I also found out no one would consider him because he showed no signs of affection toward anyone. I could understand why. So I started to visit every day, and I would sit in Walt's kennel. I would talk to him or try to get him to eat. I didn't try to touch him at first because I wasn't sure how he would react.

Five days after I had started my ritual of going to visit Walter after work, I had dozed off sitting in his kennel. I felt a wet, cold touch on my cheek, which startled me out of my slumber. I turned my head toward whatever had touched me and found I was staring at a black furry face and two big brown eyes. When I smiled at Walter, his tail started to sweep back and forth slightly, his mouth opened, and he started breathing a little harder. I expected this was an invite for a scratch. I lifted my hand slowly up and started scratching the scruff behind his ears. Then he laid his body down with his head in my lap and rolled to his side, asking for a belly rub. It brought a flood of tears to my eyes. This poor creature that had been hurt so bad in his life had grown to trust me enough to open up. That day I signed the papers, and he forever became my trusted companion.

I felt the impact of Walter and warm wet streaks all over my face. I had been gone longer than expected that day. I grabbed the big beast and pulled him to my chest, his kisses and the warmth of his thick, black fur were very welcoming. He started squirming more vigorously in my embrace the longer I held him, so I let him go. He jumped back and stuck his backside in the air with his two front legs and head on the ground, tail wagging so hard and fast his rear end was shaking. It was an invitation to play. Unfortunately, I was still tired from the day, so instead, I offered him something else he was equally as fond of. "Who wants a treat?" I asked in an exaggerated tone. Instantly he sat up, head cocked to one side, ears forward and tail swiping across the floor. I asked him again. "Who wants a treat?" This time, he started twisting in circles, jumping with his front paws in the air, working his way down the hall. He was leading me to the cupboard, where he knew his treats were stored.

After having Walt perform some tricks for his well-earned treats, I ate some leftover pizza from the night before, took a shower, brushed my teeth, put on shorts and a tank top, then slipped into bed. Walt was already lying in the bed, curled in a ball, head on the pillow. *What a spoiled dog you are*, I thought to myself. When I got in the bed, I said to him, "You know if I ever start seeing someone, you will have to start sleeping at the foot of the bed like a normal dog." He gave a big yawn and closed his eyes in response to my voice. "Yeah, I agree, that's not very likely." I turned on the TV and switched it to the Netflix app, starting the show I always fell asleep to, and clicked off the light. Right when my head hit the pillow, I drifted off into a restless sleep.

NATASHA

Every nerve in my body was alive with a burning sensation as I reached my unit. Humans had physically touched me before. It came with the territory of being a nurse. It had never affected me as it had after the deputy's embrace. Was this feeling genuine desire? Was it a sense of yearning? The deputy was bringing awareness to emotions I never thought I could experience in response to a human's affection. I wanted to release my predator side and run off the vigor I had built up. But I knew I couldn't right now, even though this feeling of the unknown was setting me on edge.

I reached Tracy's room in a rush. Her status hadn't changed since I left. *At least she wasn't getting worse*, I thought to myself. I started pacing the room. I couldn't sit down, not with all this extra pent up restlessness inside me.

I was thankful it was almost shift change. I had to get out of this environment. With all these new unclear emotions flowing through me, I needed to get away to clear my head. I needed to escape for a while. I also needed to talk to Max and Irene about the potential intruders we had to address. I was hoping Max hadn't said anything to Irene or Nik yet. I wanted to figure out who these newcomers were and what their intentions had been before jumping to conclusions.

I sat down in the chair I had brought in earlier. I rested my elbows on my knees and started rubbing my temples as if it would help release an answer to all of this hidden within my brain.

I felt a light touch on my shoulder. I already knew it was Julie. I smelled her repugnant perfume the moment she got off the elevator. She gave me a small, sympathetic smile but didn't say anything. Everyone knew Tracy and I had been close. I couldn't tell if it was because she knew I didn't want to talk about the events of the day, or because she didn't have anything to say. Regardless, I was grateful that the only words exchanged were the ones necessary for the handoff report.

I grabbed my backpack and headed out of the hospital. As I walked out of the side doors of the building, I could see my car across the street. A man stood by it, wearing a white hoodie, a ball cap, and aviator sunglasses. It looked like that man the deputy had described from earlier. I couldn't tell from this far away if he was a human or not. When I was by the deputy's car giving her notebook back to her, I couldn't smell or sense any of my kind around, but that didn't mean this man wasn't one of us. I put on the most chilling, unyielding faces I could mask and headed in the direction of my car. I didn't take my eyes off the man even once as I approached. I could tell right when I got across the street he was just a human. That thought made me relax slightly. As I neared my car, I saw the man's lips curve into a smile. He leaned back against the light pole that was next to my car on the driver's side and stared at me. A strange sense of confidence flowed off of him.

I opened my trunk and put my backpack in it. I was trying to pay the man no mind, but the arrogance radiating off him was starting to vex me. After I shut the trunk, I heard him shift and knew he was standing now.

He was still looking at me with a cocky smile that I wanted to claw off his face. If he only knew who he was messing with. In a low whisper and with extra spite, I asked, "What do you want?"

That made his grin even more prominent. "I don't want anything from you. I'm just a messenger. They have been watching you, Natalia Romanova Vasiliev. And now they are going to take quite an interest in your new little cop friend too. The one I saw you with today."

I felt my body go rigid at the sound of my birth name. My chest got tight, and I stopped breathing. I felt the lightning cracking in the back of my head. The predator was ready to lash out, but I reigned it in with as much self-control as I had. *How did this smug little prick know my real name?* Hardly any of my kind even knew that name belonged to me. It had been kept secret for decades for a good reason. Only a select few knew who I was. And to threaten the deputy on my behalf—I barely even knew her—lit a fire of rage within my very depths.

"I hope they also told you the weight behind that name and what it meant even to speak it. And I hope that wasn't a threat toward Deputy Stone, an innocent human. We just met today." I hissed at him through clenched teeth.

"Oh, they told me all about you. They told me everything. But like I said, I'm just the messenger. And as for Deputy Stone, she is just a human in their eyes. Your reaction to her earlier interested them, though." He shrugged his shoulders like it wasn't a big deal, still giving off that essence of egotism. He didn't grasp who he was dealing with and what I was capable of doing.

Whoever he was working for was dangerous if they knew who I was. They also knew how to cover their tracks, having humans do their deeds to hide their scent and whereabouts. They had probably promised him immortality, referring to the bite. Or protection from me. I knew they never would change him no matter what this human believed. He was collateral damage. He probably didn't even know where they were or what their true intentions were. He was just a simple messenger like he had said, so I wouldn't be able to get any information out of him that would be of any use to me. I straightened my posture and turned to look him square in the eyes with a fierce glare. I had seen my father use it many times. "You know, where I come from messengers are held accountable for the words they speak even if the message was originally from another's mouth. Speaking that name is very dangerous, especially in front of me, as is threatening an innocent human life." As I spoke to him, I scanned my surroundings. The parking lot was empty, and the enormous black Dodge truck parked on the passenger side of my car hid us from the road. This human knew too much, and he had hit a weighted nerve in the depths of my being.

His smile grew even broader, and he thrust his hands into his hoodie pocket. "Be that as it may, he is coming for you." He slid his glasses down his nose so he could look me in the eyes. "He will snuff out everything you hold dear and have ever cared about."

I felt a growl escape my throat. Then I moved so fast it took less than a second. I lunged, turning him away from me, and in the same motion, I wrapped my arm across his face, snapped his head back across his shoulder, and heard the fatal crack. He was dead before his lifeless body slumped into my arms. I quickly put his body into my back seat and buckled him in to make him look like a passenger. I did one more scan of the area to ensure no one had witnessed what had just taken place. Then I flung open the driver's door and got in. I slammed the door shut, then pounded my hands on the steering wheel.

I turned the key and sped out of the parking lot. I hated killing humans, especially innocent ones. It had been so long since I had killed one, and I had never done it without cause. I didn't know if this one had been an innocent person and just fell prey to whoever had filled his head with promises of power, long life, riches, or whatever else, or if he was indeed someone deserving of death. I had always felt it was not my place to judge a person's actions in life. Fate, in my eyes, would eventually catch up to everyone in the end and award them their just earnings.

In the past I had killed people, and every time it felt like ripping away a piece of my spirit. That is why some of my kind looked at me differently. They thought we were a superior race and that thoughts and energy shouldn't be wasted on the deaths of weaker, lesser beings. I didn't look at humans like that. They were just different, evolved down a different branch of the evolutionary highway. I didn't like thinking of myself as a monster, but so many of my kind reveled in that idea.

At that very moment, I wasn't very concerned about my moral compass. I needed questions answered. For the most part, humans were supposed to be kept unaware of our actual existence. This one was aware of what we were, and he was being used as a puppet by some twisted individual who knew the puppet's life would be forfeited after uttering my birth name.

I drove the entire ride home in silence. My thoughts were going in circles about the exploits that had occurred earlier in the day. My mind was exhausted, but my body was ablaze with a torrent of vitality I hadn't felt in many years.

As I pulled up the gravel driveway to my house, I saw Max sitting on the porch swing. Irene was sitting with him, her back against the side armrest, and legs extended over Max's lap. He was caressing the skin of her thighs, exposed from her running shorts. They were laughing about something and smiling at each other. I was delighted that my sister had found someone like Max because he worshipped the very ground that she walked. He was so reliable and trustworthy. I had no problem with them living together in my house. I was also put at ease since I knew I wasn't the only one now who would be looking after her well-being.

They both saw me pull up and simultaneously stood and started walking down the porch in my direction. I got out of the car and saw Irene's pace slow. She probably smelled the body that was being stored in my back seat.

"Hey sis, why are you driving around with a dead guy in your car?" She didn't stop her slowed pace till she came up to me and wrapped her arms around my neck. "Also, Max told me about your friend. I'm so sorry," she said with genuine sincerity.

My sister and I had always been close. She kept me grounded. She had followed me to Trendberge even when everyone urged her not to. It was a small place where protection was scarce, especially for two people like us. But she supported every decision I made and came with me.

We weren't actual siblings, we were actually cousins. Her father was my father's younger brother. As a result of an untimely catastrophic event, her parents were killed along with her two older brothers. My father took her in and raised her as his own. She was shorter than me, with dark brown hair. We did share the thick, wavy texture, although she kept up with hair grooming a lot better than I did. Her eyes were a lighter amber than mine, almost a golden color. Her face was thinner with sharper features than mine, and her lips were full and bright pink. Although her body was quite a bit more petite than mine, it didn't hinder the strength she carried behind her. I still would beat her every time we would spar or wrestle because her strength was no match for mine. She did, however, have a leg up on me with speed. She was faster than I was.

I gave her an appreciative smile in response to her compassionate gesture. Then I turned back to my car and gestured to the back seat with a nod. "He called me by my birth name," I said, with a gruff exhale. Both Max and Irene turned and looked at me with concern. "I don't know who he is. I have never seen him before, but he said, 'they were watching you' and 'he is coming for you.' Whoever he was working for knows who I am and isn't afraid to pull humans into our world." I let out another exhausted exhale.

"Do you think it has anything to do with the attack on your friend?" Max asked, still staring intently at me.

"Why would it have anything to do with the attack on Tracy?" Irene replied, looking from Max to me.

At her question, Max turned his gaze to me, awaiting permission to tell her about what I had said to him earlier. Instead, I closed my eyes and rubbed my face vigorously with my hand, trying to wipe away an unseen frustration within me. "Tracy was attacked by our kind. They didn't leave a great scent, but I could smell them enough. I had never sensed whoever it was before."

At this newfound information, Irene shoved Max in the shoulder. "Why didn't you tell me?" Irene asked, a sliver of agitation in her voice.

He spoke in wide-eyed defense. "I didn't want to worry you and..."

I cut him off because I could tell he was about to start floundering. "I asked him not to say anything to anyone till I found out more about the situation. I wasn't trying to hide it from you. I just wanted to know what we were dealing with before jumping to the worst scenario." Max let out a grateful sigh and nodded in my direction, thanking me for taking the heat off him.

At my response, a sly smile crept up at the corners of Irene's mouth. "And you think killing a human was not jumping to the worst scenario?" She was teasing, but there was a hint of concern in her voice. She knew I hated killing and how much it tore me up inside.

"I know. Maybe I overreacted, but I thought if someone knew who I was, they weren't stupid enough to tell him who or where they were or what their intentions were. So, I thought instead of torturing the guy for knowledge that wasn't there, I would put him out of his misery quickly. If they know me, they know you, and I refuse to let anyone hurt you." I clenched my fist, remembering that the man had said whoever was watching me would snuff out everything I cared about. I cared more about Irene than anyone on this earth, and I wouldn't let anything happen to her. "Was I wrong?" I asked, almost to myself, trying to find an approving answer to my crime. Now that I had said it out loud, a flood of guilt ran through me. *Did I act too quickly? Should I have not killed him?* My breathing started to increase. Unwillingly my feet started pacing me back and forth, and my hands shot to the back of my head. I was unraveling under the new regret that was beginning to weigh me down.

I felt a light hand wrap around my left bicep and stop me. Irene turned me to look at her. Her calming eyes and soft expression made me drop my arms to my side. I took in a deep, shaky breath. She took the sides of my face in her hands, pulling me to her, and then I felt her forehead meet mine.

"You didn't do the wrong thing. You made a judgment call. In my opinion, the right one. I know you have always struggled with the death of humans, especially at your hands, but he knew too much. I know you. I know you would never kill someone unless there was a true threat in your gut, and your gut is usually right." Irene gave me a soft, comforting smile. She always knew what to say, no matter the circumstance, to make me feel more content.

Even though I still felt a small feeling of guilt, I wrapped her in a firm embrace. "Thank you. You know just the remedy to calm me down."

Max walked over to us. "I think you did the right thing too, but now we need to figure out our next step to tracking these visitors down." At his comment, I crossed my arms and pursed my lips to one side of my face and started to chew at my cheek in thought. After a few minutes, I concluded that I would need to go to the cabin where Tracy was attacked. I didn't know if these were the same ones the human had been working for, but that was the only place I knew I could find a way to track newcomers in this area.

I turned to look at both of them, put my hands on my hips, and stated, "I am going to go to the cabin tonight where Tracy was attacked." I felt Irene's animated eagerness flow off her before the smile crept across her face. She was a bit of an adrenaline junkie and loved adventure. I saw her mouth start to open to express her excitement to join me, but I lifted my right hand to cut her off. "And I will be going alone."

She was always so dramatic. She let out a heavy, pleading sigh. "Come on!" She whined at me with the palms of her hands together in an imploring way. "This place is so boring, and I can never do anything fun! Please let me come with you?" she begged, giving me the most genuine puppy-dog eyes I had ever seen. She even took it so far as to get on her knees.

At that, I laughed and rolled my eyes. "Get up, Irene." I grabbed her under her arms to bring her back to her feet. "It could be dangerous," I told her.

"Even more reason for me to come with you! Power is in numbers, Nat. You can't deny that." She gave me a sideways smile.

I looked at Max for his support on the subject, but I wasn't going to get any from him. "Well, as little as I like your sister getting into dangerous situations, she is right. It would be better if you had some backup. While you two go check out the cabin, I will dispose of your friend's body so no one will find him."

I didn't like the fact that I could be putting Irene in danger, but it was better to have more than one set of eyes, especially on a mission like this one. We ended up settling with that. Irene and I would go to the cabin late into the night, and Max would meet up with us after he dumped the body. Thinking about Max taking care of the dead man started my mind wondering. I wondered if anyone would miss the man or if he had a family. What they thought may have happened to him. It made a slight twinge of guilt come back to the surface. I shook my head and decided it was probably best that they don't know what happened to him.

JAMIE

My dreams were plagued with horror and dread that night. I had been running from an unknown darkness. Fear blurred my vision, and my legs wouldn't move like normal. I couldn't run forward. It felt as if something was pulling my body to the ground. My legs were heavy as if they were trudging through deep dunes of sand. My veins protruded as I strained to move. I grasped at anything in front of me to help pull me forward away from the impending danger. I could almost feel its evil, menacing presence on my back. It sent a chill down my spine. My heart raced and pounded harder than it ever had. The last thing I remember seeing was molten amber eyes staring into the very depths of my center.

I felt my body lurch into a sitting position. I was breathing hard and fast, desperate to fill my lungs with oxygen. My tank top was saturated in sweat, and I felt my body shaking uncontrollably. As the hazy cloud of the nightmare faded and my conscious began to take over, I realized I was in my room entangled in the sheets. I could tell I had been thrashing in my unconscious state. One of my pillows was across the room on the floor, my comforter was kicked halfway off the bed, and my fitted sheet had come untucked from two corners. I was still a little dazed from sleep when I heard a low, deep, coarse growl. It sent an icy fear through me.

I grabbed my 9mm I kept holstered on my nightstand and turned on the lamp at the side of the bed. I turned in the direction the growl had come from. It had come from Walter. He was staring out of the window with his body stiff and rigid, haunches raised. His tail was erect behind him, and his ears pulled back, teeth bared. The curtains were pulled shut, so I couldn't see out of the window to investigate what was causing him to be on alert. It was very unnerving. I had never seen him like this. I could only think of one other time he had truly growled, and it was at a bear when we were walking in the woods.

I grabbed my phone, and it read 23:45. It wasn't even midnight yet. "Walter," I whispered low as if whatever was setting Walter on edge would hear me calling to him if I spoke too loudly. I got no response from him. "Walter!" I whispered with more intensity. He looked at me and dropped his threatening stance. "Walter, come here." I pointed to the spot next to me on the bed. He whimpered, took one last look at the window, then jumped on the bed and curled up next to me. He was still looking at the window, and I could feel his body still tense.

I had propped myself up a little on my pillow and had one arm around Walter. I petted him to try and soothe him. It was more for me to try and calm myself down. I thought about turning the TV on, but I wanted to listen and see if I could hear anything out of the ordinary coming from outside. Eventually, Walter's body relaxed, and I felt his feet start to twitch and heard him let out sleeping barks.

Walter may have been calm enough to fall back to sleep, but I was still a little on edge. I decided to get up and get a glass of ice water. Maybe that would help calm my tension. I got out of bed and made my way out of my room. I turned the hall light on and headed toward the kitchen. I still had a feeling of uneasiness in my gut, so I scanned the room before grabbing a cup from the cupboard and filling it with ice and water. Leaning back against the counter, I took a long sip. It felt good as the cool liquid trickled down my throat. I didn't realize how parched I was. Probably from sweating so much during the night.

Still scanning the room, I glimpsed my work notebook sitting on the dining table. I shrugged to myself. I guess since I was too anxious to sleep, I might as well go over it. I made my way over to the table and started going over my notes. The little intel I had jotted down didn't help me at all. I let out a huff and pushed it away in a bit of frustration. Closing my eyes, I tried to think back to everything I saw at the cabin site earlier to try and remember anything I had missed. All I could remember was the darkness of the cabin, the smell of death, and the intense fear at seeing the state of Tracy and Todd. My mind had been closed off to the environment around me. Eventually, I gave up. I had so much adrenaline earlier that I wasn't focused on my surroundings as much as I wished I had been. I couldn't remember anything useful, so I folded my arms on the table and put my head down.

I heard the click of nails on the hardwood. Walter sat next to my chair and put his head on my lap, so I sat up and looked at him. He wagged his tail at me, so I scratched behind his ears.

I was wide awake now and knew I wouldn't be able to fall asleep. Maybe since my head was clear, it would be an excellent time to go back to the crime scene to see if the sheriff had missed anything. I knew he probably hadn't, but I wanted to see for myself. It was the middle of the night, and the sheriff probably wouldn't be happy about it, but I was alert and knew if I just stayed at home, I wouldn't sleep because of whatever Walter had been growling at. I felt a little trapped in the house anyway.

After I dressed, I went to the door and slumped onto the ottoman. I laced up my hiking boots, grabbed my car keys, and Walter's leash from the hook. After I leashed Walter, I waited, still a little scared to walk outside for fear of whatever had spooked him. I looked down at Walter, waiting for his defensive stance to take over again. A slight ease spread through me when all he did was look at me and wag his tail. His legs were even dancing beneath him. I was content now that he was just excited about the walk.

I opened the front door and we made our way into the fresh night air. I turned and locked the door and ran to my car, still unsure about what was waiting for us in the dark. I opened up the driver's door to the Bronco and Walt jumped inside. He walked straight over to the passenger seat. I hopped in after him and immediately locked the door. After I turned the key and the engine roared to life, I clicked on the headlights and, out of my peripheral vision, I was sure I saw a shadow scurry into the blackness. I quickly looked over at Walt to see if he noticed it, but he was only panting in excitement, looking out the passenger window, waiting eagerly for the window to get rolled down.

After seeing his relaxed posture, I shook my head and thought that it must have been a little nocturnal animal or my imagination. Walter wasn't bothered, so I put the Bronco into reverse and pulled out of my driveway. Once I was down the road, I rolled down the windows. The cool, fresh night air felt good on my face.

As I drove, I noticed that every house we passed had the lights off. They were all soundly sleeping. I wondered if any of them knew yet about the horrific tragedy that had happened in this tranquil little town. The sheriff was trying to keep it quiet, at least until tomorrow.

My house was about twenty minutes away from the park where the cabins were located, so I decided to leave the radio off to focus. Walter had his head sticking out of the window, his tongue hanging out of his mouth and flapping in the wind. He turned and looked at me. It almost looked like he was smiling. Walter loved his car rides. It caused me to laugh; at least he was enjoying himself. Even though Walter wasn't the best guard dog, it put my heart at ease having him with me. I knew he would warn me if danger was near.

As we were driving, I couldn't help but reflect on the nightmare that had woke me up. Just bringing it back to my conscious put a discomfort in my mind. It had felt like I was trapped and couldn't get away from some looming doom. I still didn't know what it was, but the way I felt in the dream made me hope I never felt that way in real life. I also couldn't forget those eyes. The dark amber eyes that almost looked red, looking right through me. Thinking back, they reminded me of Natasha's eyes, but these were so hard, so fierce and malevolent. I shook my head to try and get the image out of my thoughts. Natasha had such soft, warm, tender eyes.

I felt the corner of my mouth arch into a smile just thinking of her. My heart fluttered, remembering I was going to talk to her again in the morning. Hopefully, I wouldn't look too ragged after this sleepless night. There was something about her that woke a part of me that hadn't been aroused before. I don't know if it was her mysterious disposition or the fact that she seemed—in all ways, I have noticed—to be a flawless individual. Whatever it was, she had my undivided attention.

I was approaching the park, so I pushed all other thoughts out of my head. I needed to remain focused right now. It got darker as I drove further into the forest; the trees blocked the light given off by the moon. I turned down the main back road of the park toward the cabins. I could hear all the nocturnal insects playing their songs to each other. That put my mind at ease a little. It's when everything goes quiet that you need to be worried.

I drove for about another mile before I turned off the road to the cabin. My headlights beamed straight into the front door of the cabin. It was wide open. I couldn't imagine the sheriff leaving a crime scene wide open like this. To help shield myself from other scenarios I could think up, I told myself that everyone had had a long day, and someone just forgot to shut the door when they left. Before I could turn off the Bronco, Walter jumped out of the window and landed on the gravel with a thud. "Walter!" I whispered loudly, worried he had hurt himself. He had never jumped out of the window like that before. But then I saw him, nose fixed to the ground heading toward the front of the cabin. I quickly turned off the car, leaving the headlights on, before I jumped out and drew my gun from its holster.

I started making my way in the direction of the cabin. My flashlight was still on and fixed to the ground in front of me, making sweeps back and forth. I didn't want to miss any overlooked evidence, but I also didn't want to trip over something and fall face-first into the ground.

As I made my way forward, a sound made me freeze where I stood. It was the same growl Walter had made in my room earlier, but this was more menacing. He was standing right outside of the open front door. His stance was stiff. His front section bowed down. His ears were back flat against his head. His lips were curled up, exposing all of his teeth. There was almost a snarl coming from his throat now. His hackles were raised all down his back, and his tail was sticking straight out. This was a more threatening posture than Walter had shown in my room earlier, and it made my blood run cold.

I didn't know what to do. My fight-or-flight instinct screamed at me to run, but I couldn't. I was frozen with fear, stuck in that spot. I could hear the blood pulsating to my head, trying to get my brain to work, but all I could do was stare at Walter. There was something or someone inside the cabin and, based on Walter's reaction, whatever it was didn't seem friendly.

NATASHA

I looked at the time on my phone when I heard a loud banging on my bedroom door. It was Max waking me up. My phone indicated it was 10:00 p.m. I had decided to catch a few hours of sleep before we went to the scene of Tracy's attack. Max and Irene stayed awake and looked up the directions to the cabin and assured me they would wake me up on time.

Although my body didn't need as much sleep as humans, I still felt like the little nap didn't give me back the energy I wanted. I lazily rolled out of my bed, still feeling sluggish. I grabbed a pair of jogger pants off the floor and pulled them on. Then I went to the closet and threw on a t-shirt and a black hoodie. I walked out of my room toward the living room. Irene was sitting on the couch with her legs crossed underneath her, reading something on her phone. When she heard me, she looked up and smiled, "I already have the directions programmed into my phone." She thrust the phone screen in my direction so I could verify that she had indeed done that. She looked at me again, and her smile disappeared. She got up, grabbed a coffee cup that had been sitting on the coffee table, and brought it over to me. "Here, drink this. You still look like crap."

Gratefully, I took the cup from her and drank the contents down. As the liquid flowed down my throat, I felt the almost instant energy it provided. I upended the cup and drank the entirety of it. Sheepishly, I looked back at Irene. "Sorry, I uh, kinda drank it all."

She smiled back at me and said, "It's OK. You look a lot better now. Besides, I don't think you've been keeping up with your needs like you should be."

She was right. I had been pretty busy and kept forgetting, but I just rolled my eyes and shoved her shoulder "OK, mom." She pushed me back playfully.

I looked around the room. "Where did Max go?"

Irene sat back on the couch and started fidgeting with some app on her phone again. "He went out back to the shed. Said he had to grab a few things. He will be back in a minute." No sooner had she said that, Max came walking through the back door.

As he walked into the living room, he started rubbing his hands together vigorously. "OK, I'm ready!" he announced in an excited tone. "I put everything I need in my truck along with the dude. Are you Ladies all set?" We both nodded, and Irene jumped up to her feet. She walked up to Max and slid her hand in his, and they smiled at each other.

The three of us walked out of the house and down to the porch stairs. I walked over and got in my car. Max and Irene went over to the passenger's side. She slid her arms up around his neck as his hands fell to her hips. Their foreheads met, and I could see he was whispering something to her. I wasn't even trying to listen to whatever lovey-dovey things the two were exchanging. It did, however, make her face brighten up, and a huge smile formed across it. She stood on her tiptoes, and they gave each other a deep, passionate kiss. It lasted longer than I wanted it to, so I pushed the horn once really quick. They both jumped at the unexpected noise. Irene scowled at me and threw up her middle finger. Max threw his head back with a loud, booming laugh. It was a good thing my house was out in the middle of nowhere, or it would have woken up an entire neighborhood. Finally, they gave each other one last peck, and Irene got in. I started the car and drove down the gravel driveway to turn onto the main street.

Irene turned on the GPS. She had it programmed to a remote area about ten miles before we would reach the cabin. We decided to park farther away and run the final distance to draw less attention.

"So," I said, raising an eyebrow in Irene's direction with a crooked smile, "what was that all about?"

She let out a happy huff. "It's private relationship stuff."

I wrinkled my nose at that. "You know it's super gross how romantic you two are," I said, shaking my head with a smile.

"Hey, just because you aren't looking for anyone and want to live a sad, solemn, lonely life doesn't mean we can't indulge in one another's love!"

I opened my mouth and scoffed at her. "I am not living a sad, lonely life. I just haven't found the right person yet. Plus, I have you two to take care of."

She rolled her eyes at my response. "Uh-huh. You could have anyone you want, you know. Yet you pour yourself into your work." She finished with a long, drawn-out breath.

I chuckled and shook my head. "When the time is right, I guess I will find someone." I had relationships in the past, but no one ever really felt right to me. No one yet had made me want to give up everything for them. Maybe I wasn't meant to settle down with someone. Who knows? It didn't bother me, though.

Irene turned on the radio, and that was the only noise for the rest of the drive. As we approached our destination, I turned off the headlights and radio. Seeing in the dark was not a problem for us. I pulled my car up under a couple of evergreens that were growing close together. Before we got out, Irene grabbed a green camo-colored hunting screen that we used to cover the rear of the car.

After we made sure the car was out of sight from anyone, we slipped into the darkness of the forest. She had memorized a path toward the cabin, so I followed her. We were silent, swift shadows. Although the ground was riddled with dead leaves, fallen branches, and undergrowth, we didn't make a sound. That was what our bodies were made to do. Slipping swiftly through the forest out of sight and sound of any living thing. The perfect hunter.

Irene slowed as we approached the cabin. When it finally came into view, I put my hand on her shoulder, signaling for her to stop. My senses were more in tune than hers, and I was born with the ability to feel the different energies emitted by living organisms. She stayed stationary right where I had instructed her to wait. I quietly advanced another twenty feet, crouching down low, letting my senses envelop me and spread out from my being. I let the wave of energy wash over me. Nothing seemed out of the ordinary. I could still slightly smell and sense old remnants of our kind in the area, but it wasn't recent. I beckoned Irene forward, signaling the coast was clear. We cautiously made our way to the door.

I turned the handle to the front door, and to my surprise, it clicked open, unlocked. When we stepped inside, I could smell the decay of old blood and death. I smelled three distinct odors that made my predatory side grow restless. One was the same I had sensed on Tracy. One I had never encountered before, and the third was somehow familiar. I couldn't remember from where in my memory it had come. I sniffed the air again, trying to place it. It was as if it was from a dream. Irene touched my shoulder, breaking my thought, and pointed to the bedroom.

When we got inside, we started searching. Quietly, we looked for any clues the deputies may have left behind. I went to the closet, but it was empty.

I found a dresser and opened it. Before I could start searching, Irene grabbed my wrist in a swift jerking motion and pulled me down low. "Something is coming," she whispered, with a quick urgency.

I could sense it too. "Quick, let's get out of here." As we hastily walked to exit the bedroom door, a pair of car headlights shone directly into the house. "Shit," I mumbled. I looked around the room. "Try the window."

Irene went to the window, but it was sealed shut. "We can just break it?" Irene suggested, shrugging her shoulder. That's when I heard a low growl. I could tell that it was a dog. That sent Irene into a defensive posture. I could feel the predator right under her skin, waiting to be released and attack. We had to get out of here.

I was about to let Irene charge forward when a particular scent filled my nose. Right as she was coiling to attack, I grabbed the back of her shirt. "Wait! Stop!" I whispered as fast as I could. She turned back and looked at me, face full of confusion. I took in another long breath and let the scent wash over me. It caused me to form an uncontrolled grin on my face. The smell was pure euphoria.

Irene slapped my chest with the back of her hand and brought me out of my daze. "What is it?" she asked with concern.

"I know who this is. I will explain later. You need to get out of here when I distract her," I said.

She looked at me, still with some confusion in her eyes. She opened her mouth to protest, but I cut her off. "Just do what I'm asking, please? I will be fine." At my request, she slowly nodded.

She went as far back into the room as she could and crouched. I took in a deep breath and got as low to the floor as I could and cautiously made my way out of the bedroom door. I stayed close to the wall, out of the car's headlights that were illuminating most of the room. I made my way forward, staying in the shadows. Dogs usually liked me well enough, so when I got close enough to the door, I softly called to the dog. He started inching forward and eventually was entirely inside the cabin, in the shadows and out of sight of the girl outside. I lifted my hand in the dog's direction, and he came over to sniff it. Then he gave it an approving lick.

All of a sudden, I heard someone running toward the front door from outside. I tried to react, but the dog was there at my feet, and I tripped over him. As I fell forward, someone came bursting through the open door. "Walt... umph!" She collided into me before I could catch and steady myself. Her intoxicating smell filled my senses and took over my consciousness. It caused me to lose concentration for a split second until I felt my back collide with the hardwood of the cabin floor. Then I felt her collapse on top of me.

She was so close to me—her face was an inch away from mine. I could feel her warm breath against my mouth from her heavy breathing. Her dark brown curly hair fell over her shoulder against my cheeks. Her eyes bore into mine with fear and confusion. I felt the warmth of her body on my hands from where I was holding her waist. I had caught her before she completely came in contact with me. The top half of her body was being held up, supported by me. Still, I felt the weight of her hips on mine. She was shaking all over, and I could feel fear emanating off of her.

I had known it was her that was outside, so I wasn't as startled by this situation. She had no idea anyone had been in here, and she was probably terrified by the discovery. I could hear her heart beating fast and hard. I didn't know what to do or say, so I just remained still, staring straight into her searching eyes, trying my hardest not to frighten her more.

She let me hold her there for a few moments, probably because she was in shock. Finally, she moved to get up. As she slid herself off me, her thigh slid down between where my legs met at that sensitive spot, and it sent such a shock through me. An unexpected sharp sigh caught in my throat. It was so quiet I hoped she didn't hear it.

She stood and walked backward till her back hit the wall. She was still visibly shaking and frightened.

"Walter, come here." She commanded the dog with a trembling voice. He trotted to her side and sat down. She knelt and wrapped her arms around the dog and buried her face in his fur. I heard her let out a quiet sniffle and knew she was trying to hide her fear and find some composure.

I slowly propped myself up with my forearms, still not knowing what to say or do. Not wanting to startle her any more than I already had, I let her regain her composure.

When the dog caught sight of me moving, he looked at me and wagged his tail. Jamie looked up from the dog's fur in my direction. She let him go, and he came over and started licking my face. I repositioned myself to a sitting position with my legs crossed and started petting the animal. I thought maybe at the dog's actions toward me, Jamie would calm down.

Jamie stood up, brushed her clothes off, and wiped her face with the back of her hand. She took in a deep breath. "What the hell are you doing here?" she hissed, her voice shaking. "This is a crime scene, and you can't be here!"

After the dog was satisfied with the attention from me, he walked back over to Jamie. I hadn't quite figured out what explanation I was going to give the deputy, but I did notice her casual attire. "Well, deputy, I don't see that you are wearing your official work uniform, so you could just let me leave and pretend like you didn't see me," I replied with a pleading, innocent smile.

She huffed at that and put her hands on her hips. "I am still an officer of the law. This makes you look suspect." She was trying to display a commanding demeanor.

I got a little offended by that. *How could she even suggest I had anything to do with the attack?* I stood up from the floor and took a step toward her. My smile was gone, replaced by a stern look. "Excuse me? I look suspect? Tracy was one of my closest friends, and you are going to have the audacity to accuse me?" I scorned a little more angrily than I intended.

That made her flinch and wrap her arms around herself defensively. "Why are you here then?" she asked, her commanding tone starting to melt away. She wasn't very good at this, and it made me feel a little guilty.

I let out a sigh and felt my body relax. "I'm sorry I scared you and got snippy. I was here to see if I could find anything out about who attacked Tracy, that's all."

Her mannerisms started to decompress slightly, but she was looking down at the floor. "So you don't trust us to do our job?" she asked. She looked more uncomfortable now than angry.

I watched her, waiting for her to look at me. "No, it's not that. I just wanted to come here and check the place out for myself." She still wouldn't look at me. Her heart rate was back to normal, but I could see something was still bothering her. I took another couple of slow steps toward her, and she shrunk further into herself. She kept stealing glances at me but would return her eyes to the floor. I reached out my hand to her chin. Using my index finger and thumb, I lifted her head so I could look at her eyes.

I couldn't read her expression, and it worried me. "What's wrong? Are you hurt?" I immediately started scanning her body for any potential injuries. Maybe she had been hurt when we collided.

"No! I'm fine," she replied quickly, shaking away my hand. "I just wasn't expecting anyone to be here. That's all. Which you shouldn't be."

A chuckle came from behind me. It startled Jamie, and she reached for her gun, but the holster was empty. Irene came from the bedroom still laughing. She reached down and grabbed Jamie's gun that had dropped when we ran into each other.

"Here, officer. you dropped this," Irene said, still with a grin on her face. "Oh, and you two can have the bedroom all to yourselves if you want." Irene ended with a teasing snicker as she headed out the door. She had clearly witnessed the entire encounter

It was dark, but I could still see Jamie's cheeks turn a bright red. She grabbed the gun from Irene and turned away while she put it back into its holster. "Thanks," she mumbled without looking up, embarrassed.

I glared at Irene with a disapproving look on my face and shook my head. It was clear Jamie had felt self-conscious. I didn't want her feeling uncomfortable. "Sorry again. That is my sister Irene. She has a terrible bedside manner," I said, trying to lighten the mood. An awkward silence filled the space between us, and it was almost palpable. I wasn't sure if I should say something first or let her break the silence. I figured she wasn't going to. "Um, I was going to look around back to see if there were tracks or anything." I shrugged, breaking the silence. I didn't know if she was going to go along with me in searching the place still, but I thought I would give it a try.

She stood in silent contemplation for a few minutes. I assumed she was trying to decide whether or not she wanted me there. I heard her take in a deep breath and let out a sigh. "I guess since you are here. You can't tell anyone you were here with me, though. I'm not even supposed to be here," she said sternly. I smiled and crossed my heart with my fingers. She rolled her eyes at my gesture and said, "The sheriff said they had found human foot tracks behind the cabin."

I gave an approving grin. "OK, great. Let's check it out then." And I headed toward the door.

JAMIE

When we got out of the cabin, Natasha took her hand off the small of my back. It left a resonating warmth that made me wish it was still there. "Walter, come," I said. He came trotting right up to my side as we made our way toward where the footprints were.

"So, is he your guard dog?" Natasha asked.

I couldn't help but let out an amused chuckle. "I wouldn't call him a guard dog, more of a companion. He probably hasn't even ever hurt a fly in his entire life. He does still make me feel safe when he is near."

"Oh, well, that was a pretty terrifying growl he gave Irene and me in the cabin. Could have scared any attacker off, in my opinion," Natasha replied.

I thought about her words for a moment. How terrified I had been when Walter disappeared into the dark corner of the cabin. "Yes, but he did eventually come to you without a fight and was probably wagging his tail," I said, shaking my head.

"True, but it's probably because he didn't sense I was a threat," she replied, shrugging her shoulders as she knelt to the ground. "Could you point your flashlight down here, please?" I did as she instructed. She gestured for me to kneel beside her and pointed at the ground. "Do you think these are the tracks your sheriff was talking about?"

I thought back to the pictures I had looked at in the sheriff's office. "Yeah, these look like the ones in the pictures."

"Want to follow them? It looks like they go this way." She pointed farther into the forest. It was dark, and I was already on edge from earlier. The entire situation had been terror replaced instantly by utter embarrassment, which left my nerves completely shot. I stared into the forest, considering whether I dare continue.

Natasha must have seen the concern on my face. "I won't let anything happen to you, I promise," she said with a soft smile.

It was a little strange that she was the one offering protection and reassurance when I was the deputy. But there was so much confidence in her bearing and voice. And that smile made me want to melt. I instantly felt safe. "OK. just don't leave me behind."

One of the edges of her smile grew even more prominent. "Promise, I won't."

We continued on, side by side, with Walter trailing after us. Every few yards, Natasha would kneel close to the ground and examine the area. It almost looked like she was smelling, but I couldn't tell. It was too quiet for me, so I decided to try and break the silence. "Are you some kind of bounty hunter along with being a nurse?"

She raised an eyebrow, and one of the sides of her lips pulled up. "Would you believe me if I said I was?"

The response took me a little by surprise. She didn't look like the mercenary type at all. "Uh, no?" I replied.

She let out a quiet laugh and stood up. "My dad taught me how to track and hunt when I was little."

I hummed in approval at her response. My dad had also taught me how to hunt and how to track an animal that had been wounded. "So is tracking people the same?"

She shrugged at my question. "I guess. People are easier to track. They aren't as graceful as animals." I thought about her reply. She was right. People weren't as elegant as animals.

We walked in the same direction for about three-quarters of a mile. Finally, we came upon a wide trail that ran perpendicular to the path we had been following. Natasha stopped. She started looking in every direction as if she had suddenly lost the trail. "Where does this path lead?" she asked me, pointing to the trail.

I looked at it and thought, trying to get my bearings of the area. "I'm pretty sure it leads to the main road."

She crouched down to the ground again. "The trail ends here. They must have had a car waiting. It looks like the tires were pretty bald, so it might be hard getting a tire print."

I knelt by her and looked to where she was pointing. She was right; there were tire tracks that looked fresh. She was very observant. "I guess I will let the sheriff know. Whoever did this was somewhat familiar with the area if they knew about this trail." I looked over at her to see what she wanted to do now. I didn't really know where to go from here. She had a frustrated look on her face. "Are you OK? I don't think there is anything else we can do tonight."

She didn't reply to me. She stood there deep in thought. I slowly walked toward her and placed a hand on her shoulder. "Are you OK?" I asked again with concern.

She shook her head like she was shaking off a daze. Then she gave a faint smile. "Yeah, I'm fine. I was just thinking. But you are right. There is nothing more we can do here tonight. Let's head back."

We started our trek back toward the cabin. I was so tired that my mind was blank. I didn't know what to make of this new information we had just found, so I let my thoughts wander to where they wanted. I thought back to the cabin and how it felt with Natasha holding my waist when I collided into her. My face was so close to hers, and her eyes were looking straight into me. That feeling I felt with my hips against hers and when my thigh slid between her legs. I could have sworn I heard her sigh, but maybe it was my mind playing tricks on me. Thinking back on it caused a warm pressure in my chest. The relief that washed over me when I saw it was her. I closed my eyes, and I could almost still feel her strong hands holding me.

I was so lost in my thoughts that when a couple of doves took flight, disturbing the branches around them, it startled me and I let out a squeal as I fell sideways into Natasha. She was so sturdy she didn't even falter at my weight. I looked down and noticed that I was now clinging to her arm with both of my hands.

I heard a quiet chuckle escape her. "I would probably be just as defensive as you are after a night like tonight, deputy. But I'm pretty sure a couple of doves won't hurt us. But if we do run into trouble, I'm sure that sound you made would scare any vicious predator away in terror." I could hear the playfulness in her voice. I looked up at her face. There was amusement in her eyes, but something else was there too, something that made my heart swell.

I felt my face flush from embarrassment, but I let out a spirited laugh. I needed to laugh after a night like tonight. "Well, it's nice to know my nervousness has been so entertaining for you and your sister." I shook my head.

I didn't want to let go of her arm. I felt so safe this close to her. Instead, I slid my right hand down her arm toward her hand. I slowly let my fingers trace down her palm. I held my breath, waiting for her to pull away, but rejection of my advance never came. As my fingers intertwined with hers, she gave my hand an approving squeeze. Out of the corner of my eye, I saw a small smile spread across her face. It made the edges of my lips curl, and all the fear from earlier in the day dissolved.

We continued the rest of the walk in silence. I was so content that most of the tiredness, fear, and exhaustion were gone. But every good thing comes to an end. As we rounded the corner of the cabin, I saw a man leaning against a truck that hadn't been there when we left.

Fright took over and pushed all those joyful feelings I had felt earlier aside. I dropped Natasha's hand and went to grab my gun, stepping in front of her defensively. Before I could pull my weapon out, Natasha spun me around to look at her. "It's OK. He's with Irene and me." She waved at the man. He stood up from the truck and opened the passenger's door. Irene got out and took the hand he offered her. They started walking toward us. A melancholy feeling passed over me, remembering I had dropped Natasha's hand. I looked down at my fingers, and they felt empty and cold now that Natasha's were no longer intertwined. She touched my lower back, guiding me toward the approaching couple.

As they got closer, Natasha provided introductions. "Max, Irene, this is Deputy Jamie Stone. She is working on Tracy's case." I reached out my hand toward Max. "And this is Irene, my sister who you met earlier, and her boyfriend, Max." Max smiled at me and took my hand in a firm shake.

"It's a pleasure to meet you. Any friend of Natasha's is a friend of mine. Although it's been a while since we have had the pleasure of meeting one of her friends," Max said.

I saw Irene quietly giggle. "It's nice to meet you officially." She extended her hand.

I took hers in mine and shook. "So, all three of you decided to work together to trespass on an open crime scene?"

They all froze and looked at each other. "I'm kidding," I said with a sheepish smile. "I'm sorry, I just have had a rough night and was trying to make a joke. Guess I'm not very good at it." I was trying to lighten the mood, but it didn't work as I planned.

Irene offered me a smile. "It's OK. I'm sorry we scared you earlier. I'm sure it was terrifying to find a couple of trespassers here, then falling into one of their arms." She winked at Natasha, and I saw her face turn a pink color and look away.

"Actually," I started, trying to take the teasing away from Natasha, "it started at my house." After my statement, Natasha spun her head around, and her eyes bore into mine with concern. Her face was as still as marble.

"What happened at your house?" she asked with interest.

Her gaze was so intense it made me feel a little exposed, and I involuntarily looked away. "Well, I don't exactly know. I woke up to Walter growling out my window. He has never done that before. Then he kept acting tense. That's why I came here. I felt uncomfortable, stuck in my house, so I decided to get out." I noticed Natasha look at her sister. Irene's smile had disappeared too. "What?" I asked, looking from one sister to the other. "Is everything OK?" The sudden change in their demeanors made me nervous.

Natasha put a smile back on her face and looked at me. "Yeah, I'm sure everything is fine. It probably was a coyote or something. Would you be opposed to me riding home with you and checking it out? My dad taught me how to run them off when I was younger." I wasn't completely opposed to her seeing me to my house, but it still made me uneasy. "Can't Max just follow me?" I still didn't want to look desperate for comfort.

Max replied, "Well, they parked a ways from here. The plan was for me to meet them here and drop them back off at their car."

Wow, they had an entire elaborate plan for the night. It made me feel a little insecure that I just decided on a whim to come here.

Irene broke my train of thought. "I can pick Nat up from your house after I get the car if you can program your address into my phone."

I looked at Natasha for approval. She gave me an encouraging smile. "OK," I said, typing my address into her phone.

Irene gave a happy grin and grabbed Max to turn him toward the truck. "I will be by to pick you up, sis!"

"Shall we?" Natasha said, gesturing toward my Bronco.

She walked over to the passenger's side and hopped in. When I opened the driver's side, Walter jumped in, and when he saw Natasha sitting there, he turned and looked at me. "Walter, get in the back." I pointed to the back seat. He jumped the console and sat down, letting out a grunt.

Natasha turned and looked at him. "I guess he isn't accustomed to sitting back there?" she asked me.

I jumped into the driver's side and started the car. I backed out on the road and started heading toward my house, thinking of how to reply to her. "No." I shrugged. "I usually don't have company, especially in my car." She gave an acknowledging "Hmm."

"So," I said, breaking the onset of silence, "Max said you don't have many friends either?" I turned the statement into a question.

She stared out the window when she replied. "No, not really. I work a lot. Plus, people look at me differently here, like they don't trust me. Maybe it's because I'm not from around here. I'm not quite sure. Tracy is the closest thing I have to a friend besides Max."

Her response surprised me and made me a little sad. She seemed like a fantastic person, and I never got a feeling of untrustworthiness around her. "I'm sorry people treat you differently. I trust you, if it counts for anything." On impulse, I put my hand on her thigh and gave an encouraging rub.

She smiled back at me. "It does count, and thank you." She reached for my hand and squeezed it gratefully. Then she let go, and I put mine back on the steering wheel.

As I turned down my street, I could almost feel the tension start to pour off her. Out of my peripherals, I could see her jaw clenched. Her eyes darted back and forth, scanning the area. It was a little unsettling. "This is it," I said, as I pulled into my driveway.

Before I could even turn my car off, Natasha was out the door. I don't think I had ever seen someone move that fast. When the car turned off, I unbuckled, opened the door, and hopped out. Walter followed after me. Natasha looked into the forest behind my house. I walked up to her. "Did you see something?" I started scanning the area she was facing, looking for any movement.

She turned her head to look at me. "No, I was only checking it out. Do you want me to take a look around?"

I looked down at Walter, who was standing at my feet, looking relaxed. "I don't think that will be necessary tonight. Walter seems pretty relaxed, so I'm sure whatever was out there earlier is gone now." I gave Walter a scratch on the head. He looked up at me, then headed toward the front door. I started following in his direction, and Natasha trailed behind. "It's super late, and unfortunately, I work tomorrow," I said with a huff. "And it is going to suck going in on no sleep." We reached the porch, and I stopped in front of the door.

She gave a small chuckle. "I already called in for tomorrow. They said Tracy was stable and improving, so I'm going to take tomorrow off."

"Is she awake yet?" I asked her. Maybe she would remember something.

She let out a sigh and looked at the ground. "Unfortunately, no. She will probably be kept sedated for a while. She had a lot of internal damage and some swelling on her brain."

I didn't like seeing her look upset. I just wanted to take away all her sorrow, but I didn't know how to do that. It sent a pain through my chest. I reached out and grabbed both of her hands in mine and gave them a comforting squeeze. "I'm sure she will be fine. Especially having people like you to look after her."

She looked at me with genuine gratitude. We stood there for what seemed like an eternity, holding hands and looking into each other's eyes. I found my gaze wandering downward and looking at her perfectly formed lips. I started imagining what they would feel like against mine. I moved my eyes back up to hers, and there was a look of longing and desire in them. It mimicked the feeling I had flowing through my body. I felt her hands slowly slide up my arms. When they reached my neck, I held my breath. As her hands cupped my cheeks, she drew me to her, and I gave in with an eager willingness. I closed my eyes and then felt her soft, warm lips against mine. It sent a jolt straight through me, and the warmth that burst from my chest almost stopped my heart. I surrendered to her flawless gentle lips as they tenderly brushed against mine. I reached my hands out and placed them on her sides. She gave an approving hum against my lips, and I felt the smile behind it.

All of a sudden, I felt her pull away, and her hands left my face, leaving my cheeks cold from the immediate removal of her touch. Worried I had done something wrong, I snapped my eyes open. Her face had transformed into a stone-cold mask as she stared out into the trees beside my house. I looked over her shoulder in the same direction.

"What's wrong?" I asked, a little worried about the way she looked.

She turned and looked back at me. "Nothing. I thought I might have heard something, but it's nothing." She had a smile on her face now, but it looked contrived—almost as if she was hiding something—and it made me feel unsettled. "You should probably get inside and go to bed. You do have to wake up in an hour or two for work," she said.

I groaned. "Please don't remind me. You can come in till your sister gets here, or I could wait out here with you." I didn't want to leave her alone outside this late if there was really something outside.

She brushed a loose lock of hair that had fallen over my eyes behind my ear and then cupped my face with her hand. She gave me a warm smile. "Go in and get some sleep. I will be fine. Besides, my sister should be here any second."

I was still worried about leaving her outside alone. I went to protest, but when I opened my mouth, her lips were on mine before I could get a word out. I smiled into the kiss in approval. It didn't last long, but it still was intoxicating enough to make me feel dizzy with lust.

"Go inside. I will be fine, I promise. I will text you when I get home," she whispered against my lips after she slowly pulled away.

I was so lightheaded from the kiss that all I could do was obey. "OK." I smiled at her with what must have looked like the most childish, giddy smile anyone could ever have. I unlocked the door. Walter trotted in first and I followed. Before I shut the door, I turned around and said, "Please let me know when you get home, and drive safe."

She nodded her head. "Of course. Good night, Deputy Stone. Sleep well." She grabbed my hand and kissed my knuckles, and it sent another flood of butterflies through my stomach.

After I had shut and locked the door, I turned and rested my back against it. I haven't smiled this big in so long. I put my fingers to my lips, where I could still feel hers, and grinned even wider. I was so happy and realized I probably wouldn't be sleeping at all tonight, and if I did, I hoped my dreams would be filled with the beautiful nurse who had stolen my breath away.

NATASHA

As soon as I heard Jamie walk to her room for bed, I slipped into the tree cover surrounding the house. I had heard and smelled him. I knew he was out there. It made my blood boil. I followed his tracks and started gaining on him. Then I saw him. He had no idea I was on his trail. I knew he was one of Tracy's attackers by his scent. He was already shifted into his predatory form, and I guessed he was young since he was transformed and still couldn't sense my presence. He had no reason to be like that with no threat right now.

I quietly snuck up behind him and grabbed his throat. It happened so fast he didn't even realize what was going on before I slammed him against a nearby tree. The tree's thick trunk groaned and bent at the power I had smashed his body against it with. He snarled at me with a savage rage and burning in his eyes. He was definitely young, because I was able to hold him there as he was, and I wasn't even transformed.

I squeezed tighter around his neck and bared my teeth at him. "Who are you?" I demanded angrily.

He swung an arm at me and growled. I caught it with my other hand, and I squeezed even tighter around his neck. "Who are you?!" I boomed with a rage-filled command. He started clawing at my hand around his throat. I loosened my grip just enough to allow him to suck in air for him to speak.

His eyes moved to mine. They were so cold, evil, and filled with hate that it caused me to snarl at him. "You have five seconds to tell me who you are and why you are here, or I will kill you and not lose a second of sleep."

"We are here to claim what's yours; your land, your inheritance." he hissed.

Years ago, our kind had fought for territory all the time, but in recent years it hadn't been a problem with the diplomacies that had been forged. It was also suicide to threaten our particular territory.

I slammed him against the tree again and kneed him in the gut. "Who is we?" I demanded.

He let out a laugh that flamed the rage in my chest. The predator in me hummed at my surface, ready to kill.

He growled. "You are out of your league, Natal..."

I cut him off before he could finish, and slammed him into the ground as hard as I could. I felt some of his ribs break. I snapped the arm I had been holding into an unnatural angle and felt it shatter. He let out a wail of pain. "Tell me again that I'm out of my league, you piece of shit. You have no idea who you are dealing with. You told a human about us. You told him a name that should never be spoken. And you got him killed."

He let out a laugh again. I punched him in the face and felt his nose break. He groaned in pain. "My boss just wanted to see how you would deal with the human—to kill him or spare him. You actually surprised him."

I gritted my teeth together. *How could these assholes use humans as pawns?* "Who are you!?" I roared at him again.

He looked me right in the eyes, and his mouth curled up into a smile. "I guess I'm just the decoy. Your actions with the human piqued the boss's interest." He pursed his lips together in the form of a kiss. It sent a sudden fear through me. Lightning cracked in the back of my head. I let the change wash over me. I grabbed his face in my hand and smashed his skull as hard as I could a nearby boulder. I didn't know if I had killed him or not, but I didn't care. I had to get back to Jamie's house. I moved through the trees so fast I didn't care how much noise I made. All I saw was red from the rage that was taking over my body. It was hard to stay in control with the anger pulsating within me.

As soon as I saw the house, I sped up even more. I saw my car parked on the street. Irene was sitting in it. When I stopped in front of the house, and let my sense seep out of me. I was looking and feeling for any sign of something present that shouldn't be there. At the site of my state, Irene came running. Before she got to me, I circled the house on high alert. When I got back to the front, Irene had a look of intensity on her face.

"Nat, what the hell is going on? Why are you in your form? What happened?" she asked worriedly.

I couldn't sense anyone else around. That little shit had played me. I let out a deep, primitive howl of frustration and kicked a stone close to my foot. I took a few deep breaths and pushed the predator back inside, which caused a splitting headache. Irene ran to the car and grabbed a canister. When she came back, she offered it to me, and I drank.

"One of the intruders was here," I said, taking another drink. "I ran him down. He said something about them being here for territory. He made it sound like the others were back here at the house when I caught him." Irene looked at me with an unmoving face, soaking in all the information I was giving.

"Where is he now?" she asked me.

"Back there." I pointed in the direction I had been. "I may have killed him," I said with a frustrated huff, and slammed my fist against the ground.

"Let's go check anyway. Come on," she said, nudging me in the direction I had pointed.

When we got to where I had tracked him, the boulder had a pool of blood on it, but the body was gone. "Damn it!" I snarled in frustration. I started pacing, kicking at rocks, and punching a tree.

"Nat, stop! Calm down," she said.

I turned around and saw her grab something off the ground. "What is this?" she asked. It was a folded piece of paper. She unfolded it and read it out loud. "*Thank you Natalia. You have shown your hand. Always so caring. I will be keeping an eye on you all.*"

After she read it, she handed it to me. I reread it and then crumpled it up and put my hand against my head. "I never should have reacted like that. I never should have..." I trailed off. *I never should have kissed her or shown affection for her.* I felt another growl escape me. "Stupid." I said out loud to myself.

"Nat, what is going on? What does that note mean?" she asked, looking very concerned.

"We need to get back to the deputy's house. I will explain when we get there." We started running back to the house. When we got there, I did a few more laps around the perimeter, making sure nothing was out of the ordinary. I focused on the inside, but could only sense her and Walter's energies inside. Finally, I motioned for Irene to go to the car, and we both got in.

I felt a swell of emotions wash over me. I had just dragged Jamie into the middle of a potential turf war I knew nothing about. Guilt started to pulsate through me. I started shaking and breathing hard. I didn't even know what they wanted or who they were, and they already were after my weaknesses. They attacked my best friend and threatened Jamie. I put my hands on my face, and without thinking about it, I whispered, "What have I done?"

Irene touched my shoulder. Her voice was calm and soft. "Nat, talk to me. What happened? We can get through this together, but you need to talk to me."

I felt my eyes get hot and wet. I can't remember the last time I cried. I don't even remember if I ever had. I kept the tears from falling and wiped my eyes. *Who were these people? What did they want?* Everything was out of control right now. I had never had to deal with something like this before. I took a deep breath, dropped my hands from my face, and looked at her. "Irene, I kissed her. I kissed the deputy."

Her mouth dropped, and her eyes went wide. She stared at me. Then her mouth formed into a broad, open smile. She clapped her hands and squealed with delight. "Oh my gosh! I knew it! I knew you had a crush on her! I'm so happy!"

I grabbed her hands to stop her celebration. "Irene, stop! They must have seen it too, and then how I reacted to the threat must have confirmed how I felt. This is a mess. What if they take her or kill her? It will be all my fault." I let out a defeated sigh. "I can't let that happen, Irene." I was so frustrated with myself.

She gave me a sympathetic smile. "We won't let anything happen to her, Nat. We just have to work together and figure out what these trespassers want."

I was glad I was taking the next day off, because I was exhausted. "I'm not going to be able to see her again," I said with a sad realization.

"Excuse me? And why not?" asked Irene in a demanding tone.

"If I distance myself from her, maybe they will leave her alone. Besides, if there is a turf war, I can't have a human on the side and try to keep everything a secret and try to keep her safe at the same time. It's for the best."

"Nat," she said, grabbing my face and turning me to look at her, "unfortunately the cat's out of the bag. Even if you don't see her again and distance yourself, they know you care about her. It would probably be safer for her to be closer to you so you can keep an eye on her rather than distancing yourself from her. And we can cross the other bridges as they come. We can all take turns keeping an eye on her when you aren't." She smiled at me. It made me feel a little better, but I was still upset with myself.

"I'll have to think about it. I don't even know what I was doing kissing a human. Especially one I just met." I shook my head.

"Well, do you like her?" Irene asked.

"Of course I like her. I have never felt so scared for another individual in my life like when I thought they were at her house and were going to take her," I replied. "I don't even know why, because we just met." I closed my eyes and hit my head on the back of the car seat.

"OK, well, you haven't been with someone in a long time. You deserve a chance at happiness too," she told me with a smile.

I reciprocated the gesture. "Thank you. I don't know yet, though. I don't want to drag her into a fight that she never asked to be a part of. It's not fair to her." I didn't even know what this fight was over. I moved down here to get away from the politics and drama, and now I was facing enemies that wanted something I couldn't offer. I had no idea what to do.

"Well, Nat, what is fair to her should be her decision, not yours. But speaking of territory threats, I think it's time to call Nik and tell him. We can't fight a battle by ourselves if that is what they truly want. It is still his territory," she informed me.

I let out a heavy sigh. "I know we need to. Will you tell Max to call him when you get home?" The last thing I wanted to do was tell Nik about what was going on and ask for help, but it was necessary at this point.

She gave me a curious look. "When I get home? Why can't you tell him when WE get home?"

"I can't just leave her by herself right now, Irene. I don't know if they are going to come back," I replied through a long exhale.

"I will stay here with you. You can take a nap in the back, and I will take the first watch," she responded.

"Irene, this isn't your responsibility. I brought the danger to her front door, not you." I didn't want to put Irene in danger as well.

"It's important to you, Nat, and what's important to you is important to me. I'm not leaving you alone in this," she replied, "Now get in the back. I will drive down the street out of view and wake you up if there is trouble."

I was grateful she was willing to help me, but I still didn't want her to feel obligated to help. I went to open my mouth to protest, but she pointed to the back seat. I was so tired I didn't have the energy to argue, so I crawled over the center console. I rested my back against the driver's side door and crossed my legs, stretching them out along the back seat. I sent Jamie a text telling her I got home safe to put her mind at ease, then folded my arms and rested my head back slipping into a dreamless sleep.

. . .

I had decided to keep my distance from Jamie until I figured out what I was going to do with the situation. Max had gotten in touch with Nik and let him know about the events that had transpired. Nik told us to keep an eye out and that he would be sending help when he could. I was not looking forward to whatever support he had to offer.

It had been a couple of days since I had kissed Jamie. It took every ounce of will not to try to communicate with her, but I needed to figure out what had to happen to keep her safe and figure out who these intruders were. I was surprised and a little hurt that she wasn't trying harder to get in touch with me. Maybe she had decided the other night was a mistake. That, to me, was hard to believe. I could smell how much she wanted me, and could sense the yearning behind her kiss and touch. The desire blazed off of her that night. It made my entire being thirst for every ounce of her, crave her touch and lips, hunger for her taste. I wanted to drown myself in her. If I hadn't sensed the intruder in the woods, I don't know if I would have been able to take myself away from her. I don't know if I would have been able to control myself.

We had taken turns watching her house at night. Since that night, there had been no signs of anyone around her home or anywhere else. I didn't know if that was a good thing or a bad thing. The calm before the storm, maybe? Or they had decided to pack up and leave. The latter was a far-fetched wish. They wouldn't have given up that easily, which made me frustrated and on edge.

I had to work that morning. I got up and did my usual morning routine. I took a quick shower, downed a cup of my morning fix, brewed a cup of coffee, and headed out the door. When I got outside, I took a long, deep breath of the cold, crisp morning air and walked to my car. I got in and started the long drive to the hospital. As I got closer to my destination, I felt a tightness in my chest, like something wasn't right. I parked in my usual spot. Instead of sitting in the car, I threw back the remaining bit of coffee and headed to the building.

As I walked through the doors, I could feel something was wrong. Instead of waiting for the dreadfully slow elevators, I took the stairs. There were no cameras in the stairwell, so I took the flights as fast as I could, which took less than a second at my full speed.

As I burst through the doors to the critical care unit, I saw a group of people in and around room one. It was Tracy's room. I saw the crash cart hooked up to her, and my coworkers were performing chest compressions on her. I had seen this done many times before, but it looked so brutal being done on such a petite body like Tracy's. I heard Dr. Hubber's voice. "Give her another gram of epi. Check for a pulse."

"There is no pulse," said a nurse by the bedside.

I saw James, another nurse who worked on the unit. I walked briskly up to him. "What the hell happened?" I demanded. "She was improving. They were going to extubate her and take the intubation tube out today."

He didn't even look at me when he replied. "We don't know. She seemed fine all night, and then about forty-five minutes ago, she coded. We couldn't get a pulse and she wasn't breathing."

My heart sank. They had been coding her for forty-five minutes. I hadn't seen many people come back after being coded for that long. I knew deep down there was nothing I could do to bring her back, nothing at all.

I hear Dr. Hubber's voice again. "OK, give her one more shock, and if we don't get anything, I'm going to call it." It made me angry that he was giving up, but I knew she was gone. Even the bite couldn't save her at this point. And I grew anxious, and a feeling of despair washed over me.

I heard the crash cart charging up. When it pinged, letting the nurse controlling it know it was fully charged, she told everyone to clear and delivered the shock. I saw Tracy's body jerk in response.

I saw her heart start beating in her chest, but I knew it was just the epinephrine forcing the heart muscle to contract. Eventually, it would stop again. I watched the heart monitor as her heart rate spiked and then slowed, till eventually, there was a flatline.

"OK, I'm calling it. Time of death 6:27 a.m." He quickly walked out of the room and then out of the unit. There was a solemn, stagnant silence from everyone in the room. No one moved. I didn't even know what to do. I wanted to yell and scream and kill whoever had caused this. There was a heavy pain inside me. My inner self was screaming. *How could this be happening? How could this happen when she was improving? She was getting better.*

I could hear the sounds of soft sniffles and weeping as people mourned our fallen coworker. Everyone loved Tracy. It was such a loss to have such a precious, pure life taken from this world. I was finally able to make my feet move. I walked over to Julie, who had been the nurse caring of her that night. She stood at Tracy's bedside. Her eyes were closed, and her head was bowed. I could see tears streaming down her cheeks. I put my arm around her shoulder to try and comfort her. I felt her turn and look at me. Her eyes were full of sorrow and guilt. "I did everything I could," she whispered through a soft sob. "I don't know what happened. She was stable all night. It's like something just stopped her heart." She turned back around to sob quietly into her hands.

As my head started to clear from the shock I just witnessed, fear crept into the back of my mind. *What if Julie was right? What if something had stopped her heart?* I got right by Tracy's bedside and leaned over her body. I focused all my senses on her. I closed my eyes and took in a deep breath. I even siphoned off a little of my predator side. I never tried this around humans regularly, but I knew I was in full control and wouldn't let any other part of it present itself. Then I could smell it in her blood. I could detect multiple chemicals and drugs, but there was something else that shouldn't have been there. It smelled like propranolol. It was a heart medicine used to slow the heart down and make stronger contractions and decrease blood pressure. *Why would a medication like this be in her?*

I ran back to the computer and opened up Tracy's medicine record. There was no prescription for her even to be getting propranolol. So why was it in her system? Anger filled me. Someone must have overdosed her on this. If she was given enough, it would have stopped her heart. I quickly went back to James. "Did anyone else go into her room tonight besides Julie?"

He still didn't look at me. "I don't think so. I don't know. I wasn't paying that much attention to anything like that," he replied coldly.

"So no one else besides the nurses and doctors were in the unit last night?" I asked him.

He had a thoughtful look on his face as he tried to remember. "No, there were no other people in the unit last night." I turned around, frustrated. But then I heard him say, "Wait, yeah actually, maintenance came in early this morning. Something was going on with room fifteen's airflow, so they were fixing it. They're gone now. Why?"

I didn't reply to him. I turned and walked away toward the break room and started pacing. Someone did this to her. Someone murdered her in cold blood. I couldn't sense that any of my kind had been around here, so they probably hired a human. He must have disguised himself as a maintenance person. I started to feel the rage take over my body. I needed to figure out who it was. I knew there were cameras all over the unit. One of them had videoed who the person was. I needed to get to the security footage, but the only way to access it was through security, and I knew they wouldn't just let me look at it. I needed someone with authority. I needed to call Jamie. I knew it was her case, so they would probably be willing to let her look at the footage. I needed to convince her I thought it was someone who did this intentionally. My train of thought was interrupted by my manager's voice.

"I know we just lost Tracy, but we need to keep working. Other people need us. Take a minute, and help get that room cleaned. ER is holding a patient waiting for an open room up here." And without getting a reply from me, she turned and walked back to her office. The bitch can't even let us mourn for one of our own. Obviously, patient care was just a business in that woman's eyes.

I got up and left the break room. I needed to call Jamie and let her know what happened.

JAMIE

It had been three days since the midnight investigation at the cabin. I had told the sheriff about the tire tracks and trail we had found. He wasn't happy I had been out so late by myself at the crime scene, considering I left out the fact Natasha and her crew had been there. He sent Chance to investigate the trail more, but we didn't get anything from the new information. Like Natasha had stated that night, the tires had been too bald to leave any tread indentation in the soft earth.

We were at a dead end in the investigation, and Tracy was still nonresponsive as per the last transmission from Natasha. I hadn't seen her since that night. We had only texted a few times, and they were very brief, professional exchanges. It seemed as if she was acting distant toward me, and it upset me. I thought there was a connection between us the night that we kissed. She seemed just as eager to touch and kiss me as I had been toward her. I didn't know if it was intentional for her to be keeping her distance or if she was truly busy with work. I didn't want to push her and act clingy. Instead, I poured myself into the investigation and did everything I could to take my mind off her.

I sat at my desk with pictures from the crime scene and witness testimonies spread out all over the top of my desk. I tried to find any little hidden detail we could have missed. I had been over all the evidence with a fine-tooth comb to no avail. We had no new leads at all. Out of frustration, I slammed my hand down on the desk and exhaled deeply. I closed my eyes and rubbed my forehead. I was getting nowhere in this case, and I felt useless.

As I wallowed in my defeat, I felt my cell phone buzz. Without looking at the screen, I answered it. "Deputy Stone here," I said with more frustration in my voice than I wanted. When I heard Natasha's voice on the other end, my heart swelled, but I was immediately put on alert by the tone in her voice.

"Deputy, I have bad news. Tracy passed away this morning." My heart sank in response to her words. Everyone I had talked to said Tracy was such a virtuous person, and even though I didn't know her, it still made my heart ache. I knew that Natasha was close to her as well, and I knew she would be hurting over this. I wished I could have been there for her.

"I'm so sorry, Natasha," I said softly. "What happened? I thought she was getting better?" I asked her. It seemed all the updates I had gotten pointed toward Tracy recovering.

She was talking fast, but I could hear the sorrow in her voice. "I think someone injected her with a lethal dose of a beta-blocker. I think whoever attacked her the night at the cabin came back to finish the job. I need you to come down here to help me look at the security footage and see if someone besides hospital personnel went into her room last night. I don't think they will let just a nurse look at it." I thought about her words before I replied. It seemed too early to have the autopsy results back. How would she know if someone overdosed her on something?

"Why do you think someone killed her? Did they do the autopsy?" I asked.

"No," she replied flatly, "I just have a gut feeling. She was getting better. We were going to try and take her off the ventilator today because she was doing so well. Someone doesn't just go downhill that fast without a push."

I tried to work the information out that she just gave me, but she sounded rushed. I knew there would be an autopsy because the sheriff had said the attack was possibly a murder attempt, but it probably wouldn't be done for a while. I wasn't even sure if the security at the hospital would let me look at the footage without probable cause and evidence. I guessed it couldn't hurt to try and see what I could do if she genuinely thought someone had murdered Tracy. "I can't guarantee they will let us see the footage without having a warrant or evidence from an autopsy, but I will head down there and see what I can do."

She let out a small sigh of relief to my response. "Thank you. You can come straight up to the unit when you get here. I will see you in a little while."

"OK. It might be like an hour or so, but I will be there. See you soon." Then the line went dead without another word. She still sounded very distant from me, but I was too eager now to get down there to dwell on it.

I immediately got up from my desk and went to the sheriff's office. I didn't even knock before I burst through the door. Surprised, he looked up from the files he was going over. "Deputy, most people knock before they enter."

"I'm sorry, Sheriff. Natasha called me. She said that Tracy unfortunately passed away this morning. She thinks there was foul play, that someone killed her." I was almost out of breath. I didn't know if he would go for it without any real evidence, but it was worth a shot. He usually backed me up on cases.

His face was unmoving. "Why does she think there was foul play? I doubt the autopsy has been done yet. They haven't even contacted me about the girl's death."

"She has a gut feeling, Sir. She wants to review the video feed of the floor to see if anyone besides the nursing staff or doctors went into the room. Tracy was getting better. There is no way she could have just taken a turn that bad. I trust her judgment." I was trying to sound as confident as I could.

He looked back down at the files on his desk and ran his fingers through his hair, then looked back up at me. I could tell he was trying to process the information and figure out what he wanted to do with it. Finally, a resolute look crossed his face, and he let out a sigh. "OK, Deputy. You won't have a warrant. But I can't stop you from asking their security officers nicely or asking around down there. Call me if you find anything."

With a nod, I turned and headed out of his office, grabbing my bag on the way out. I decided to take my Bronco today, since the last time I took the cruiser a stranger had eyed it pretty hard.

I drove the entire way in silence, trying to rehearse how I was going to ask to get access to the footage. After I gave up with that, my mind wandered to Natasha. I knew she was going through a hard time, but she sounded so removed from me, far away, like the other night had never happened. I tried to push that thought out of my head. *She was trying to be professional because she was at work. That had to be it.*

When I got to the hospital, I went straight to the ICU floor. I walked through the unit doors and saw Natasha on the far side of the nursing station at a computer. Just seeing her caused me to smile, and I felt my stomach flutter.

As I approached, she looked up at me. Her expression was one I had yet to see on her face. It was almost expressionless, a stone mask I couldn't read. I smiled hello, but I got nothing in return. She got up from her chair and walked right past me in the direction of the elevator. "Come with me. The security room is in the basement." Her voice even had a cold tone about it. It cut through to my heart, and I could feel a pain there. Now I was sure she was over the other night and had moved on. *How could she be so callous toward me?*

I pushed that thought out of my head. I was here to do a job. I needed to find out what happened to Tracy. "Wait," I said, stopping before I went out the doors. She halted and turned around. Annoyance was written all over her face. "Can I talk to anyone that was here when the event took place? Someone who witnessed it?"

Her face was unmoving when she replied. "I was here. Everyone else that was part of the incident and on the night shift is gone." Not giving me time to respond or protest, she turned around and went straight to the elevator.

I practically had to run to keep up with her swift strides. As we waited for the elevator, her gaze was fixed straight ahead of her, not even glancing at me. I decided to break the silence. "How are you dealing with this? Are you OK?"

Her posture was still. The elevator door opened before she replied. We both stepped in, and she hit the button to take us to the basement floor. When the elevator door closed, she replied, "I just want to figure out what happened and who did this." She had built up a vast wall and was determined not to let me in. I touched her arm lightly with my hand. Her entire body went rigid at my touch. I knew she wasn't looking for empathy right then, but I couldn't help it. "If you need anything, someone to talk to, please don't hesitate to let me know. You're going through something hard, and everyone needs someone to talk to."

I felt the elevator jerk to a stop. Natasha still wouldn't look at me. She replied in a detached tone. "Thank you. Security is this way."

I followed her around several corners until we arrived at a door labeled SECURITY. She knocked on it. I took a step in front of her, since we were relying on my authority to get us access. A young white man who looked like boredom had taken over his persona opened the door. "What can I do for you?" he asked in a monotone voice.

I took a breath and tried to sound as in control as I could. "I'm Deputy Stone with the sheriff's department." I flashed my credentials for him to inspect. He looked them over lazily. "I'm working a case involving a woman who was attacked. She was brought to the ICU and passed away earlier this morning. It would be of great help to the investigation if you could help me out."

His interest had been piqued by the information I shared with him. "How can I assist with your investigation, Deputy?"

I smiled, knowing I had his attention. "As part of the investigation, the sheriff wanted me to look at security footage. We want to see if the woman's attacker came back and visited her at all during her stay. See if anyone out of the ordinary had gone into her room at all."

His eyes widened. "Of course. Anything to help." He opened the door to the office and led us to a back room. "You can go through all the footage from the past three days here. Unfortunately, after three days, it records over itself."

Then he looked at Natasha as if he just noticed she was there. "She was the nurse taking care of the patient. I want to see if she can recognize anyone. That is, if it is OK with you that she comes in too?" I smiled at him.

He shrugged his shoulders. "Yeah, that's fine." He then showed me how to pull up different cameras, how to rewind, slow down, and fast forward. I graciously thanked him again, and he left us in the room alone to go over the film.

I went to grab the remote and felt Natasha's hand go over mine. We both quickly pulled our fingers away. "Umm, I think it's best that I go through the footage, considering it's my case." I tried to sound as unbothered about the other night as she was, but deep down I still felt troubled.

"Go back to four this morning. We can start there," she said.

I flipped through all the cameras in the unit area till I found one that was angled toward Tracy's room. I pushed the rewind button till it was at 04:00, then I pressed play. "What exactly are we looking for? I'm guessing an unfamiliar face?" I asked Natasha.

She watched the screen with such intensity that I didn't think she heard me. Right before I opened my mouth to ask her again, she said, "James said that there was a maintenance group working in one of the rooms last night. So maybe look for someone in a maintenance uniform."

I realized I had been staring at her, watching her beautiful eyes scan the screen. Even with the stern look on her face, she was still one of the most ravishing human beings I had ever seen. She must have sensed me watching her because she turned to look at me. "What?" she asked me. The sharpness was gone from her voice, and it made me feel a little more at ease.

I shook my head. "Nothing, sorry." I looked back at the screen, but wished I knew what she was thinking. Maybe then I could figure out why she was acting so numb toward me.

We had been watching for about thirty minutes. I had all but zoned out staring at the screen, so Natasha made me jump when she said, "There!" louder than expected. On the display was a figure in a brown shirt, khaki pants, and a ball cap. "That's a maintenance uniform. I can't see his face," Natasha said, moving closer to the screen.

The person on the screen slipped into the room. About ten minutes later, the man slipped out. He had no business working in that room. "He must have known where the camera was. Look how he is avoiding it and is keeping his face out of view." I gestured toward the man on the screen.

Natasha took the remote and switched to a different camera angle and rewound it to the same time. We saw the same figure still managing to keep his face away from the camera. She switched from camera to camera until the person was out of the hospital. She slammed the remote down on the table a little too hard and let out a frustrated exhale. "We have nothing," she said with frustration.

I could see the tension running from the muscles in her face down her neck. "Natasha, we do have something. We know she was probably murdered. That guy had no business being in there, so we have a lead. Maybe the person left something behind. I need to call the sheriff and get some people down here." I tried to sound as positive about the situation as I could.

She didn't reply to me and instead stood up out of the chair. I followed her out of the room. As we passed the security guard, he stood up. "Did you find everything you needed, Deputy?"

I smiled at him and replied, "Yes, we did. Thank you so much for your assistance." I followed Natasha out of the security office toward the elevator. She still wasn't acknowledging my presence, and it was starting to rub me the wrong way. I didn't have to come down here to help her. She wasn't even acting grateful. She wasn't even acting nice to me. When we got in and the doors closed, I decided to be straightforward. I had seen this done plenty of times in movies and TV shows, pushing the emergency stop to get a bit of privacy. I slapped the red button, and the elevator jerked to a halt. Wow, I couldn't believe that worked.

I turned to look at her. "What is going on with you?" I asked, pulling as much sternness to the surface of my voice as I could. I could still hear a minor pain in my voice slip out.

"What do you mean?" she replied, not looking at me.

I stepped in front of her so I was standing in her line of sight. "Why have you shut me out? I know this is hard for you, but you can hardly look at me. What did I do?"

She lowered her eyes slightly, so they were even with mine. I could see pain and sorrow in them. She took a deep breath in, and her shoulders slumped. "I just want to find who did this to Tracy."

The response frustrated me. She was blocking. "Natasha, that is not what I'm talking about, and you know it. I'm talking about the other night."

She was still looking into my eyes, now. "Everything I'm doing is to protect you." She reached around me and pushed the emergency button again. It started going up and stopped on the first floor.

"What does that even mean?" I didn't understand what she meant by her protecting me. "I'm the one who is supposed to be protecting you and the citizens."

She exhaled a heavy sigh. "Nothing. It's complicated." The elevator pinged and the doors opened. She held the doors open so they wouldn't shut before I got out. "This is your floor. It seems like you have some phone calls to make. You need to catch a bad guy."

She was right; I needed to get the wheels turning on the case now that we may have a lead, but I hesitated. I wanted an explanation. But the elevator started dinging, informing us the doors needed to shut. "Yeah OK, you're right." I walked out of the elevator. Before the doors closed, I turned back and saw her head was hanging low, and her eyes were shut tight as if she was in pain. I didn't understand why she was doing this. It looked like it was just as agonizing for her to act distant from me as it was for me.

I couldn't do anything about it right then. I called the sheriff to tell him my newfound information. He told me to come back to the station, and he would take care of getting in touch with the local authorities to help with the investigation. I tried to protest because I wanted to be part of the investigation at the hospital and lead it, but he objected. When I got off the phone, I walked out of the hospital to my car and headed back up north toward the station.

· · ·

I was exhausted by quitting time. The sheriff had me working on paperwork for the entire rest of the day. I hated paperwork, and it was as tiring for me as working the streets.

It was past sunset by the time I left the station. I slowly walked to my car and pulled out my cell phone, debating whether or not to text Natasha. I wanted to see how she was holding up. I wanted to be there for her. But I slid my phone back into my pocket. It seemed like she didn't want to talk to me, so I tried to let it go.

I got into my car and started the drive home. As I pulled into my driveway, I felt my phone buzz in my pocket. After turning off my car, I pulled out my phone. It was a text from Natasha. *I am sorry about earlier. A lot has been going on lately in my life. Maybe if you aren't too busy tomorrow, we could get coffee and talk.* I jumped out of my car and made my way to the front door. A warm sensation formed in my stomach, and I felt my lips curve into a smile. Maybe she would finally open up to me. At least this text wasn't as stand-offish as her other texts had been.

Before I texted back, I fumbled in my pocket for my keys and unlocked my front door. I walked in and turned on my front room lights and started texting back without looking up.

Before I could send the text, I heard a man's voice from across the room. "Good evening, Deputy. It's a pleasure to meet you finally."

I was so startled I dropped my phone. My hands went to grab my gun, but before I could get it out of the holster, I felt someone grab me from behind and pin my arms against my back so tight I couldn't move. Then I felt a sharp pain in my neck. I knew I had been injected with something. I was terrified. I tried thrashing to break free, but the grip on me was too strong.

I looked up to where the voice had come from. A man sat in the chair across the room, smiling at me. The smile, full of venom, looked more like a sneer. I tried to put on a brave mask, and I looked right into his eyes. I had seen those eyes before, those dark red, amber eyes, cold and empty, staring straight into me. They were the same eyes from my nightmare. A cold chill went down my spine and fear clutched at my chest. My body grew heavy, and my mind became fuzzy. My entire world started going dark and I knew I was in trouble. I tried desperately to hold on to consciousness, but I felt my body collapse even more and grow even weaker. I don't know why I did it, but the last thing I remember was saying Natasha's name, and then my world went black.

NATASHA

I got a text from Max around lunchtime that said the help had finally arrived. I hoped the aid would be of some use to us. I had let him know as soon as Jamie left about the events that took place with Tracy's death and about the person I saw on video going into her room. He agreed it was probably someone finishing the job. I decided to leave early, so I told the charge nurse I had a family emergency.

On the drive to my house, I reflected on the morning with Jamie. I hated closing myself off to her, but I knew it would be best this way, for now, to keep her safe. It hurt me more than I thought it would. When she touched me in the elevator, I wanted to embrace her, breathe in her scent, and let it fill me, seek comfort from her touch, and get lost in her lips, but I knew I couldn't, not until this entire thing was over.

I turned onto the gravel driveway leading to my house and saw a car I didn't recognize. It must be the help that was sent to assist us. I parked next to it and walked up the porch and through the front door. I stopped and glared at the face that was looking at me from the couch as I entered.

"What are you doing here, Kyle?" I asked through clenched teeth. I hadn't seen or talked to him since I moved down here. He was a stuck up, spineless man who I didn't care for in the slightest.

He smiled and scoffed at my question. "That's not quite the greeting I was expecting for an old friend you haven't seen in years."

"We aren't friends. I thought I made that very clear when I left. Why are you here?" I repeated, still standing by the door. If this was the help that was sent, I almost felt insulted.

He stood up from the couch and made his way toward me. "We heard you had some intruders in the area and thought you might need some help."

He stood in front of me now, still smiling. "And Nik sent you? The little brown-nosing weasel with your head so far up Nik's ass you can't think for yourself?" No one had ever really liked Kyle. He was a yes man to his very core. He would do anything to get in good graces with people, even if it meant turning on his best friend.

After my comment, his smile was gone, and his eyes bore into mine. "Maybe he wouldn't have had to send me if you took your role seriously and weren't such a human-loving pushover."

I clenched my fists, ready to strike. "You want to see just how much of a pushover I am?"

Max jumped between us before fists started flying, "Enough! Both of you! Kyle, you know who she is, and you will respect her, or so help me. I know you are here on behalf of Nik, but so am I, so you need to remember your place."

Kyle was still staring daggers at me. "Then she needs to remember her place too, and who she really is, and not take leisurely vacations and act like everything is a game."

I was ready to fight him, prepared to assert my dominance and show him how much of a game I knew it wasn't. "Oh, I know who I am, Kyle. It seems you have forgotten what I am capable of."

Max still stood between us. "OK. Sit down, both of you. Kyle, you know she could kick your ass, but right now we have bigger things to deal with."

Kyle let out a breath and put a grin back on his face. He turned away and sat back down on the couch. "You're right. We do."

I resisted the urge to say anything more and sat on the chair across from Kyle. We did need to figure out what to do, and if Kyle was the only help we had, I had to make the best of the situation even though he knew how to get under my skin. "So what does Nik have to say about this, and how are you supposed to help us?"

Kyle reached and grabbed a cup off the coffee table, then took a quick drink. "We have heard of a group growing bigger and starting to become more brazen in trying to take our territory. The last we heard, they were east in West Virginia. They haven't made any huge moves yet, but it's only a matter of time. Their leader supposedly goes by Phantom."

I heard Irene chuckle as she came in through the kitchen. "Phantom? Really? How much more cliché can you get?"

It was a little amusing that someone by the name of Phantom was going around trying to take our territory. "Who is Phantom really, and when you say their group is growing bigger, do you mean they are changing humans?" I asked with concern.

"Yes, they have been changing people. We haven't been able to find Phantom yet. His group is very fluid and moves around a lot. It's like trying to catch smoke," Kyle replied.

Turning a person required permission on someone's territory. As far as I knew, no one had permission to turn anyone lately. "I can't believe they are turning so many people. I met one of the guys, and he seemed to be recently turned. You think this is them?" I asked him.

"That's what I was sent to find out. If they do know who you are, that is dangerous for everyone. You might want to think about moving back or going into hiding somewhere else," Kyle said with a stern look in my direction.

I hated hiding and running. I didn't leave my home to hide, even though that was my excuse. I needed space. I wanted some control over my own life. "I'm not going anywhere. I'm not going to give in to this prick's threats. He killed my friend and threatened my, umm, another friend. They have been using humans to do their dirty work." I gave Kyle a frustrated look.

He looked at me curiously. "Human friends? Have they attacked any of you? And why would they be using humans?"

I stood up and started pacing. I couldn't sit still right then. I knew it was strange for us to consider humans our friends, but they were my friends. "Yes, human friends, and no, they haven't attacked any of us yet. They sent a human to try and threaten me, and they sent a human to kill Tracy. I guess they are using humans because we can't track them."

"That's very unsettling that they are so bold as to freelance humans so openly," Kyle said.

I turned to look at him. "Since you are Nik's liaison, what should we do with them? Hunt them down?"

Kyle sat and contemplated for a moment. "No. If we try to be too aggressive, they might make a big scene. We should wait and see. Keep an eye out and try and figure out their next move."

His response infuriated me. I knew he didn't think much of humans, but a gruesome murder had been committed on our land. "You don't think brutally attacking a couple in a cabin is a big scene?" I asked. "What more do you want them to do to get our attention?"

He jumped at my loud reply. "Nat, an animal could have done that. It didn't bring any attention to our world. They are playing a game, and they want you to overreact."

"They knew my name! They killed a close friend of mine and threatened Jamie! They have made this personal, Kyle!" I felt rage poring through my veins. I needed to get out of the house. I needed to get away. "I'm going on a drive. If you think of a logical plan, let me know." Before any of them could respond, I stormed out the door, got into my car, and started driving. I knew of a remote cove in a nearby lake where I would go and clear my head from time to time.

I pulled up under the trees and got out. The forest above me provided much-needed shade. The water was so still and blue. I took in a deep breath, and the fresh air started clearing out some of the anger that had been poisoning me. I sat down on a large boulder and looked out across the lake, taking in the scene. I shut my eyes and listened intently, trying to get lost in the sounds of my surroundings. I could hear all the noises of the forest. Every individual insect buzzing, all the different heartbeats from the many animals around, the crunching of leaves under a deer's feet, ants crawling up a nearby tree. It was nice clearing my mind and letting my instincts take over.

I had been sitting there for a few hours before I brought myself back to reality. The sun had just fallen over the horizon. I felt relaxed and calm from my meditation. I didn't want to think about the intruders and what we were going to have to do now. Maybe running and hiding somewhere else was the best for me. But then my mind went to Jamie, and I started to feel guilt surround my heart. Maybe Irene had been right. Maybe keeping her close was safer than keeping my distance. I knew I thought that for selfish reasons. I wanted her around for my benefit. I pulled out my phone and decided to text her. I had tomorrow off, so I was going to see if she wanted to get coffee. Hopefully, my actions from earlier in the day didn't drive a wedge too far between us.

I sat there a little while longer. I heard the nocturnal essence of the forest come to life. It was different from the daily sounds. It was more alive, wilder. Then I heard my phone ping—a text. I looked at the screen and saw it was from Jamie. I clicked to open the text. What I saw sent dread through my body, and I felt my heart stop. Then rage filled every inch of me. I started shaking uncontrollably. It was a picture of Jamie bound and gagged. Her eyes were shut, so I assumed she was sedated or knocked out. There was a message under the picture. *Come to her house. We need to have a little chat.* I let out a savage roar and let the predator wash over me. In my blind rage, I couldn't tell if I was in control or my other side had taken over. I got in my car and pushed the pedal down as hard as I could. I called Irene on my way to Jamie's house.

I heard her on the other line. "Nat, where are you?"

"They have her, Irene. I'm going to her house. Meet me there." I could hear the primal animal in my voice, drowning out my human side. I hung up without saying another word.

As I got closer to the neighborhood, every nerve in my body lit up with a fury like I had never felt before.

I slammed on the brakes in front of Jamie's house. A man stood on the front lawn, relaxed as could be. He was shorter than Max, more the height of an average human male, and his body was slim but not skinny. His hair was combed back over the top of his head and slightly to the side, but not slicked down. I could tell he was older because he had grey flecks in his hair and had a well-kept peppered beard. When he saw my car, a crooked smile formed on his face, and it only ignited the fire taking over my body. I was out of the car before it even stopped, and in his face before he could even blink, gripping his shirt collar in my hands. "Where is she!?" I growled furiously at him.

The man chuckled. "Touchy, touchy." And he looked over at the porch.

I turned my head in the direction he was looking and saw another man come out of the house half dragging Jamie. She was trying to walk, but it seemed she was still sedated and couldn't keep her footing. She had a blindfold over her eyes, and a gag in her mouth. Her arms were tied tight around her back, and her feet were bound together.

Seeing her in this state and being dragged from her own house filled me with such a wrath-filled frenzy that I was on the brink of losing it. I didn't care who I killed. I let go of the man and was about to attack Jamie's handler when I saw him put a long claw along her throat. Jamie recoiled at the pressure. She still couldn't stand on her own, so the man kept jerking her to her feet.

I turned my attention and fury back toward the first man. It was clear he was the one in charge. He had a smug smile on his face. I bore all my malice and hate into the look I gave him. "If you don't let her go now, I will kill you right here, right now."

"I believe introductions are in order," the man said, as if he hadn't heard a single word I said. It made my anger blaze even brighter.

I cut him off before he could continue. "I don't give a shit who you or your little group is. I will bleed all of you dry before any of you know what happened. Let her go!"

He let out a laugh. "Boy, aren't you a spitfire! The amount of energy you have in you is outstanding! You have so much more raw power rolling off you than the last time I saw you." He shook his head and put his hands on his hips like he didn't have a care in the world.

I had never seen this man before. Nothing about him registered with any of my memories. I wasn't going to let him get into my head. I growled at him.

"Regardless of whether you remember me or not, we are going to negotiate. I have something you want," he said, pointing at Jamie. "And you can offer me something I want."

I started to breathe hard, and I felt the little control I had slipping away. I wanted to kill the man. I wanted nothing more at that point. I couldn't even comprehend the words he was speaking to me. I just had one thought in my mind: end him.

I hadn't responded to him, and that made the man drop his smile and smugness. It was replaced by a sinister, emotionless, cold mask. "I know who you are. I know your legacy, and I want it. I almost had it once, but I wasn't prepared for the power that runs in your blood. You are lucky you survived back then. I'm back for it, and you will give it to me. I have no problem killing a human for it or anyone else in my way. I'm prepared this time."

I remembered now, the smell in the cabin that I couldn't place. This man was there the night my family was murdered. He had taken my siblings and mother from my father and me. I felt a feral part of me I hadn't felt in a long time start to creep in. I didn't care now if I lost control. My body started recoiling for an attack. My teeth bared, ready to tear into his throat. Then I heard a yelp.

It was Jamie. I snapped my head in her direction. She had a deep slash on her cheek now and blood was running down her face. Her pained cry pulled me back in control. "You are going to regret coming here and threatening me. You kidnapped Jamie. You killed one of my friends. You killed my family!" I hissed.

He shook his head. "You killed one of mine, so I killed one of yours. An eye for an eye. And that family business is ancient history. Now you know I mean business. And your little human pet is my leverage."

I glared at him. "Even if I wanted to give in to your demands, this territory is not mine to give. I'm just its protector for now."

That smug smile was back on his face. "You are the heir to it all, not just this minuscule piece of land. You have a say, and you will give me what I want, or I will take everything from you." He looked at the man holding Jamie and nodded to him. I moved so fast the man didn't even see me.

I knocked Jamie onto the ground out of the man's grasp and was behind him. My hand had ripped through the flesh of his back and penetrated his chest cavity. My fingers were wrapped tight around the strong muscle that was still pumping blood through his body. I ripped it out with a fierce growl and crushed it in my hand. He saw the entire event transpire before his life left his body, and then I let the body slump to the ground.

Irene, Max, and Kyle were there now in their predator forms. I knew they had been close earlier. The man that had been talking to me before had already vanished. There were six more of our kind newly turned out of control, attempting to fight back. After two of them were cut down by Max with no effort, the rest ran off into the woods, and the three took off after them.

I released the heart I had crushed in my hand and let it fall to the ground. I bent over the man's body and used his jacket to wipe as much blood off my arm as I could.

When I stood and turned, I saw Jamie. She was still bound on the ground, but the blindfold was now off her eyes. She stared at me, eyes wide, and I could see fear and terror in them. It made me freeze, and I didn't know how to react next.

JAMIE

As I fell out of my captor's hold, I couldn't catch myself because my arms were tied too tightly around my back. I landed on the hard ground right on my hip, and it sent a sharp pain down my leg.

I was still groggy from whatever they had injected me with, but I was trying to get free in any way possible. Finally, I was able to use my shoulder to nudge the blindfold off my eyes to try and figure out my surroundings. I blinked, trying to adjust my eyes to the little light my porch gave off. I saw someone standing in front of me. Their back was turned toward me. It was a woman. Her hair was wavy, dirty blond, and in a ponytail. It looked familiar. A man lay on the ground face down at her feet. I saw an enormous bloody hole in his back, and it sent a shock of fear through me. *Was he dead?* He had to be.

The woman turned around, and all I could do was stare. It looked like Natasha but different. Were the drugs they injected me with making me hallucinate? She was taller, and her entire body was broader. Every muscle in her was bulging, hard, and defined. Her veins protruded from her snow-white skin. Her body looked as if it were humming or vibrating. I couldn't explain it. The features on her face were much sharper than usual and more defined. Her eyes were still an amber color, but darker, and the tone in her irises looked as if they were dancing like they were on fire and alive. Her lips parted slightly, and I saw her cuspid teeth—they were an inch longer than they should have been.

Who was I looking at? What was I looking at? My brain supplied an answer, but I couldn't believe the explanation it came up with. *A vampire? Was I having a dream?* I couldn't tell if this was reality or not.

She started taking slow steps toward me. Her eyes scanned my body from head to toe. Then they stopped at my eyes. It was her. I knew it was her. There was no menace in her untamed eyes, only worry and sorrow. She knelt beside me and reached out her hand toward my cheek. I saw long talons protruding from her fingertips, and it made my body instinctively retreat from her. My fight-or-flight instinct was coming alive, and the prey inside of me was screaming for me to run, to flee as fast as I could. After I flinched, I saw sadness and pain in her eyes. She wasn't a danger. She was there to help me.

She moved around me to my back, and I felt the tension of the rope around my wrists release with a snap. I brought my hands to my front and started rubbing my wrists, trying to get feeling back in them. After the numb tingling sensation went away, I turned my body around to face her again. I still wasn't quite sure if I was awake. She looked at me as if she was waiting for me to move or say something first. I reached my hand out slowly because I was still somewhat nervous.

She didn't move as I cupped her face in my hand. Her skin was cold and hard, like marble. I rubbed my thumb along her cheek, and she closed her eyes. She reached her hand up and put it over mine, soaking in my touch. Then she opened her eyes and looked at me. Maybe she was some kind of monster or vampire, but it was still her. It was still Natasha.

Her eyes wandered down to my cheek. She ripped off part of the bottom of her shirt and pressed the cloth against my cheek. I was suddenly reminded of the pain that was there. The touch made me flinch, and I inhaled sharply through my teeth.

"I'm sorry. It's still bleeding." Her voice was even different now. It was a rough, primal rumble from deep in her chest, but not threatening. "Hold this here with pressure." She took my hand and placed it against the cloth on my cheek. I did what she instructed. Her presence was so powerful. I knew I was frightened, but I trusted her.

She stood up and unclipped a canister attached with a carabineer to a belt loop on her pants. She took three long swallows from it. When she took it away from her lips, there was a thin line of dark red left behind. It was more confirmation of my previous theory of what she was. Then she took in a deep breath and shut her eyes. Just like that, her body melted into the form I knew.

All I could do was stare. I couldn't wrap my mind around what was happening. It wasn't possible.

She started coming back to me. I was still trying to process the change I had just seen when I heard her ask, "Are you hurt? Can you stand?" in the soft voice I was used to hearing.

I couldn't answer right away. Her voice had changed. Her physical being had just transformed right in front of my eyes. I rubbed my eyes and shook my head. I looked back into her gaze, trying to find an answer. There was still a concern in her look but there was also a warmth.

"I think I am fine physically." I couldn't feel any of my injuries at this point. I knew that could just have been the adrenaline that was surging through my body. I didn't know if I was mentally well, though. If what I had just witnessed was my imagination or not.

She came over and undid the rope around my legs and then put her arm under mine. I tried to stand, but once I put pressure onto my right side, I collapsed and a cry of pain escaped my lips. The pressure shot pain down to my toes. I would have fallen to the ground, but Natasha was there and caught me.

She put my left arm around her neck and her right arm around my back. She then swept my legs off the ground with one swift movement. It was so effortless. She carried me up the porch stairs as if I weighed nothing, pushed the door open with her foot, and carried me inside.

I felt her carry me over to my couch and set me down with the utmost easy. Her hand brushed over the side of my face, and she kissed my forehead. Then she knelt in front of me, placed her hands on my thighs, and pressed her forehead against mine.

"I'm so sorry about this." Her eyes closed, and her brows creased together. Her voice had so much sorrow and pain in it. "I wish I could take you out of the equation. This is all my fault." I watched as she bowed her head down.

I didn't know what was going on or what her words meant, but I did know she just saved my life. She just showed me something that she probably hadn't shown many people before. Her eyes had told me everything. I reached my hand under her chin and lifted it so I could look at her. "Natasha, you have no reason to be sorry. You saved me. I thought you didn't want me in your life anymore."

She swiftly but gently held both of my cheeks and lightly placed a kiss on my lips. "I could never want you out of my life."

I smiled against her lips at her response. "Good."

She stood up after our exchange. "I need to go check on the others," she said as she headed toward the door.

"Wait!" I realized Walter was missing. *Why hadn't he been next to me? Why wasn't he barking or going crazy with all the commotion?* "Where is Walter?" I tried to stand up. As I took a step, my leg gave out. Natasha was there and braced me before I could fall. Her movement was so fast I almost couldn't see her.

The anxiety gripped my chest. After everything that had just happened, I needed to know he was alive and well.

"You need to sit down and rest," she told me.

"But Walter. Where is he? I need to find him." I started to get even more frantic. I had no idea where he was.

"OK, relax Jamie, I'll go find him. But please, stay here, on the couch." Then she stood and moved so fast to the back I almost couldn't wrap my head around it. It looked like she was flying. I heard the back door open and close.

I pulled my entire body onto the couch and leaned my head back against the armrest. I took in some deep breaths to try and slow my heart rate down. As my body relaxed, I started to realize how tired I was. I knew I had been knocked out for who knows how long, but I was exhausted and was beginning to feel the soreness all over my body. I didn't know if it was from everything that had happened or if the drugs were still affecting me. I closed my eyes, trying to understand what was happening.

My thoughts were interrupted when I heard the back door open. My eyes instantly snapped open. I saw Natasha walking into the front room toward me with a bundle of fur in her arms. I must have had a look of concern on my face because before I could say anything, she put my mind at ease. "He is OK, I promise. They used a tranquilizer on him." She laid him down on the dog bed in the living room.

A sense of relief washed over my body. I was so happy he was safe and that they hadn't hurt him. Natasha came over and sat down on the couch beside me. I had so many questions I wanted to ask her, and she knew it. "Jamie, I will answer any and every question you have, I promise. But I need to see if Irene and Max are OK. I promise nothing will happen to you." She wasn't looking at me, but I could hear the guilt in her voice. I put my hand on her thigh and squeezed. She turned and smiled at me, then walked to the door and outside.

Max and Irene were here too? I sat up on the couch and looked through the window. Natasha stood in the middle of the front yard. Then I saw three shadows emerge from the forest. They moved with the same speed as Natasha, stopped when they reached her. All three were in a form Natasha had been in. *Were they whatever Natasha was too?* I saw what I thought was Max and Irene. Another man carried a body over his shoulder.

Natasha spoke to them, but I couldn't hear what she was saying. All of a sudden, they melted back into normal-looking people. Max walked over to the body of the man that had been at Natasha's feet earlier. He picked him up and threw him over his shoulder. He and the other man walked to a truck parked in front of my house. They threw the two bodies into the bed of the truck. Then they went and grabbed two other bodies from my lawn and put them into the bed, then covered the bed with a tarp. Irene ran off into the woods. Max and the man got in the truck and drove off. I saw Natasha come back to the house.

The door opened and Natasha walked through. "Are those guys dead?" I asked, just now realizing how bad that was.

"Three of them are, including the one that was holding you captive. He was going to kill you. The other one isn't dead, just unconscious," she replied to me with a hint of anxiety in her voice.

My mind was racing a hundred miles an hour again. Three dead guys had been on my front lawn. I didn't know what questions to ask because my mind was everywhere. "Are you OK?" she asked me.

It pulled me out of my thoughts. There was so much underlying concern in her voice.

Was I OK? I thought to myself. *I was alive; Walter was alive; she was here.* "Yeah, I think I'm OK. Maybe? I don't really know what is going on here. I was kidnapped and drugged. There were dead men in my front yard, and then you, you were something else. You looked different and then changed, and Irene and Max were different… well I think that was them. I don't know right now if I'm dreaming or if all of this is real."

She strode over to the couch and sat down by me. "Yes, what you saw was real. You aren't dreaming. And the dead guys were the same as us, but they weren't good people."

"The same as you? What does that mean, Natasha? Are you some kind of vampire or something?" I half expected her to deny it and give me some other explanation of the events that had taken place.

She was quiet for some time, staring at the floor. "I guess vampire is the closest explanation to what we are that humans have come up with, so yes, we are vampires," she replied, still not looking at me.

I let out a long breath and started to feel light-headed. This couldn't be real. I could feel my body starting to shake. My vision narrowed, and my chest tightened. *Vampires. This couldn't be real.* Natasha turned on the couch and looked at me. "Take deep breaths, Jamie. Slow your breathing down. Deep breath in and out, in and out." As she coached me through breathing, my body started to relax. A panic attack was the last thing I needed right now.

She still had guilt and sadness written all over her face. "I understand if you are frightened by me because of what I am, but I promise I would never hurt you, and I promise I will never let them get near you ever again."

I was still a little shaky, but I reached out and grabbed her hand. "Natasha, I'm not scared of you. You saved me. But I did just get kidnapped and drugged. There were dead people on my front lawn. And now I know that vampires exist. It's just a lot to take in right now." I wanted her to look at me, but she had turned her face away from me.

I scooted as close to her on the couch as I could get. I reached out for her cheek again. It was warm, soft, and smooth now. I turned her face toward me. "I'm just scared of the situation. I have so many unanswered questions. I don't even know if I am awake right now. But I know I'm not scared of you."

She still had a look of uncertainty in her eyes, so I leaned forward and let my lips touch hers in a reassuring kiss. She turned her body toward me, and I felt her arms slide around my lower back and pull me closer to her. She deepened the kiss, and I felt the desire behind her lips. It was the same feeling that had just ignited in my chest.

I didn't know if it was the adrenaline that was fueling this need, but I wanted her close. I slid one of my arms around her back and the other up her neck and through her hair. I pulled her even closer.

Our lips moved in tandem, the hunger for one another's touch driving us. I had to pull away for a moment to catch my breath. I felt her nip at my lower lip, and it sent a yearning down my front to my core.

Everything that had happened earlier that night disappeared as I got lost further in her. I usually didn't move fast with people when it came to physical intimacy, but after almost dying and learning vampires did exist, I needed something to distract my mind. I needed her to touch me, to hold me. I needed her lips against mine. I needed all of her.

I leaned back on the couch and pulled her with me. There was no resistance. I felt the pressure of her body against mine, and it gave me a sense of comfort and longing. Her lips tasted so good. I let my tongue run along her bottom lip, and I felt her push her hips into me in response. One of her hands had found its way under my shirt, and I felt her warm touch against my ribs. I pulled at her hair to slightly raise her head so my lips could find her jawline. I left a trail of hot, wet kisses down her jaw till I got to her throat. I nipped and sucked at her neck, and in response her body tensed, and I heard a low groan escape her. Her hand clenched the skin on my side tightly, and I felt her body grind against me, searching for friction. I had my hand under the back of her shirt and I raked my fingernails down the length of her back. I let her lips find mine again.

There was an eagerness behind her kiss that was almost wild, and I wanted to give in to it so badly. Her lips parted, and I slid my tongue between them, searching for hers. When I felt it slide against mine, I grabbed her tighter, trying to deepen the kiss.

Her hand slid down my side till it finally reached my stomach right above my jeans. She unbuttoned them, and I sucked at her lower lip, encouraging her. I was utterly lost in her now. I wanted all of her. My hips arched up, trying to find her hand. My lips moved against hers. I held my breath as I felt her smooth fingertips start their slow descent down the sensitive skin. Right before her hand met where I needed it the most, I felt her pull away. In an instant, the weight of her body on top of me wasn't there. Her presence was gone.

I sat up, startled. She was on the other side of the room. Her breathing looked out of control, and she was grabbing the back of her head, crouched over. I thought I did something wrong or that I may have hurt her. "Oh my gosh! Are you OK? I'm so sorry. I didn't mean to push you. I just…"

She cut me off. "No, no, no. It's OK. It's not your fault." She sounded almost in pain, her teeth were clenched, and her eyes squeezed firmly shut. "I just can't do this right now. I can't lose control." I was worried about her. I was about to get up and go to her to offer comfort, but she stopped me, lifting her hand in my direction. "Just stay right there for a second." I didn't understand what was happening. But I listened to her and stayed put.

"Can I do anything for you? You look like you are in pain." I wanted to help her but didn't know what I could do.

She didn't answer me, but her breathing started to slow, and her hands began to move away from her head, but her eyes were still tightly closed. She opened her eyes as she replied. "I'm sorry. I wasn't in pain necessarily. I felt like I was about to lose control. This night has taken a lot out of me, and my instincts are a bit on edge." Once she had gained control, she came over and sat down beside me.

I had no idea what she was talking about. "Your instincts?" I thought that was an excellent place to start with my questions.

She gave a little smile at the question. "Yes, my instincts. I am guessing your opinion of what vampires are is based on popular fiction books and movies?"

She wasn't wrong. I had read and seen plenty of fiction based on vampires. "Yeah, but you seem a lot different. You physically changed. You are warm right now, which means your heart pumps blood, so your heart beats, right? But then you were cold and had claws and took on a different form."

She softly took my hand and placed it on her chest. I felt a heartbeat, but it was a lot slower than a normal human's heartbeat. "Yes, I have a heartbeat. We are not immortal or undead like stories make us out to be. We do, however, live for a very, very long time. That may be how we became known as immortal. When we shift into our other form, our skin gets hard, tough, and cold. It's a defensive mechanism, like a shield. And instinct is what controls our predator side, I guess. When we feel threatened or angry, upset, or get way too excited..." She smiled after the word excited. "Sometimes that side of us tries to work its way out on its own. If we lose control of it, it would not be an ideal situation. But as long as we are in control of it, everything is fine. Mostly it's used for hunting or when we are in an unsafe, threatened situation." I pulled my hand away from her.

"Hunting? Like hunting people? Is that what real vampires do? I saw you drink something red from your canteen. Do you drink blood to survive, from people?" My rapid-fire questions came flooding out of me like word vomit. *Did they kill people for their blood?* That thought made me scared for not only myself but for my community as well.

She was quiet. I could tell she was trying to figure out how to give me the answers I wanted. "Yes, we do drink blood. That part of the stories is true. Irene, Max, and I, along with the others in my clan, mostly hunt animals for blood. I also get bagged human blood from a supplier. We can eat human food, but we need blood to survive. If we don't get enough of it, our predator side will take over and go looking for it. But we don't have to kill when we drink from an animal or person if we are in control."

It was a lot of information for my brain to handle all at once. I was curious about something, though. "So, if you bite someone to drink their blood without killing them, do they turn into a vampire?"

She shook her head. "No, and yes. Just because we bite someone doesn't mean it turns them. If we want to turn someone, it has to be a bite meant to turn someone. There is a specific hormone and enzyme in our bodies. If it gets into a human's blood, it takes over and changes their body makeup and DNA. We have to will the molecules out of our blood to our saliva, which, for some reason, is very painful and exhausting. Then we have to have the will to stop biting the person before we drain them."

She was so open about her world with me. It made me feel more comfortable. "Have you ever changed someone into a vampire?"

She looked away from me back to the floor. "Yes. Twice, a long time ago. Changing humans is frowned upon in my world. You have to have permission to do it." There was sadness and shame in her voice when she told me.

Another question popped into my head. I was a little scared to ask it but wanted to know. "Have you ever killed a human before?"

She turned her head around to look at me. I couldn't read the expression on her face. Then she turned it back to the floor and let out a long sigh. "Yes, I have. Please don't ask me how many. But know

I would never hurt a human or a vampire unless it were necessary." That was a little worrisome, but I was glad she was honest with me.

I decided to steer my questions in a different direction. I didn't want to push her with that subject. It seemed to upset her. I would have kept on the topic if I hadn't felt safe with her, but I did feel safe. "Those other vampires tonight—were they hunting me? Did they kidnap me to drink my blood? I thought you said your clan hunts animals."

She slowly turned her head again to look at me. I saw guilt in her eyes. Her brows furrowed, and her lips formed a hard line. The muscles in her jaw were flexed hard as she clenched her teeth. "They aren't part of our clan. Some vampires do hunt people and drink their blood. But they went after you because of me." There was a wave of anger behind her voice. "They saw us kiss the other night and wanted to use you as leverage. I got a warning from them the night we kissed that they knew I cared about you. That's why I have been keeping my distance lately. I thought maybe if I kept away from you, they wouldn't go after you."

I felt hurt by what she had just said. Not because I had gotten dragged into the middle of this but because she kept it from me. "Why didn't you tell me, Natasha? It's not fair to me if I'm in danger and you keep me in the dark. It also hurt when you just stopped talking to me, more than you can know. I thought I did something wrong." It looked like my words hit a nerve a little harder than I wanted.

She bowed her head down and drew in a deep breath. "I couldn't tell you about it. It's a law in my world to keep humans in the dark about us. Even if I could have, I thought the less you knew, the less danger would follow you. I'm so sorry I hurt you. It hurt me, too, trying to keep my distance." I could tell she was genuinely sorry for it by the pain behind her words.

I reached out my hand and took her arm. I found her hand and interlaced my fingers in hers. "Why do they need leverage against you?"

She took in a deep, shaky breath. "Because of who I am."

"Who are you?" I asked out of curiosity. The only thing I truly knew about her was that she was a nurse and wasn't originally from here.

She was silent. I didn't know if she was going to answer the question or not. "No one is supposed to know who I am. Only a handful of vampires know who I am. Right now, can we save that question for later? I will tell you in time, I promise, just not yet."

My curiosity was spiked, but I knew it was making her uncomfortable talking about it, so I tried to lighten the mood a little, "So what are you? Some secret vampire princess that can bring peace to the world?" I nudged into her shoulder softly.

She cocked her head sideways to look at me. I saw a small smile form on her lips. "What if I was?"

"Hmm," I replied slowly, pretending I was deep in thought. "Well, I guess I would be the luckiest person in the world, having just dry-humped a legendary princess."

She laughed and grabbed one of the couch pillows and threw it at my face. "Shut up," she said through her laughter. I caught the pillow before it hit me. I tossed it onto the floor, and wrapped my arms around her neck and pulled her into a kiss. "Thank you for being honest with me."

She put her hands on my sides and with ease, lifted me in front of her. My legs rested on either side of her thighs, straddling her lap. She looked into my eyes intently, and her face turned serious. "Jamie, you can't say anything about this to anyone. Please promise you won't. The more people who know you know about our world, the more danger you are in."

I stared into her eyes for a while before I answered. It was finally hitting me that I wasn't in a dream and that all this was real. "I won't tell anyone. I promise. I trust you."

For some reason, fear took over me again. The terror I felt when I saw those men in my house and the horror when I knew they had drugged me. I wasn't in control of any of that situation. They had gotten to me so effortlessly. "What if those vampires come back for me?"

Her face went still and hard, and I saw the amber color in her eyes start flickering like flames. There was a growl behind her voice. "I won't let them touch you ever again."

NATASHA

I convinced Jamie to move to her room from the couch. When we got there, she went into the bathroom to do her nightly routine and get ready for bed. I could tell she was limping from where she fell on her hip, but she wouldn't let me take a look at it. She could be a very stubborn individual.

I walked to the window in her room and stared out, scanning the forest. I knew Irene was out there keeping an eye open for the intruders, but I was still anxious about them coming back.

Max and Kyle took the dead vampires' bodies to dispose of them. They were able to knock one of the others out without killing him. Kyle wanted to interrogate him, so they took him back to my house.

Jamie was taking all the new information a lot better than I thought she would. I wasn't sure at first if I wanted to give her all the information about my world, but I knew after what she had witnessed, she would probably go looking for answers, and that would have been even more dangerous for her. At least if I was candid and answered her questions honestly, I wouldn't have to worry about her seeking out answers and getting in more trouble. Of course, there were some things that I couldn't tell her or wasn't ready to say to her right now, but I decided to be forthright about my world.

Irene, Max, and I had decided that when I couldn't be around to protect her, we would take turns no matter where she was. I still hadn't told her yet that we planned on basically stalking her twenty-four hours a day. But now that she knew about the dangers she could be in, I was hoping she wouldn't be too opposed or put off with me spending so much time with her.

I heard the bathroom door open, and she walked into the room. I turned away from the window to look at her. She was wearing short, navy blue sleeping shorts and a black tank top. My eyes uncontrollably scanned her body from her feet up. I noticed she wasn't wearing a bra, and my eyes hovered there for a moment too long. I heard her chuckle. "Do you like what you see?"

I tried to hide it by clearing my voice. "I, um, was making sure you didn't have any injuries."

She laughed again. "Uh-huh." It was clear I had been caught. She walked over to her bed and pulled down the covers. I watched her slide into the sheets. She laid her head against the pillows and pulled the covers up to her stomach.

I felt a little embarrassed that I had been caught staring at her and needed to say something to prevent the blush that was growing up my neck. "Can I get you anything before I go to the living room?" We had already established I would spend the night, and I was under the impression I would sleep on the couch.

"No, I don't need anything," she replied. I nodded my head and turned toward the door. "Wait! Natasha," she hesitated before continuing. "Will you stay in here tonight with me? The bed is big enough for two people, and I would feel safer. Please?"

I could hear the plea in her voice and felt the corners of my lips curve up in a smile. "Yes, of course, I will. And you can call me Nat." It was a little selfish of me to agree to stay in her room with her. Yes, I could keep a better eye on her, and I knew nothing would happen physically between us that night, but just having her close to me made me feel a sense of excitement.

I turned off the bedroom light and walked over to the opposite side of the bed. I laid down on my back on top of the comforter. I laced my fingers together behind my head and closed my eyes. There was silence in the darkness for five minutes before I heard Jamie begin to move. Her head softly landed on the front of my shoulder, and her arm slid across my stomach. I unlaced my fingers and wrapped my arm around her back, and put my other hand on her arm that was over my midsection. I breathed in her scent and was overcome with a sense of pleasure.

"Did you just smell me?" Jamie asked, breaking the silence. *How many embarrassing things could she catch me doing tonight?*

"Uh, no, I was, um, yawning," I told her, trying to cover it up.

"Yeah, no, that wasn't a yawn. You were smelling something," she insisted.

I let out a sigh because I knew I had been caught yet again, "OK, OK. Yes, I was smelling you. Your smell is…" I didn't know how to describe it to her without sounding like a creep.

"My smell is what? Do I stink?" she asked, leaning her head over to her arm and taking a sniff.

I snorted a laugh at her gesture. "No, you don't stink. Your smell is kind of intoxicating to me. I like it." I shrugged. It was true, and I didn't know how else to describe it to her. "It's hard to describe if you haven't sensed something like it before."

"So, it's like how I like the smell of freshly cut grass, and right before it rains, kind of thing? Or is it like smelling an expensive perfume?" she asked.

I chuckled. "Not really. It's more of a pleasure-triggering sent." I felt her smile on my shoulder. "I told you it's hard to explain to a human because you can't smell certain things."

"Vampires have heightened senses?" she asked, curiously.

"Yes," I replied. Our senses were far more heightened than humans. They were more enhanced than any animal, which was one of the things that made us such good hunters.

"All of your senses?"

I smiled. "Yes, all of our senses. Sight, smell, hearing, touch, and taste." I replied. "More so in our predator form."

"Are you faster and stronger than humans too?" she questioned.

"Yes. Also, more so in our other form," I answered. We were one of the most physically strong creatures to walk this planet.

"What is a vampire's' weakness? I know from movies and books there are crosses, holy water, wooden stakes through the heart, garlic, the sun. Are those all true?" she asked.

I huffed at her question. "Why do you want to know my weaknesses? Are you going to try to get rid of me in my sleep?" I asked her teasingly.

"No," she replied quickly. "If those guys come back, I don't want to be helpless."

I was quiet for a moment. I still felt responsible for what they had done to her, and it filled me with guilt that she wanted to know how to hurt a vampire because she felt so insecure about it. "Jamie, I won't let them hurt you." I tightened my arm around her in a reassuring grip. "But I will answer your questions as I promised. Crosses and holy water are a myth. Of course, a wooden stake would kill me if someone were able to penetrate my skin and get it to my heart, which is highly unlikely. Our skin is pretty much impenetrable. But a wooden stake through any animal's heart would kill them. Garlic is a no—I have yet to see it negatively affect any vampire, but the smell is very repulsive to us. The sun does hurt us. We don't spontaneously combust when we walk in it. It's more like having an extreme allergy to the sun, but if we stay in it for too long, without protection, it can kill us. We have formulated a specific sunscreen that protects us. A vampire's main weakness is silver."

"Silver," she repeated inquisitively. "I thought silver was a werewolf thing?"

"It is also a vampire thing," I told her.

She lifted herself up with her free arm and pushed on my stomach to support herself with the other. I could see her face in the dark, but I knew she couldn't see mine. Her eyes were full of shock and awe. "Wait, werewolves are real too?"

It made me giggle how intrigued she was. "Yes, werewolves exist, but they probably aren't the typical werewolf you think they are. Most legends and myths are formulated from some truth, and over time they are exaggerated and changed along the way."

"So then all the fairy tales and stories I was told as a kid are real?" she asked me.

"Well, maybe not all of them, but a lot are, yeah. Some are just a little different."

"Have you met any?" she asked enthusiastically.

"Any what?" I asked her.

"Any, you know, werewolves or witches or supernatural beings."

I thought about how to reply to her question. I had met many different creatures in my life. Some were my friends. Some were not. "I have, yes. But most werewolves live in Canada or wilderness areas. They stay away from humans for the most part. And witches are all over but keep to themselves as well. Each race has its own governing body. We all live in harmony as long as the different species keep to their laws. We all respect each other's legislation. As long as this happens, no one disrupts the balance."

"So you aren't like mortal enemies?" she asked, as she lay her head back down and replaced her arm across me.

I shook my head. "No, we are not mortal enemies. We all work together, sometimes when the balance gets disrupted. One of my best friends is a werewolf."

She was quiet for a long moment after that. Then she asked me a question that I wasn't quite prepared for her to ask. "You said that vampires live for a long time." I hummed in agreement to her statement. "How old are you?"

I mulled the question over for a while. I was a little frightened at stating how long I had been walking this earth. What if she thought differently about me? I knew humans and vampires looked at time and years differently. "For all intents and purposes, I am thirty years old." I decided not to answer directly.

"So you were thirty when you got turned?" she asked me.

I was a bit puzzled by her question. Then I realized she didn't know vampires could be born. Yet another pop fiction inaccuracy. "No, I wasn't bitten. I was born."

"Vampires can be born? When were you born?" She was so full of questions.

"I was born a while ago." I didn't want to get too specific just now about my actual age. "And yes, vampires can give birth. We are still living creatures. We aren't the undead like I said earlier."

I heard her yawn. "I think those are all the questions I have tonight. I will come up with some more tomorrow. I'm getting tired," she whispered through a sleep-filled voice.

I kissed the top of her head, and she gave me an approving "Hmm." It was only a matter of minutes before I heard her breathing slow and form the shallow, even respirations of sleep. At that point, I felt my eyelids growing heavy. I sent a quick text to Irene, asking if she had seen any of the others come back. She replied that all was quiet, and nothing unusual was happening. After her reassuring response, I closed my eyes and drifted off into sleep.

. . .

I was woken up by a whimpering, moaning sound. I realized Jamie was no longer by my side. I looked toward her side of the bed and saw her body facing away from me. She was clutching the sheets and grimacing. Sweat had soaked through her tank top. She was shivering. I placed my hand on her shoulder and shook her. "Jamie, wake up. It's just a dream." My touch and voice woke her in a frenzied state. She sat straight up, breathing fast and heavy. I scooted close to her and turned her face to look at me. "Are you OK?" She looked around the room, taking in her surroundings as if trying to figure out where she was.

Once her eyes fell on me, she threw herself into my chest and wrapped her arms around me. She buried her face into my neck. I slid my arms around her and pulled her closer to me. She was still shaking. "It's OK," I whispered into her hair. "It was just a bad dream."

The poor girl was so scared. I wished I could take away all her fear, but I didn't know how, so we just sat there wrapped in each other till her breathing evened. "That man was in my dreams. The one who was in my house. His eyes were so cold and filled with so much evil." I felt her nuzzle my chest, trying to get even closer. I slowly started rubbing up and down her back, trying to soothe her fear.

Anger crept into my mind. He had frightened Jamie so much that he was intruding on her dreams. I wanted nothing more than to destroy him. I knew that was extreme, but what he had done was worth nothing less. When I found him, I would end him.

I looked out the window and saw the sun starting to creep over the horizon. It was Saturday, and both Jamie and I had the day off. It was good we didn't work today so we could come up with a plan to keep everyone safe. I needed to get back to my house and talk to the rest of my crew. I also wanted to see if Kyle had got any information out of his prisoner. I didn't want to leave Jamie here alone, so I was hoping she would be willing to come with me. Eventually, she pulled away from me. Her arms were still around my back. "Are you OK?" I asked her.

She looked into my eyes. Hers looked wet, like she was about to start crying, and they ate at the inside of me. "Yeah, I will be fine. It was just the dream." She took in a deep breath "What are we going to do now?"

I reached over and grabbed my phone. It read 6:30 a.m., and I saw a missed text from Irene. It was sent at 5:00 a.m. She said everything was clear and that Max was picking her up so she could go home and clean up. She told me to come back to the house when we got up. She must have been talking to Max and Kyle throughout the night. Maybe they were able to come up with a plan or get information out of the vampire they caught.

"Would you be willing to come with me to my house?" I asked her.

She pulled out of our embrace. "Yeah, let me take a quick shower." She slipped off the bed and walked toward the bathroom. Then she turned around, ran back to the bed, and climbed over to me. She wrapped her arms around my neck and pulled me into her. "Thank you for staying with me last night, and for this morning." I wrapped my arms around her and held her tight. I loved having her in my arms. She leaned back and gave me a peck on the lips. Then she got back off the bed and walked in the direction of the bathroom.

She started stripping her sweat-soaked clothes off before she got through the bathroom door. I didn't think she was trying to be a tease on purpose, but seeing her bare skin sent a warmth straight to the pit of my stomach, and I felt my cheeks flare. I had to turn away before I started getting any ideas. Then I heard the door close, and the water start to flow. I finally let out a long exhale and slumped over on the bed—the things I wanted to do to her. But I had to shake those thoughts out of my head. The main thing on my agenda was to keep her safe.

She didn't take long to take a shower and get dressed. Then she grabbed a bagel and a cup of coffee. She offered me some. I declined the bagel, but gladly accepted the cup of coffee.

The beginning of the drive was quiet. Jamie nibbled on her bagel as she broke the silence. "Do all vampires drink coffee?"

I smiled at her question. "I don't know. Not every vampire is the same. We all have different likes and dislikes. I love the taste of coffee, but caffeine doesn't affect us."

"Why not?" she asked.

"Why doesn't caffeine affect us? I guess because our metabolism is so fast, it burns off before it can get into our system." At least I assumed that was the reason. I never really paid attention to the physiology of vampires when my instructors taught me. I didn't care back then.

"What about alcohol? Does that affect you?" she asked, taking a sip from her cup.

"It does if we drink a high enough proof and a lot of it in a short amount of time. We burn that off pretty fast, too, though," I replied. Alcohol wasn't my thing. Irene and Max enjoyed binge drinking for fun, but I never understood the hype in having one's inhibitions tested. I liked having control over my actions.

She nodded her head at my response. "Who was the other man last night with Max? I have never seen him before."

"He came down here to help us. When we figured out it was other vampires that were causing trouble, we asked the clan leader for help." I still hadn't told her we knew it was vampires that had caused all the new mischief that had been happening.

I felt her gaze fall on me, and intense energy suddenly flowed off of her. "So it was them that attacked Tracy and her boyfriend?"

I clutched at the steering wheel tighter. "Yes. They did that to get my attention. Then hired a human to finish Tracy off after I killed one of their men." I clenched my jaw, remembering how angry I was that Tracy and Todd had been caught in the crosshairs of an angry vampire who was trying to piss me off. I could never get their forgiveness for it, but I sure as hell could avenge them.

I felt her energy change to a more sympathetic flow. She touched my arm softly. "I'm sorry they did that to you. What does the guy want from you?"

I huffed out my response. "That's the thing. I don't even know. I mean, he said he wants our territory, but I'm just the protector of it down here. I can't just give it to him." She rubbed my arm in comforting strokes. It felt so soothing when she touched me, and some of the anger melted away.

The rest of the drive was in silence. I didn't know if Kyle knew I was bringing Jamie, but I didn't care. I knew he didn't like humans. I knew he wouldn't be pleased when he found out I told her everything, but she had a right to know after what she went through.

We turned onto the gravel driveway to my house. "This is nice," she said, admiring her surroundings. "It's so remote and beautiful."

I stopped the car in front of my house. "Thank you. We can somewhat be ourselves out here in the middle of nowhere." I got out and went to her side of the car using my speed. I opened her door and helped her out. She still had a little limp, and I didn't want her to hurt herself more.

"I will never get used to how fast you can move," she said, taking my hand as she got out.

I smirked at her. "I have a lot more talents than just moving fast." I didn't let go of her hand when we started walking toward the porch.

Irene came out of the house, skipping toward us. She came up to me and gave me a quick hug. "Nat, I'm glad you are OK." She then turned to Jamie. I could feel she was contemplating if she should give her a hug or not. In the end, Irene wrapped her arms around Jamie. "I'm so sorry about everything that happened to you. I can't imagine how frightened you were."

Jamie accepted the hug and wrapped her arms around Irene. "Thank you. It is just a lot to take in, I guess." I had texted Irene earlier that morning, letting her know I had told Jamie about us.

Irene slid out of the hug and grabbed both of Jamie's hands and squeezed them reassuringly. "We won't let anything happen to you. Yesterday took us by surprise, but we won't let it happen again." Jamie smiled. "Thank you, Irene." Irene returned the smile and turned, leading us to the front door.

Jamie returned her hand to mine. I could feel her starting to get anxious. Maybe of the unknown, perhaps because she had never been to my house. I whispered in her ear, "Everything is going to be alright. I promise." She looked up and smiled at me.

JAMIE

It felt a little strange knowing I was about to walk into a house full of vampires. Having Natasha at my side gave me courage. We walked up the porch, and she opened the screen door for me. When we walked in, I saw the man from last night, the one who left with Max, sitting on the couch.

He already had a frown on his face, and when he looked up and saw me, his face contorted into a venomous scowl. I held my breath when he got up and bolted toward me. Natasha was in front of me in one brisk movement.

"You brought her here? A human?!" He spit the word "human" into her face like it was some repulsive insect.

She grabbed him by the front of his shirt and growled at him through bared teeth. She whipped around, kicked open the screen door, and threw him out so far, he cleared the porch stairs. I was amazed that he was able to alter his body in mid-air so he would land on his feet. But Natasha moved with so much speed that by the time his feet hit the ground, she had his throat in her hand and, with one swift drive, slammed him into the ground on his back.

"How dare you come into my house and insult my guest!" Her voice boomed with fury. He gasped for breath as her hand squeezed tighter around his throat.

"I see your temper hasn't improved with your time away," he said, clawing at her arm and trying to pry free from her grip as she squeezed tighter. She took her other arm and punched it so hard into his side that something cracked, causing him to howl in pain. He tried to wrap his legs around her, but she lifted him by his neck and slammed his head into the earth with such ferocity it left an indent in the ground.

His eyes came to life, his body started to vibrate, and his canine teeth extended through the sneer on his face. He let out a groan of rage. "She is human, Natasha. She isn't supposed to know about us and she shouldn't be here!" The sound that came out of his throat echoed that of a snarling animal.

Irene came out and put her hands lightly on my shoulders. "Max!" she shouted back toward the house. I couldn't tell if I was frightened or not at this point. The pure power that Natasha had was mesmerizing. I couldn't take my eyes off her. She was so phenomenal. I had never had someone defend me like this before. It was endearing, even though she was hurting this guy.

She lifted his head off the ground and brought his face close to hers. "This is my house, Kyle! My rules! She is with me and if you have a problem with it, leave! If you touch her or threaten her, I promise I will end you!" she threatened through clenched teeth. Her body started to vibrate, and I could see her muscles begin to strain. *Was she changing?* I thought to myself. For some reason, it sent a jolt of adrenaline through my body. Not out of fear, but almost from excitement.

Right then, Max stormed out of the house toward them. "Nat! Enough! Get off of him." She turned to look at him. I could see the change in her face, the more prominent features, her irises dancing. She was still baring her teeth, and I could see they were longer now. Then her eyes fell on me. Slowly the rage dissolved from her expression. "Irene, please take Jamie inside. I need to have some words with Kyle."

I didn't know what words she was going to have with Kyle, but they probably weren't going to be pleasant ones.

I let Irene turn me around and direct me into the house. She led me over to the couch and had me sit down. "I'm sorry about all of that. Nat is very protective, and Kyle is, well, he's a douchebag," she said. "Can I get you anything?"

My brain was still trying to catch up to what I had witnessed. "Are they OK?" I asked her with genuine concern. I Just saw Natasha almost choke the life out of the guy and slam him so hard into the ground it left an indentation of his skull. I guessed vampires were stronger and probably had a higher pain tolerance than humans.

She walked out of the room toward what I assumed was the kitchen. "They will be fine. Just a little scuffle is all. Kyle was stupid to get in Nat's face like that. She could easily tear him to shreds if she wanted." She came back in with a glass of water and handed it to me.

"Thanks. But I heard something break when she punched him." The guy didn't like the fact that I was human, but it still sounded like it hurt and made me feel a tiny bit sorry for him.

"Yeah, it probably broke some ribs, but he had it coming. He can be a little prick sometimes when people don't respect his word. Fortunately for Nat, she outranks him and is a lot stronger. Don't worry. We heal fast. It might hurt him for a little while, but not too long." She winked at me then took a sip out of a dark coffee cup. I didn't know what was in it—blood, coffee, water. The thought of them drinking blood made my stomach a little queasy, but I knew it was necessary for their survival.

A long silence filled the room and it made me uncomfortable. "Do you have any other human friends?" I knew Natasha and Kyle had both said humans weren't supposed to know about them, but that seemed lonely if it was just the three of them.

She shook her head and set her cup down on the coffee table. "Nope, you are my first real human friend I have had who knows about us. I guess I have had acquaintances, but none of them ever knew about me." She smiled at me. It was a warm, welcoming smile, and it made me feel more relaxed.

It seemed like Natasha was friends with Tracy, and she was human, but they worked together and saw each other a lot. "Do you have a job?"

Irene shook her head again. "No, Nat and Max don't want me having one. They say it's too dangerous."

I felt sorry for her. It must be so lonely. "Those two have jobs. Why won't they let you get one?"

She chuckled at that. "They work together and use that as an excuse for 'having each other's backs' if something happens. I guess if

I got a job at the hospital, they might let it fly, but I'm not really into death and dying and people being hurt. It's too depressing for me."

I couldn't imagine staying in the house by myself all day. I would go crazy with boredom and loneliness. "Do you get lonely staying here all alone?"

She smiled at me. "Sometimes. It's not like I'm on house arrest, though. I get out and go places. But Max is all I need. He gives me anything and everything I could ever ask for. With him, I want for nothing. Nat is good company too. She is my best friend."

Before I could respond to her, I heard footsteps on the porch, and Max came in through the screen door followed by Natasha and Kyle. Kyle was cradling his side where Natasha had punched him.

Max went over to Irene, who stood and let him sit down. As he fell into the chair, he wrapped his arms around her and pulled her into his lap. Both were smiling at each other. They were so happy together, and it made a warmth flow through my heart. Natasha came over and sat down beside me. She placed her hand on my thigh. I instinctively put mine on top of hers and curled my fingers between hers. Out of the corner of my eye, I saw her smile.

Kyle walked past everyone over to the fireplace on the opposite side of the room and plopped himself on the raised hearth. I could feel his eyes leering at me, and it made me feel uncomfortable, so I scooted closer to Natasha. She took her arm and put it around me, protectively. "Knock it off, Kyle," she threatened, narrowing her eyes at him.

Irene's smile left her face, and her voice was assertive in response. "OK, guys, I thought you hashed this out outside. We need to figure out the next step. Nat, who was that guy last night? He disappeared into the woods before we could get a close look at him, and he didn't leave a trace behind. Was it the Phantom?"

I felt Natasha take in a deep breath and release it before she answered. "I guess it was the Phantom, but I think it's Malcom."

I had never heard any of them mention that name before, but everyone else in the room went completely silent. They all stared wide-eyed at Natasha.

Max was the first to reply. "Are you sure? We thought he died during his revolt that night. There's no way it could have been him."

Natasha shook her head. "I know. I was little then, but it smelled like him, and he said he knew me. How else would he know my real name, what I was entitled to? Plus, they never found his body after that night. It makes sense. This guy said he had tried before, and this time he was ready."

Kyle was next to voice his concern. "Nat, if it is Malcom and he has come back again to try another revolt, you need to tell your father. This is serious."

I was completely lost. "Who is Malcom, and what revolt?" I wanted to ask a million more questions, but those two topics seemed to be the most pressing.

I looked at Natasha for an answer, but it looked like she was too lost in her thoughts. My answer came from Irene. "Malcom used to be one of Nat's father's close advisors and friends. He got power hungry and tried to overthrow him. In the process, both our families were killed." There was a sadness behind her voice.

"A lot of people were killed because of his treachery," Max added through his clenched teeth.

This new information made me even more confused. "Aren't you and Natasha sisters? So you have the same dad? And why was he trying to overthrow him?"

This time it was Natasha who spoke. "Technically, Irene and I are cousins. My dad, Nik, is the leader of our clan. Irene's dad was his younger brother. My dad believed in peace with humans and all the other beings that roam the world. Malcom, however, thought we were the superior beings. My dad wouldn't listen to him, so he revolted. He wanted to take control. Little did he know how much power was in our family's blood. I don't remember much about it or Malcom. I was too young. All I remember was fire and an explosion. Both of Irene's parents were killed along with all her siblings. My mother died, and so did my older brothers and sister. Nik took Irene in and raised her like a daughter." Her voice was distant. I placed my hand on her leg and squeezed, trying to offer some comfort.

"So, your dad is in charge of your clan? How many clans are there?" I asked her.

"There are a lot. But there are five main houses or families. Our house is the most powerful one. All the other clans fall in line with the five main houses and their rules. The house rulers work together to keep the peace amongst ourselves. If Malcom was able to take down the most powerful vampire, who knows how many others would have followed him." She still sounded afar.

I was still caught up on the fact that her dad was one of the few in charge of the entire vampire world. I would have to ask her about that later.

"So why is Malcom after you then?" I asked Natasha.

"I'm the last heir to my father's empire. Without me, our bloodline dies unless he has another kid. I guess Malcom thinks if he gets to me, it's a way to get to my father." She shrugged with her response.

My mind was trying to put everything together. We had a Hitler vampire trying to overthrow one of the leaders of the vampire world. He was going after me to get to Natasha to get to her father. Then out of nowhere, a thought popped into my head. Without thinking, I blurted out, "Oh my gosh! You are like a vampire princess!"

I heard Max laugh so loud I felt the vibrations in my chest. "A princess?! There are many things Nat is, but I would definitely not call her a princess." He was still laughing.

Irene hit him in the chest but was laughing as well. "Oh come on, Max. It is kind of set up like a monarchy."

Max pulled her even closer. His lips were almost on hers. "So does that mean you are a princess too?"

She put her arms around his neck and said, "I will be whatever you want me to be."

At her response, Max looked over at Natasha and me and raised one of his eyebrows up and down. "Get out of here, Max," Natasha said, chuckling, and then I saw a book go flying out of her hands in the direction of his head.

Irene snagged it out of the air with cat-like reflexes and used it to block their faces. It was apparent they had started making out behind it. I found myself laughing as well. It took a little edge off all the overthrowing-an-empire talk from moments ago.

Kyle spoke next. "OK, we need a plan. I will call and get some more reinforcements down here. We should wait to go after him till we get more numbers. We don't know how many people he has with him and I don't want to go in blind. But Nat, you really should call Nik and talk to him."

She took her arm away from around my shoulder and rubbed at her face with both her hands. "I know I do. I will call Nik tomorrow."

I wasn't sure what my next move would be. We didn't really have any answers or plans right then, and I didn't want to be continually looking over my shoulder, waiting for a vampire rebel to snatch me up. I wasn't scared to admit that I was frightened to be alone. I was only human, and it's not like I was rolling in money and could buy a bunch of silver to have forged into weapons or bullets. "What do I do?" I whispered to Natasha.

She reached her arm back around me and pulled me close to her. "Would you be opposed to staying here with us for a while?"

Of course, I wouldn't be opposed to being as close to her as I could. "No, I wouldn't, but I can't leave Walter alone at my house, and I would need to go get clothes and some other things for my stay."

She smiled and kissed the top of my head, but before she replied, Irene spoke up. "Max and I can go up and get Walter. We can also grab some of your clothes and all the things you need if you make a list."

I looked at Natasha questioningly. Why couldn't I go up and get everything? Max saw my expression. "We weren't able to get a lot out of our prisoner, but he did lead us to believe they are staying in the deep forest up around where you live. The farther away from that area you are, the better."

"What about my job?" I did work up there, and I couldn't skip out on work every day.

"One of us will be near you all the time," Natasha told me, trying to reassure me everything was going to be OK.

I still didn't feel comfortable, even if I knew I had a secret vampire bodyguard. I still felt like I would be exposed. I looked in her eyes for even more reassurance.

"I promise everything will be OK." She smiled at me.

I returned her smile. I did trust her, but I still had a terrible feeling lingering in the back of my mind. I knew that movies and books portrayed vampires and myths differently than how they really were. Still, in every single story, it was pretty consistent that something terrible always happened to the human in the story, and I was the human in this story.

NATASHA

Irene and Max had left for Jamie's house to pick up everything she had requested. Kyle had disappeared outside somewhere to make some calls for help, which left Jamie and me alone. I could feel her tension and anxiety. All this new information was a lot to process.

I asked if she wanted to go outside and sit on the porch swing. It was cramped and stagnant inside, and being in fresh air usually helped clear my mind. Maybe it would help her. She was quiet for a long while after we made our way to the porch. I hoped all this information hadn't scared her too much. When she sat down on the swing, her posture was stiff. She folded her hands in her lap. She gazed off into the distance, not looking at anything particular. I sat down and left about half a foot between us. I didn't want to push her to talk or interrupt her thoughts.

I used the silence to give myself time to reflect on the situation. I didn't want to get involved in a war, but if it was Malcom and he was back to try and overthrow my father, it was inevitable. Maybe it was time to take up my role as his second in command. Perhaps I did need to start learning at my dad's side. I never wanted to be the heir to his legacy—I wasn't supposed to be. I was the youngest in the family. It was a lot more responsibility than I felt like I could handle or wanted on my shoulders. I always felt like an outsider in my father's world. That's how I ended up here. I shut my eyes and let out a loud breath of frustration.

Jamie moved closer to my side and laced her fingers around mine. "I'm sorry about your family. I never knew." She leaned her head against my shoulder.

I couldn't believe how fast I had fallen for her, especially since she was a human. In all my years I had never had feelings like this before, but I didn't mind.

"It's OK," I replied. "It was a long time ago. I was so young. I don't really remember it too well." It was true that the memory of my family was stretched a little thin. I remembered my mother. She was beautiful and so full of love. She was the kindest person I had ever known. My older siblings had been involved with helping my father run things, so I didn't spend a lot of time with them. Irene was closer to my age, so I spent more time with her. We had grown up together. The memories were so long ago it seemed like a different lifetime. I didn't want to talk about my depressing past right then, not with how happy she made me feel being this close. "What about your family?"

She turned her head and looked at me. "What about my family?"

"I don't know. Tell me about them. You know all the deep, dark secrets of mine. What is your family like?" I was genuinely curious. I had never gotten this close to a human before. I wanted to know everything about her. Plus, changing the topic would take my family out of the spotlight.

She sighed, thinking, and turned her gaze out into the trees. I felt her shoulders shrug against my body. "Well, my dad used to own the local outdoorsmen shop and my mom taught at the town's high school. When they retired, they moved an hour and a half west onto a farm. They like their privacy. My older brothers and one of my older sisters joined the Navy. They are stationed outside of the country. My other older sister is an architect and lives in California. I have a pretty cookie-cutter family. Not too much excitement."

I nodded my head, taking in the personal information she divulged. "So, you are the baby of the family, too, huh?" I smiled and nudged against her.

She looked back up at me. "Yeah, I am."

"Why did you stay here and join the sheriff's office? All your other siblings left."

She closed her eyes and relaxed more into me. "I guess I don't like big cities or going too far away from home. Plus, I like helping people, and working for the sheriff's office seemed like a good choice to accomplish that."

I was satisfied with her answer, so I rested my head against hers. I was completely content with just sitting there with her. It had been so long since I had felt as relaxed as in that moment. I couldn't help but smile to myself. She must have felt it. "What?" she asked.

"Nothing. I'm just enjoying sitting here with you," I replied.

"So now that I know you are a princess, can you grant me anything I want?" she asked me with a teasing giggle.

I couldn't help but let out a laugh. "First of all, genies are the ones that grant wishes, not vampire princesses. Secondly, technically, I'm not a princess."

She turned and gave me a pouty, pleading look at my response.

It made me laugh even more. I raised an eyebrow and looked down at her. I was curious about what she would request. "OK, OK. If I were a princess and could grant wishes, what wish could I grant you?"

A sly smile crept across her face. She jumped up and pulled me to join her. I let her lead me toward the front door. "Where are we going?" I asked, because I couldn't read what was going on in her head.

We walked through the front door, and she stopped me at the hall. "Which one is your room?" she asked me, still sporting that cunning smile on her face.

I started to understand her motives. In one quick move, I swept her up and threw her over my shoulder. She let out a high-pitched gasp at the unexpected motion. I used the arm that wasn't holding her to pinch at her side playfully. She squirmed and laughed uncontrollably. Her response made me start giggling. I carried her to my room, and when I got in, I shut the door and set her down.

When she stood up straight, her eyes scanned my room. I had the master bedroom of the house. My bed was a king-size four-poster bed made of solid dark oak, centered on the far wall. I had a matching bookshelf that ran the entire side of the closest wall, filled with books I had collected over the years.

She walked over to the bookshelf and started surveying the bindings, running her fingers over the spines and reading the titles. "Wow, you have a lot of books," she said through a haze.

I didn't know if that was a good thing or a bad thing, "Yeah, I have always loved reading, and I've had a lot of time to collect them."

After she was done looking over the books, she made her way toward the bathroom. I didn't know why her exploring my room made me so nervous. Maybe it was a sense that I wanted to impress her and didn't want my personal space to disappoint her. She was even more surprised by my bathroom. I had a jacuzzi bathtub separate from the double-headed shower meant for two people.

"I am definitely using this someday," she said, running her hand over the edge of the tub. She then walked over to the shower and opened the door. "A shower meant for two people?" It was more of a question than a statement. She looked over her shoulder and raised an eyebrow at me.

I smiled. "It came with the house. There is almost too much room for just me." It was nice having such a large shower. I never really used the tub. I never got the thrill humans got from soaking in warm water.

When she finished admiring the bathroom, she made her way to my bed and sat down. She pushed her hands into the mattress a few times, testing the firmness. "Your bed feels amazing."

The bed was amazing, one of the most exquisite beds someone could invest in. I had realized long ago to not skimp on the necessities of life. Especially since I have lived as long as I had. "Thank you. I am all for pampering myself when I can," I paused and curved one side of my lips up, "and others."

She rubbed the surface of the bed right next to her as an invitation for me to sit there. I eagerly made my way to the spot. When I sat down, I delicately captured her hand in mine. "Jamie, are you OK?"

She looked at me with a puzzled look on her face. "Am I OK with what?"

I wanted to make sure she was OK, mentally, with everything she was going through. This was all new to her. I knew from working as a nurse that significant changes in One's life sometimes could negatively affect a person's mental state. "Are you OK with everything you have just been through and with everything you have learned? You got kidnapped yesterday and just found out about this secret vampire hierarchy."

She stood up and turned to face me. She put her legs on either side of me, straddled me on the bed, and rested her backside on my thighs. Her arms slid around my neck, and her beautiful golden eyes stared intently into mine. "I'm not going to lie to you." She inhaled deeply. "It does scare me. And yes, I do feel very overwhelmed with everything. It's an entirely new world for me. I'm a deputy who is supposed to be brave and strong and protect people, but I feel completely helpless, weak, and useless in your world. And usually in the stories…" her brows furrowed together, "the human ends up with the short end of the stick."

Her last statement sent a pain through my heart. Of course she was frightened and scared, and I hated that it was because of me that she felt this way. I had dragged her into this world, and her entire life changed overnight. I lowered my head and averted my eyes. A feeling of shame took hold of my chest. Then I felt one of her arms slide away from my neck and her fingers under my chin. She lifted it, so I was forced to look at her again. "But, being with you gives me courage. I feel safe when I'm around you. I trust you. I also feel safe around Irene and Max and even Kyle, although I know he doesn't like me being human."

That comment lifted my spirits slightly. I wrapped my arms around her back and pulled her close to me. She put her forehead against mine and closed her eyes. I inhaled deeply, taking in her scent. I didn't even care if she knew I was smelling her.

Then I felt her soft lips gently touch mine. I smiled into the kiss, and she pulled me deeper into it. I let the euphoric feeling cloak me, take me over entirely as our lips moved against each other. It made me dizzy with pleasure. I could feel her breathing start to quicken, and her hold around my neck got tighter. She was getting lost in the kiss just as I was.

A physical need to explore her body overcame me, a need to learn every inch of her. My hands found the hem of her shirt and slid up the smooth skin of her back, slowly, in anticipation for her to pull away, which never came. She was so soft and warm. I traced up and down the length of her back, my fingers memorizing the curves of her muscles, the dip in her lower back, feeling her back dimples as the pads of my fingers brushed over them. I felt her tongue slip past my lips, an invitation. My eagerness had been awakened. I greeted her with my tongue, grazing it with every motion of her lips.

Then I felt her suck my lower lip, and her teeth nip at it, the teasing gesture encouraging me. I dug my fingers more firmly into her back, pulling her so close there was no more room between us. Her breathing got heavier against me. Then abruptly, she pulled her lips away from mine. She was still close enough that I could feel her warm breath against my mouth. "Are we moving too fast?" she asked through an exerted whisper.

I pulled away even farther, so I could look into her eyes, searching for what she meant. I honestly didn't know if we were moving too fast. I had never been intimate with a human before and was unsure if humans had a particular time they waited. I had overheard many conversations from humans having one-night stands or sex on the first or second date. Maybe those times were just for the sole purpose of sex. Even I had participated in activities just for the pure pleasure of it. What Jamie and I had was different though. I didn't want this to happen just for sex. I wanted her, even after such a short time knowing her. I had developed strong feelings for her and, to me, this wasn't just about the physical pleasure. I had never put a time restriction on it before. If I felt like I was ready, I was ready. And right then, I was more than ready. I could smell desire and eagerness. Sense the yearning that was flowing off of her, and it made me ache for her. But I wasn't going to force Jamie into anything. I wasn't going to make her feel as though we needed to do this right then.

"I don't know. Do you feel like we are moving too fast? I don't want to do this if it makes you uncomfortable and you aren't ready. I have never been with a human, so this is new territory for me."

She smiled at me. "I have never been with a vampire before, so it's new territory for me as well. I just don't want you to think this is only about sex for me. I have never developed feelings for someone this fast before, and that is new territory as well, and it's a little scary."

I could see the uncertainty and worry in her expression about how I would react to what she had just said. I smiled at her and pecked her on the lips, reassuringly. "The feeling is mutual. I have feelings for you too, and I don't want this to be strictly a physical thing."

She gave a soft smile and pulled me into a hard kiss. I felt all of her resolve and uncertainty fade away in the kiss. I knew she was ready. Her mouth moved against mine longingly, and it made me hungry for more. I stood up, and her legs instantly wrapped around my waist, not wanting to allow any more space between us.

I turned us around and worked my knees on the bed, crawling up to the head of it. I bent us over till her back was resting on the sheets. She released her legs from my waist, and her hands searched down my sides. She found the bottom of my shirt and pulled at it, desperately tugging it up. The kiss was broken just long enough to allow her to pull it over my head. Then she discarded it over the side.

A new expression masked her face and it made me freeze, thinking I had done something wrong, so I pushed myself up onto my knees. My torso loomed over her. She stared at my body, and I saw her lips part just slightly. Her arm reached out, and she touched my abdomen. She started lightly tracing every line and swell created by the muscles there. I had never had anyone look at me the way she was right then. It made me feel vulnerable, and I don't think I had ever felt that way before. I didn't want to move. I didn't want her to stop. Everywhere she touched left a trail of a warm, tingling sensation. Her eyes followed the line her fingers traced.

Her hand moved up my body, lingering in certain places, retracing over different areas till it finally reached my neck. My gaze never left her eyes. I searched for her reaction. I wanted to know what she was thinking. Her hand eventually stopped on my cheek. She cupped it, and then her eyes met mine. She smiled. "You are the most beautiful woman I have ever laid eyes on."

Warmth spread across my chest. I leaned forward and placed my hands on the mattress on either side of her. I held my body up and hovered above hers. I lowered my head, gaze fixed on her eyes, waiting for her to permit me to keep going. It came when her hands reached behind my neck and pulled me to her. Her lips crashed into mine with a hard, desperate longing that I could feel throughout her entire body. Her hands moved to my back and traced the muscles down till they were right above my pants line and then worked their way back to my neck, exploring every detail. I melted into her touch.

I wanted her to be in control, so I let my body stay above hers until I felt her hands slide down and pull at my hips, bringing my body in contact with hers. The connection of her center against mine sent a rush of eagerness through me. I could feel the desired heat radiating off her, and it made me lust for more of her. My hands ran up her sides, taking her shirt with them. Our lips parted, so I could pull it completely over her head. Just the brief moment apart was too long. My lips were drawn back to her like a magnet. Then I slipped my hand between her back and the bed till I found the clasp of her bra.

It took a simple flick of my wrist, and it was undone. In her eagerness, she pulled it off and tossed it aside. Her hips started to rock just slightly against mine, encouraging me. I moved my lips down her jawline to her neck, right on her pulse. Her heartbeat quickened. I kissed it and then nipped at the spot, and her hands clenched at my back in response. I sucked at the spot and got a quiet moan as a reward. The sound riled me. It was so innocent, so pure, so raw, and I wanted to hear more. I could feel the animal inside me stir, but I was in total control right then.

I moved down her neck, leaving a trail of wet kisses, sucking and softly biting, then soothing with my tongue. Finally, I got to the swell of her breast and lifted my head to admire how perfect they were. My eyes moved down, taking in her firm, defined, petite stomach. I placed my hand on her abdomen and moved it slowly up, relishing in every aspect of her, till I was at her breast. The flesh in the center was already hard, and that sent a sudden tightness to my stomach. I leaned back down and touched my tongue to the stiff center and flicked it. I heard her suck in a sharp breath. That was the only encouragement I needed before I put my mouth around the center and sucked. Her grip on my back tightened. I nibbled and flicked at it with my tongue, and I could hear the hitches in her breathing grow sharper.

My hand traced up and down her side. On the next pass, I slid my hands down, catching her running pants and underwear with my fingers, and slid them past her hips. She arched her lower back off the bed, allowing me to pull them down her legs and out of my way. After the barrier was gone, I gently used my fingernails to trace back up along her bare thighs. Her legs spread just slightly, inviting me to explore.

I knew vampires were a lot stronger than humans, and my instincts were already on high alert from how worked up I was. I needed to be gentle and not get too aggressive with her. It was so hard, though. Everything about her like this made me weak. Desire writhed within me. Her scent, her touch, her breathing, her motion—all of it made me desperate for her.

I could smell how wet she was before my hand was even at her center. The eagerness I had to get to it was almost uncontrollable, but I wanted to go slow. She already was out of her element, and I didn't want to push her. I moved my lips back up to hers and I could feel the desperation behind her kiss. She wanted it, wanted me, and I wanted to give her everything.

The next time I ran my hand down her leg, I shifted it to her inner thigh. She felt the shift and spread her legs even further. I ran my hand up her inner thigh but didn't aim for her center. My hand found her stomach and traced along the sensitive skin. I felt her hips rocking, trying to find some kind of friction. "Please," she whispered through her heavy breaths, "don't stop." That was the permission I was waiting for.

I raised my head up away from her. I wanted to see her face when I touched her, wanted to know what she was feeling. Slowly, my hand slid down her center and I gradually ran my finger through the saturated flesh between her legs and reveled in the sound that escaped her mouth. Her eyes closed tight, and she bit her bottom lip as my finger passed over her clit. Her hands gripped tight around my back.

I made several long, slow strokes with my finger, lingering on the bundle of nerves that made her hips roll with my touch, circling that spot at the end of each stroke. I gradually quickened my pace, and her breathing got faster. I felt her chest rise and fall against mine—the rolling of her hips encouraging my motion. I found her lips again with mine, desperate to taste her.

I had to hold back the burning desire that ached in me, but how she was responding was stirring my very core. With my next stroke down, I slowly slid my finger into her. I heard her breathing catch, and her fingernails dug into my back. I pulled out and then slid into her again. Each time I did this, her hips rolled with my movement and I needed more. On my next thrust in her, I added a second finger, and felt a moan escape her into my mouth. I quickened the pace of my thrusts. With each one, I felt the muscles inside her tighten around my fingers, encouraging me deeper and faster.

Her lips started getting erratic with their movement between her heavy breathing, so she buried her face into my shoulder. I curved my fingers inside her, searching for that spot on the front wall and found it. When I did, I felt her teeth try to bite into the hard muscle on my shoulder. It was so surprising to me that I felt a warm tightness in my center, and my hips bucked into her uncontrollably.

She still hadn't climaxed yet, but I was so eager to get her to come that I placed the pad of my thumb on her clit and moved it in rhythm with my fingers, working the sweet spot inside her. The next moan out of her made my mouth water, as my thumb touched the bundle of nerves. Her hips started to move frantically, unpredictably. She was almost over the edge. Then I felt her back arch off the bed into me. Her arms gripped me tightly, her teeth dug hard at my tough skin, her entire body went stiff, her breathing stopped, and all I felt was the pulsating thrum of warmth around my fingers inside her. I didn't cease my movement as I pushed her over the climax. As the first wave of pleasure rolled over her, she let out a loud, high moan that was pure ecstasy for me and made me want to lose control, but I knew I couldn't or I would hurt her. I worked in her as wave after wave of pleasure rolled over her. I sensed the pure bliss of energy flowing off her, hear it in her exhilarating breaths, feel it in her quivering legs that had tensed around me. I gradually started slowing my pace till the pulses stopped, and her grip on me began to loosen. I let her ride my fingers through the last waves of pleasure until she was finished. Her breathing was heavy, and I could feel her skin saturated in a thin film of sweat.

After I felt her entire body relax I pulled out of her and went to push myself up, but she gripped my back even harder to keep me where I was. "Please don't. Just lay here for a minute," she whispered. It still sounded like she was trying to catch her breath. I was content with laying on top of her while she came down from this high. Her face was buried in my shoulder, and I could feel her breathing was still slightly labored. Her arms were wrapped tightly around me, holding me close.

After her breathing slowed and her heart rate was back to baseline, I propped myself up so I could look at her. I wanted to make sure she was OK. I got so lost in her that I couldn't tell if I was too rough with her. When I met her eyes, they were half-lidded, but there was a smile on her face. "Are you OK? Did I hurt you at all?" I quietly asked with concern.

She lifted her head off the bed and gave me a peck on the lips. "I'm more than OK. And no, you didn't hurt me at all." Then I saw her look at my shoulder. "Did I hurt you?" Her finger traced across my shoulder.

I could see the worry in her face. I smiled at her concern. "No, you didn't. My skin is almost impenetrable unless you have crowns made of silver. Are you sure you are OK?"

She pulled my head down into another long kiss. I could taste the afterglow on her lips, and it was satisfying. "I am perfect. That was amazing. I don't think I have ever been this exhausted after sex before," she whispered through my lips.

I broke away from her lips and rolled over onto my back, pulling her into me. She rested her head on my shoulder and put her arm around my body. "Well, vampires can live for a long time, which allows us to master certain activities."

I felt her chest vibrate against me with a laugh. "OK, big head."

I scoffed at her. "Also, it takes a lot for us to get tired, and I can sense when you are enjoying something, so sensitive spots are not a guessing game for me." I had heard stories of people who fake orgasms or had to finish themselves because their partners didn't have the stamina. But I can feel if someone is enjoying something or not, and I can last a very long time, which is excellent when it comes to sex.

She looked up at me and rolled her eyes. "So how many opportunities did it take for you to master it?"

I knew she was teasing me, so I raised an eyebrow at her and replied with a sideways smile, "I never kiss and tell."

She laughed and shook her head. "Well, you are pretty much perfect in every way," she said through a yawn.

I hummed at her comment. I had done many imperfect things in my long life. I didn't know if I necessarily regretted the decisions I had made, but some of them I wasn't proud of. "I can promise you I am far from perfect," I replied, feeling the smile fall from my face.

She scooted in closer to me. "Everyone makes mistakes. But that doesn't take away from how amazing a person can be," she said, her voice tired.

I had my arm wrapped around her and was stroking a pattern up and down her back with my thumb. I could feel the exhaustion in her. Not just from the pleasure she had experienced, but from the events that had taken place in the past week. She let out a tired sigh. "I want to return the favor right now, but I feel as though you may have worn me out beyond function."

I smiled and kissed the top of her head. Honestly, seeing and feeling her climax the way she did was all I wanted and needed to feel pleasure. I expected her to be too tired after. "It's OK. Sex with a vampire will do that to a human."

I felt her giggle and grip me tighter. It was only a matter of minutes before her breathing shallowed and grew into a slow, steady rhythm, and she was asleep.

Once I knew she was in a deep sleep, I stealthily crawled out of her hold so as not to wake her. I was still riding a high from our time together and couldn't just lay motionless right then. I walked to the kitchen and went for the refrigerator, grabbing my canteen taking three long swigs. It did little to settle me. I thought about taking a shower, not just to cool me off, but to wash off the smell of intercourse that surrounded me. But I didn't want to wake Jamie, and it wouldn't calm me much or remove the scent from Jamie. Max and Irene would still sense it.

I decided to go outside. As much as I wanted to stay in the house to be closer to Jamie, I needed to calm myself down a little more. As soon as I walked off the porch, I heard Max's truck drive up the gravel path.

The truck pulled up and parked. Max got out of the driver's side, and Walter followed after him. Walter ran up to me, wagged his tail, then jetted off to explore the open space that surrounded my property.

Max grabbed a suitcase from the bed of the truck while Irene jumped out of the passenger side and started walking toward me. As she got closer, I saw her hesitate, and then her eyes went wide. A massive smile formed on her face. "Oh my gosh. You dirty girl, you!"

All I could do was shake my head at her. I knew she would pick up on it fast. Max came up behind her and raised an eyebrow at me, and a crooked smirk formed on his face. "We leave you alone with the human for three hours, and you defile her," Max said, wiggling his eyebrow.

I shoved him hard in the shoulder. I knew they were going to give me crap for it, but I didn't care. I would do anything for Jamie at that point. "Enough guys. She is sleeping right now. Don't wake her up. She's had a hard week and needs her rest. And don't say anything to her about it, OK?"

Irene laughed at my comment. "Yeah, right. You probably sexed all the energy out of her. That's why she's asleep. You know humans don't even come close to the amount of stamina we have." She started thrusting her pelvis in the air, making a humping motion.

"OK, Irene. Both of you get it out now. I don't want you saying anything to make her feel embarrassed or uncomfortable," I scolded. I was hoping they wouldn't tease Jamie. I could take their tasteless remarks, but I didn't know if Jamie would be OK with it yet.

We walked up the porch and into the house. As we stepped through the door, Max took in a big sniff. "Wowee, would you smell that! You must have had a good ol'' time, girl!" He winked at me.

"Quiet!" I hissed. "I don't want you to wake her up."

Irene came up behind me and put her arms around me in a big hug. "I'm just so happy that you have found someone to make you happy." She kissed me on the cheek, then let go. "How was it, by the way?" she nudged my shoulder playfully, giggling.

I couldn't hold back my smile, and looked away from her. "Oh, so she was that good, huh?" She jumped on my back and gave a little squeal and a tight squeeze.

Max was the next to chime in. "I am happy for you too. But I'm starving, so if you want us to stop giving you crap, you need to feed me."

I rolled my eyes at him and walked to the kitchen. "OK, I will make food as long as you leave it alone around Jamie. Please? And go get Walter from outside. I don't want him running off." Irene gave my cheek one more kiss and jumped off, heading to the door to get Walter.

JAMIE

I was roused from a deep, pleasant slumber by the aroma of something cooking that made my mouth start to water. When I opened my eyes, I looked around the room and had to reorient myself. I was in Natasha's room. I reached my arm out only to find the other side of the bed empty. I grabbed my phone to see how late it was. The bright screen showed 7:00 p.m. It had been almost two hours since I had fallen asleep in Natasha's arms.

I closed my eyes, remembering back two hours ago. The way she had touched me. Every touch was precisely where I needed it to be. Every stroke was the speed I needed it to be. Every kiss was how I wanted it to be. Everything she did to me was perfect, executed flawlessly. I had never been touched the way she had touched me. I had never been brought to climax that fast and with that much ferocity. It's like she knew every sensitive part of my body—where to touch, when to touch, and for how long. Just thinking about what she had done to me made me want more. I felt a warm pulse flow to my stomach just thinking about it, which woke me entirely out of my slumber.

I scooted off the bed and found my clothes on the floor. I thought about going out to lure her back to the bed naked but decided not to, just in case anyone had come back. When I pulled my shirt back over my head, my stomach growled from the smell of food cooking. I opened the door, and only got a few steps before a familiar big black bundle of fur jumped on me. If I hadn't been so used to him doing this every time I got home, Walter would have knocked me over. I was glad to see him. I knelt and hugged him, burying my face in his fur.

After I felt like he had a sufficient amount of my time, I made my way down the hall, following the smell of cooking food. I got to the living room and saw Irene and Max sitting on the couch. When Irene saw me, she shut her laptop and smiled at me. "How was your nap?"

she asked. I couldn't tell if there was a little more behind that smile or not, but it seemed a bit suggestive to me.

"It was nice. With everything that has been going on, I haven't been sleeping very well," I replied.

I saw her look at Max and grin, then back at me. "I bet you haven't," she giggled.

At her comment, I figured they knew what Natasha and I had done while they were gone. I felt a warm flush instantly creep up my face. "Irene!" I heard Natasha snap from the kitchen. Then her head popped into the living room from around the corner, and she glared at her sister.

Irene sat back further into the couch and threw her arms in the air. "What? I was only asking how her nap was," she said innocently, still sporting a suggestive smile on her face. Then she winked at me. I couldn't help my lips from curving into a smile before I turned and went into the kitchen.

Natasha was now in front of the stove, stirring something in a huge frying pan. "Hungry?" she asked me without turning around.

At her question, my stomach let out another loud grumble, which made her laugh. "I'm famished. No thanks to you." I heard her huff an amused laugh. I walked over to the stove to see what she was stirring in the pan. It was some sliced sausage mixed with onions, peppers, and mushrooms. "That smells and looks amazing." I complimented her.

I saw her smile at my approval. "I hope you like Polish sausage and veggies," she said.

I had never really been a picky eater. Unfortunately though, the one food I didn't like was in everything people cooked: cheese. Just the smell of it would put me off. But it didn't seem like that was on the menu tonight. "I love all of it," I replied.

She turned her head to look at me and kissed me. "Could you grab the plates and silverware and take them to the table for me please?" she asked, as she gestured to the stack she had already pulled out.

I grabbed the stack and took them over to the table, placing them in five spots. She came behind me with the hot pan and divided up the food equally. "Dinner's ready," she called to Irene and Max.

I wasn't sure if I would be able to eat the mountain of food she had just piled on my plate. It's like she could read my mind, because she uttered her next words to me with amusement. "If you can't eat it all, I will finish your leftovers." I would have been amazed if she could finish my leftovers after finishing the heap on her plate. It still was hard for me to get over the fact that vampires could eat regular food at all, based on all the stories I had been led to believe. "Do vampires need more food than humans?"

She shrugged her shoulders at my questions. "Yeah, I guess. Our metabolism is faster like I said earlier."

My curiosity grew. "Can vampires strictly survive on blood if they didn't want to eat human food, or do they have to consume both?"

She cocked her head to the side and pursed her lips as if she were thinking about her response. "Yeah, we can survive solely on blood. If a vampire did that, they would have to drink a lot of blood though, to keep up with their body's needs."

"Have you ever done that?" I asked curiously.

She smiled and turned her head toward me. "Yeah, I have done it a few times. We are a lot stronger when we strictly stick with blood. But I will admit my lust for flavor outweighs my desire for power and strength. Food, to me, tastes better than blood." I nodded my head with approval at her reply.

I guessed Kyle was going to be joining us from the fact there were five plates. "Are we going to eat without Kyle?" I asked Natasha.

She took the empty pan and put it into the sink. "Yeah, he texted me that he was on his way. Told us to go ahead and eat if he wasn't here by the time the food was ready." She came back over and pulled out a chair for me. I sat down, and she scooted me closer to the table. Then I heard Max and Irene come in. Irene sat down on my left, and Max sat next to her. Natasha took the seat on my right. When everyone had sat down, we all began to eat. The first bite I consumed was so overwhelming with flavors my taste buds almost didn't know how to respond. "Oh my gosh Nat! This is so good!"

She smiled at my compliment and nodded her head. "Thank you."

Irene then piped up. "Yeah, Nat is the cook in the family. I don't know how she does it, but everything she makes turns out amazing."

"I have had lots of time to master it feeding you two bottomless pits," Natasha said, wiggling her fork at Max and Irene.

I heard the front door open and assumed it was Kyle. He came into the kitchen and sat down in front of the plate that had been untouched. When he sat down, I saw him grimace a little and clutch at his side. Nat must have broken his ribs pretty severely.

Natasha looked up at him. "So?" she questioned him between a bite.

Before he answered her, he picked up his fork and shoveled a heap into his mouth. After he swallowed, he replied, "Well, Nik said he would send three people down to help us investigate. He doesn't believe it was Malcom you saw and that it was probably some imposter or power-hungry new guy."

Natasha set down her fork and leaned back, letting out a loud, frustrated huff. "Of course he doesn't believe it was Malcom. He never believes anything I say." She crossed her arms and shook her head.

"Nat, you need to talk to him then. Maybe hearing it directly from you will be more believable," Kyle replied, then scooped another fork full of food into his mouth.

"He wouldn't believe me if I went up to him and told him the grass is green or the sky is blue," she said, rubbing her temples with her fingers.

"Well at least he is sending help and didn't completely ignore the threat. I am actually surprised he isn't taking it more serious based on everything that has happened."

She picked up her fork and started eating again. I didn't know how strained her relationship with her father really was. I was curious, but didn't want to bring it up here in front of everyone.

"So, now what do we do?" I asked, directing my question toward Kyle. I was surprised that he responded to me.

"Well, Isaac, Jason, and Shae will be here Monday, and then I guess we will do some surveying in the area they are staying in. Then try and figure out who the new intruders really are and what they want." He said, looking into his plate, continuing to eat.

I heard Natasha let out a groan and fall back into her chair with a loud thud. I turned to look at her, worried. She had her head tilted back and eyes closed. "Great," she quietly hissed through clenched teeth.

It made me a little worried. "What's wrong?"

It wasn't her I got a reply from. I heard Irene give her a teasing chuckle. "It's Shae, her ex. Nat broke her little heart and Nat hasn't really talked to her since."

Natasha let out a loud exhale. "I didn't break her heart, Irene. We decided to go our separate ways, that's all. It wasn't even really a relationship, just a fling."

"Uh-huh. Try telling Shae that then," Irene said.

I couldn't help but grow a little anxious. One of Natasha's ex-girlfriends was going to be here. A vampire. I had a million different thoughts flood my mind at once. *What if Natasha realized she still liked Shae?* I wasn't even close to being as strong as a vampire or as appealing. I was just a human, after all. *Or what if Shae got jealous and wanted me out of the picture?* Or maybe I was overthinking things and needed to stop getting myself worked up over nothing.

I felt an elbow nudge my left side. Irene must have sensed my tension. "Trust me, Jamie. You don't have anything to worry about. That was a long time ago. Plus, I have never seen Nat fawn over someone as much as she has you." She then looked at Natasha and winked.

Natasha put one of her hands over her face. I could tell she was blushing because it went all the way down her neck. "Irene, there is no possible way you could embarrass me any more than you have in the past five minutes."

Irene raised an eyebrow toward Natasha. "Is that a challenge?"

Natasha slammed her palm down on the table. "No it's not!" I could tell she wasn't angry because there was a hint of laughter in her voice. "Man, you can be such a pain sometimes."

I saw Irene smile and continue eating. I hadn't realized it, but I made it through about half the food that was on my plate, but I was full. Natasha had cleared her plate entirely. "Are you full?" she asked me.

"Yeah, I can't eat another bite."

She reached over and took my plate. She walked over to Max and scraped the rest of my dinner onto his plate. He looked up and nodded his head, thanking her. "Want to go outside for a little?" she asked me.

"Yes, please." I smiled and followed her out. It was completely dark by now, and I could hear all the insects of the night alive and thriving. We walked over to the porch swing and sat down next to each other. I let my head rest on her shoulder and intertwined my fingers with hers on her lap. We sat in silence for a long while before I was able to work up the courage to bring up Shae. "So, Shae. How long ago did you guys date?"

She turned to look at me. "It was a long time ago. You have nothing to worry about. I promise."

"She won't be some jealous ex-girlfriend, will she?" I asked her, only half-joking.

I felt her shoulder move from the small chuckle she gave. "No, she won't be jealous. She is with someone else and has been for a long time now. We didn't end on great terms and haven't seen too much of each other since."

That put my mind a little more at ease, but I was still a bit nervous about seeing her. "So, what are we going to do tomorrow while we wait?" We had a full day till help would come down. I didn't know if they planned on looking more into it or were going to wait.

"Well, those three are going back up north and, at a distance, see if they can lock down the area of where the intruders are staying," she replied.

I didn't want to just stay locked at home while they risked everything. I knew I was just a human, but I wished there was some way I could help. I voiced my concern. "So what are we going to do? I don't want to stay cooped up in your house all day like a damsel in distress."

I felt her go a little rigid and sit up straighter. I looked at her because I didn't know what just set her on edge. Her eyes were averted away from me, and she just looked at our hands in her lap. "Well, umm, I was going to see if you..." she trailed off and took a deep, nervous breath in. It made me grow anxious.

What could possibly make her this nervous? Was there something she wasn't telling me? "Nat, what is going on?" I tried to get in the line of her sight with my face, but she turned away even more.

I could see her brows furrowed together, and lips pursed. "Well, I was wondering if..." she trailed off again.

The next voice I heard wasn't hers. It was Irene's voice yelling from the living room. "She wants to know if you will go on a date with her. She is a little out of practice and nervous."

"Shut up, Irene! I've got it!" Natasha yelled back at her.

I heard Max boom with laughter. "I haven't heard someone drowning that bad since the Titanic sank!"

"And you're a dick, Max!" Natasha yelled back, slapping the side of the house.

I couldn't help but let out a laugh. "Nat, were you that nervous to ask me out on a date? We slept together, for goodness' sake." I wrapped my arms around her and kissed her cheek. Her blush was such a deep shade of red; it looked like a horrible sunburn.

She lowered her voice and sheepishly said, "I know, but I haven't done that in a long time and didn't know if you would actually want to go on one with me or not."

I couldn't help but keep smiling at her and embrace her tighter. "Of course I want to go on a date with you. I do like you, you know. Like, I like, like you."

She turned her head toward me and smiled. "Good, because I like, like you too." Then she gave me a peck on the lips. "What would you like to do for our date then?"

I thought about that for a while. You could never go wrong with a movie, and I loved movies, but that would take away from talking time to get to know each other better. "How about a coffee date? We never went on one earlier," I suggested.

"OK," she said. "Coffee date it is." She wrapped her arms around me this time and kissed the top of my head.

We sat outside a little while longer till the bugs started getting to be too much for me. Fortunately for vampires, bugs couldn't bite through their tough skin. She led me back into the house. It seemed Max and Irene had already retired to bed since the front room was empty. I didn't know where Kyle was staying, but he was out of sight as well. She guided me down the hall to her room. Even after my long nap from earlier, it wasn't enough to ward off my exhaustion. When we got to her room, I rummaged through the suitcase Max and Irene had packed for me, found my hygiene bag, and headed to the bathroom. I was still in awe at how big and luxurious her room was.

After I finished all my pre-bedtime activities, I headed out of the bathroom. When I got out, I saw her sitting at the bedside. She stood up and smiled at me. "I'm going to take a quick shower and get ready for bed."

I walked over to the other side of the bed and slid myself into the comfort of her sheets. The thread count must have been super high. They felt so heavenly. "OK," I said through a yawn and pulled the comforter up to my neck. "Don't keep me waiting long." She smiled back at me in response and went into the bathroom and shut the door. I was already feeling the heaviness of sleep taking over my body when I heard the shower start running.

I must have dozed off because the next thing I remembered was feeling Natasha push her body against my back and her arm slip around my waist. I felt an approving, "Hmm," escape my throat. It made me feel so safe wrapped in her arms. That would be my first restful night since I saw the gruesome murders that started this entire endeavor. I whispered through a sleepy smile, "Goodnight, Nat."

I felt her breath on my hair. "Sweet dreams." And then I slipped into a pleasant slumber.

NATASHA

I woke up with Jamie still cradled in my arms. I smiled because she was still there, which meant she hadn't been thrashing around in her sleep having nightmares like the other night. I lifted my head to glance out the window. There was the faintest of light shining in. It must have been around 6:00 a.m.

I usually got out of bed as soon as I woke up, but I was enjoying holding Jamie close to me this morning. It just felt so right with her here in my arms. She stirred and rolled over. She buried her face into my chest and scooted closer to me. Her breathing was still slow and steady, so I knew she still wasn't awake yet.

After lying in bed for another fifteen minutes, I felt her lips press against my collarbone. "Good morning," she said in a still sleep-filled voice. I pulled back so that I could look at her. Her eyes were still half-closed.

I couldn't help but smile at the sleepiness that still lingered over her. "Go back to sleep. It's still early," I whispered.

She pushed away from me into a full body stretch. As her arms reached as far above her head as they could, she yawned, and I heard a squeak escape her throat. I couldn't help but laugh at the sound. She grabbed her pillow and swung it at my face. "Don't make fun of me."

I grabbed the pillow before it could reach me and slung it off the bed. Then I rolled over on top of her. She instantly slid her arms around my neck and smiled up at me. I lowered my head, capturing her lips with mine. After a long deep kiss, I felt her smile. I pulled my head away. "What?" I asked.

"I could get used to waking up like this every morning," she replied.

I would never object to waking up every morning kissing her. I wanted to stay in bed with her all day, but I was ready to get up. I was eager to take her on our date. "I'm going to hop in the shower."

I gave her one last peck on the lip and heard her groan in disapproval as I slid out of bed and made my way to the bathroom.

After I finished my shower and morning bathroom routine, I came back into the bedroom and saw Jamie was already dressed in light blue tight-fitting jeans that formed perfectly to her legs and ass. She had on a white and green flannel shirt with a white tank top undershirt. I guess I was staring a bit too long because when my eyes made it up to her face, one of the sides of her lips was curled up into a cunning smile. "You could take a picture. It would last longer." All I could do in response was shake my head and scratch the back of my neck.

The peck on my cheek left a warm sensation as she walked past me to the bathroom. I couldn't help but follow her with my gaze. I knew she could tell I was staring because she put a little sway in her hips, and before the door shut, she looked back and winked at me.

I went to my closet and picked out a pair of dark blue jeans and a plain black, long-sleeved shirt and slipped on my black Vans shoes. After I made my way down the hall into the living room, I saw Irene sitting crisscross on the couch, and Walter lying beside her, his head in her lap. She scratched behind his ears while she read a book. When they heard me come in, Walter lifted his head to acknowledge I was there, then set it back down in her lap. "I see you made a new friend," I said.

She looked up at me from her book and smiled. "I'm actually thinking about getting my own! He is so sweet and cuddly. Aren't you, Walter?" she said as she took his face in both her hands. He licked her face in return, and she let out a happy giggle.

I heard my door open, and Jamie came walking down the hall. Her black, wavy hair was down, and it framed her beautiful face perfectly. I couldn't help but smile at her. Irene must have seen because I felt her punch my leg. She whispered, "You're drooling a little." In response, I turned and scowled at her.

As Jamie came down the hall, Walter jumped off the couch and trotted up to her, wagging his tail. She knelt on the floor and petted him. I could feel the strong bond between them. It was so powerful for an animal and human to have that bond.

After she stood up, Walter walked back over to the couch and jumped up and rested his head back in Irene's lap. I smiled at Jamie. "You ready to go?"

She walked up to me and grabbed my hand with hers. "Yep, let's go."

I could feel the joking humor radiating off of Irene, but she just smiled and said, "Have fun, you two."

We left the house hand in hand. I guided her to the passenger side of my car and opened it for her. "Thank you," she said with a smile as she got inside. After I got in the driver's side, I started down the driveway and turned onto the main road.

I decided to take us to a small, independently owned coffee shop downtown instead of a big chain coffee shop. It had a hipster atmosphere to it. After we pulled in the parking lot and entered the establishment, I saw her eyes scan the inside and then look at me. "I didn't know you were a hippy at heart." She nudged into me playfully.

I chuckled at her jest. "Hippies don't judge people," I said. That wasn't the main reason I brought her here. It usually wasn't crowded and had more space than the other coffee shops I had been to. I didn't have social anxiety, but, outside of work, I didn't really like being around large groups of humans. Even though we didn't look like stereotypical vampires, humans still picked up on a vibe we gave off, and I would get wary looks a lot of the time.

I led her up to the counter and ordered a black coffee for myself and two egg and sausage croissants for us. She ordered a white chocolate mocha with whipped cream on top. I handed the barista cash and told her to keep the change. Jamie went to go pick out a spot to sit while I waited at the counter for our order. She sat down at a corner booth by the window. The sunrise shone through the window just right, forming an almost halo around Jamie.

"Nat!" I heard the barista yell. I grabbed the tray with our breakfast and made my way over to the booth Jamie had picked out. I sat across from her and set our tray down between us.

She reached for her coffee cup and took a sip of it. Her eyes closed and she smiled as she let the warm liquid flow down her throat. The satisfaction that was on her face made me smile. I took a sip of my coffee next. Before I could speak, she said, "So Shae."

The statement almost made me choke on my coffee. I know we talked a little about her the night before, but I guess I knew she would want to know more about my ex. I wasn't expecting it now and so suddenly though. I took in a deep breath with my coffee cup still in my hand. "What about Shae?"

She shrugged her shoulders. "I don't know. I don't know much about your past dating history. You said you are old, and I'm not naive enough to assume you haven't been intimate or dated people before. I'm just curious about it, that's all." I smiled at her statement. I liked people that were honest and straightforward.

I was quiet for a while, trying to figure out how to explain my short affair with Shae. "Well, Shae and I were a thing a long time ago. It was during one of my rebellious phases. I was tired of listening to my father's rules, so I secretly left his manor."

I saw her start to chuckle and it accented her dimple. "So you were a teenage runaway?"

I had been a "teenage runaway" more than once. I hated living in my dad's manor under his strict rules. I always had someone with me and never had privacy anywhere. "I guess I was one. Shae's dad was high up in the ranks with my father's men, so she and I were acquaintances growing up. I went to her place, hoping she would give me a space to stay and keep it a secret." I saw her looking down at her coffee. I couldn't tell what she was thinking. I could feel a bit of anxiety coming from her.

"So she let you stay with her?" she asked, not looking up at me.

I couldn't tell if she was uncomfortable hearing this story, or angry with me. She seemed like she didn't want the answer. But she asked, and I told her before that I would always be honest when she asked me questions. "Yes. I did stay with her. At that time, I was carefree and very lustful when it came to my physical needs. She offered me a place to stay and more."

I saw her lower her head even more and her jaw clench. I couldn't tell what the feeling was that she was putting off now, but it was so powerful it made me feel uncomfortable. "Jamie. This was a long time ago. None of it meant anything. I was rebellious." I was starting to get worried because she still wasn't looking at me. Her posture was stiff and rigid. "Jamie?" I asked, reaching my hand across the table to her chin. "Are you OK? I can stop if you want me to. I don't want you to feel uncomfortable."

She looked up at me and smiled. I could tell it wasn't a sincere smile. She was trying to hide an underlying emotion. "Jamie, are you upset with me?"

She reached up and grabbed my hand with both of hers. Her smile lightened "No! Of course I'm not upset with you. I guess I'm just a little jealous is all." She looked out the window, averting her eyes from mine and looking a little ashamed.

I cupped her face with my hand and turned her so we were facing each other. "There is nothing you have to be jealous of. That was in the past. I'm very taken with you. You have my complete, undivided attention. I want to be honest when you ask me questions." I couldn't tell if humans felt jealousy the same as we did. I had envied others before.

"I know," she replied. "I am just a little scared. I'm only human, normal, boring, nothing special, and your world is everything but normal."

I couldn't help but laugh. "Jamie, you are not boring, and you are very special to me. I have zero interest in anyone else. My history with Shae and anyone else is just a blip in my past, nothing more." I reassured her with a smile. She seemed to relax into her seat more and took another drink of her coffee.

Now that she knew a little about my dating past, I was curious about hers. "What about you? Tell me a little about your past dating history."

I saw her lips curve into a smile. "Well, there isn't a lot to my past dating. Growing up being into girls in a small town like mine didn't leave me much room for dating. There was always a lot of gossip, and it was kind of taboo. In high school, I had a thing with a girl named Kristy, but nothing too crazy happened between us. She was too scared people would find out. When I went to college at the nearby university, I was in a relationship. Rylie and I were together for about a year and a half. She was two years ahead of me and, when she graduated, she moved to Seattle, thus ending our relationship. I was young and heartbroken and thought it was the end of my life," she laughed and shook her head, "but then I got over it. Dated a little, went a little crazy. When I graduated and got a job with the sheriff's office, I didn't really have time to date, and the gay pool around here still is slim pickings. And that's pretty much that." She shrugged and picked up the sandwich in front of her and started nibbling on it.

Before I could say anything else, the front door opened. I knew it was another vampire before he walked through. Jamie turned her eyes to the door. There were too many people in the café for me to act in any defensive manner. Before I could get up and sit by Jamie, the man swiftly made his way to our booth and sat down beside her. I could feel the anger wash over me.

"Good morning, Nat," he said through a smile. "That is what your friends call you?" I didn't reply to his statement. I was too preoccupied with how close he was to Jamie. I didn't know if he would make a scene in public or not, but I knew I would not let him hurt her. I would do everything in my power to prevent that.

I saw he left room between them and wasn't touching Jamie, so I met his eyes with my own. "You'd better have a damn good reason for ruining my breakfast," I growled through gritted teeth.

His eyes didn't leave mine. I could tell he was an older vampire, not a newly turned one, but not as old as me. His tone was soft and calm. "My boss sent me to talk to you. The other night, he feels, was a bit of a misunderstanding, and he would like to have a calm one-on-one talk with you."

Before I could reply, Jamie cut in. "A misunderstanding? You drugged me, and hog-tied me like I was an event at the rodeo."

The vampire was not impressed by her comment, and it sounded like venom being spit out of his mouth as he whipped his head around to face her. "How dare you speak to me!" he harshly whispered at her. I heard her let out a quiet whimper from the now tight grasp he had on her leg.

Anger shot through my body, but before I could reach over, he turned his head to me and said, "If you even think about it, I will cut her femoral artery before you have a chance to reach me, so please sit down." He glared at me. Then I heard a click of metal, and the vampire's posture went rigid. He slowly turned his head and looked down to his side, and my eyes followed.

Jamie had pulled her gun out and had it dug into the vampire's side. It was still concealed under the table so no one could see what was going on. "I just turned the safety off, you asshole. All I need to do is pull the trigger."

The vampire smiled at her. "You haven't learned much about us. That little human weapon isn't strong enough to hurt me."

I felt helpless. I knew if I made a move, the vampire could kill her in less than a second. Yes, I could get revenge, but I didn't want to lose Jamie. All I could do was sit and watch their standoff, hoping he wasn't stupid enough to actually cause a scene.

She leaned closer to him, which brought her face within inches of his. There was spite written all over her expression. I had never seen this side of her, and I could hear pure malice in her voice. "I have learned something, you prick. You share the same weakness as werewolves. After you attacked me the last time, the first thing I did was go out and buy silver bullets. They are tough to find, but I work for the sheriff's office, so it was doable. I wasn't going to let myself be caught off guard and defenseless again. I'm not stupid."

I couldn't tell if Jamie was telling the truth or bluffing, but I could feel her fear and anger radiating off of her. My heart started beating out of control. I wasn't in control of any part of the situation in front of me. I had to have faith that Jamie had either gotten silver bullets and wasn't afraid to shoot, or she was good at bluffing.

The vampire squinted his eyes at her. I could see the uncertainty in his face. He didn't know if she was bluffing or not, either. "You're lying."

Jamie clenched her teeth hard and shoved the gun deeper into the vampire's side. "Want to try me? I am not afraid to shoot and kill you here. This town, they know me as a deputy. They don't know you. You are an outsider. I can easily make it go away." I was impressed at how Jamie had completely taken control of the situation, and even though I could feel the fear in her, she didn't let it show in her outward appearance at all.

The man took his hand off of Jamie. He looked back and forth between us. I knew instantly he had given up and believed what Jamie had said. "I will tell my boss some other time then."

He went to stand up, and as soon as he was away from Jamie, I grabbed his arm, tight, digging my now extended talons into his skin. He gave a quiet yelp in response. "Tell Malcom to get the hell out of my territory or I will tear him limb from limb," I whispered through closed teeth. I still didn't let go when the vampire tried to leave. "And if you EVER touch her again, I will rip out your heart." The vampire jerked his arm out of my grasp, and hastily walked out the door.

As soon as I knew the man was gone, I moved around the table to Jamie's side before anyone could blink. All the color had drained from her face. I took the gun out of her now limp hand and put the safety on, then set it on the booth next to her.

I took her hands in mine and could feel her shaking uncontrollably. "Jamie?" She was staring in front of her at nothing. "Jamie?" I asked again, moving her chin so she was looking at me.

Right when her eyes met mine, tears started flowing down her cheeks. "I'm sorry. I was just so scared, Nat."

I pulled her into me and let her quietly cry into my shoulder. "Jamie, you have absolutely nothing to be sorry for," I said as I stroked her back, trying to calm her down. She was still shaking uncontrollably. I could feel the terror rolling off her, and it made my heart ache.

I held her till her shaking and crying stopped. I pulled away from her so I could look at her. "Are you OK?" I asked.

She sat back a little and used the palms of her hands to dry her eyes. Then she grabbed the gun and put it back in her waist holster. "Yeah, I'm good." She exhaled deeply and looked back at me. I still was worried about her, but she smiled at me. "Nat, I promise I'm good now, but can we leave?"

I wanted to get back home as well. "Of course. Let's go." I stood and made my way out of the booth, and when she got up, I defensively put my arm around her. She accepted it gratefully, and I felt her tension lessen as she leaned into my side. We made our way outside, and I walked her to the passenger's side and helped her in.

The first part of the drive was quiet, but then I got curious. "Did you really go out and buy silver bullets?"

I heard her let out a nervous laugh. "Absolutely not. There is no way I could afford to buy real silver bullets on my salary. That's why I was so terrified. I'm a horrible poker player and liar, and was scared he wouldn't believe me."

I couldn't help but exhale a soft laugh. "Well, you even had me fooled. But maybe you should have some just in case."

"You wouldn't feel worried about me having silver bullets?" she asked.

Of course, I didn't like the fact she would be carrying my kryptonite around with her twenty-four/seven, but my main priority was her safety. "No. I wouldn't be worried. I trust you. I know someone who manufactures them. I will put in an order for you."

She looked at me and smiled. "Thank you, Nat."

"Of course," I replied. "By the way, you were an absolute badass. You took over the entire situation and had that guy scared, legit scared. It was actually very sexy." I know that during the event, I was scared and angry, but looking back at it now, it was kind of a turn-on at how strong she had been.

I heard her let out another laugh. "How did you get sexy out of that situation? I was terrified."

I chuckled. "I guess I like a girl that can be authoritative and powerful. You didn't look terrified at all." I reached my hand over to hers. She had calmed down by then.

The rest of the drive was in silence. I still had no idea what we were going to do. I couldn't believe Malcom had the nerve to send his henchmen after me in public. I needed to get to the house and talk to the others. We couldn't just sit back and see what would happen. This needed to be dealt with now before it got out of hand, and someone else got hurt.

JAMIE

I was exhausted by the time we got back to Natasha's house. I had the most significant adrenaline spike in my life when I decided to try and fake that vampire out. Now I was coming down from it, and the crash was hitting me hard. I had a throbbing headache and felt weak and exhausted. I plopped myself down on the couch. Nat told me that Irene and Max went out, and they took Walter with them so he wouldn't have to stay at home alone. Kyle wasn't at the house either. She told me to rest while she went into the back to make some phone calls.

I had just gotten comfortable on the couch when I heard a sudden knock on the front door. After everything that had happened earlier, the noise made me sit up, startled. I looked around, waiting for Nat to answer the door, but she must have been busy on the phone still. The knock came again. I slowly stood up and made my way in the direction of the door. *Surely those other vampires wouldn't be stupid enough to come to her house.* They also wouldn't be knocking on the front door. I was two steps away from the door when the knock came again. I slowly grabbed the handle and twisted, cautiously pulling it open.

A woman stood on the other side of the screen door. She was very tall with broad shoulders. Her skin was a dark tan color, like she had spent a lot of time outside under the sun. I could see scars covering the exposed surface of her arms. Her curly hair was a thick, dark brown color and hung down loosely over her shoulders, almost touching her hips.

It was her face that made me aware of the fact that she wasn't a human. Her eyes were a bright yellow/ golden color that almost glowed. When she looked into my eyes, I could tell they were a predator's eyes. The features that surrounded them were primal, and when she smiled at me, her mouth was full of pearly white animal-looking teeth. From the looks of it, there were more in her mouth than should have been.

She was wearing baggy jeans with a cut-off flannel shirt and a tan tank top under it. Everything about her made me want to curl up on the ground in a fetal position and hide from her dominant presence.

"You must be the human I have heard so much about." Her voice even had an animal edge to it. It reminded me of what Nat sounded like when she was in her vampire form. This woman's voice, however, seemed wilder, edgier, and raspy. I didn't answer her. I felt exposed with my humanity being brought into the spotlight. She was still smiling at me, which made me feel even more vulnerable.

Then I heard footsteps coming up behind me. "Lylith! It's so good to see you!" Nat walked by me through the screen door and embraced the woman in a hug.

In response, Lylith slapped her arms around Nat. "Nat! it's been too long, old friend! But I may have scared your friend," she replied, nodding in my direction with a pure apologetic tone.

"Oh, Jamie, I'm sorry. This is one of my oldest and closest friends, Lylith. She is a werewolf," Nat said, giving me an enthusiastic smile. "Lylith, this is Jamie, the one I told you about." Lylith reached her hand out, inviting me to shake it. I grabbed her hand without hesitation. *Holy crap, I was meeting a real werewolf.*

"It's a pleasure to meet you finally. Nat has told me so much about you." I could tell now her smile was genuine and not the smile of a predator about to pounce on prey. "I'm sorry if I frightened you. I don't spend much time around humans and forget that I can be intimidating at first."

"It's OK. We just had a long morning, and I wasn't expecting visitors. I have been a little on edge since," I replied. I was curious why Nat hadn't mentioned Lylith before. I guess she had said that one of her closest friends was a werewolf.

Lylith moved her bright, golden eyes back to Nat and raised an eyebrow. "What happened earlier?"

Nat gestured for Lylith to come inside, and we all sat down. Nat sat next to me, and Lylith sat across from us on the floor, legs stretched out in front of her, arms propped up behind her supporting her torso. "Malcom sent one of his goons to try to talk to me while we were getting coffee. He threatened Jamie, but she pulled a gun on him and told him she had silver bullets." When she mentioned silver bullets, a sternness fell across Lylith's face, and her gaze fell on me. She made me feel so naked. I shrank into Nat, trying to seek protection. Nat reassured her, "She doesn't have silver bullets, Lyl. She was bluffing."

Lylith let out a laugh. "And I'm guessing the brute believed her? Maybe you should invest in some silver." She shrugged. "But please, make sure you aren't pointing it at my kind." She turned her attention back to Natasha. "So, you are certain it is Malcom? And he really is trying to take your territory?"

Natasha started rubbing the back of her neck. "I'm almost one hundred percent sure it is Malcom. And as far as I know, he is after my legacy. I don't know what that means. I guess he wants to start where he left off so many years ago. Take over my father's house."

Lylith shrugged her shoulders. "Why not just go find him and ask?"

Nat took in a deep breath. "Well, that's kind of why I asked you to come. We haven't been able to pinpoint his whereabouts, and I don't know how many followers he has. Kyle told my dad about everything, and all he is doing is sending three people down here, and he wants us to sit on our hands. We do know they are hiding out up north around your territory. I thought if we work together, we can figure out what all this is about."

Lylith chuckled. "I'm guessing you haven't talked to your dad about inviting the wolves into this little debacle."

"No," Nat replied hastily. "Otherwise, your father would be involved in it. I thought it would be best to handle it at a lower level than going all the way to the top. You and I get along great. Our parents are obligated to. You know it's different."

I was confused now. Nat had told me that all the different factions of creatures got along. The way she was talking now made it sound like there were issues between them. "I don't understand. I thought you said everyone got along."

Lylith let out another laugh. "When it comes to supernatural politics, everyone 'gets along,'" she said, using her fingers to air quote, "but dislike each other at the same time. They are complicated relationships. It's like how liberals and conservatives get along."

I guess it sounded like a typical government and diplomatic approach. "So, your dad is high up in the werewolf community?" I asked Lylith.

I saw Lylith turn and smile at Nat, but the response came from Natasha. "Lylith's dad is the alpha of the North American Pack."

I knew that alphas were leaders of packs. I had seen the Discovery Channel enough to know every real wolf pack had an alpha, but the way Natasha said it made it sound like there was only one pack in all of North America. All the stories I had ever heard of before made it seem like there were many packs everywhere. "Is there only one pack in North America?"

Lylith brought her legs into a crisscross fashion and her arms out in front of her. "I see you haven't given your woman a lesson on werewolves," she said, looking at Natasha. Then she turned her gaze back to me. "Yes, there is technically one big pack in North America. We are spread out in smaller communities run by the alpha's family, mostly his children but some of his siblings."

I felt Natasha slip her arm around my shoulder, "Every decision goes through Lylith's dad since he is the alpha. Lylith resides down here in the US. He stays somewhere in Canada. Since it is such a significant territory to cover, he puts people like her in charge of smaller packs."

It was like all my childhood stories were coming to life. "So do you share territory, or how does that work?" I asked.

Lylith replied, "In a sense. We have made boundaries and can enter each other's boundaries based on criteria. But we are in charge of protecting the area we have claimed. It has worked to keep fighting and wars at bay for a long time now."

"So you will help Nat with finding this guy?" I asked her with a hopeful tone.

She looked at me, thoughtfully. I couldn't tell what she was thinking. "Yes, I will. I have to talk to my people that came with me and see how they feel about it. If it is Malcom, I feel like he could ruin the balance of everything. The werewolves would be in danger too, especially so close to our turf." She stood up, and Natasha followed suit.

We followed Lylith through the front door and down the porch. Nat hugged Lylith again. "Thank you for coming, and thank you for helping me with this."

"Of course. You have helped me plenty of times in the past. I hope we can get this taken care of without incident. I will talk to my brother and the others that came with me. Tomorrow when we meet up, we can figure out where to go from here." She then turned her attention to me and held out her hand. "Again, it was nice to meet you. I hope we have many more positive encounters in the future."

I shook her hand. This time I noticed how warm it was. "It was nice to meet you too," I replied. Then she turned and started walking toward the forest that surrounded Nat's property.

Natasha guided me back in the house to the couch. She sat down and reached her hand out, inviting me to sit next to her. I had so many questions to ask. Now that my eyes had been opened to a world hidden beneath the life I had lived for twenty-eight years, I couldn't think of where to start. I plopped myself down next to Natasha. My mind was going over all this new information so in-depth that I almost didn't realize Natasha was laughing. "What?" I asked her, turning my head to look at her.

"Nothing. I can feel so much curiosity pouring off you," she said with an amused look.

I knew she had the ability to sense how other people were feeling, but I still wasn't quite sure how strong it was. "You know it's not fair that you can feel my emotions." I nudged my shoulder playfully into her side, and it just made her chuckle even more. "Of course, I'm curious. I just met a real werewolf that is going to be in charge of all the werewolves in North America someday?" I was assuming that was how it worked for them too, with the eldest child taking over when the parents died.

"If Jackson ever dies, yes, she will become the alpha of the pack. Lylith was born with the alpha gene. Not all the alphas' offspring inherit it, though," she said.

"Are werewolves not immortal like vampires?" I asked. I remembered her telling me vampires could live a long time but eventually would die.

She shook her head. "They aren't immortal. They can live for a very, very long time like vampires. Jackson has been around for centuries, though, and still has the energy of a pup."

I still had so many questions I wanted answered. "Why did she look like that? It's hard to tell if you or Irene or any of the vampires aren't human when you aren't in your vampire forms. Can werewolves not look like humans? Do they have the ability to turn into wolves, or do they walk around like that?"

She smiled at my questions. "Well, she was born a werewolf and is very old. Her bloodline is long and strong. Most born werewolves can hold a kind of in-between form like that, not taking a complete human form. They are stronger like that. Honestly, I don't know if she can take on a true human form now. Werewolves that have been bitten can't do that, though. They either look like a human or turn into a wolf. And that is the answer to your next question. They can turn into wolves, bigger than normal wolves."

I nodded to her statement in understanding. "You said that when vampires bite someone, it has to be an intentional bite for a person to turn into a vampire. You have to will it. Is it the same with a werewolf?"

I saw her face form a more neutral look. "No. No matter how a werewolf bites a human—human form or wolf form—they will turn, as long as blood is drawn. That's another reason they don't interact much with people. Their laws about turning humans are laxer. As long as they take responsibility for whoever they turn. When a person first becomes a werewolf, it's hard for them to control their emotions. Their emotions are what control the wolf. When they are born, they are taught how to keep it in check from a young age. When they are bitten, it takes a while for them to keep it under control. Having a newly turned wolf in a city around people could cause an issue if they turned uncontrollably in the middle of a group of humans, if you know what I mean. They keep mostly to the woods and to themselves, in remote places."

That made sense to me. "So they can turn into a wolf whenever they want? It's not just during a full moon?"

That question brought another smile to her face. "Yeah, they can turn whenever they want. During a full moon, however, it does call to them even more. They are very powerful during a full moon. A lot of bitten werewolves that haven't learned control succumb to the moon and change unwillingly. Most werewolves take the time to turn during it and get out all of their primal energy. But, even I feel the power emitted during the full moon."

"So they have control when they are wolves?" I asked.

"They are in control as long as they are willing to turn and are the reason they turn. If the animal takes over and forces its way out, they lose control," she replied.

I guessed that part was more like the stories I had heard about werewolves. "Does it hurt them?"

She tilted her head to the side with a questioning look. "Does what hurt them?"

I shrugged my shoulder against her. "For them to turn into a wolf?"

"Hmm," she said. "Well, I can't speak for them. I have never turned into a wolf before." She laughed.

I gave her a playful nudge. "Come on," I said. "You know what I mean."

"Well," she said, taking in a deep breath, "I can say it hurts us to change forms. I would assume if one of their bodies changes so drastically so fast, it would cause some sort of pain."

I hadn't realized it would hurt her. She always seemed so strong, like nothing could hurt her. "It hurts you to change?"

I felt her inhale deeply beside me. "Our bodies physically transform almost instantly. It used to hurt terribly, but I have done it so many times and for so long now, that I have grown used to the pain. With power, there is always sacrifice."

I didn't like knowing she went through pain just being her. "Do you have to change?"

She was quiet for a minute. "Yes. The longer we don't change, the more restless we become, and the more likely it is we lose control. It's a part of who we are." She turned to face me with a worried look. "Does that upset you?"

"Why would any of that upset me? It's who you are. I just don't like that you are in pain," I replied.

She smiled at me. "I told you, I have grown used to it. It's a part of me."

I wrapped my arms around her arm closest to me and leaned into her. She put her head against mine. I wondered what other trials she had to face on the daily just being her. The front door flew open, interrupting my thoughts. Walter bolted in and jumped right into my lap. Then Max and Irene came in. Irene's face formed an enormous smile.

"Is Lylith here?" she asked Nat in an excited, loud voice.

Natasha lifted her head in Irene's direction. "She was here earlier. I asked her if she would be willing to help. She's talking with whoever she brought down with her right now. They are staying in the woods out back."

Irene clapped her hands and squealed with excitement. "I'm going to go see her! I haven't seen her in so long!" And without another word, she was back out the door.

Max smiled and watched as she left the house. After the door closed, he turned his attention back to Natasha. "So, you recruited the wolves without approval from Nik?"

Natasha shot Max a sideways glance. "I am in charge of this area, and I will defend it how I see fit."

"Nat, your father is still in charge of the house. This is his territory technically," He replied sternly, shaking his head.

"His territory that he entrusted to me. He was made aware of the issues that have taken place down here and has done nothing about it. It's my responsibility to defend this area," Natasha replied, her tone cold. I had never heard them talk like this to each other.

"You should have told him what was happening down here yourself. Kyle is naïve when it comes to things like this. He is a yes man and won't push your father when he needs to be pushed." Max huffed as if this was a repeated conversation.

I felt Natasha let out a long exhale. "He won't listen to me, Max. You know this."

Max's raised his voice this time as he replied to Natasha. "No, I don't know this, Nat. This is serious. Stop acting like a child. Talk to your father!"

Natasha stood and was instantly an inch away from Max's face. There was distaste in her voice when she spoke to him. "If you are so concerned about the wolves helping, you tell my father. He has always listened to you over me." Her next move was out the front door. She moved so fast that it took my brain a few seconds to catch up to what my eyes had seen. I didn't know if I should follow her or stay there.

Max let out a sigh and scratch the back of his head. Then he looked up at me. "I'm sorry about that." And without another word, he headed toward his room. I was left alone in silence.

I was curious about what had happened between Natasha and her father to make her not want to talk to him and why she thought he wouldn't listen to her. I decided to go outside and try and find her to make sure she was OK.

When I got outside, I saw her sitting on the porch swing. She had her elbows on her knees and her head in her hands. I didn't like seeing her so upset. I made my way over and sat by her. I started rubbing her back but didn't say anything. Maybe she just needed some quiet time, time to think. "Do you want me to leave you alone?"

She instantly lifted her head and looked at me with concern. "No, of course not." She reached for my hand and held it. "I'm sorry about inside with Max. It's a touchy subject for me."

I didn't want to push her to talk about it, so I left the subject open so that if she ever wanted to talk about it, she could. "If you ever need to talk about it, I am all ears. You shouldn't keep things bottled up like that."

She smiled at me and rubbed her thumb over my knuckles. "Thank you, but right now probably isn't the best time for me to talk about it when I'm still riled up. But I would love your company right now."

I wanted to do anything I could to help her. If it was sitting on the porch in silence with her, I would stay out here as long as she needed. I pulled my legs onto the swing and leaned my head against her shoulder and relaxed into her, enjoying the calmness that swept over me whenever we were this close.

NATASHA

Jamie had fallen asleep while we were out on the porch, so I carried her to my room and tucked her into bed. She could use a nap after the morning we had. I knew Max had been right about talking to my father, but I wasn't ready to try and have that conversation yet. If he hadn't believed Kyle, he wouldn't believe me. Hopefully, teaming up with Lylith would solve everything.

It was around two in the afternoon. Irene had come back a while ago in good spirits from visiting Lylith. After I told her Max was in their room, she went to find him and never came out.

I lay on the couch with a book to try and get my mind off everything, and suddenly the front door swung open. I knew it was Kyle. I could feel the anger radiating off him before he got on the porch. "Wolves?!" he yelled at me, slamming the door shut behind him. "You invited the wolves?!"

I sat up from my comfortable resting position. "Shut up, Kyle. Keep your voice down. Geez." I glared at him. "Yeah, I invited my friend Lylith to visit. What of it?" I knew Kyle wasn't particularly fond of werewolves, but in his defense, it was because of stories he had heard about rough rogue ones. He had never actually spent time with any.

He huffed and squinted his eyes at me. "Lylith? I know the only reason you would invite her and a pack of mutts would be to help with this. You didn't even ask Nik about it, did you?"

I was still trying to keep calm. I didn't want to get Kyle even more worked up than he already was. "Kyle, listen. They have territory here too. Nik only sent us three people. We have no idea how many people Malcom has recruited, and we need the numbers and strength. Nik isn't taking this as seriously as he should. Even you should be able to see that."

He inhaled and let out a long breath, pinching the bridge of this nose. I could tell his posture was relaxing a little. "Does the alpha know about this?"

"No," I replied. I knew the fewer higher-up people that knew about any of this, the better. My answer seemed to satisfy him a little.

"Okay. So, what is the plan?" Kyle asked.

"Lylith came over earlier, and I told her about everything that has transpired. She agreed that she and her people would help. She went to talk to them and said she would be over tomorrow so we could formulate some plan of attack." I replied. He calmed down a lot faster than I thought he would. He sat down in the love seat by the couch and relaxed into it.

He rubbed his temples with his fingers. "That sounds good. We need to make sure this stays between us and no one else." It was clear the entire situation had been weighing on him a lot more than I thought.

"Kyle, what's going on? You never agree with me this easily." Something was going on inside of his head. He hated werewolves, and to agree that easily to meeting with them and working with them was out of character for him.

He let out a heavy breath and rubbed his face. "Nat, I believe it is Malcom. If he has come back, he is going to be strong, especially if he is going after you as aggressively as he has been. If he is strong enough to turn so many people into vampires and keep hidden as he has been, we are up against something powerful. The fact that Nik isn't helping and isn't taking this more seriously isn't good and scares the hell out of me. I think he is in denial. No matter what evidence we give him, he doesn't want to believe it. As much as I am not thrilled about working side by side with wolves, we are going to need the help."

I had no idea Kyle felt this way. "Tomorrow we can go over everything with everyone and figure out a way to find him and stop him." After I said that, I heard movement from my room. Jamie was up. Kyle could hear her, too, because he looked toward my bedroom.

Before she came out, he leaned forward and spoke in a low, quick voice. "Nat, we need to keep her safe. Especially since she is practically your girlfriend, he is going to try and get to her." I saw him hesitate and run his fingers through his hair. I also felt a warm flush make its way up my cheeks at the word girlfriend. Jamie and I hadn't talked about the specifics of our relationship yet. We haven't had time. He didn't seem to notice my flush. "I also feel like there is something more to it than that with her. It just seemed out of character that he didn't kill her when he had the chance. Maybe he just wanted leverage, but who knows? There could be something else behind his motives."

Before I could ask him what he meant by *he thought there could be something more*, I saw Jamie making her way down the hall. His change of heart got me thinking. Maybe he had grown up and was a trustworthy person and a reliable ally.

Jamie came into the living room with a sleepy look on her face. I smiled at her, and she yawned. "Why did you let me sleep so long?" she asked.

As she stretched her arms above her head, her tank top pulled up and exposed the smooth skin of her stomach. I found myself staring but was brought out of it by the sound of Kyle clearing his throat. I looked at him, and he stared at me with a teasing half-grin. He had caught me staring at her, which sent another blush creeping up my face. At least Jamie hadn't seen me checking her out again.

After Jamie had finished her stretch, Kyle stood up and nodded at her. "Hope you enjoyed your nap. I'm going to take my leave now." He made his way through the kitchen to the back. I had an office space where Kyle was staying while he was here.

Jamie came and dropped down on the couch next to me. Instinctively I wrapped my arm around her, pulling her into me. She rested her head against my chest. "What were the raised voices all about?" she asked me.

I took a long breath in, taking in her scent, and then exhaled. "Oh nothing. Kyle wasn't happy when I told him Lylith and the other werewolves were down here. He came around, though, after some encouraging word."

"He doesn't like werewolves?" she asked.

"No, not really. He has never spent time around werewolves. He doesn't understand them. But after our talk, he was OK with them helping us." I didn't want to talk about those future plans right then since we didn't even know what we were going to do yet. I swung my legs up on the couch and extended them across the length of the cushions and lay back, pulling Jamie down with me. I did it so fast it that she let out a startled squeal as she came to rest on top of me.

It was nice having her lay on top of me. She didn't weigh much, but just the small amount of pressure her body created against me felt comforting. She lay her head down on my chest, and I felt her wrap her arms around me as best as she could.

"So, what do you want to do for the rest of the day?" I asked her. I didn't feel like leaving the house and just wanted to spend time with her alone. I was hopeful she was in the same kind of mood. She lifted her head to look at me. Her eyes were so beautiful. I could drown in them.

"How about we just put on a movie, make some popcorn, and cuddle?" she suggested.

I was in complete agreement with that. "Out here or in my room?" I asked.

A thoughtful look enveloped her face, and then I saw her lips form a sly smile. "How about your room?"

The corners of my lips curved up in response to her suggestion. I'm glad she wanted to go to my room. We wouldn't get interrupted in there and could spend alone time together. She had to go to work tomorrow, and Irene agreed to watch her while we had our meeting about a plan of attack. After today, I wouldn't be able to see her again until tomorrow night.

I grabbed her sides playfully and loved the reaction I got. She squirmed and let out a high-pitched laugh. I was a lot stronger than her, so no matter how much she squirmed, she couldn't get out of my hold. I couldn't help but giggle at how much she was laughing.

"OK, OK, I give up! Uncle!" she cried breathlessly through a laugh. I stopped my tickling attack and let her fall on top of me as she tried to catch her breath. "That was mean." She told me as she sat up.

"It was cute. I love when you squirm." I replied.

"No, you just like asserting your dominance over me because you are stronger and a bully." She smiled at me.

I let out an uncontrollable chuckle to her response. "My dominance? I will show you how dominant I can be." I raised an eyebrow at her and gave her a sideways smile. "You'd better run!"

She jumped off me and ran down the hall in the direction of my room. I could hear her playful giggle even after she got into my room and slammed it shut. It made me chuckle to myself.

Before I went to my room, I headed to the kitchen and threw a bag of popcorn into the microwave.

As it began to pop, I heard Irene's bedroom door open and shut. Then Irene strode into the kitchen. "So what do you two have planned? You look far too happy right now," she said, leaning against the counter with a grin on her face.

"What do you mean?" I asked.

"Nat, I haven't seen you this happy in a very long time."

I was generally a happy person. Not many things made me unhappy. I shrugged at Irene. "For the most part, I am always happy."

She grabbed my shoulder and turned me to face her. Then she smiled at me. "Not like this. Yeah, you usually are content and not unhappy with life. But ever since Jamie came into the picture, you have been genuinely happy. You haven't been this way in years."

I knew that Jamie made me happy, but I guess I didn't realize it had affected me as much as it had. Just thinking about it made me smile. Irene gave my shoulder a little shove. "Look at you! Nat and Jamie sittin' in a tree, K-I-S-S-I-N-G." She laughed playfully.

I shoved her back. I couldn't help but grin. "Shut up. So what if she makes me happy? I'm allowed to be happy, right?"

She leaned back against the counter. Her laugh turned into a small, soft smile. "Yes, you are allowed to be happy. You have more reason than most people to be happy. I love that you have found someone that makes you this blissful. I also totally approve of her. She is pretty great, and I will do everything in my power to protect her."

Hearing her vocalize her approval sent a warm pulsating feeling through my heart. I was so thrilled she had my back. The microwave dinged, informing me the popcorn was done. Irene grabbed a bowl and handed it to me. "Don't have too much fun with movie night." She winked at me and strode back in the direction of her room.

I poured the contents of the bag into the bowl and walked back toward my room. When I opened the door and walked in, I saw Jamie sprawled out across the top of the bed in nothing but her underwear. I felt an instant warmth in my lower stomach and felt my breath catch. *Geez, this girl made me so weak.* I froze, my eyes scanning every curve and bare inch of her body. I didn't even care when I felt her eyes staring at me. I wanted to take in every ounce of her. I felt desire wash over me, and all I wanted at the moment was her. I set the bowl down on the table next to my door.

Not taking my eyes off her, I made my way toward the bed. The smile on her face curved wider, causing her dimple to deepen, and the hunger inside me grew stronger. I crawled onto the bed slowly, still scanning her body, till my eyes fell in line with hers.

I finally stopped when my body loomed over hers. I stared into her eyes, full of need and longing, and realized we were never going to get to the movie tonight, which was completely fine with me.

I woke up to a vexing buzzing sound in my ear. I growled and reached in the direction the noise was coming from. My hand was stopped before it could reach the source of the sound. I felt warm, smooth skin, and it brought a smile to my face. Jamie was sitting on the side of the bed.

"I'm sorry." She whispered frantically, fidgeting with her phone, trying to turn the sound off. "I didn't mean to wake you up."

I scooted myself to her side and pulled her back down into me. I was still so groggy from sleep that the only sounds I could make were disapproving grumbles at her as she tried to break free. She laughed as I wrapped myself around her, holding tight.

"Nat!" she giggled. "I need to get up and go to work."

I huffed my protest as she wiggled out of my grasp. She gave me one more peck on the lips before she walked to my bathroom to get ready for her day. After she shut the door, I rolled out of bed to make sure Irene was awake, since it was her responsibility to keep an eye on her today.

After I knocked on her bedroom door, it only took a couple of seconds for her to answer it. She was already dressed and had a grin on her face. I looked past her and saw Max was still unconscious in bed, snoring loudly. "Don't worry, *mom*. I'm all ready to go." She pushed by me and headed to the kitchen. I followed her to try and whip Jamie up something for breakfast. I popped a bagel into the toaster and turned on the coffee pot.

By the time Jamie came into the kitchen, I already had a cup of coffee and a cream-cheesed bagel waiting for her. Her face lit up when she came in and realized I had it already made for her. She kissed me in exchange for her breakfast.

Irene grabbed her thermoses out of the fridge, and we made our way out the front door. Since it would take Jamie a while to drive to work, we had to wake up extra early this morning. There wasn't even a glimpse of dawn in the sky. I was OK with that. Darkness was when we were at our strongest.

I walked Jamie to her Bronco. She set her coffee cup in the drink holder and her bagel on the dashboard.

I was still worried about not being the one to keep an eye on her. I trusted Irene would keep her safe, but I couldn't help but worry. Jamie could tell I had doubts about it because when she turned back to me, she cupped my cheek with her hand.

"Everything will be fine. I promise I won't go anywhere by myself or do anything stupid. Plus, Irene will be there."

Malcom's men had already been impulsive with how they were doing things. I wasn't sure it was safe enough for Jamie to be in public. But I knew I needed to be here to discuss with everyone how we were going to go about finding Malcom and his crew.

I hear Irene yell from her car. "It's OK, Nat. I promise I won't let anything happen to her!"

I looked Jamie in the eyes. They were so soft and inviting. I smiled at her. "I know she will protect you, but I need you to stay as safe as you can."

She stood on her tiptoes and wrapped her arms around my neck, pulling me into a deep kiss. Her lips tasted so good that I didn't want to pull away, but then she did and placed her forehead on mine. "I promise I will stay safe, and if anything out of the ordinary happens I will let Irene and you know."

"OK," I replied. Then she got in her car, and they both drove down my driveway and pulled onto the main road.

As I watched them pull away, I heard footsteps behind me. "I have never seen you so smitten before. It's a little gross." Lylith walked up beside me and gave me a small shoulder check.

I couldn't help but laugh because just a few days prior, I gave Irene this same speech. I playfully shoved her. "I guess I am a little infatuated. I don't know why or how she makes me feel the way I feel."

I saw her shrug her shoulders. "Maybe you two are soul mates?" She lifted an eyebrow at me and gave me a half-cocked smile. She was a romantic and knew I didn't believe in that kind of stuff. "Or maybe it is just love at first sight?"

The next thing I heard was Max's signature laugh from the porch. "Love at first sight? Lyl, you know Nat isn't about the lovey-dovey stuff." I turned and saw him leaning on the porch rails sporting nothing but his boxers.

I had never been into romance and soul mates and love at first sight. Maybe it was because I had never experienced it. In all the years I had been alive, this was the first time I had a glimpse of the possibility of it. Max and Irene claimed they were each other's soul mates, but Irene was a hopeful romantic. I turned and smiled at Max. "Maybe all it took was a human to make a believer out of me."

I heard Lylith take in an exaggerated gasp and grab my shoulder. "On everything holy! Who are you and what have you done with my best friend?"

I laughed at that and wrapped my arm around her shoulder, leading her to the house. "I don't know, she makes me feel more different than I ever have before. It's hard to explain. It's like we are meant to be."

After we all had breakfast, Kyle left to go pick up Shae, Isaac, and Jason from the airport. Their flight wasn't supposed to get in till 10:45 a.m., but it took over an hour to get to the airport. I used this time to talk with Max and Lylith alone to get their input about how to find Malcom. Lylith suggested that we search the northern forest at night, since both werewolves and vampires were strongest then, and retreat here during the day. Max suggested that we have continuous scouts, half searching during the day and the other half searching at night. Both had their merits and flaws. Of course, no decisions would be made until the rest got there.

We made our way to the living room to wait for the others to arrive. I heard Kyle's car pull up. Max and I got up and walked outside. Lylith decided to stay put.

"Holy freakin' crap, Natasha," Shae said as she got out of the car. I had mixed feelings about seeing Shae. I had seen her only a few times since we broke up. It was just a fling, but I knew she had developed strong feelings for me then that I didn't reciprocate. I heard she had been with someone now for quite a while, so I was thinking positively.

She ran up the stairs and hugged me. It was a much different reaction than I thought I was going to get.

"Shae! It's been a long time."

She patted me on the back a few times. "Yeah, it has! I hear you have been jumping around, still trying to stay away from dear old dad. I guess some things never change." She pulled away and grinned at me. Shae was shorter than me. Thin and lean. She had jet black hair—one side of her head was shaved, and the other swooshed over the side and hung down to her ear. She had earrings all up and down her ears and a bar through one of them. Her nose was pierced, as well as her lip and tongue. Her style was drastically different. "You have changed since the last time I saw you," I stated as I looked her up and down. "Sporting a somewhat grunge punk look nowadays, I see."

She laughed at my comment. "Well it has been a long time since you have seen me. I guess I like this style for now."

I never really understood the attraction people had to fashion trends. It seemed like too much time and energy that I didn't want to spend, trying to pick a clique to fit in with. I dressed in a way and did things that were comfortable for me.

The next to come up to me was Isaac. I remembered him from when he was just a little boy. His mother and my mother had been close friends when they were growing up. He came up and extended his hand for me to shake. He had always been somewhat formal. "Nat, it's good to see you." I accepted his hand and gave it a firm shake.

"Likewise." I replied.

I had never met Jason before. I had heard about him, though. He wasn't a born vampire, which surprised me that my father had grown to trust him as much as he had. He had been bitten and changed by one of my father's workers. Her name was Rachel. She had lusted over him when he was a human, and got permission to turn him into a vampire. Ever since then, he made his way up the ranks pretty fast.

"Natasha, it is good to finally meet you. I have heard a lot about you," he said as we shook hands.

"I'm sure you have," I replied. I wasn't quite sure how I felt about this guy. He was unknown to me and that made me nervous. Especially since we were going to be working with werewolves and Jamie would be around.

I still wasn't sure if Kyle had told them I had recruited Lylith and her pack. I knew Shae would be OK with it. She and Lylith got along great, and Isaac would most likely be fine with it. I didn't know how Jason would react, though.

Shae was the first to speak as we walked through the front door. "Well, well, look what the cat dragged in." I felt the instant tension given off by Jason and Isaac, but Shae didn't seem phased by it at all.

"Hello, Shae," Lylith said, standing up and walking over to us. The two gave a friendly hug. Jason and Isaac just nodded at her, still clearly uncomfortable. "I see your counterparts aren't as comfortable with me around as you are," Lylith stated, observing Isaac and Jason's tension, eyeing them up and down.

Isaac had been around werewolves before, but not many times, and as far as I knew, Jason had never dealt with them.

"Jason, Isaac relax, she's a friend. Plus, her bark is worse than her bite," Shae said, winking at Lylith with a smile.

I saw Isaac grin slightly and felt him relax. But Jason was still tense and rigid. "But she is a werewolf," he whispered. I saw his eyes turn into a glare.

Something inside me hardened at this statement. I was not about to have this turn into a fight before we even got started. I needed him to realize quickly who was in charge and that we all were going to be working together on the same side. I turned to him, stone-faced.

"Listen up, Jason. This is my home. She is welcome here, and she will be helping us. I know her and would trust her with my life. I don't know you, so if you think for a second you are going to get away with any childish bullshit in my house just because you are my father's man, you are dead wrong. I am not one to be messed around with. Do you understand me?" I growled the last words at him.

A look of fear and submission quickly replaced the menace that was in his face a few seconds earlier. I didn't like making people fear me, but I needed him to understand I was in charge and I would not tolerate unwelcomeness from anyone.

"He understands." Kyle came up and grabbed him by his collar and pushed him past me. "Apologize now," he told Jason, as he positioned him in front of Lylith.

It was almost as though Jason's strong persona melted away into a child's form as he shuffled up to Lylith, "I am sorry for what I said. I understand you are going to be helping us." He didn't look at her, and I couldn't tell if it was because he was scared of her or ashamed of himself.

Lylith looked at me, confused, as if she was asking what she should do. I didn't know what to tell her, so I just shrugged my shoulders.

"Umm, apology accepted. I know we are all on the same team," Lylith finally said to him.

"Jason and Isaac will share my room with me. Shae, you get the guest bedroom down the hall. They need to freshen up. Then we can all sit down and talk," Kyle stated, as he guided Jason and Isaac out of the living room toward the back.

After they had vanished in the back, I heard Shae and Max start laughing. "Geez Nat, I think you made the kid wet his pants!" Shae slapped my back. "When did you become an authoritative hard ass?" I didn't think it was too authoritative. I just didn't want this entire thing getting off on the wrong foot. I wanted to protect Jamie and find Malcom.

"I don't need a little child coming in here thinking he is going to run the show just because my father gave him a job. This is my territory, and I will not let someone like him jeopardize this or the people around me," I said sternly.

"Wow," Shae said with a smile, "Kyle was right. You really do like this human if you are getting all uppity in charge like this."

I felt a flush run up my cheeks. "It's not just because of her," I fired back.

Max laughed. "Yeah? Then why is your face all red, and why so defensive?"

I huffed at both of them and saw them fist-bump. At least Shae wasn't acting like an ass because I was seeing a human, so I smiled. "Go get cleaned up. I know you had a long flight," I told Shae. Max followed, and they parted ways at his door.

Once they disappeared down the hall, I heard Lylith speak. "Well, that could have gone a lot worse."

"Yeah, but that was just introductions. We haven't even gotten to the 'trying to get everyone to work together' part," I replied, and sat down on the couch.

I was still worried about Jamie. I hated not being the one watching her, and Lylith could sense it. She came over and sat down beside me and put her hand on my thigh. "Nat, everything is going to work out. You and I have been through more than enough to know that even *if* the odds are against us, we will come out on top." I nodded my head, trying to cling to her words and reassure myself she would be safe.

JAMIE

The sun peeked its way over the horizon as I pulled into the parking lot of the sheriff's station. Irene had stopped tailing me a while back. I still felt a little awkward having someone follow me and keep tabs on me when I couldn't see them. I wished that I could have her by me the entire day. That would make me feel a lot more comfortable. Before I got out of the car, I texted Irene. "I can't see you."

I felt my phone almost instantly vibrate. I opened up the text, and there was an eye and a ghost emoji, followed by, "That's the point! But I can see you!" A winking smiley face appeared after the words. I smiled at her response. At least I could get in touch with her fast if I needed to. I also sent Natasha a text letting her know I made it. When I got into the building, it was empty. I was the first one there, so I turned on the lights and made my way to my desk.

I wasn't quite sure what I was going to be working on today. I already knew who killed Tracy, but I couldn't say anything to the sheriff about it since it was vampires. Maybe he would still make me follow up on whatever little leads we had. I guessed I could do that and pretend like I didn't know anything. I grumbled to myself and let my head rest against the desk.

"Rough morning already, huh?" Chance had come in without me even hearing him. I practically jumped out of my seat and felt a scream get stuck in my throat. My heart nearly stopped.

"Chance! What the hell? You can't just sneak up on people like that. Geez!" I scowled at him.

"Whoa, geez. I didn't mean to scare you. Why are you so uptight today?" he replied as he walked to his seat.

"Sorry, I just had a long weekend," I told him. I already was high strung, and that just made my anxiety go even higher. I took in a few deep breaths to try and bring down my heart rate. Once I could no longer feel my pulse in my head, I turned on my computer and opened up my email. There weren't any important ones that caught my eye.

"So what do you think the sheriff will have us do today since that chick's murder is at a standstill?" Chance asked.

The way he said his statement ticked me off. Chance had been with the sheriff's office for about six months. He was young, tall, and muscular, and had been the star quarterback for the high school. I would have thought he was on steroids had it not been for drug tests we had to go through occasionally. He also thought of himself as somewhat of a playboy, and he acted like an immature jerk half the time.

"You don't have to be such an ass about it, Chance. Someone brutally murdered her. Have some respect," I scolded.

"Whatever." He replied to me like it didn't matter at all. "He probably will have us just rounding the city today."

"What do you mean by us?" I asked him. We never really did drive-arounds together because the city was so small, and we were short-handed anyway. The last thing I wanted to do was share a car with him all day.

"Friday, Sheriff said because of the recent events, he wanted us using the buddy system." He shrugged as he started typing something on his computer. Great, not only did I have evil vampires after me, but I also had to share a day with Chance.

Another forty-five minutes passed before Sheriff Davis walked in. He walked over to Chance and me. "Since we don't have any new leads, I want you two in the cruiser today driving around, making sure nothing is out of the ordinary." Before I could stand up and protest, he had already made it to his office and shut the door.

I slammed my hands down on my desk hard enough that everything rattled on it. "Come on, Stone, alone time with me isn't that bad." He gave me a sly, cocky smile. "Maybe I can even convince you being with a man is better than being gay." He winked at me, leaned back in his chair, and folded his hands behind his head. The look on his face was so disgusting it made my stomach churn.

If we hadn't been at work, I would have smashed his nuts in, but unfortunately, I couldn't. "You're disgusting." I tried to emphasize how much distaste I had for him. He was so pig-headed it didn't faze him.

Now I was frustrated more than anything. I texted Irene, letting her know what we had planned for the day. She texted back a thumbs up.

I walked over to the wall where the cruiser keys were and grabbed them. "Let's go," I said to Chance, and walked out of the office without even looking to see if he was following.

"Wait!" he shouted after me, while he tried to gather up all of his things and catch up.

After I got into the cruiser, I slammed the door and started it. I had every intention of driving off without him, but I knew the sheriff would not be happy about me disobeying his orders. So I waited till Chance made his way to the car. After he got inside, he asked, "Why can't I drive?"

I slammed the car in reverse and peeled out of the parking lot. "Because I said so," I replied. The rest of the drive was in silence as I drove us to the downtown section of our little city.

There was nothing out of the ordinary to me, and I knew if there was it would be vampires, and I really didn't want to run into them.

"What does the sheriff expect us to be looking for?" Chance asked with an irritated edge. I was so annoyed that I just grunted back at him.

"What's your problem?" he asked me with a sneer.

Just the fact he asked me that made my blood boil. He had always given me shit about being gay and making comments about how he was a real man, and he could turn me straight. I had thought it was just because I'm one of the only girls that hadn't slept with him.

"What's my problem? The problem is you're an asshole and a pig." I growled.

He scoffed at my response. "Whatever man. You're just a little fag, and I don't care what you say."

I slammed on the brakes in front of the local grocery store. "screw you," I said before I got out and slammed the door. It was about lunchtime, and I was hungry. There were enough food places nearby. I didn't know where I was going, but I just started walking.

I heard the passenger door slam. "Wait! Stone! The sheriff doesn't want us patrolling alone!" he yelled after me.

"I don't care. Go get lunch. I need a break from you," I yelled over my shoulder without looking at him. Then I felt my phone buzz. It was a text from Irene. *Is everything OK? You look a little irritated.*

I didn't need Irene to get involved in this. *Yes,* I replied to her. *My partner is just a little prick, and I needed a short break from him.*

OK, she replied. *I got your back,* she sent with a smiley face.

I was still a little restless from how mad he had made me, so I walked into the grocery store to look around and see if I could get my mind off it. I went to the back to the fresh food section. They made oven-baked chicken daily, and the smell had drawn me in that direction. I heard my stomach growl as I got close. As I stood there deciding which one I wanted for lunch, I noticed a man come up beside me. I didn't take an interest in him; I just smiled at him and saw him smile back.

"Can't decide on what to get?" he asked.

It caught me off guard. I turned to look at him again. I had never seen him before, and that was a little strange because our city was so small. And me being a deputy meant I knew pretty much everyone that lived here. When his eyes met mine, I knew I could be in trouble. His face was too perfect, and he had familiar amber eyes. The smile on his face screamed predator. I was 99.9% sure he was a vampire. I used every ounce of willpower inside me to force myself to remain calm. I gave him the best smile I could at the time. "No. They all look good. This place makes the best," I replied while pulling out my phone. I sent Irene a quick text that just said *SOS*.

The man smiled back at me. "Well, I guess I will have to try one."

I nodded in his direction as a reply and turned my attention back to the chicken. I could still feel his eyes boring into me as if I was a meal, which made my heart start pounding. For all I knew, that is how he was looking at me. I knew he would probably be able to hear my heart beating so hard and fast out of fear, so I quickly grabbed one and walked as fast as I could to the front. When I got to the checkout line, my phone vibrated with a text. Irene had replied to my SOS text, *Head toward the post office when you leave.* The post office was about three blocks away. There were a few buildings between here and there.

As I waited for the cashier, I saw the man in a line a couple of registers away. He still had a venomous smile spread across his face, looking at me.

After I paid and had my bag in hand, I walked out and immediately turned left. Unfortunately, the man finished right when I did. I wanted to run for my car. That's what my instincts told me, but I trusted Irene, so I continued walking in the direction of the post office. The man was about thirty feet behind me. My phone buzzed again. *Go down the alley between the two buildings before the post office.* I knew what alley she was talking about.

Right when I turned, hands gently but firmly grabbed me and swung me to the ground against the building behind a dumpster, hiding me. When I looked up, I saw Irene, but she had transformed. The next thing I knew, Irene had the man in a chokehold against the wall. The man had changed as well, but I could tell he wasn't half as strong as Irene.

"Who are you, and why are you following her?" She was only an inch away from the man's face as she hissed out the question. The man reached to try and grab Irene. With her free hand, she grabbed one of his arms and snapped it in an awkward angle. It caused him to growl in pain. Irene tightened her grip around the man's neck to keep him quiet. Then she lifted her knee and thrust it right in his groin with a force that would have broken stone. The man made a gruff noise but couldn't keel over like his body wanted to because Irene had such a stronghold on him. "Now let's start over. Why are you following her?" Irene asked him again.

I had never seen her like this. She could be scary and stern when she wanted to be. I was still hunched over on the ground, keeping as low and out of sight as I could.

She loosened her grip around the man's throat so he could talk. "OK, OK!" he gasped. "It was orders. I had no choice."

Irene then head-butted him in the nose, and I hear another crack. The man tried to scream, but she gripped her hand hard around his throat again, muffling the sound. "Who gave you orders?" Irene asked in a cold, stern voice. It was almost scaring me how good she was at intimidating this guy.

"What the hell, bitch? You ain't getting anything more from me!" he managed to squeak out. "Why are you protecting a human anyway?"

She pulled his face closer by his throat and gave a low growl. "Because she is my friend. If you threaten my friend, I take it personally." Then she slammed his head against the wall, and his body slumped to the ground. His head hit the wall so hard there was an indent in the concrete and cracks formed around it.

That had to have killed him. Irene turned around, looking very predatory. I knew she wouldn't hurt me, but her form still startled something deep down in my being. I guess my face showed it too, because she quickly shivered and then was back to normal Irene. She took a drink out of the canteen at her side. When her eyes met mine, there was a worry in them. She didn't move toward me yet. "I promise I won't hurt you," she said to me in a soft voice.

I shook my head to break my thoughts and smiled at her. "I know Irene. I know you wouldn't. You're too sweet of a person. Plus, Natasha might kick your ass."

She chuckled and moved toward me slowly. She offered me her hand to help me up. As soon as I was standing, both her hands cupped my face. Her hands were petite, a lot smaller than Natasha's. Her eyes scanned every inch of my face. Then she stepped back and looked me up and down. "You aren't hurt, are you? I'm sorry I had to put you on the ground like that. I wanted you to be out of sight if anything happened." I nodded at her.

Then I looked past her at the man on the ground. She followed my gaze. "Is he dead?"

She shook her head. "No, he is still alive. I should kill him, but I will be able to track him now."

I felt an instant worry and distressed feeling wash over me. I didn't want her to leave me today and chase after him. I reached out my hand and grabbed her arm. "No, please don't leave me alone today." I had absolutely nothing to defend myself against vampires, and faking silver bullets probably wouldn't work again.

She gave me a reassuring smile. "I promise I'm not leaving you. Now when I go out and look for them, I can follow him. But we need to get out of here before he wakes up. It might be best if you go back to the station. Maybe try and get off a little early. I didn't think they would go after you this fast in public." She grabbed my hand and led me out of the alley, ushering me toward the cruiser that was still parked in front of the grocery store.

Chance was leaning against the passenger side. I forgot I had the keys. When he saw us walking toward him, he stood up fast. He had an annoyed look on his face. "Where the hell have you been, Stone?" Then he eyed Irene up and down. A glimpse of disgust formed on his face. "Getting a little tail on working hours, I see." He scoffed at me.

I hear Irene laugh next to me. "Little boy, if she was getting some, it's more than you have ever gotten. You seem like the kind of guy that needs to compensate for some—" she hesitated and looked him up and down, "shortcomings." Her eyes landed on his crotch.

"Excuse me? You don't know me," he started before Irene interrupted him.

"And I'm glad I have never gotten the opportunity to," she said before turning to me. "Remember what I told you." She gave me a tight squeeze then turned and walked down the street.

Before Chance could say anything to me, I got into the cruiser and started the engine. He slumped himself in without saying a word, and slammed the door. I drove us back to the station, and decided to take Irene's advice to leave a little early.

When we got to the station, I went straight to the sheriff's office and knocked on the door. I heard his gruff voice. "Come in."

As I walked in his office, he looked up from his computer in my direction. "Deputy Stone. Find anything on your cruise?" he asked.

"No, sir, but I got a worrisome text from family. I was wondering if I could take off a little early and make sure everything is OK." I had never asked to leave early, never had been late, and hardly ever used sick days, so I was hoping he would be OK with me leaving early.

He coughed and cleared his throat. "Yeah sure, we don't have too much going on today. Keep an eye out for yourself, Stone."

I nodded at him and left his office. As I walked to my desk to grab my stuff, I texted Irene and told her I got permission to leave early. She sent back a thumbs up emoji. I got in my car and pulled out onto the main road. I hadn't driven a mile before I saw Irene's car behind me. That set my mind at ease a little more. I hadn't realized how anxious the encounter had made me from earlier, and I could feel my hands still shaking.

Before I even knew it, I was turning onto Nat's driveway. I pulled up, and before I could even get out of the car, I saw the front door open. Natasha was opening my car door before I could even unbuckle. She practically pulled me out of the vehicle.

"What happened? Are you OK?" Her hands were on my shoulders, and her eyes were scanning over my entire body. She had the most distressed look on her face.

I smiled as well as I could. "I'm OK, Nat. Irene was there and took care of it." I heard Irene's car door shut, and she made her way over to us. Natasha inhaled and then let out a long breath, which made her relax slightly.

"I told you, Nat, I would take care of her," Irene said, stopping by Natasha's side.

Natasha pulled me into a full strong hug and held me there for a moment. Then she broke away, but slid her hand down my arm and intertwined her fingers with mine. She looked at Irene. "What the hell happened?"

Irene bit her lip and looked at the ground before she answered. "He followed her into the grocery store. I didn't want to follow and make a scene in public, so I told Jamie to lead him down an alley. When he turned to follow her, I...let's just say I interrogated him. He didn't give me anything, though. I was going to kill him but decided since I knew his scent, I could follow him, so I just knocked him out."

I felt Natasha tense up beside me as Irene told the story. Her breathing started to deepen, and I felt a small tremor start in her hand. "He shouldn't have even gotten that close to her, Irene," she said through clenched teeth.

I didn't understand why she was getting mad at Irene. She dealt with the guy and kept me out of harm's way. "Nat." I moved in front of her, so she was looking at me instead of glaring at Irene. "It's OK. She protected me and now she can track him. Nothing happened, I promise."

When her gaze fell on mine, her eyes softened. "If I would have been there..."

I cut her off. "If you would have been there, what? You would have confronted him in public and made a scene? Irene did the right thing. She was in complete control."

Her posture drooped, and her eyes fell. "Yeah, but—"

I grabbed her cheeks with my hands. "Yeah, but nothing Nat. I'm here now with you, safe." She closed her eyes and let her face rest into one of my hands.

After she took a deep breath, she turned and looked at Irene and gave her a genuine smile. "I'm sorry Irene, I know you did everything you could to protected her, and you did the right thing."

At least Nat was calming down and not about to blow up at Irene. I felt Natasha turn me toward the house and possessively put her arm around me. Irene walked up next to Natasha.

"Nat, to me, Jamie is family now. I will do everything to keep her safe." Then she ran in front of us toward Max, who was standing in the doorway. He welcomed her with open arms and wrapped her in a hug when she reached him.

I felt Natasha kiss the top of my head, then whisper, "Are you sure you are OK?"

Physically, I was OK, but the fact I was still being hunted made me uneasy. I knew they would protect me, but I was still worried about what would happen if they were outnumbered or couldn't get to me in time.

I took in a deep breath and decided to be honest with her. "Physically, I am good. I'm still uneasy about the fact I have vampires tailing me in broad daylight. I just wish I had something to defend myself with." I felt her arm grip me tighter, protectively.

"I talked to my friend about getting you some weapons, including silver bullets," she said. "But I would never let anything happen to you. I wish I would have been there today."

I stopped us before we got to the porch and turned to look at her. "Nat, I trust you with my life. This is just new territory for me." I wrapped my arms around her to try and reassure her I felt safe, which I did when I was with her, here at this house. I pulled away from her with another growing concern on my mind. "Is everyone in the house?"

She could feel my growing anxiety at meeting everyone. I felt her body shake as she chuckled. "Yes, everyone is here, and don't worry. They will be nice."

She guided me up the porch stairs and to the door, where I took a deep, anticipatory breath. As we walked through, my eyes instantly scanned the room. On the far side of the room, I saw Kyle, who gave me a wave and smile, sitting next to two other men.

"Jamie, that is Jason and Isaac." Each man waved in my direction at the mention of their names. Isaac gave a smile, but Jason kept an unmoving look on his face. Then I saw Lylith sitting on the floor with a younger man who looked like a replica of her, and a woman with short blond hair. "This is Lylith's little brother, Ryan, and her second in command, Sasha." They both smiled at me. They seemed friendly enough.

Lylith got up off the floor and embraced me in a hug. "I'm glad to see you made it back in one piece." She pulled away but still had her hands on my arms. "We are going to get these guys and stop their harassment."

I smiled back at her. "Thank you, Lylith."

Then my eyes fell on a woman who was sitting on the armrest of the couch. She was gorgeous and had a punk look about her. Her smile was warm and inviting when she looked at me, and her eyes were a soft, light amber. "This," Natasha said, gesturing toward the woman, "is Shae."

She slowly made her way toward me and embraced me in a hug. "It's so nice to meet you finally," she said happily.

Her response was not what I expected from an ex of Natasha's. "It's nice to meet you too, Shae," I replied, trying to project as much friendliness as possible.

After all the introductions had been made, I felt a little more relaxed. I still stayed as close to Natasha as I could, making sure there was some kind of physical contact between us.

"OK, so after today's events, we are going to start our reconnaissance tomorrow. Only recon. Make sure you are prepared, but I don't want to engage without our full force. We're going to break for now. Make sure to prepare whatever you need tonight and get some sleep."

They must have already discussed most of the details, because it was way too short of a meeting. It was kind of sexy seeing Natasha in an authoritative, commanding role. I had always been attracted to people in powerful positions. Just how her physical presence and demeanor almost demanded respect right then brought a smile to my face.

After everyone had left the house to prepare for the next day, I sat down on the couch. Natasha dropped down next to me and put an arm around me. I snuggled into her, "So, what is the plan you guys came up with?"

She took in a deep breath. "We decided to do scouting in three different groups continuously so we wouldn't miss anything. I was going to go out with the first group in the morning since I could track Malcom and another one of his guys. Max was going to watch you tomorrow but," she shook her head, "I'm probably going to end up going with you and have Max lead tomorrow after what happened today."

She was pretty much leading this entire entourage. She couldn't do that if she was always with me and poring all her attention on me. I don't even know if everyone would be able to get along without her. "Nat, you need to go with them tomorrow. It's more important."

I felt her arm tighten around me. "No, you are more important. Max can lead tomorrow."

I looked up at her. Her head was down, and she was looking at the floor. I put my hand on her cheek and turned her to look at me. As much as I would prefer her looking after me, I knew she needed to be with the group tomorrow. I smiled to reassure her I would be OK.

"Nat, Max can watch over me tomorrow. The faster you guys find Malcom and his goons and stop him, the faster this is over with, and the sooner everyone is safe. You are the leader of this. You brought all of them together, and if you want this to work smoothly, you need to be here running the show."

She closed her eyes, and her brows creased together. She placed her forehead against mine. "I can't keep you safe if I am not with you," she whispered.

"When you bring down Malcom, you will be protecting me and everyone else," I replied. Before she could protest even more, I captured her lips with mine in a deep kiss. I felt her body begin to relax next to me, and I melted into her.

When we pulled apart, she still was holding me close. I heard her whisper. "OK. But will you please just stay here tomorrow?

Don't go to work." It was the most pleading voice I have ever heard from her.

I wanted to so badly, but I couldn't. "Nat, I can't just put my life on hold out of fear. I need to go to work."

I felt her exhale sharply. "You're so stubborn." She pulled me even tighter toward her. "Are you hungry?" At her question, my stomach made a loud growl, and I realized I never did get to eat lunch, and it was already five in the evening. She chuckled at the sound. "Come on. I'm making pasta."

She led me by the hand into the kitchen. I pulled one of the bar stools over near where she was cooking over the stove. It was amazing how she could go from being the leader of a supernatural raiding party one second to being so domestic the next. It made me chuckle.

She turned her head and smiled at me. "What's so funny?"

"Nothing. You look sexy cooking, that's all." I winked at her, and I saw a slight blush make its way up her face as she turned back to the stove, but I could see a smile on her lips.

It seemed like she was relaxed enough. I really wanted to ask her about her relationship with her father. "So, can I ask you a question?"

"Anything," she replied.

"It's about your dad." I saw her freeze for a moment, then go back to cooking.

"What about him?" she asked, not looking at me.

"You have never really talked about him to me, but whenever you mention him, it seems like you two have a strained relationship." I didn't really know how to go about talking to her about this, but I figured straightforward would be the best.

She didn't answer me right away. I guessed she was deciding if she wanted to tell me about it or how she wanted to talk about it. Then she took in a deep breath. "Yeah, we do. After my other family members died, he hid me away from the world and gave me a fake name. I guess he wanted to secure his legacy. I never wanted to be the one to take his place, to lead people. He never made time for me. I hardly every saw him and he treated me like property. I hated constantly being surrounded by guards, hidden away from everyone and everything. I felt caged. So when I got old enough, I ran. My father chased me for a while, but I was too allusive." She gave me a sideways smile. "Finally, he gave up on chasing me. We made a deal. I had to go off the grid, blend in, and take one of his own to help protect me, act like a territory protector. If I agreed to his terms, he would stop chasing me. Max had been a friend of mine since I was born, so I decided I would be fine with him tagging along. Dad wanted me in the most remote territory of his, so I was still somewhat hidden. I was OK with that as long as I had control over my own life. He doesn't listen to me or trust me because he thinks I still act like a child because he never gave me the time of day to get to know me. He never looked at me as his kid, just some kind of relic to keep safe."

I felt so sorry for Nat. Her father was more worried about keeping her alive to take his place than treating her like his daughter. I wrapped my arms around her stomach and rested my head between her shoulder blades. I felt her turn around in my arms to face me. "I'm sorry, Nat," I whispered, looking into her eyes.

She gave me a warm smile. "It's really OK. I'm not bothered by it anymore."

"So, Natasha isn't really your name?" I asked her.

I felt her chuckle. "No. It's not my birth name. My father made it illegal for anyone to mention it. After a while, people forgot about me, and the name. That's how he wanted it."

"Am I allowed to know your name?" I knew I was starting to get personal, but I felt like I deserved to know, now that I was a part of her world.

She ran her fingers through her long, dirty-blond hair. Her lips pursed together, and I could tell she was having an internal argument with herself whether she wanted to tell me or not.

Then a look of resolve crossed her face, and she leaned close to my ear. "Never tell anyone you know this. Never use it, ever." She took a long breath in and whispered even softer, to where I could barely hear her. I felt her lips brush against my ear. "Natalia," she whispered. Her breath tickled my ear, and the fact that she was trusting me with something like this made my chest warm.

"Thank you." I whispered. I wrapped my arms around her neck and gave her a long, soft kiss. I felt her hands slide around my lower back and pull me closer to her. I was safe here with her, and it made me all too aware of how scared I was to leave the house the next morning.

NATASHA

I woke up startled, breathing heavily, and drenched in sweat. I couldn't remember what the nightmare had been about, but Jamie was in it, and there was a terror flooding my chest. I never had nightmares because I was at the top of the food chain. There was usually nothing a vampire had to fear that would cause bad dreams. I turned to look at Jamie, but she was still soundly asleep. A heavy breath escaped my lungs.

I didn't want to fall back to sleep and feel that fear again. I moved my body flush with Jamie's back and wrapped my arm around her, pulling her close into me. My movement hadn't woken her, but her arm moved to rest on mine, and I heard her let out a quiet sigh.

I was dreading the morning. I still didn't want to leave her side, but I knew I had to get rid of Malcom. Only then would they stop harassing her. My body must have tensed up at the thought.

"Are you OK?" I heard Jamie ask through a sleep-filled whisper as she turned around in my arms.

"Yeah, I'm fine. Just had a dream is all. Go back to sleep." I kissed the top of her head. She curled into me and buried her head into my chest and was fast asleep again.

I had no idea how long I had held her that morning, taking in her entire being. When her alarm went off, she broke out of my grasp, frantically searching for her phone. It was entertaining at how fast she woke up and moved in response to the noise. I couldn't help but chuckle.

"I'm sorry," she whispered as she turned the alarm off.

"It's OK," I told her, softly stroking her bare back. "I've been awake."

She smiled at me, then leaned over and kissed me. "I'm going to take a shower." She slipped out of the covers and walked toward the bathroom.

I got out of bed too. I wanted to make sure Max was up. When I got to his door and knocked, it was Irene who answered. "Is he up yet?" I asked her through a yawn. I heard grumbling from behind her.

"Max! Get out of bed!" she yelled at him over her shoulder. "He will be ready to go when it's time." She smiled at me. I lifted a questioning eyebrow at her. "Nat, I promise he will be."

"He better be," I replied.

I walked to the kitchen to make Jamie some breakfast and coffee. When Jamie walked into the kitchen, she had a smile on her face, but I could feel tension surrounding her. "Are you OK?" I asked.

She came over and gave me a hug. "Yes, I'm fine. I'm just a little nervous about today. I know Max will be there, but I do still have worries."

I started stroking her back. "I know. Tomorrow I'm going to pick up some things that will give you more protection. Max will be there, though, and will take care of you."

"Yes, I certainly will," Max exclaimed, making his way into the kitchen with a big grin on his face. "I am an expert at being a bodyguard. Isn't that right, Nat?" he said, winking at me.

While Jamie drank her coffee and ate her breakfast, I pulled Max into the living room out of earshot. I put on the sternest face I could because I needed his full attention. "Max, I need you focused today. I need you to protect her."

He put both of his big hands on my shoulders and looked me straight in the eyes. His smile was warm and assuring. "Nat, I promise I will do everything in my power to keep her safe today. I have never let you down before."

He was right. We had been through a lot, and not once had he wavered. "Thank you," I told him.

I heard Jamie walking our way. "OK, I need to get going if I want to get to work on time," she said.

We all walked out front and said our goodbyes. I didn't know why, but I had a strange, uneasy feeling deep in my gut as they drove away. But I trusted Max, and I knew he would take care of her.

I made my way back inside and went to the fridge. The headache had started when I was pulled out of sleep by the nightmare. I hadn't changed or gone hunting in a while, either. After I grabbed my canteen from the fridge, I took four long gulps of blood. It subdued the urge.

"I told you, sis, you need to make sure you are taking care of yourself on a regular. If you aren't, you won't be able to defend Jamie or any of us, and I need you at your full potential," Irene scolded as she walked into the kitchen.

I knew I needed to do better at keeping myself reliable and fit. "I know, Irene."

She came over and grabbed my arms. "This is serious. Not just to protect Jamie. Everyone is looking to you. We can't afford to have you falter."

I shrugged her off. "I know, Irene. Now you sound like dad and Kyle."

"What about Kyle?" Kyle said as he walked into the kitchen.

"Nothing, just getting a lecture from Irene," I told him. "I need you to make sure Isaac, Jason, and Shae are ready. Irene, can you go out and see if Lylith and her guys are prepared?" They nodded at my requests and went their separate ways.

We had decided that the first day's group would include Kyle, Shae, Lylith, Sasha, a couple of other werewolves, and me. I went out front and sat on the porch swing, waiting for everyone to get there. Lylith had driven down a Tahoe, so we were going to pack into my car and hers.

As everyone started to make their way to the vehicles in preparation to leave, I checked my phone to see if Jamie had texted me to let me know she made it to the office. I didn't have any new texts, but she could have been busy and forgotten to let me know. "Irene," I called to my sister.

"Yeah, what's up?" she asked as she skipped to my side.

"I want you to stay here and keep an eye on Jason and Isaac. Make sure they stay away from the wolves, please" I told her.

"Sure thing."

"Oh, and have you heard from Max yet?" I asked

I felt her set a hand on my shoulder. "Nat, relax. They will be fine," she told me, giving me a reassuring smile. "But no, not yet."

I sent Jamie a quick text, asking if she had made it and slid my phone into my pocket. "Alright, everyone. Let's head out."

Kyle and Shae were going to be riding with me. "Shotgun!" I heard Shae yell and run to the passenger front door.

In response, Kyle shook his head. "Childish," he whispered under his breath.

Once everyone was in their designated car, I pulled out onto the road with Lylith following me. There was a parking lot near the cabins where Tracy had been attacked. We decided that it was going to be our starting destination.

Kyle was quiet in the back, looking out the window. Shae broke the silence. "So have you deflowered her yet?" she asked, punching me in the shoulder.

I felt my cheeks flare. "Umm, that is none of your business, Shae. geez," I snapped back.

I heard her laugh. "So I will take that as a yes. You dog. So, you really do like her?" I didn't have to look at Shae to know her eyes were scanning me.

I felt an uncontrollable smile form on my face. "Yeah, I do. I have never felt this way about someone before, never felt so protective. The feeling is hard for me to explain. I feel more alive with her. It's as if I have been aimlessly walking through life with no direction. When she came into it, a veil was lifted, and I could truly feel and see for the first time."

I heard Kyle groan in the back seat, "Ew, I don't need to know about your sex and love life, Nat."

Shae let out a loud laugh this time. "Oh come on, Kyle, it's cute! I am so happy you have found her." Shae grabbed my arm and gave it an affectionate squeeze.

"Yeah, but it's a weakness, Shae. She is just a human. Not that I have anything against her. I actually have grown kind of fond of her," Kyle said.

Shae reached back and smacked Kyle on the leg. "Come on, Kyle, she isn't a weakness. If anything, it's made Nat stronger. I have never seen her more determined before. I like that she's taking the lead. It's nice to see her like this. She has something worth fighting for." I did have something worth fighting for now, something that made me stronger. I would do anything for Jamie. That was a fact.

I heard Kyle let out a sigh. "Yeah, I guess you are right about her acting like a leader now."

Shae blew a raspberry with her lips. "You are such a party pooper, Kyle. Always have a stick up your ass. Can't you just be happy for them?"

"OK, OK, sure. I'm happy for you two," he said, clearly uncomfortable talking about relationships and the topic.

I flashed Shae an approving smirk.

She now knew about Jamie and how I felt about her. I had heard she was with someone but didn't know any of the details. "So I hear you are with someone," I said in her direction.

I saw a broad smile form on her face. "Is that a question or a statement?" she asked me.

I chuckled at her response. "Well, you know all about Jamie."

I saw her nod out of the corner of my eye. "Yeah, Jessica and I have been together for a while now."

"Tell me about her. Why didn't she come with you?"

"She isn't the warrior fighting type. She is kind of like you in the fact that she likes humans. She owns a nonprofit corporation that helps children with cancer. She didn't come down because I don't want her anywhere near Malcom." She rubbed my arm, sympathetically. She had been close to all my siblings before Malcom blew them up. I completely understood why she wouldn't want her significant other near Malcom. But it made me feel even more guilty because I wasn't protecting Jamie right then. Shae must have been able to tell it bothered me.

"Nat, taking him down will protect Jamie more than if you were just following her around all day," she said, trying to reassure me that what I was doing was the right thing. I was trying to believe her and convince myself. I knew I had to get rid of him.

Before I knew it, we were pulling into the parking lot. Shae enthusiastically jumped out of the car and stretched. "Oh, nature. I love it!" she said gleefully. I grinned in her direction, pulling out my phone. The screen displayed no new messages, so I sent Jamie another text, asking if she was OK. Then I texted Max to ask if they had made it. He never ignored my messages. Lylith pulled up next to my car, so I slid my phone in my pocket.

Everyone piled out and came to stand in front of me, waiting for orders. I had never really been in a position of power, or in charge of anyone before. I guess my dad was getting what he wanted now. "OK, we are going to spread out, but in the buddy system. Never be out of earshot or eyesight of your buddy." The night before, Irene had put together some maps with paths for us to follow. I handed them out to everyone. "OK, If you find anything, do not attack. Call us, and we will regroup. Got it?"

Everyone either nodded or replied with a *yes*. As we started to walk in the direction we were assigned, my phone started buzzing. Relief washed over me. It had to be a reply from Jamie or Max. When I pulled out my phone, it was Irene's name that was on the screen. I clicked the green answer button, but before I could say anything, Irene was speaking frantically on the other end. "Nat, I can't get ahold of Max. I texted and called and nothing. He never goes AWOL like this. I tried calling Jamie, too, but she didn't answer."

I stopped moving, stopped breathing. I took a couple of deep breaths to try and center myself. They probably were in a situation where they couldn't answer their phones, I told myself. That had to be it. "Irene, slow down. We don't know anything is wrong right now. We need to stay calm." I was saying that more for myself than for her. I took in a deep breath. "I will go to the station and see what's going on. I need you to stay there, though. I will let you know anything that I find out."

I heard silence on the other end of the line. "Nat, if anything happened to Max—" I heard her growl on the other end. There was fear and hate in her voice.

"Irene, I know, but we don't know anything yet. They could just be busy right now." I tried to reassure her. I didn't know if I was doing an excellent job because I was on the verge of freaking out.

"OK," I heard Irene say, "let me know when you find anything out."

The phone went dead on the other end. I was too scared to breathe, too frightened to move. It wasn't in either one of their natures to not answer or reply. I felt a hand on my shoulder and finally was brought back to reality.

I heard Shae's voice. "Nat, is everything OK?"

I didn't answer her. I found Jamie's number in my phone and clicked it. Every ring sounded like a hammer in my ear. Then I heard her voice message. I felt myself starting to unravel. I tried her number three more times. Then I tried Max's number. All I got was his voice message. After I dialed his three more times without a response, I felt like I was falling.

"Nat? What is going on?" Shae asked. There was a hint of franticness in her voice.

I turned to her. "No one can get ahold of Jamie or Max." I felt my breathing getting faster. Anger and rage started filling my conscious, but I didn't care. If something happened to either of them, I wanted blood. I wanted the change to happen.

"Nat!" I heard Shae's voice through the fog of red. "Nat! Calm down." I felt hands on my shoulder. "Nat, listen to me. We will go drive by where she works. Figure out if it's just a technicality or misunderstanding before you vampire out. Please don't lose control right now," she pleaded.

I took a couple of sharp breaths in to try and calm down. "OK," I replied. I could hear the harshness in my voice. "You need to drive." I handed her the keys. I told Lylith to keep on track and that Shae and I were going off course for a while and she understood.

After we got in my car, I directed Shae toward the sheriff's office. My heart sank when we drove by the parking lot, and Jamie's Bronco wasn't there. I saw a younger man standing by the cruiser, talking on the phone. "Pull in, Shae. Pull up to him." I saw the man stare at us till we drove up next to him.

"Can I help you?" the kid asked.

"Do you work with Jamie Stone?" I asked him.

"Yeah, she works here. Why?"

"Did she show up today?"

I saw his body go a bit rigid. "No, she didn't. She didn't even call in. What's going on?"

I was assuming this was the prick Irene had told me about from the day before, but he had genuine concern in his voice. I didn't know if I should tell him no one could get ahold of her. It would put them in danger. But it would also give me more players looking for her if they knew she was missing.

"She has been staying at my house for the past couple of days. She left for work this morning, but I haven't heard from her, and it appears she didn't make it." I saw a hint of fear mask the guy's face.

"Wait here, let me go get the sheriff." He turned and started running toward the building.

"Go," I told Shae. "Go now," I said through gritted teeth. I was so angry I felt the door handle crack under my grip.

Shae touched my shoulder. "Nat, I need you to keep in control right now. Where are we going? I'm with you, but we need a plan."

"Just drive!" I yelled. I didn't know where to start. My head was throbbing, and I couldn't think. My mind was a swirl. All I could feel was rage and fear. I started losing control of my breathing. I felt another emotion clench tight around my heart, and my eyes started burning. Sadness? Fear? I didn't know. My chest was aching.

My lungs were on fire. It felt like something was constricting them. "What's happening to me?" I whispered. I grabbed my head. I felt like I was going through an emotional overload, and I couldn't catch my breath. "Shae," I tried to say, but it just came out as a low choke. Then I felt the car stop. My head was in my hands. Suddenly my door opened, and small, strong hands grabbed me, pulling me out.

"Nat, look at me!" Shae said in a stern voice, shaking me. "Please look at me," she begged.

I focused my gaze on her. I didn't know what was happening to me. Fear, anger, sadness, helplessness—emotions I had never really been able to feel before were flooding my consciousness all at once. The last time anything ever came close to this was when m family was taken from me.

I felt her arms wrap around me and a lump form in my throat. I couldn't hold it in anymore. I let it build, and a cry came with it. I buried my face in her shoulder and screamed. At least I think I was screaming. I felt tears flowing down my face. I couldn't stop the sounds coming out of my throat, or the tears streaming down my cheeks. Jamie was somewhere I couldn't find. Shae held me, comforting me till I was finally able to control myself. I gained control of my breathing. I looked in her eyes, desperate for an answer. "What do we do, Shae?"

Concern was written all over her face. "I don't know, Nat. Take some deep breaths. We need to figure out where to start, first of all." She handed me a canteen. I took a drink, even though I knew the predator had no control over this breakdown. This was all me. This was my heart breaking.

Shae helped me sit down on the ground. I needed to think, think about where to start. Think about what to do. I was in charge, and I was having an emotional breakdown. I needed to center myself. I pictured Jamie's smiling face. I tapped into how she had made me feel the other night, and my breathing started to slow, my muscles began to relax. I started gaining more control of my mind. *OK, self, think.* On our way up, we didn't see any crashes or runoffs. I started taking deep breaths, trying to focus even more. Where else could we check? "Her house," I said out loud.

"Her house?" repeated Shae.

"Yes." That was the next place we needed to search. That was the only place I could think of to go.

She nodded. "Are you OK? I know this was a lot to take in."

I took a couple more breaths, but I was OK. Not entirely back, but steady enough to continue looking. "Yes. Let's go," I said. We both stood and got in the car.

"Which way?" Shae asked with a determined look.

I directed her toward Jamie's neighborhood. As we approached her house, I could see both cars in the driveway. Max's truck was smashed. I was out of the car before Shae stopped my car, and I ran to Jamie's first. I looked for any signs of her. I took in the smells. There were about five different vampires I had never smelled before. The scent was off and foul, not right. It didn't smell like it was of this world. It made me want to gag. Shae was at my side almost instantly.

"The hell is that?" she asked, covering her nose.

"I don't know," I replied. Anger was brewing in my chest.

I ran to Max's truck next. Even more vampire smells surrounded it with that same strange, putrid smell. I also smelled blood, Max's blood. It took a lot for a vampire to bleed—especially one like Max. which made me even more worried.

I hear Shae's voice. "Want to go check the house?"

I was already headed toward the front door.

I burst through the front door and saw the house was in ruins. I focused all my senses on her home, on everything that was in it. I took two deep breaths in and out. Nothing living was in the house now, besides myself and Shae.

I walked to Jamie's room. It wasn't as tossed as the front couple of rooms. The bed was still made, so I went and sat down on it. I had no idea what to do. I had no idea what they were planning on doing with Jamie or Max, or if the two of them were even still alive.

I felt helpless. More helpless than I had ever felt in my life. I couldn't protect her. And now I had no idea where she was. Shae walk in. She tapped on the door before she entered. I felt her sit down next to me and place an arm around my shoulders. "Did you talk to Irene yet?" she asked in a soft voice.

"No," I replied. I didn't know how to tell Irene that Max was missing. That his truck was smashed, and his blood was in it. I didn't know what my next move should be. I felt another wave of anger wash over me and felt a yell come out of my mouth. I slammed my fists on my knees. "Shae, what do we do? I need to get them back."

I heard her exhale and felt her start to rub my back. "First you need to call Irene and tell her. She is probably going to want to come up here. Maybe calling everyone here will help too. We can track them better from here."

She was right. At least we knew where the last place they had been was. "Shae, can you call Lylith and have them come up here, please?" She gave me a small smile and nodded her head, then left to make the call.

I took in a long breath before I touched Irene's number to call. "Nat?" I heard her voice over the phone. I could hear the anticipation in her voice.

"Irene, I need you to come to Jamie's house." I couldn't hide the anguish in my voice.

"What happened? What did you find?" There was desperation in her questions.

"We found their cars empty at Jamie's house. Max's truck has been trashed. No sign of them. We stopped by the sheriff's office, and she never showed up to work this morning. I need you up here now."

I could already hear her car's engine revving in the background. "On my way." Then she hung up.

I walked over to Jamie's dresser and found a picture of her on her first day with the sheriff's office. Her smile was the same. She was such an amazing, innocent person who wanted to do nothing but help people. *How could someone do something like this to her?* I heard Shae's footsteps come up behind me.

"They are on their way up here. What do you want to do?" she asked.

I wanted to kill each and every one of them. I wanted them to suffer. I felt my arms start shaking and my fists clench. I should have been with her. I should have been there to defend her. I left her vulnerable. I exhaled. "I should have turned her." I didn't mean to say the last part out loud.

"What?" Shae asked. "Did you just say you should have turned her?"

"Yes. Then she wouldn't have been so defenseless," I said through clenched teeth.

"Nat," I felt her put her hand on my shoulder. "Did she want to be turned?"

"I don't know. We have never talked about it, but I should have." I felt empty and angry.

"Nat, I know it's hard right now, but we will find them both, and we will punish whoever did this. We need to clear your head, though, to think of a plan. We can track them now, Nat."

"Yeah, we can track them, and kill them." I heard the venom in my voice. I was in no compassionate mood. None of them would find mercy with me.

I walked past Shae and went straight out the front door. I was going to do anything necessary to get them back. When I got outside, I let the change wash over me. I welcomed it like an old friend. I went to Jamie's car and was able to pick up her scent right away. I followed the trail to the back of her house. It was Jamie's scent mixed with that rancid smell, which set my predator side on edge and made me let out a loud, defensive growl. We were waiting for the others before following the trail. I was hyper-emotional and angry, but I wasn't stupid enough to walk into an ambush without back up.

I heard tires squeal. It was either Irene or Lylith. When I ran back to the front, I saw Lylith, Irene, Isaac, and Jason. Irene was in Max's truck. I saw Kyle, Lylith, and the other three werewolves by Shae. I was assuming they were getting a run down. When Irene got out of Max's truck, all the color was gone from her face. I ran up to her and grabbed her in a hug. It was an attempt to comfort her, but I needed it too. "We will find them, Irene. We will get them back." I felt her start to shake and pulled away to look at her. Her eyes were distant, and there was a look of terror on her face. "Irene?"

I could see tears begin to form in her eyes. "Nat, this is worse than I thought." Of course, it was worse than we thought. I never knew anyone would be able to take down Max. I thought Jamie was protected.

"What do you mean?" I asked her.

She gestured to Max's car. "Could you smell it?" she asked.

I was assuming she was talking about the stench. "Yes, I could. What is it?"

She clutched my arms. "That is the smell of blood magic."

I stepped away from her. I didn't know much about magic, never really cared for it. But I did know that blood magic had been banned centuries ago. It was very powerful, from the stories I had heard, but hard to control. It also required taking life in order for it to work. At the words blood magic, the others turned their heads in our direction. Lylith was already investigating the smell.

"She is right, Nat. I could never forget that decaying stench," Lylith said, spitting on the ground as if to try and rid the smell from her sinuses.

I shook my head, "Malcom is using blood magic? How? He is just a vampire, not a mage."

"Maybe that's why it took him so long to come back after us. He was learning how he could use it for himself," Irene said, her voice lost, defeated.

"Nat, we can't fight him like this. We don't even know how or what he is using it for," Lylith said to me, earnestly.

Regardless of her plea, I had made up my mind instantly. I knew Malcom was a monster, and I knew Jamie and Max didn't have much time. I had no hesitation at all to go after them, no matter the consequences. The longer they were in his grasp, the less likely they were to survive. I would sacrifice my life for either of them. "I'm going, and if anyone else wants to come with me, feel free. I will not leave them to be tortured and tormented."

Shae instantly walked over to me. "I'm coming too."

"Obviously, I'm coming," Irene said.

Lylith nodded. "I got your back Nat, always. I already called and told the rest of my pack to come up here. I just told my brother to let the alpha know. He needs to know if this kind of magic is being used near his land." I nodded at her response.

"I'm coming with you," I heard Kyle say, without faltering at all. I put a hand on his shoulder. "No, Kyle."

He glared at me and knocked my hand away. "Yes, I am. You still don't trust me?"

"I do trust you, and that's why I need you to go talk to Nik. I need you to tell him what is going on here. He cannot just sit on the sideline anymore, and you need to make sure he knows that." I knew the alpha would take this seriously. My father needed to be involved now as well, and since Max wasn't here, Kyle was the next person that could convince him.

"OK," he said through an exhale. "But Nat, be careful." He placed a hand on my shoulder and gave it a hard squeeze.

We waited until the rest of our company reached the house. I could feel Irene nipping at the bit, and I was feeling the same way. We both drank as much blood as we could to give us as much power as possible. I knew our rage would also fuel us.

"You know this is a suicide mission," Lylith said.

"There is no better mission to take on than a suicide one," I replied. We all were able to latch onto the scent. I had already returned to human form. No one wanted to transform yet. We all needed to conserve energy. We had no idea what we were about to encounter and needed to be at our strongest. "Let's go."

JAMIE

I woke up with the worst headache I have ever felt. It was as if there was a little man in my head, pounding on my brain with a hammer. I felt cold, damp stone beneath me. I tried to sit up, but couldn't. Thick metal clasps were tight around my wrists, making them throb with pain. My ankles were fastened together with metal cuffs as well. My entire body ached, and my joints were stiff. I could feel unseen bruises all over my body as if I had been dragged and thrown around like cargo. At least I was alive.

It was so dark I couldn't see anything. I felt a swell of panic forming in my chest. *You can't freak out right now, Jamie*, I told myself. I took a couple of deep breaths in, trying to push away the fear.

The sound of rough, ragged breathing coming from somewhere near was suddenly brought to my attention. I didn't know who or what it was coming from. One of the last things I remembered seeing was Max's truck behind me getting crunched by five creatures and then him getting ripped from the driver's seat like a rag doll. "Max?" I whispered.

I got a groan in response. "Yeah." I could hardly hear him. It sounded like he was in a lot of pain. I tried to move toward him, but an instant pain shot through both of my arms from my shoulder. I cried out in agony. I was chained to the wall, and my arms weren't going anywhere. "dang."

"Jamie, are you OK?" I heard Max ask through a pained whisper.

"I'm fine. I can't move. I'm chained to the wall. Do you know where we are?"

I heard him cough, his breaths ragged. "Underground. It looks like a cave."

I remembered there were supposedly a ton of underground caves further north that hadn't been explored before. People said that they stretched for miles. This must be where Malcom had been hiding all this time.

"How are we going to get out of here?" I asked.

"I don't know. I'm too weak to move right now." I could hear his teeth gritting together.

Then I heard footsteps coming toward us. A man walked through the entrance to our makeshift prison cell, carrying a lantern. It was the same man that had approached Nat and me in the coffee shop. I saw a crooked smile form on his face. "How are those silver bullets helping you now, human?" he asked rhetorically. He then signaled toward both of us. "Bring them," he ordered the men by his side. They looked like some sort of vampire, but far more malevolent. Their eyes were pitch black, not the amber color I had seen in other vampire eyes. All of their teeth were sharp and elongated. The skin on their faces was stretched tight across their skulls. They looked more like demon monsters than vampires, and fear encapsulated my heart. I felt bony, cold hands dig into either of my arms and wrench me up. I let out a pained scream. It felt like they ripped my shoulders out of their sockets.

"Leave her alone," I heard Max growl, then a loud crunch and Max cry out in pain.

They started dragging me so fast I couldn't even get my feet under me to walk. I took in a deep breath to fight back the painful cries that wanted to escape my mouth. As I breathed in, I smelled a foul odor like decaying death, and my stomach rolled. I couldn't help the vomit that came up. I turned my head to the side, and vomited all over one of the creatures dragging me. It made an animal-like hiss, and I felt instant pain on the side of my face. The hit dazed me, and all I could do was let them drag my limp body.

I was barely holding on to consciousness from the strike I had received when an enormous lit cavern came into view. We were dragged through the opening, and it took my eyes a few moments to adjust to the light. On the back wall, I saw a man sitting on a stone that had been carved into a seat. Max and I were dragged in front of him and thrown onto the ground. I tried not to let out a cry, but a pained squeak escaped my throat through grit teeth. I had never been in so much pain before. I heard the man—I was assuming he was Malcom—let out a huff of amusement. "It was stupid of Natalia to leave her plaything in such a weak state."

Max let out a faint growl beside me. My eye was starting to swell from the hit to my face and I could hardly see out of it, but I turned to look at Max. He looked terrible. His body was battered and bruised, and dried blood was on his face. I didn't know vampires could look that beat up. He had thick rings around his neck, wrists, waist, and ankles. Where the rings were contacting his skin, I could see him burning. Silver, I was assuming.

I scanned the rest of the cavern. I saw plenty of the demon vampires, as well as regular-looking vampires. Then my eyes fell on an even more disturbing scene. Humans were hanging from the top of the cave by their feet, dozens of them. They all had large, deep gashes from ear to ear under their chins. They had been bled dry. I saw one of them with the maintenance uniform from the hospital. He must have been the one who killed Tracy. There was another hanging in the front of the row with blood still trickling down into a bucket. I could tell he was dead from the glossed-over look in his eyes. I turned my head away, clenching my eyes shut and trying to hold down more vomit.

Max must have seen the same thing. "What are you doing here, Malcom?"

I heard Malcom chuckle. "Can't you see, Max? I'm creating an unstoppable army. A new breed of vampire." He gestured to the creatures that were scattered below him. "They feel no pain, they obey without question, and they are powerful, as you have already witnessed. But unfortunately, they survive strictly on blood, unlike us, and to keep a population as big as mine fed, well," he pointed to the humans, "sacrifices must be made."

Max pulled himself more onto his knees. "They're abominations. What you are doing is forbidden. Blood magic was made illegal centuries ago for good reasons! You won't be able to control it. This killing is madness!" Malcom was in front of Max before I could blink. His boot cracked into Max's face and toppled him over.

Malcom grabbed Max by the hair and brought his face inches away from his own. "I don't take orders from you!" he hissed. "I have spent years perfecting this, and no one will stop me, not even you. It's only a matter of time before I take over all the houses and put humans in a place where they belong." Then he shoved Max's head against the ground.

His gaze turned to me next. His eyes were amber, but they were cold and evil and full of some darker presence. It made me instinctively lean away from him. He had a smirk on his face. "Jamie, the one who stole the heart of the future vampire queen. How quaint." His eyes scanned every inch of me intently. It looked like he was trying to find some answer to a riddle. "What is so special about you to make her act like she has been, hmm? I have never seen her act so pathetic before."

I was terrified, but I turned my face away from his gaze because he made me angry. It made me mad that he would talk about Nat like that, angry that he had hurt Max, angry that he had killed humans the way he did. Then I felt fingers grab my face in a vice grip and yank my head back in his direction.

"Do not look away from me when I talk to you, pest!" I felt another sharp pain on the side of my face where the back of his hand hit me. I saw a white flash, and my vision went dark for a split second. An uncontrolled whimper snuck out of my mouth. I felt warm liquid start to trail down my face, and at this point, I could only see out of one eye. I growled. "What do you want from me?" I screamed at him out of frustration. A metallic taste started to fill my mouth.

He turned and looked at one of his demons. "You know these vampires just need to bite flesh, and a person turns into one. Not like us, where we have to will it to happen. One bite and the person becomes this beautiful new vampire and part of my new planned world. Another one of my children."

Was he going to turn me into one of those creatures? I started to feel panic flood my chest. He would make me fight Nat. *Was that his plan? Turn me against her? Would it make her hesitate?* I couldn't become part of his zombie vampire army.

He must have seen the fear in my face. "Don't worry, dear. I have better uses for you. You are my golden ticket. You are Natalia's strongest weakness, the only thing that can keep her at bay."

As I started to realize what he was going to use me for, guilt took over. I didn't want to be her weakness. I would rather die than be a bargaining tool to hurt Nat. "You will never break her, you asshole." I glared at him.

Then I felt his boot smash into my side. I felt a crack, and the air was knocked out of my lungs. It must have broken my ribs. I sucked in sharp to try and stifle my cry. I didn't want to look weak in front of this bastard and give him the satisfaction of knowing he hurt me. "See how weak you are? Talking to me like that won't do you good. She should have turned you into one of us. Then you wouldn't have been such a burden."

I wished I had silver at that point to drive through his heart. But the only thing I could think of was spitting in his face. Maybe I could bait him into killing me so Nat wouldn't have to worry about me anymore. But the only thing it earned me was a solid fist to my gut and back hand across my face. I toppled over to the ground, too weak and in too much pain to move this time.

I saw Max writhe next to me and yell as he tried to go after Malcom, but the ring around his neck lurched him back, and three of the creatures started beating him.

Malcom grabbed me by the face again and jerked me to my knees. It hurt to breathe. As my chest was forced to straighten, it caused pain so sharp and terrible that my vision flashed white again, but I couldn't fight back. I was forced to look at him, forced to stare at him. He looked straight into my eyes. I saw a wicked smile form on his lips. "I will offer you a deal." He was so close I could feel his breath on my face. It was cold and smelled like a festering wound. "If you chose to be mine, I would spare your precious Natalia. She won't be killed when I take over, only exiled."

I wanted to save Nat, but I couldn't trust a word he said, and I would rather die than stand at his side. It hurt for me to talk, but he needed to know where I stood. "Let me make myself very clear, Malcom." I didn't know how intimidating I sounded given the state of things. Still, I would let my opinion be heard by this monster, and let him know I would never support him. "I might be weak, and I might be your prisoner, but I will never join sides with a tyrant like you, no matter how much abuse you put me through. I will always fight for the innocent, and I would never turn my back on people that I care for. You can take your offer and shove it up your ass. No deal. Nat is stronger than you could ever be, and she will stop you. I have no doubt." His smile turned into a sneer, and I felt him shove me to the ground hard and kick my stomach again.

Malcom stood up and turned away from us, walking to his makeshift throne. "You both have spirit. I will give you that. But nothing can save you now. If you think this is torture you haven't even seen what I can do to you. Get them out of my site," he instructed his guards.

I felt myself get hoisted up. My legs wouldn't work. They were being dragged behind me. I felt every time they hit a rock jutting out of the ground, but I was already in so much pain that it didn't bother me. When we got back to our little cave cell, I was thrown on the ground and heard a clinking noise as they chained me back to the wall. Then I heard a thump where they dropped Max's body. Within a matter of seconds, we were swimming in darkness again.

I could only lay there and try not to move. The slightest movement sent pains through my body. I felt myself breathing hard, trying to catch my breath. It hurt, but my body was gasping for oxygen. I had never been worn out from getting the crap kicked out of me. In fact, I had never gotten beat up before like this. I decided to try and sit to open my lungs up better. I was able to get through the pain and prop my back against the wall.

I heard Max groan through the dark. "Jamie, are you OK?"

I had injuries everywhere, and as I felt the adrenaline wearing off, even more underlying pains started to surface. My face was probably unrecognizable and throbbing by how many hits it had taken, but I was pretty sure I had no life-threatening injuries. "I'm alive, just banged up. What about you?" He had taken more, harder hits. As hard as Malcom and those monsters hit me, I think they were holding back, but not with Max.

"Surviving."

"Max, what are those things? How did he make them? What is blood magic?" I had so many questions running through my head. I didn't know magic was even a real thing, and blood magic sounded even worse.

I heard him take a deep breath. "Dark magic is evil magic used by the most sinister of people. But by using it, it kind of siphons off someone's soul and starts to make them lose who they are." I heard him let out a shaky breath. "But blood magic is the strongest type. To use any type of blood magic, life has to be sacrificed. Any product or magic created by it has a stench because it's unnatural and ruins the balance of life. It's tough to control. The user even starts to rot and wither if it's not used right." That must have been why Malcom's breath was cold and smelled putrid.

He must have been sacrificing people to create those things. "Didn't you say it was outlawed or something? How did he even know how to do it?"

"I don't know," he said. "All the leaders of the factions came together long ago to outlaw it. Civil wars using it almost destroyed the world. It was so catastrophic that everyone decided to put their differences aside and put an end to it. They destroyed any remnants of it. Malcom must have figured out how to use it. I have no idea how, though."

I could tell he was in pain, and talking and thinking wasn't helping his cause. I needed something to get my mind off my pain. I pictured Nat. How beautiful she was, how caring she was. Her warm, comforting, dancing amber eyes. Her enchanting smile that brought butterflies to my stomach every time I saw it. Her dirty-blond hair hanging perfectly no matter what she was doing, the comfort and safety of her arms whenever they were around me. I felt tears burning at the corners of my eyes, thinking of her. She was so powerful and robust, and all I was, was a human. I tried to stop the oncoming cry to no avail. A hitching sound escaped my throat as I inhaled. Then a flood of tears ran down my face.

Max's chains clinked together as he tried to sit up. "Jamie, what's wrong?"

"I'm her biggest weakness, Max. She is going to come looking for me, and she's going to get hurt or die because of me, and I can't do anything because I'm a weak, helpless human!" I blurted out through tears. Since my arms were chained too tightly behind my back, I couldn't wipe them away, so I just let them fall.

"Jamie," Max said through the dark in a soft voice, "you are not Nat's biggest weakness. You are her greatest strength. I have never seen her so determined, so strong before in all the years I have known her. You have given her a strength I didn't think she had inside her. You can't give up. Plus, you are not weak. I don't think I have seen a human take a beating like you just did and still be conscious. You stood up to Malcom, and you didn't just roll over at his order."

His words gave me some hope. "But Max, I can't fight. I'm just a human that can't fight against vampires or demons or magic." Then I heard Malcom's words again. *Natalia should have turned you.* "Max, can you turn me?"

His voice was fast, harsh and loud. "No!" It startled me and caused me to jump, jerking the side Malcom had kicked. I sucked in a quiet cry of pain. "I'm sorry Jamie, I didn't mean to be that forceful, but I can't change you. I won't do that to Nat."

I was confused. If he turned me, I could help Nat. "Why can't you?" I was desperate to be of some help.

I heard him suck in a breath. "First of all, I don't think I am strong enough right now to change you. But also, when a vampire changes someone, there is usually a connection formed between those two, a bond. And when people are as close as you two are, it's said the bond becomes even stronger. I would never take that away from her. If I bit you, you and I would share a bond, which would never allow for you and Nat to share the 'Sire' bond."

"But Nat and I already have a bond," I replied to him.

I heard him chuckle, then wince in pain. "Yes, clearly, you two have a strong bond already. It's pretty much tangible when you are together. If I changed you though, it could change that—maybe even take it away—and I don't want to risk it."

I wanted the bond with Nat to stay. I loved how she made me feel, but I couldn't live in a world where she didn't exist. "But Max, what is the point if she is dead or I am dead?"

"Deciding to become a vampire needs to be something you think about. It's not just a split-second decision. It changes your entire life, Jamie," Max said. "Plus, it's not instantaneous, the change. After you are bitten it takes anywhere from two- to-seven days for your body to change, so it wouldn't help us. They would either kill us or lock you up before we could do anything."

I knew it was a lost cause arguing with him. I wanted to keep talking, though, to get my mind off things. "Have you changed anyone before?"

"Yes," he replied. "It was only because of orders from Nik. When he finds humans that earn his favor, he asks his' men to change them for him."

"Nat said she had changed people before. She seemed like she doesn't like talking about it." I was curious why she got so defensive about it when I was talking to her earlier.

"She has. It was more of a way to rebel against her dad. Nothing good came of it. But that is her story to tell," he said. "Not mine."

My head was aching. Now it was hurting and filled with magic, demon vampires, and human sacrifices. I wanted Nat to come save me, but I also didn't want her to come. I wanted to see her again, wanted to feel her lips against mine, wanted to be comforted in her arms, hear her soothing voice. I knew if she did come, it would put her at risk. She could be killed, and I couldn't live without her.

"Max?"

"Yes?"

"Is she going to try and find us?" I knew the answer, but I needed to hear it.

He was quiet for some time. All I could hear was his ragged breathing and the thumping in my head. "Yes," he finally said. "She is probably on her way now. She would do anything to keep you safe."

I let out a shaky breath. "She is going to get hurt, Max. What if she is by herself?"

I heard him laugh. "I know Nat. She has probably recruited an army by now. If she is coming, she is bringing help. She isn't that daft."

That put my mind at ease a little bit, but I was still worried. They didn't know about the monsters that Malcom had created. If she was coming, I wanted to be able to help her. But we were both so weak; I didn't know if either of us would be able to help. "Can we help them at all?"

"I don't know. The only thing I can think of is to build your strength. Rest."

I leaned my head back against the wall. Rest did sound good right now. Even though I felt my entire body aching, and the ground and walls were cold and wet, exhaustion was starting to take over my mind. I pictured Natasha—absolute perfection—before darkness engulfed my consciousness, and I drifted off into a dreamless sleep.

NATASHA

Including Lylith's pack, there were twenty-five of us in total. It was a large enough number I thought to take out Malcom and his men. None of us were sure what we were going to be up against based on the fact he was using blood magic.

Lylith and I decided it would be best if we all stayed in one big group instead of splitting up. We followed Jamie's scent instead of trying to hunt a single vampire. I knew wherever she was, Malcom would be. The track took us for miles deep into the forest. We decided to stay in our human forms to conserve our energy.

I had regained complete control of my emotions by that point and was level-headed. A determination was the only thing I felt. As we made our way, we came upon a small opening in the ground. Jamie's scent path went past it, but I could sense something inside.

"Wait," I called to the others. "Lylith, can you tell how far this tunnel goes?" I would have tried, but wolves had a much stronger connection to nature than I did.

She nodded, came over, and knelt at the opening. After she placed her hand flush against the ground and closed her eyes, I saw her ears start twitching. She stayed in that position for a long moment. Once she was satisfied, she stood up, brushed her hands together, and turned to me. "It looks like an underground cave system—huge. I could only reach partway into it, so it probably goes on for miles."

So this is where Malcom had been hiding. "Lylith, he is down there. I am sure of it. Do you think we could enter here and have access to everywhere in the cave system?"

She shrugged her shoulders. "Most likely. I could sense living beings down there and a couple of big caverns. No one is near this opening."

It was a small entrance, not guarded. I was assuming Malcom would have the significant openings protected. "What do you think?

Want to go in through here? It's small, but I feel like it's less likely we will run into anyone for a while."

"Sure, sounds good to me," Lylith replied. "I want to keep a couple of my guys out here, just in case something goes down." I nodded at her request.

Once she selected who would stay back, we were ready to go in. "OK, everyone. We don't know what to expect down there. Keep on your guard. If anything looks or feels out of the ordinary—anything at all—speak up." My sense of others' energies usually was excellent, but I didn't know how they would do up against these foul-smelling vampires. I didn't know if I would be able to sense their presence or not.

It felt like we had been prowling around in the tunnels for hours. We were taking things very slow and being as careful as we could, trying not to make a sound. I had no idea if Malcom knew we were there or not, but I wasn't taking any chances by barging headfirst into a trap.

After a few hours had passed, I felt an overwhelming presence of people gathered together in one central location. I could also feel Jamie. I didn't know how, but I could. I knew she and Max were there. I stopped our group and signaled for everyone to hide behind whatever object they could find. I knelt by Lylith. "I can feel something close, Lyl. A lot of somethings. Jamie and Max are there too."

I felt her put a hand on my shoulder. It grounded me. I didn't realize how tense I had become. "I can feel it too."

"Irene, are you good?" I whispered. She had been unusually quiet on our entire trek. I felt so many emotions and energies radiating off her, so powerful that it was giving me a headache when I would focus on her.

"I'm fine," I heard her say in a low rumble. I could tell she was ready for blood. She hadn't shifted yet, but it was humming right under her skin. I didn't know how much energy she was expelling to keep it there, but I needed her level-headed.

"Irene, I need you clear."

"I told you I'm fine," she snapped back at me.

I turned back to Lylith. "What do you think? It could be an ambush. We are all experienced, but sometimes quantity is better than quality."

I heard Lylith's low, raspy chuckle. "Quality will always be better than quantity, Nat. We can take them."

"OK, let's keep going then." I signaled for everyone to pick up where we had left off. As we came around a turn, a faint light could be seen in the distance. I heard Irene let out a low grumble. "Easy, Irene. We need to be careful here. Let Lylith and I go first."

The light grew more prominent as we approached. It looked like a sizeable, spacious opening. I could tell there were many creatures in it by the noise and energy. We approached slowly. As we got to the opening, I could see vampires and other demonic-looking vampire creatures forming a half-circle around a forty-foot shelf on the back wall of the cavern. They were all facing our direction. It was clear they had been expecting us.

"What are those things?" I heard Jason ask from behind me.

"A product of blood magic," Lylith replied with disgust.

I stopped everyone at the entrance of the cavern. I didn't know if they were going to attack, but I wanted to get a lay of the room before we entered. I smelled death everywhere. I saw that humans had been strung up and bled dry on the far side of the room. I couldn't tell if it was for the blood or ritualistic. I didn't care, because it was disgusting and evil. I glanced at the barricade the vampires had formed. There were about thirty-five on the ground. The demonic ones were in the front, closest to us. They looked wild, untamed, and it sent a chill down my spine. The predator in me was writhing to get free, but I kept it suppressed for the time being. There were other normal-looking vampires toward the back of the group, closest to the cliffside. I could feel Jamie close, but I still couldn't see her.

I looked up toward the shelf that the vampires were protecting. As I felt an uncontrolled growl slip out of my throat, I heard Irene let one out too. My eyes landed on Malcom.

He had a smile on his face that wasn't a welcoming one. It was an evil, malice-filled smirk. His arms were spread out above his head. I took deep breaths to try and keep calm.

"Welcome, Natalia Romanova Vasiliev, to my temporary abode," he shouted, "I see you have brought the mongrels with you as well."

I heard some of the werewolves behind me growl, but Lylith just laughed next to me.

"This is wrong, Malcom! You won't get away with it." I tried to sound as authoritative as I could.

"Who's going to stop me? You and your ragtag team?" he gestured in our direction. "You aren't strong enough to beat my creations. Besides, I have something you want." His grin grew even more sinister. He looked behind him. Four of his monsters came into view, dragging two bodies. They both had bags over their heads, but I knew it was Max and Jamie.

Max was stripped down to his boxers with silver clasps around his neck, waist, wrists, and ankles. I could see from where I was standing the damage it had already caused him. His body slumped to the ground as the creatures dropped him.

"Max!" Irene yelled. I saw Max's body move in response to her voice. I grabbed her by the arm before she could run. The creatures in front of us recoiled into a defensive position at the sight of Irene.

"Irene, wait! He is alive. Just wait a second. We don't know how powerful those things are," I said. She looked at me with a type of anger in her eyes that she had never given me before. I couldn't risk us losing a kind of formation. Those things were ready to attack anything that came their way.

I looked back up to the ledge at Malcom. The next two creatures dropped a smaller body. I knew it was Jamie. I heard a muffled cry as her body hit the ground hard. I could feel life inside her still. Every instinct within me was clawing to go to her. To change and fight for her, but I knew I couldn't. I had to control myself. I felt a hand on my shoulder. It was Shae's. A comforting touch to try and calm me.

"What do you want, Malcom?" I tried to hide the disdain in my voice and the worry. I tried to be as stoic as my father looked when he was in council meetings and giving orders.

"I want you and your father to cooperate. Give me your allegiance, or I will take it from you. I will rule this world the right way. Your father has become weak and complacent. We are the strongest beings, and it's time someone brought us out of the dark to rule, where we belong." His smile had turned hard, dark. I felt something in him, pure evil.

"That's not going to happen, Malcom. This world is for everyone. What you are doing is wrong." I responded. I saw his face ice over. He turned to where Jamie was on the ground. She had managed to prop herself up on her knees. He knelt beside her, and I felt my heart stop as he took the covering off her head. Her face was swollen, black, and blue. One of her eyes was swollen shut. Dried blood was on her face and down her neck. They had tortured them both, and it made my heart break. I felt my hands clench. My entire body was rigid, and I started to shake.

Malcom grabbed Jamie by her chin and moved her head so her eyes were in my direction. I saw the slightest smile form on her face, and for some reason, it hurt me even more, because right then I couldn't do anything for her. Then I saw him whisper something in her ear. He stood up, and then the back of his hand crashed into her already swollen face, causing her body to hit the ground hard, a pained whimper escaping her. The change washed over me instantaneously, and a roar escaped my throat, one I had never made before. I felt something deep in my chest snap, and a building of some kind of potential energy. I had never felt it before, whatever it was, but I was too focused on what was happening in front of me to pay it any mind at that point. I felt everyone else in my group change. Lylith's massive wolf form was growling next to me, hackles raised, teeth bared, coiled low and ready to pounce, and Irene was prepared to attack at my other side. Everyone else ready to advance at my command. The monsters in front of us responded to our sudden change.

They were tense and rigid, making enraged hissing sounds. "That's enough, Malcom!" I yelled.

He turned and glared at me. "No, I don't think it is. I don't feel you understand the gravity of this situation. I have all the power in my hands. You're in no position to be making demands here." He snapped his fingers, and six of the demon vampires screamed and started charging toward us. Lylith, Sasha, Irene, Shae, Jason, and I ran out to meet them. The others I signaled to hold back.

It was like hitting a wall as I collided with the vampire I had set my eyes on. I was so stunned by the power behind it; I found myself with my back on the ground, and the demon vampire straddling my waist. It had its cold, bony hands gripped tight around my upper arms. I was able to get my hands on its shoulders to push it up and keep its snapping mouth away from my face. As I looked in its eyes, I saw nothing but pure malice. *What were these things?* It was powerful, stronger than anything I had ever fought before, and cold. I used all my force and was able to throw it off me. I jumped to my feet, but almost instantly, it had wrapped its arms around me tight, trying to crush me. I felt all the air leave my lungs as it lifted me off the ground. I threw my head back and brought it forward as hard as I could into where its temple should have been. It stunned it just enough to where it released its grip slightly, and I was able to break out of its grasp.

I backed up into a defensive stance, and it charged again. At the last minute, I moved out of the way, grabbed its arm and used the force of its momentum to run its head straight into the cave wall. As it collided, it made a loud cracking sound. Usually, that kind of force would have killed anyone, even a vampire. All it did was make the creature let out an ear-piercing scream. It turned to look at me with hate and rage in its eyes. Black liquid ran down its face from a gash created by the collision. It had hardly hurt it at all.

I didn't know how everyone else was doing, but these things seemed like they only acted on impulse and couldn't react very well. It came at me again, swinging its sharp claws in a rage-fueled fury.

I focused on blocking and dodging, trying to figure out if it had a weakness. I tried to get jabs in, but it didn't seem to faze the thing, even when I would put my full force behind it. I extended my talons and tried to claw at its body, but when I swung with all my might and finally made contact, it barely broke its skin. Normally, that would have sliced right through an entire cow. It was so fast, and it was exhausting trying to dodge its erratic attacks.

The only other thing I could think of was that it had a brain. Maybe breaking its neck would do the trick to kill it. It had so much speed; it took a while for me to get it into a position where I needed it. Finally, it charged straight at me. I danced to the side of it, swung my legs around its back, and wrapped my arms around its neck. I felt its long claws rip into the skin on my arms. But I was so focused on what I was doing that I didn't notice it. It was thrashing around wildly, knocking me into the wall, trying to get me off its back, but my legs were around too tight. I was able to get my hand around its face, and with every ounce of energy in me, I snapped its head back behind its shoulder and heard a faint pop, which caused it to stop moving.

I released my grip and dropped to the ground. To my amazement, the creature started melting into a black, tarry substance. "What the hell?" I yelled as I scrambled to my feet. Malcom made a whistling sound, and the other creatures retreated to where the rest were standing.

I looked around at everyone else to make sure they were OK. Lylith had killed one and was helping Jason. But no one else had been successful in killing one. We all had gashes and looked out of breath, which was unusual for both werewolves and vampires. We fell back to the rest of our company.

I looked up at Malcom, who had a smirk on his face. "What the hell are those things!?" I yelled at him in frustration.

"Welcome to the new world of vampires, Nat. The most powerful you will ever see, as you have just experienced. You can't beat them," he replied to me in a cold, monotone voice.

"You won't get away with this. This is forbidden. All the factions will be against you! You can't fight us all!" He was crazy if he thought he would be able to get away with this. These weren't living things. They were mindless monsters, and no one would stand for this. He took away their free will the moment he had created them.

"You're outpowered here, Nat. All you have to do is swear your allegiance to me, and you can have Max and Jamie back. We can walk side by side into this new world I am creating." He spread his arms out in front of him with a welcoming gesture. Lylith growled next to me.

"This is so wrong," I heard Shae say from behind.

"We can't let him do this, Nat," Jason whispered to me.

They were right. I couldn't let Malcom get away with this, but I wasn't expecting to fight things like this. He had all the cards. He had Max and Jamie captive and an army of demon vampires I hadn't expected to be part of the equation. I didn't think he would kill Max or Jamie. He needed them as leverage. But I wasn't sure how we would defeat these things.

"You're weak and pathetic, Malcom. You hide behind your puppets and force them to do your dirty work. You have always been a coward! I will never follow you! If it's a fight you want, then a fight you will get!" I didn't know if we could beat these guys, but I was going to do everything in my power to save Max and Jamie and take these things out. Everyone who was with me rallied behind me, ready to fight.

What I didn't realize was how low Malcom was willing to go. "Oh, Natalia, you think courage can save you, but you're wrong." I saw him pull something from behind his back. It was a long knife, and I could tell from the reflection of light it was silver. He walked up behind Max and knelt beside him. He smiled at me with a look of evil, and then I saw the tip of the blade appear out of Max's chest. It was like watching something in slow motion. Max's eyes never left Irene's, and the soft, loving smile never left his face. It felt like time had stopped and I couldn't breathe or move. Max was my best friend. *How could this be happening?* I thought to myself.

I heard a loud, pained scream, but it seemed so far away. It was from Irene. I had never heard her cry like that before, but I couldn't take my eyes off Max. Then Malcom stood up and kicked Max. His body fell from the cliff. I felt a sharp pain in my shoulder. Lylith had her teeth latched onto me to wake me up from my daze. Reality flooded over me. Shae and Jason were holding Irene back. She was screaming and thrashing, trying to break free. I saw the herd of vampires running at us. I had no idea what we were going to do.

Then I felt the potential energy inside my chest from before erupt inside of me. I had never felt this kind of power, but somehow I knew to direct it toward my hands. I let the energy flow through my body. I pointed my hands at the advancing vampires. I saw my hands start to glow, and then a burst of energy shot out. Every vampire it hit instantly turned to ash, about ten of them.

I looked at my hands, which now looked normal. A strange feeling of power flowed through my body that I had never felt before. *What the hell was that?* I thought. When I looked up, everyone was looking at me with wide eyes. Even the advancing vampires had stopped. I looked up at Malcom. The look on his face was one of pure astonishment. He wasn't expecting this. I wasn't either, but this was it. I reached deep down inside me to whatever it was and aimed at him this time. He dodged the power I shot at him.

The advancing vampires had regained their senses and ran at us again. I was able to blow them away with a few more energy shots. After all the vampires on the ground were gone, I looked up at the ledge where Malcom had been. He was gone, and so was Jamie. I was about to run after them when a sudden weakness washed over me, a heaviness, and I fell to one knee.

Shae ran up to me and grabbed my arm. "What was that?" she asked, trying to pull me to my feet.

I felt exhausted. "I don't know, but it worked," I said breathlessly. I saw Irene was already by where Max had landed. I was too scared to go to her. I didn't want to know what was waiting. "Shae, go make sure Irene is OK. I need to go get Jamie."

She tugged me and eventually got me to my feet. "No, you can barely stand right now. How are you going to fight Malcom? Whatever you just did drained you."

I grabbed her shoulder to steady myself. "I don't care. I can't leave Jamie alone with him anymore. You saw what he did to Max, what he already has done to her. He has no mercy. Make sure Irene is OK."

"Nat," Shae said with pain in her voice.

I knew I was spent, but I was hoping I could pull off what I had already done. "Shae, please. She is everything to me. He already took Max away from me. I can't let him hurt her anymore."

I felt her hand slide off my arm. She reached her hand around my neck and brought her forehead to mine. "Stay alive. I will be right behind you." Then she ran in the direction of Irene.

Lylith strode up to my side. She grumbled at me in her wolf form. "Are you ready for more?" I asked her. She bumped her body into me and bared her teeth as if to say, *Let's kick his ass.*

"We are with you, Nat," Isaac said, walking up to me.

"Yeah, we are. For Max," Jason said through clenched teeth.

"Let's go," I said, taking off in the direction Malcom had run. I could feel Jamie now. I don't know how, but I could feel her presence inside me. She was scared and in pain. It's like she was calling to me, pulling me toward her. It brought on rage, and I let that fuel me, give me energy, and let it drive me.

JAMIE

So many things had just happened at one time. Nat had been there, right in front of me, with a small army. She had come to rescue us just like Max told me she would. Those creatures had been so strong. As I watched Nat fighting, her movements were so fast and fluid. It was like watching a dancer. It worried me at first because it took her a minute to grasp how strong the creature she was fighting was, but eventually she was able to kill it. Those things were so savage and reckless; it was as if they didn't care about getting hurt or killed. They just wanted to kill and destroy, no matter the cost.

I still couldn't tell if I had imagined the knife sticking through Max. Malcom had stabbed him without any hesitation with a smile on his face while he did it. Max was such a good, kind, lighthearted guy, and for Malcom to have stabbed him so easily made me sick to my stomach. I couldn't let myself believe he was dead. Max was strong. After everything I had seen them put him through, he had to survive. He was the only reason I was able to endure the torture that we had been put through. I couldn't help but shed a tear, not knowing what had become of him.

I also remembered the words Malcom had whispered to me after Nat had told him off. *She will be your torture, but you will be her death.* Just remembering those words sent another shiver down my spine. He was so heartless and cruel.

I was still trying to wrap my mind around the explosion Nat had produced from her hands. I could tell no one had expected it, not even Nat herself. Not even Malcom had expected it, which is why I had been thrown over one of his henchman's shoulders, bouncing as he ran down a tunnel following Malcom to try and escape. I tried to tense my body because every time my body would jerk with the vampire's running movement, I felt pain everywhere, especially where my ribs had been broken.

It had been so dark in the tunnels that I couldn't see anything, and we were moving so fast I didn't know how far we had gone. The only upside was that I wasn't being dragged this time. I didn't think my body could handle being dragged at that speed.

All of a sudden, my carrier stopped, and I felt a cool breeze. It felt so good, considering I had been kept underground in a stuffy cave for the past couple of days. I looked up and saw it was night. The moon shone bright and full overhead. Nat had said full moons made werewolves stronger. Hopefully that would help my rescuers tonight.

I knew we were outside, but I couldn't see where we were going because of how I was being carried. We were running through a forest. The smell of pine filled my nose. I couldn't see anyone following us yet, but I only had one good eye to use. Even though the moon was full and bright, it was still dark out, and my night vision wasn't meant to spot creatures that were meant to hunt, chase, and fight at night.

"Stop!" I heard Malcom growl at the vampire carrying me. "Throw her in the back and make sure she is cuffed."

I heard metal hinges creak and felt myself get heaved over the vampire's shoulder and thrown through the air. As I landed, I felt the cold, hard ground underneath me. I was so sick of being thrown around like I was an inanimate object. It hurt so much. "You know Karma is a bitch, you asshole," I spat at whoever threw me.

He climbed up after me and wrenched me around as he pulled my arms even tighter behind my back. I felt the cuffs around my wrists bite even deeper into my skin, and I winced in pain. "Keep your mouth shut." He reached for my legs and bound them together tight too. Then he knocked me back against the ground forcefully and climbed out. I heard the door slam hard, and it made my ears ring. As my eyes started to adjust to the darkness, I was able to see I was in the back of a metal vehicle. It reminded me of the bulletproof trucks that banks used.

As I looked around the truck, I noticed it was empty other than me. There was nothing I could use to try and get free. Then I felt the vehicle lurch forward. It was so sudden, and I had nothing to grab on to and brace myself. The motion tossed my body toward the back doors of the truck. I was about to collide headfirst into the back, but I maneuvered so that my shoulder took the full impact. I felt an excruciating sharp pain shoot down my arm, and it hurt to try and even move my fingers. I became lightheaded from the pain. I did everything I could to hold on to consciousness. I was sure I dislocated my shoulder. I took in a few deep breaths and rolled onto my good side, and managed to get my legs into a position where I wouldn't be thrown around as much with the speed and turns of the truck.

I was so tired and I hurt everywhere. I had been beaten and tortured, and witnessed one of my close friends get stabbed with a knife. I had watched as vampires and werewolves fought demons to try and save me. I couldn't help but start to cry. My world had been turned upside down, and there was nothing I could do about it. I was helpless and weak. All I could do was wait for either Nat to rescue me or for Malcom to kill me.

My head and eyes grew heavy with exhaustion. I had been fighting so hard while being a prisoner, just to stay alive and stay positive. But I didn't know if I wanted to hold on anymore. Maybe if I just let myself go, it would be better for everyone. Then I remembered Nat. She was worth fighting for. She had fought so hard for me already. I had to survive—had to do anything and everything I could to stay alive. For Nat, and Max, and Irene, and all those fighting to rescue me.

Then the entire truck jerked, like something significant had landed on it. The truck swerved, and it took every ounce of energy to keep myself from flying across the back. Then I heard the sound of metal screech and whine under pressure. One of the back doors was ripped off its hinges and flew through the air. Through the opening, I saw bright, amber eyes dancing in the dark, but I wasn't afraid. I knew who they belonged to. I felt a lump in my throat and tears run down my face. "Nat," I said through the choke that escaped my throat.

She was instantly at my side. I felt her cradle me in her arms with such care and softness that I felt safe, so safe. I nuzzled my face into her neck. Relief washed over me. I knew that we weren't entirely out of harm's way, but just being in her arms gave me a sense of safety. She jumped off the back of the truck, and I barely felt us land on the ground. The truck sped off into the night.

When we were on the ground, she ran farther into the woods. We got to a tree with a vast trunk, and she set me down and knelt behind me. She grabbed the metal cuffs, then I heard a crunching noise, and instantly the pressure around my wrists was released. I felt a sigh escape my mouth. She moved around to my front and started gently rubbing the red marks where the metal had torn into my skin. It wasn't until then that I noticed she was breathing hard like she was tired and out of breath.

I opened up my mouth to speak, but before I could get a word out, a massive wolf trotted up beside us. It touched its nose against Nat's shoulder. It was so large that I felt my body involuntarily recoil back into the tree trunk, and I took a sharp breath in. At my reaction, the wolf laid down in front of me and crawled closer, placing its head softly on my thigh.

"It's OK. It's just Lylith. She won't hurt you," Nat said in her raspy vampire voice. I needed to get used to the change in her voice.

I guessed it was a natural reaction my body had. I was so high on the ledge before that Lylith hadn't looked so large. After Nat reassured me it was Lylith, I reached out my good arm and scratched between her ears. I heard a low rumble in her throat that seemed like an approving sound. It made me smile. "Thank you, Lylith."

"Lyl, have everyone gather here. They are going to come for us," Nat said with an urgent tone. Lylith huffed an approving sound, stood up, and trotted off into the dark, leaving us alone.

I felt Nat's hand on my cheek. Her thumb started to gently stroke it. Her skin was cold in this form, but it was comforting. "I'm so sorry for all of this," She said. Her voice was filled with guilt. I wished there was a way I could tell her it wasn't her fault and I didn't blame her for anything. But then she pulled me into a tight embrace. It felt so good—she felt so good—being wrapped up in her. All I wanted to do was get lost in her embrace. I went to wrap my arms around her, but I felt a sudden pain shoot through my injured arm. I let out a pained yelp.

She instantly pulled back. There was so much worry in her face. Her eyes scanned me from head to toe, searching for whatever had caused my pain.

"I think my shoulder is dislocated," I told her, gritting my teeth through the pain.

I saw her face change. There was rage and anger in her features. Her teeth clenched hard together, and her nose flared. Her eyes looked beyond me into the dark, searching for whoever had done this. Seeing her in her vampire form, angrier than I had ever seen her, sent a strange feeling through me. I wasn't scared, though; it was more of an exhilarating feeling. She was so strong and fierce.

She quickly calmed herself down with a few deep breaths. "Which shoulder?" she asked.

I signaled to my right shoulder. She lifted her hands to my shoulder, and her hands brushed against my shirt. "Do you have any sentimental value to this shirt?" she asked, scanning my face.

I shook my head in response. I had no idea what she was going to do, but I trusted her.

She ripped off the sleeve of my shirt all the way through to the neck hole, exposing my shoulder completely. She touched it so gently; I could hardly feel her touch. I was so focused on her face and the intensity of it. I was entirely sure I was falling in love with her. The past couple of days that I had been locked up and tortured had suddenly vanished now that she was here.

She finally exhaled after examining it. "It's dislocated. I need to set it." Her eyes met mine. There was a pleading in them. I could tell she didn't want to hurt me, but my shoulder needed to be put back in place before nerve and muscle damage occurred. I had seen people get their shoulders set before. It looked painful.

I nodded to her. "It's OK, I trust you. Just tell me what I need to do."

She picked a thick twig up off the ground. She ran her hand along the length of it and stripped off the bark, revealing a smooth surface. "I need you to bite this. It's going to hurt. I'm not going to lie. But I will make it as fast and as painless as I can."

I took the twig and placed it between my teeth and exhaled sharply, preparing myself. She grabbed my right bicep with one hand and put her other hand on my shoulder. "Relax your arm for me." I did as she instructed. "On the count of three. Take deep breaths in and out. Focus on your breathing." I started focusing on my breathing as she told me to. In and out, I closed my eyes, and my body instinctively started relaxing. I heard her voice. "One." Then I felt my arm jerk up and back.

"Ahh!" I let out a scream at the unexpectedness and bit down hard on the stick. There was an instant sharp pain followed by a low aching throb, but it felt better. "You didn't count to three," I said, spitting the stick out.

"Are you OK? I'm sorry. I just needed to make sure you stayed relaxed before I did it to avoid nerve damage. I didn't want you tensing up when I got to three." She was so amazing. I couldn't wait any longer. I wrapped my uninjured arm around her neck and pulled her into a hard kiss. I needed her. I needed that feeling of her lips on mine. I had never kissed her while she was in this form before. I felt the power flowing off her as our mouths crashed together. There was a hunger behind her lips as they moved against mine, an eagerness behind them. It was so different, yet so familiar, kissing her like this. I ran my tongue along her teeth and felt her elongated canines. As I grazed them, I felt a shiver run through her body. I felt her hands slide up my shirt over my ribs. The trail left warm tingling trails even though her skin was cold. Then She touched where I had been kicked. I twitched from the pain.

She slowly pulled her face away from me. When I opened my eyes, she was looking straight into them. Even though she was in her predator form, her gaze was soft and comforting. "As much as I want to continue, we're going to be expecting company soon," she said. She unbuttoned her flannel shirt and slipped it off, revealing a black tank top. In this form, her already muscular body was even more pronounced and defined.

I couldn't help but smile, "I thought we needed to stop. Why are you undressing?"

I heard a low, throaty laugh rumble within her. Then she fashioned it into a makeshift sling around my injured arm and neck. "This will help support your shoulder for now." She was so gentle, even in her hunter form.

She gave me one last slow kiss before she pushed herself up. As she stood, her arm shot out to the tree to balance herself. She leaned against the tree to keep from falling over. Her breathing was heavy. "Nat, are you OK?" I gasped in surprise.

"I'm fine," she replied in her raspy voice. She turned to face me and gave me as much of a reassuring smile as she could. "I need you to stay here for now, no matter what happens. Out of sight. Please?"

I could tell she was lying to me. She looked exhausted, drained, even in her vampire form, but she had determination in her voice and look. Whatever she had done earlier must have taken quite a lot of energy out of her. But I knew I couldn't stop her. "Please be safe, Nat, and come back to me."

"Always," she said through her smile.

I watched her walk a ways, then stop. She was still as a statue for a while. Then I saw her head snap to the side. All a sudden, a dark figure darted out of the shadows and collided into her. She was ready for it, though, and came out on top. But then I saw another one dart out. "Nat!" I yelled to warn her. It gave her enough time to jump out of the way of the oncoming demon. She danced around them, keeping out of their grasp, her movements amazing. And even though she was exhausted, she still stayed one step in front of them.

But then another one came out of nowhere and hit her from the back. It knocked her to the ground. "Nat!" I yelled again, standing up this time.

"Stay there!" she yelled at me, as the other two descended upon her. She struggled but was able to knock one off her. She was losing. One was on her back, completely wrapped around her. The other one was in front of her, trying to knock her down, clawing at her, kicking her. How could I sit here and do nothing? I was about to leave the safe haven of my tree when, out of the corner of my eye, I saw a large figure come into view, and heard a loud growl.

Lylith jumped over Nat, grabbing one of the demons by the head and throwing it about one hundred feet. It allowed Nat to get out of the grasp of the other one. She punched it hard enough to get it away, and then she got into a defensive stance. Lylith and Nat were standing back to back now, surrounded. But they were both so strong as they worked together that none of the demons could get a hit on them.

I could hear and see other fighting taking place in the forest around us now. I crouched back down and hid, since there was no way I could take on these creatures or vampires. Then I felt a big hand grab my arm tightly and yank me up. "Nat! Lyli—" Before I could get out Lylith's name, another hand clasped tightly around my mouth, muffling it. Then I was getting dragged across the forest ground. I fought desperately, trying to claw and kick my way out of the monster's grasp.

"Shut up and hold still, you little shit." It was the vampire who threw me into the back of the truck.

I saw Nat. She and Lylith were both fighting to get through the demon vampires that had descended upon them. I could hear Nat growling. She kept knocking them down, but every time one went down, another one appeared in her way. I was getting dragged farther away from her. I felt tears start to flow down my cheeks in frustration and desperation. I couldn't get taken away from her again. Not like this. Not when she was right there.

I felt him lift me off the ground, and I did the last thing I could think of. I kicked my leg back as far as I could and rammed it with all the force I had directly into his nuts. I heard him let out a grunt and his grip loosened just a little. His hand fell away from my mouth. "Nat!" I screamed out in desperation.

I looked up and saw her eyes lock on me. Those red, amber dancing eyes staring at me in determination. "Jamie!" she yelled back. Every muscle in her body coiled as she tried to fight her way to get to me. I was willing her to be with me, for those things to get out of the way.

"Nat!" I yelled again.

NATASHA

I was fighting desperately to get through to Jamie as I watched the vampire drag her farther away from me. Lylith was at my back. I couldn't just leave her backside defenseless. "Lylith we need to get through!" She growled in response, telling me she was trying. There were just too many, and they were so strong. I was already weak, but I knew I couldn't give up. I couldn't stop fighting. I couldn't let them take Jamie away from me again.

Suddenly three of them simultaneously rammed into Lylith, toppling her over and knocking her away from me. They had split us up. "Lylith!" I turned, trying to get back to her, but the demons had taken the opportunity to encircle me and separate us. They were on her, biting and clawing, and she couldn't get her feet under her to stand up. I could hear her growls and yelps as they slashed into her. Jason was the one who came to her rescue. He ran full speed and grabbed one off her, throwing it against a tree with so much force that the tree snapped at its trunk and fell, crushing the demon. In the same motion, he kicked another one hard in the face, knocking it off Lylith, giving her time to spring up. Now they were back to back defending each other.

My backside was left defenseless. Every time one would attack me from the front and I would move to defend myself, another would slash at my back. I was exhausted, and I was trying to split my attention between keeping an eye on Jamie and the vampire dragging her off and fighting these creatures that had surrounded me.

I tried to make my way in the direction the vampire was dragging Jamie, but I was slow, trying to fight off these things. It was a never-ending assault. I could feel blood trickling down my arms and back and legs where they had been able to claw through my skin.

Then I saw a big, grey wolf come up behind the vampire who had Jamie. It was Sasha. She sank her fangs deep into the vampire's shoulder, yanking him back. He let out a wailing scream. Sasha threw the vampire several feet and jumped in front of Jamie, separating her from him. She gave a loud, defensive snarl in his direction.

Something caught my eye from above. A creature jumped through the branches in the direction of Lylith and Jason. "Jason, watch out!" I called out. Before he could react, the creature landed on him and sank its teeth deep into his neck. I heard Jason scream in agony as the beast ripped a chunk of his flesh away with an ear-piercing screech. Lylith was on the creature in the blink of an eye, and crushed its skull between her powerful jaws.

Jason's body slumped to the ground, quivering, as blood gushed from the enormous gaping hole in his neck. Lylith stood her massive body over him defensively, knocking any creature away that approached. In between attacks, she would lower her head and nuzzle him to try and get him up.

One creature ran at me. I grabbed its arm and swung it hard into two others in front of me. All three toppled over. I ran in the direction of Lylith and Jason. Then claws dug into my back. Without looking, I grabbed its head and swung it over my shoulders, slamming it hard against a boulder.

When I reached the two, Jason was almost gone. His injury was so devastating that none of us could heal it, not even with blood. I knelt beside him and placed my hand on his shoulder. I could hear Lylith whimper through the defensive snarls as she attacked the others that came near. She knew he was a goner but didn't want to leave him alone in his final minutes of life.

"Jason, I'm so sorry I got you into this." I felt guilty; it was my fault. He put his hand on my arm and smiled. Lylith nuzzled the side of his face one last time. He moved his hand to touch her face.

"Thank you," he said through a gurgle of blood, and then I felt his life energy leave him.

Anger, pure anger, flowed through me. Lylith looked over her shoulder in the Jamie's direction. Sasha was there with another wolf and Isaac. Lylith grumbled at me and looked in that direction again, encouraging me to help them.

"I'm not leaving you alone," I snapped at her. She let out a snarl and nipped at my feet.

"Fine," I said, "but don't die." She huffed in response. I ran toward Jamie, dodging attacks. Before I could get to her, something crashed down on top of me. Two creatures had jumped out of a tree and caused me to lose my footing. Before I could get up, three more were on me. One was on my back. Each of my limbs had a creature grasping it, digging their claws deep into me. I groaned in agony. I tried fiercely to escape their grip, but I was outnumbered. Then another creature joined in, and all I could do was struggle helplessly and watch as Sasha, Isaac, and the other wolf defended Jamie.

Three normal vampires appeared through the forest. I thought they had all driven away with Malcom. One pulled a gun from his waist and aimed at Sasha.

"Sasha, move!" I screamed. She jumped away from the first shot, but as she landed, she let out a yelp and hit the ground as a second shot rang out. I screamed, struggling even more. Another shot was fired, and the other werewolf dropped. Three more shots were fired at Isaac. I saw his body jerk, but he landed behind a tree, which left Jamie defenseless. A loud growl escaped me, and I started fighting frantically, trying to break their hold. I felt the claws of the creatures dig into me even further.

As the three vampires approached Jamie, I saw her try to scoot away from them, but it was hard for her to push herself up with only one arm. I scanned the forest frantically to see if anyone was free or near enough to save her, but everyone was involved in their own fights.

One of the vampires grabbed Jamie by her unslung arm and lifted her to her feet. My heart was beating so fast, and I felt stinging in my eyes as tears of frustration formed. I couldn't lose her again. "Jamie! Please don't hurt her! Please! Let her go!" I begged through a yell. One of the creatures kicked me in my stomach, but I could hardly feel it. All my attention was on Jamie. The vampire that had shot Sasha, the other wolf, and Isaac looked over his shoulder at me.

Jamie looked at me too. Fear was in her eyes—a desperate, pleading look. I felt helpless. I couldn't do anything.

Then I saw him extend his long talons, and he smiled at me. "Malcom sends his regards," he said, as he plunged them deep into Jamie's stomach. She let out a low, grunting gasp.

Time stopped. Everything around me stood still. My chest was constricted, and I couldn't breathe or move. I didn't know if this was reality or my mind was playing tricks because of my exhaustion. I felt numb everywhere. The man let go of Jamie, and her uninjured hand went to the now gaping holes in her stomach. Her eyes left mine and moved down toward the injury. Blood trickled through her fingers, ran down her stomach and dripped on the ground, staining the dirt around her feet. Our eyes met again as her legs buckled beneath her. Then her body hit the ground.

I heard a long, loud howl from somewhere behind me, then a snarl. Something pulled one of the creatures off of me. I was too absorbed in what was happening to Jamie to realize it. One of the vampires kicked Jamie in the side, and that was the final straw. Deep down within me, I felt a snap like before, but this was different. The energy pooled from the depths of my being. I knew what it could do, and I released it. Energy radiated through my entire being, and I let it extend off of me.

The creatures that had been holding me were instantly turned to dust. The three vampires that had hurt Jamie sprinted in the opposite direction in fear after they witnessed what had just happened to the creatures holding me. I pursued them out of instinct.

It didn't take me long to catch them. I saw nothing but red and I was filled with hate. The three turned and fell to the ground when they knew they weren't going to get away from me. They surrendered, begging for their lives. "Please show mercy," one of them said.

I showed them none. I had no sympathy for them. The fear in their eyes almost made me laugh, but all I could form was a scowl. "Like the mercy you showed Jamie and Max? You will get none from me." My voice was hollow and filled with hate. I shot out another energy blast, and they became nothing, just three piles of ash on the forest floor.

A sudden feeling of heaviness and weakness fell over me. I fell to my knees, shaking. That last blast had taken almost everything out of me. I was breathing heavy, ragged breaths. My body was completely depleted of energy, I turned and hobbled to my feet to make my way back to Jamie. I had never felt this weak before.

"The sun!" I heard a familiar voice scream from a distance. "They can't be in the sun!" It was Shae. I noticed the sun had started to make its peak over the horizon. I couldn't concentrate on that now. I saw Lylith, now in her human form, kneeling next to Jamie and holding her hand. Another werewolf cradled Jamie's head. Other wolves stood around, some in their human forms, some not.

As I reached Jamie, I dropped to my knees on the opposite side of Lylith. I could hear Jamie desperately gasping for breath. I looked over at Lylith, who had tears already streaming down her face. I felt Jamie's hand grab for mine. She was shaking, "Nat, Nat. You're safe," she whispered through her breaths.

Pain shot through my chest, and tears started falling. She was bleeding out, and all she cared about was my safety. "Of course, I am," I told her, cupping her face in my free hand.

Shae finally made her way to us, yelling something about fire killing the creatures, and the sun catching them on fire and killing them. But when she skidded to a stop, her mouth dropped open. Her eyes moved back and forth from Jamie to me. "Nat! Do something!" she yelled, desperately.

She came over to me and shook my shoulders. "Nat!" she yelled at me again.

"I don't know if I can!" I screamed back. Usually after a fight, my vampire body would start healing itself by now, but I had wasted so much energy that my injuries were still seeping blood, not healing at all. "I don't know if I'm strong enough to do it right now."

She knelt beside me, and I could hear the desperation in her voice. "Nat, you have to try! You have to do something!"

She was right. I inhaled a ragged breath. "Jamie." I wanted her permission before I tried, but I got no response. She was still breathing, and her heart was still beating. "Jamie!" I yelled louder through my tears. She squinted her eyes open and smiled at me and grumbled something incomprehensible.

"Nat, you have to do it now," Lylith said through clenched teeth. I wasn't sure if I would survive changing her, or if I would be able to stop biting her, and Lylith knew this.

My eyes never left Jamie. "Lyl, I need you to keep her safe no matter what." That meant if I lost control, she had to keep me away from her, by all means necessary. She nodded her head, agreeing with my terms.

I closed my eyes and focused, willing the enzymes to go where I needed them. My mouth started to water. My predator was getting restless, knowing what was about to happen. I hadn't bitten someone in a very long time, but I was hoping I would be able to stop. I felt the venom glands in my mouth fill and knew it was now or never. I wrapped my arms around her body and pulled her to me. I leaned over to where her neck met her shoulder. I could smell her blood, feel her pulse. My mind started to grow foggy with lust, but I had to save her.

I sank my teeth deep into her flesh. I heard her inhale sharply and then moan, and her body tensed in my arms. I felt the venom release into her blood system. You never forget the feeling of turning someone.

I had done it. She would turn now. I tried to pull my mouth away, but then I tasted her blood on my tongue. It was so overwhelming. I had never tasted anything like it before, and a need for it took away any other inhibitions. I felt it flow down my throat, and I instantly needed more. My teeth latched harder onto my prey to keep her still. I wrapped my arms around her tighter, drinking in more. I needed more. I drank in the warm liquid, desperate to drink as much as I could.

"Nat!" I heard through a haze of red.

What? What was happening? There was blood. It tasted so good and was so satisfying.

"Nat!" I heard it again. It was even closer and louder this time. Then I felt a heaviness hit my chest. I was on my back, and someone was hovering over me. I hissed defensively. She was mine.

"Nat!" Lylith was straddling me, shaking me. Then she punched me across the face hard enough to knock the blood lust out of my mind.

"Ouch!" I said. I shook my head, trying to shake off the rest of the haze. I opened my eyes and saw Jamie. The sight of her brought me back to myself. My head ached like it was splitting in half. An uncontrolled growl escaped me from the pain.

I still felt Lylith's hands clenching my arms. "Lyl, I'm fine." I could hear the rasp in my voice. She turned my head to look in my eyes. I was now in my human form. "I promise." I felt her release her hold on me. I was so weak. I tried to pull myself to Jamie, but I wasn't able to move very far. Shae and Lylith both pulled me back to Jamie's side. I could still feel life in her. She was breathing, and her heart was still beating, but it was weak.

When a human was bitten, it usually took a few days for them to turn completely, but if the person being bitten was injured at the time of the bite, the enzyme would rapidly heal the wounds, making the host viable. I looked at Jamie's stomach wound, which should have stopped bleeding. I waited a couple of minutes, but still nothing. She was getting worse. I felt panic start to well up in my chest. "It's not working," I muttered through gritted teeth.

Shae put a hand on my shoulder. "Give it time, Nat."

I shrugged her hand off. "It should have started working by now." This couldn't be happening. It always worked, especially from someone with my bloodline. I must have used up too much energy earlier. "Jamie!" I screamed. As upset as I was, I felt a weight wash over me, a heaviness. My vision started to grow dark. Finally, the exhaustion caught up to me, and my body was shutting down. I touched Jamie's face. "I'm so sorry."

I looked at Lylith pleadingly, tears streaming down my cheeks. "Lylith, I need you to save her," I blurted out through my cries. Even with my diminished vision, I saw Lylith's entire body go tense. A stone-cold look clouded her face, and her eyebrows furrowed tightly together "Lylith! Please!" I begged her. I saw her nod her head slowly, but her teeth were clenched tightly together.

My body collapsed, but Shae caught me. I saw Lylith bring Jamie's wrist to her mouth. Her eyes never left mine as she sank her teeth into Jamie. Jamie gave another low, soft groan. I knew a wolf's bite was a sure thing, especially from an alpha's bloodline. Their bite changed people almost immediately, and was usually completed within an hour. Maybe it was selfish of me to have a werewolf turn her, but I didn't want Jamie to die because of me. I needed her to live at any cost.

I didn't know how Lylith would feel about this, if she would be angry with me for putting her in this position, or if she was OK with it. Hell, I didn't even know if I would survive to know. I could feel Lylith's gaze boring into me. It was sorrowful. She felt sorry for me, for what her biting Jamie could do to the relationship Jamie and I shared. If it changed her, she would have a connection with Lylith, and Lylith would be in charge of her after she turned. At least she would be alive. I moved my eyes to Jamie's face. She was still breathing. She almost looked peaceful. I didn't know if it was because my vision was fading or if she really was at peace. Finally, the darkness took over.

. . .

My mind was a haze, and my head was throbbing. I opened my eyes and slowly scanned the room. The bookshelf, the bathroom door, the familiar soft sheets. I was in my room. Everything was familiar. What had happened; how did I get here? I remembered being... I couldn't remember where I had been or what I had been doing. I moved my body slightly and felt all the gashes in my back scream. I saw bandages on my arm. The flood of memories came back. "Jamie," I whispered. I could hardly speak. I still felt so weak. I tried to push myself up, but a spell of dizziness washed over me and caused me to fall back against my bed.

Out of the corners of my eyes, I saw someone move at the sound of my voice. A tall, broad figure stood in front of my window. "Max?" I said lowly. My voice was hoarse and weak. The last time I saw Max was when he was falling off a cliff with a knife through him. As the person walked closer, my vision started to clear. It wasn't Max. I clenched my teeth and hands. "Father."

I tried sitting myself up again. I was able to get myself positioned so my back was resting against my headboard. If he would have just believed us from the beginning, maybe none of this would have happened. He had never believed me or trusted me with anything.

He slowly walked over to the side of the bed. There was worry written on his face. His brown hair peppered with grey hadn't changed. Neither had his fierce amber eyes.

"You need to rest and recover. You did a lot of damage to yourself," he said.

I was in no mood to listen to his lectures on resting or doing what was best for me. I needed to check on the others to make sure everyone was alive and well. I ignored him and started scooting toward the edge of the bed. One of his big, strong hands grabbed my shoulder and stopped me. "Natalia, stop!" he commanded. "You need to rest! You expelled all your energy, and you need to gain it back, which takes time."

I knocked his hand away and glared at him. "No, I don't. I need to make sure everyone is alright. This is all your fault. If you would have just believed us in the first place—that Malcom was back and after us—maybe none of this would have happened."

He shook his head at me and sat down on the edge of the bed. "You need to rest, child."

Anger erupted in my chest. "I can't rest because I have to check on my friends! The people who risked their lives because you wouldn't take us seriously!" I snapped at him. It made my head throb even worse, and another dizzy spell washed over me.

He looked into my eyes and then I saw the old him. The stone cold authoritative figure I was so used to growing up with. "You brought this on yourself, falling for a human, sacrificing our people to save a human. You went in without proper backup. Without knowing the situation," he scolded.

"I had no choice!" I spat back at him. "He took Jamie and Max! He was torturing them because of me, because of you! He was using blood magic. Did you know about this?"

He inhaled. "You had a choice, Nat. If you wouldn't have gotten involved with this human—"

I cut him off. "Her name is Jamie. And you have always been fine with sharing a world with humans and interacting with them. You always taught me this world is for everyone."

"Sharing a world with them and interacting is one thing Nat, but getting involved with one is another. Max wouldn't have been caught in the middle of it. Malcom wouldn't have been able to find leverage on you, and you would have had a clear mind about how to act with him encroaching on my territory."

"Get out!" He didn't move. He just looked at me. "Get out!" I yelled again.

He slowly stood up and walked to the door. Before he opened it, he said, "You need to get your rest. Find me when you are ready to talk. We have a lot to discuss." He walked through the door and slammed it shut.

I fell back against the pillow. My head was screaming by then. He was right. If I would never have met Jamie, Malcom wouldn't have been able to get to me that easily. A light knock on the door brought me out of my thoughts. "I told you to go away!" I yelled.

The door opened anyway, and I saw Lylith walk through. Worry was written all over her face. Right when she saw me sit up, she ran to me and wrapped her arms around me in a firm embrace. "Don't ever scare me like that again. I thought you were good as gone." Her voice was raw. She squeezed me tighter.

I wrapped my arms around her. "You can't get rid of me that easily, Lyl. How long was I out?"

She pulled away. "Three days. It was hit and miss for a while. We didn't know if you would make it." She handed me a canteen, and I gratefully took it and downed the contents within.

I still felt weak, but it cleared my head a little. I set the canteen on the nightstand. "Nik didn't try to kick you guys out, did he?"

She smiled. "He did try. But surprisingly, Kyle stopped him. Kyle told him this was your house and property, and your rules stated the werewolves were welcome here, and he would make sure your rules were carried out. Nik couldn't argue."

At least Kyle was growing a pair. It was a relief that I could trust someone close to my father. "Good, I'm glad."

My thoughts wandered somewhere else. I was scared to ask what happened with Jamie, but I needed to know. "Lyl." I could even hear the pleading in my voice. She sat straight up. I saw a strange look in her eyes. Her brows furrowed together, and her lips formed into a tight, thin line.

Worry clutched at my heart. "Lyl, is Jamie..." I couldn't get the rest out. "Is Jamie..." I clenched my teeth and shut my eyes, taking in a deep breath.

Lylith's look softened a little. "She isn't dead, Nat." She grabbed my hands, but looked down at the floor.

"So…" I paused, taking in another breath, "she's a werewolf?" I had mixed feelings about how it would affect our relationship now, but I was relieved she was alive.

She lifted her head and looked at me. "No. No, she isn't a werewolf," she replied.

I was confused, a little shocked. *Did my bite work after all? Was it just delayed because of how injured she had been?* "So she is a vampire?"

Lylith slowly shook her head. "No." She took a deep breath in. "Her body rejected both our bites. I can't explain it."

I tried to get to the edge of the bed. "So, she's fine. I need to go see her." I was surprised she wasn't here next to me, but I didn't care at this point. I needed to see her.

Lylith's hand grabbed my shoulder and stopped me. I still felt weak, and I took in a few heavy breaths. I couldn't fight her hold, though. "Wait," she said, and exhaled a long breath. "She is alive. But barely."

"What do you mean barely?" I couldn't believe neither of our bites turned her, and now I was being told she was barely alive. "Where is she?" I tried to move to the edge of the bed again, but Lylith wouldn't let me.

"Nat. She is being cared for but you need to rest."

The same words my father had just told me. "No, I don't!" I barked at her. "I need to go see her." I took in a couple of breaths to calm myself down. "Please, Lyl, I need to see that she is alive. please?"

She lowered her head and exhaled again. She was tired and looked emotionally drained, I could tell. I remembered Sasha and another werewolf getting shot trying to protect Jamie. At the time, I couldn't tell if they were dead, but I wasn't sure if I wanted to ask yet. "Fine," she finally said.

She helped me to the edge of the bed and put one of my arms around her shoulders so I could support most of my weight on her. As we stood up, another dizzy spell washed over me. "Whoa." I wobbled a little, but Lylith supported me and kept me upright.

"You alright?" she asked, wrapping her arm around my waist for more support.

"Yeah, I'm good." She helped me hobble to my bedroom door. "Where is she?"

"She is in your back office. Nik and my dad brought an entire medical team in to take care of her. After Nik found out you bit her, he wanted to get rid of her. I intervened and wouldn't let him because I had bitten her too. When the alpha found out about my bite, it became a political issue." Thank God Lylith had intervened. Werewolves never turned their kind away once someone was bitten, especially by the alpha's blood.

"But I thought you said neither of our bites turned her. Why are they so interested in keeping her alive?" I asked.

"They did blood work on her and found both our enzymes in her, but they were dormant, nonactive I guess, but still present. They have never seen it before. I'm not good at medical lingo. They didn't change her, but the DNA is present in her blood. It's questionable who is responsible for her," she said. "Since they were present in her blood, and she still isn't awake, and no one knows what is happening to her, both Nik and my dad wanted to keep her under surveillance. This has never been seen before, Nat."

I had no idea what this meant. It made my head hurt even more, trying to understand it. "So she isn't awake yet?" I asked.

She stopped before she opened my bedroom door. "No. She still hasn't woken up since we bit her. They say she is in some kind of hibernation state."

"Lyl, what the hell does that even mean? Humans can't hibernate. Their bodies aren't set up like that." I had been a nurse for a long time. I knew how fragile human bodies were and how maintaining homeostasis was imperative for a human body to live.

"I know, Nat. I'm just warning you, so when you see her, you don't freak out. I guess her vital signs are super low but holding steady. Her metabolism has all but shut down to accommodate for it."

I needed to see it for myself. Lylith had never really been around medical areas, so it was hard for her to explain what was going on.

We made our way into the hall. We passed Irene's room. I was still too weak to feel energies in my surroundings, so I couldn't tell if anyone was in there. I was too scared to ask about what had happened to Max right then. I didn't know if I could handle what happened, so I avoided the question. As we made our way through the house to where they had set up a makeshift hospital room for Jamie, I noticed it was completely empty and quiet.

The door to the room was shut. I stopped us before we went in. I didn't know what to expect and needed to take a few moments before continuing.

"You good?" Lylith asked.

"Yeah, let's go." She reached out her hand and turned the doorknob.

As we walked in, I noticed a strange scent in the air. I couldn't tell what it was, but I had never smelled it before. The room was frigid.

Someone was typing away at a computer at the far side of the room. "Hey, you can't be in here," the man said, as he got up and started walking in our direction. He stopped in front of us. It was a human doctor that my dad used a lot. Supposedly he was a genius medical doctor.

"Get out of my way," I growled at him.

"I'm sorry, but only people who have been cleared by Nik can be in here."

"Or the alpha," Lylith added, with a hint of disdain in her voice.

The man looked back and forth between us. I didn't have time for this. I reached out my arm and shoved the guy to the floor, knocking him out of the way.

"Hey!" he yelled.

"My house, my rules." I spat at him. I knew he was under orders from my father, but he didn't need to act so entitled, especially here in my home where anyone and everyone was welcome.

I looked up and saw her, Jamie, lying in the bed. She had no life support equipment attached to her, but had a vital sign machine monitoring her. Her vitals were all low. Her heart rate of 30, blood pressure 60/30; her temperature was low as well. I lightly touched her cheek. "She is freezing cold."

The doctor got up and walked over to us. "Yes. I have never seen anything like this. Her body is in kind of a hibernation state. It seems like it's working like a bear when they go into hibernation."

She looked like she was sleeping, but she was so pale. There was a bandage on her neck where I had bitten her. There was another one on her wrist where Lylith had bitten her. Her face was still swollen and bruised from the torturing she had gone through, but she looked better than the last time I had seen her. She was covered so I couldn't see the wound on her stomach. "Human bodies weren't made to do this. They weren't meant to stay alive like this," I said, shaking my head.

"I know," the man replied, "but somehow her body is keeping her alive. Even though her vitals are low, they seem stable, and her brain is still active. Her vital organs aren't shutting down either. She is a medical marvel!" he said excitedly.

It made me angry how excited he was getting about her state. "She's a victim!" I snapped at him.

"Nat," Lylith scolded me.

"I'm sorry," the man replied. "Her injuries are healing slowly. It's as if her body is going through a change, some kind of metamorphous though."

"Like she is becoming a vampire or werewolf?" I asked. This had never happened when people change to either creature. Usually, it was the opposite.

"No, something else. I can't figure it out. Yes, both species DNA are present in her blood, but something is keeping them inactive, and I can't pinpoint it." "We won't know anything till she wakes up."

It was too much to think about right then. I was just relieved she was alive. "Can you leave us, please?" I asked him.

He looked between Lylith, and me. Lylith signaled to the door. He bowed and walked out the door.

Lylith pulled a couple of chairs over for us. We both sat down, and I reached for Jamie's hand. It was so cold. She had always been so warm and full of life. Now she was barely holding on. "Lyl, this is all my fault. My dad was right." I squeezed my eyes shut.

"This is not your fault. I know vampires have a different opinion about humans than werewolves do, but you can't help who you fall for—vampire, human, werewolf. It happens. Plus, regardless of if you met Jamie or not, Malcom still would have attacked. He still would have created those things. We still would have gotten involved because it was in our territory, and a battle still would have ensued. The difference was, we were stronger because you brought us all together."

I was still terrified to know the outcome and casualties from the fight. I was responsible for them even if Lylith told me the battle was justified. I took in a deep breath. "How many?" I asked in a quiet voice.

Lylith slowly turned her head toward me. But I couldn't look her in the eyes. "How many what?" she replied questioningly. She knew what I was asking, but she was scared to say, I could tell.

"Lyl," I said, looking into her eyes.

She took a deep breath in and then let it out. "Jason. Isaac succumbed to his wounds yesterday. Shae was injured, but is fine. Sasha is gone, along with five other werewolves." I saw tears form at the corners of her eyes.

It pained me to see her so wounded. "I'm so sorry I brought this upon you and your pack."

"No," she said. "It wasn't your fault. I told you. They volunteered to go. I knew Malcom needed to be stopped. I just wasn't expecting him to have done something as preposterous as this." She bowed her head down.

I knew Sasha and Lyl had been close. I placed my hand on hers. I tried to offer as much comfort as I could. "He will pay for this," I told her through gritted teeth.

I felt her hands clench. "Yes, he will."

I had realized she never mentioned anything about Max. I didn't know if that was a good or bad thing. I was scared even to ask. "Lyl," I said.

She lifted her head to look at me. She had a sorrowful look in her eyes. She knew what I was going to ask. Before I could say anything, she slowly shook her head. "He didn't make it," she whispered through a choke.

I had figured he hadn't but hearing it out loud hit my heart like a hammer. He had been my best friend for so long. The one person I could rely on and counted on to always have my back. He had taken care of me. He knew me better than anyone, and now he was gone. The one person who could keep me level-headed. I felt numb and hollow, empty.

"I'm so sorry, Nat. I know he was family to you. I'm so, so sorry." I felt her wrap her arms around but I couldn't lift my arms.

Then I remembered Irene. She probably hated me. I shot up out of the seat. I needed to check on her. Make sure she was alright. "Irene," I said out loud.

Lylith grabbed my arm, pulling me back down to the chair. "She hasn't been taking it great. She's been staying with me in my trailer."

"I need to go see her. She probably hates me."

"No, she doesn't," Lylith said. "She doesn't blame you at all. She blames Nik and Malcom. But she also understands Max did what he felt was necessary. It was his choice, and she knows that. The only reason she hasn't been able to stay here is because she was terrified that she would walk into your room, and you would be dead. She will be happy you are awake finally."

I wanted to stay with Jamie. I wanted to try and wake her up, but her condition wasn't changing, and I didn't think it would change anytime soon. I needed to check on my sister. I needed to be there for her. I leaned over and gently kissed Jamie's lips. "Please come back to me," I whispered to her. "I can't live in this world without you." I stood up straight and looked at Lylith. "Take me to Irene. I need to talk to her."

JAMIE

I felt like I was floating. I was surrounded by nothing but white, and it was so bright. *Was I dead?* I didn't know what dying felt like, but I didn't know where I was, so maybe I was dead. The feeling wasn't normal for me. I tried to remember what happened and how I got there. I remembered seeing Natasha fighting so hard to get to me. She had six demons holding her back. They were hurting her, and I couldn't do anything to help her. At that moment, that was the only thing that mattered. She was in pain. I tried to reach for her, but then I felt the vampire yank me to my feet and felt something thrust into my stomach. Looking down I saw there was so much blood—blood flowing out of deep holes in my abdomen, and then to the ground. I remember thinking that I was so tired and maybe now I would die. Maybe I had died. I was the reason all this chaos was happening. They came to rescue me. Two werewolves and Isaac got shot trying to defend me. Max had gotten stabbed and thrown off a cliff. Maybe being dead would be for the best. I remembered closing my eyes. *Just go to sleep and never wake up*, I told myself.

But then I felt pain, a sharp pain in my neck, then a slow burn down my arm and chest, but within seconds it was gone. I felt another pain in my wrist, this time a throbbing, deep pain. A tingling sensation shot up my arm, but within seconds it too was gone. *Why was I in so much pain? I had tried to live a good life. Be there for people who needed me. Help the weak and those that needed it. I just wanted to help Nat, be a part of her life, have her be a part of mine. Why was it so hard to be with someone I cared about?* I heard yelling and screaming, crying. I couldn't move, though, and I started to feel cold all over.

Then I was floating. No, I was being carried. Cradled in someone's arms. More yelling and screaming, commands this time. Then everything faded away. Now I was here. Floating in an empty abyss. *Was this my hell I was supposed to live in for eternity for my sins?*

Alone and unable to move? Reliving those last minutes of being helpless when Nat and the others needed help? I couldn't feel the pain anymore, but I couldn't move.

Then I saw something in the distance, something floating toward me. It was shining brightly. I could tell it wasn't evil or going to hurt me, so I wasn't scared. As it approached, I could make out a face. It was smiling at me, a warm, brilliant smile, but it was so bright that I had to squint my eyes. "Grandma?" No, it wasn't my grandma, but she looked so familiar; I just couldn't place her face. It almost felt like I knew her, in a different time, in a different life. She reached her hand up to my cheek. Her hand was so warm when it touched me. I heard someone speaking in my head; I didn't know if it was her or not. "Wake up now, child. You have much to do."

I felt a sudden burst of warmth from her hand. And my vision was flooded with white bright lights. Then it went dark. I heard my name being called in the distance. It was a familiar voice. As I focused on it, it seemed like it was getting closer. My eyelids were heavy as I tried to open them, like waking up after a long, heavy sleep. Then I saw Nat's face, hazy and fuzzy at first. But it was her, her amber eyes staring straight into mine.

NATASHA

My property had been turned into a makeshift campground. Most of the vampires had set up camp closer to my house. I saw a large trailer in the middle. That had to be my father's. He always was one for luxury. It was a good thing I had a lot of land, and it was in the middle of nowhere, or we would have drawn attention. The wolves had set up camp around and in the forest.

As we approached the front door of Lylith's trailer, Irene came crashing out the door right into me. Her arms wrapped tight around me, and we both fell to the ground. I could feel her body shaking and trembling with her cries. She was trying to say something, but I couldn't understand through her sobs.

I wrapped my arms around her and pulled her tighter into me. "I'm so sorry, Irene. I'm so, so sorry." I squeezed my eyes shut. It was comforting having her near me. I was so glad she was safe.

After we lay on the ground wrapped in each other for a few minutes, she pushed herself up and dragged me to my feet with her. "I'm sorry I knocked you down. I was just so scared you wouldn't make it." She grabbed my hand, and I let her lead me into Lylith's trailer. I still was pretty weak, but I had Irene to use as support if I needed it.

Lylith stayed outside. "I will let you two have some privacy. I need to go see my father and discuss some things anyway." She turned and walked into the forest.

Irene led me to a couch, and we sat down next to each other. She laid her head on my chest, and I wrapped my arms around her.

I could tell she had started crying again. She had lost the love of her life. They had been together for so long. They were meant to be together forever, I thought. Two jigsaw pieces fitting flush, and he had been cut down right in front of her eyes. Her entire family had been slaughtered by the same man when she was little, and now this. "I can't believe he is gone, Nat. How could Malcom do that to me again? Max was such a good person." I could feel her entire body trembling with each sob.

"Then you!" She started banging her fists on my chest. It hurt, but she needed to get out her frustration; she needed this after everything I had put her through. "You almost left me too! What were you thinking? You could have died! Then I would have nothing Nat! I have already lost so much. You can't do that to me, ever again!" she screamed.

I didn't know what to expect from Irene regarding her being angry with me about Max's death. But she wasn't. She was mad that I put myself in harm's way.

"I promise I will never leave you, Irene. I'm sorry I scared you. I had to try and protect everyone, though."

She finally started calming down. She sat herself up, wiping away the tears smudged all over her cheeks. She had loose hair strands stringing down her face, so I brushed them all behind her ears.

She took in a few breaths and seemed like she was composed enough to talk. "He was still alive when he landed on the ground," she said. "I got to him before he died. He died in my arms." She looked down at her hands that were folded in her lap now. Tears ran down her cheeks again. I hated seeing her so upset like this, the pain it was causing her to relive what had happened. "He told me to make sure you didn't blame yourself."

I felt so guilty. I felt as though this entire thing was my fault, and my heart ached from all the destruction and death I caused. As if Irene could hear my thoughts, she lifted her head to look me in the eyes. "It's not your fault, Nat. Don't blame yourself. Max was doing what he does best, being a protector. His death and everyone else's were the doing of a monster." She clenched her hands into fists. "We need to stop him before he causes more harm and death. Those things he made are unnatural and evil."

I nodded my head. "I know Irene. We need to stop him. But I don't know what Nik will let me do. I don't know what I can do to help. So many people just died doing something I asked them to do. I can't have anyone else die at my hands."

She pursed her lips together. "Nat, no one could have foreseen what he did, what kind of evil shit he was conjuring up. No one. Nik couldn't even have seen that. But he could have done something earlier to help and maybe—" She trailed off and took a deep breath in and closed her eyes. "We can't undo the past now," she said it in a whisper, almost speaking to herself, then looked me in the eyes. "You saved us out there. Whatever you did."

I still wasn't even quite sure what I had done. "Irene, I don't even know what I did. It just happened. I don't even know if I could do it again. Besides, people still got hurt and died. It wasn't enough to save the lives we lost."

Irene reached up and grabbed my shoulder. "It's in you, Nat. You just have to find whatever it is and not use up all your energy doing it. Whatever you did was raw. It needs to be fine-tuned, tamed, but you're strong, even stronger than Nik. I have never heard of his powers being near what I saw from you."

I didn't want to talk about the power surge right then. Especially when I didn't know what it was. I knew Nik would know, and he was probably the only person who could help me. Thinking about that unsettled my stomach, so I changed the subject. "What happened after I passed out? What happened to Malcom and his men? How did everyone get out of there?"

She looked back down at her hands. A look of remembrance washed over her face. "Malcom ran off with his lackeys. Those demon-vampire-looking things ran off too. They are flammable, though. Shae was able to light a couple on fire. Light them on fire, and they are good as dead. They also can't be in the sun. It instantly burns their flesh."

So old myths were true with these new vampires. I wondered if anything else from legend was real. "And holy water?" I asked with a teasing edge to it.

I saw one corner of Irene's lips curl up slightly. "I don't know. No one thought to check. But feel free to try when we see them again." Then her expression got serious again. "After they all cleared out, Lylith grabbed Jamie and Jake grabbed you. Shae came to find me and helped get Max's body. We made it back to Lylith's car, but you and Jamie were both in bad shape. I was a wreck. I didn't think you were going to survive. You weren't healing at all, and neither was Jamie. Shae called Kyle on the drive back, and he said he was with Nik, and they were on their way down. When we got back to the house, Lylith and Shae set you and Jamie up for blood transfusions. You didn't respond for the first day. It was questionable if you would make it or not." She paused for a second before she continued. "Lylith called the alpha down. Once Nik got here and found out you had bitten Jamie, he was furious. When he learned she hadn't turned, he tried to have her killed. Lyl stepped in. She said she had bitten her too and had a say in what would happen to her. Nik didn't care and still tried to get rid of her." I felt anger growing in me. My dad was an asshole. "When the alpha got here, he didn't take any of Nik's crap. He said if Nik wouldn't help her, he would. He didn't care if she wasn't changed. The alpha's blood had bitten her, and he would take responsibility for her. Well, long story short, they ended up having to compromise. Both species' DNA is present in her now. They have never seen anything like her before, so they agreed to keep her alive till she woke up, then figure out what to do from there." She took in a deep breath. "I don't know what's going to happen when she wakes up, Nat. I almost wish she would have turned into a were-wolf." She put her hand on my leg.

The last time I turned someone into a vampire, I did it in rebellion against my father. I didn't ask his permission. I didn't think he would take it as far as he did. To make an example, he killed them in front of me—something drastically out of character for him. I knew one thing now, though. I wouldn't let him touch Jamie. If that meant sending her away with the alpha and Lylith, then so be it.

Irene started again. "On day two of you being out, your body started healing finally. Slowly though. Life started flowing slowly back into you. That's what Lylith reported to me. I avoided the house because I was angry with Nik, and there are too many memories of Max there. I was also scared I was going to lose you, that if I walked into your room, you'd be dead." She took a deep, shaky breath in. "And now I guess we are gearing up for war in your backyard."

Wow, I didn't realize how close to death's door I had been. "Do you know what they are planning on doing now?"

She shook her head, "No. I took myself out of it. I wasn't in the right state of mind to contribute, and I didn't want to hear any of it. I needed to mourn. Needed time to heal unseen wounds." Irene had always been smart and level-headed, even when her world was falling apart around her. She had one of the sharpest minds I had ever seen. Most people would be vengeful and seek retribution.

I leaned into her and gave her another hug. "I need to heal, too, emotionally and physically. I need to recover my strength before I get into it." I couldn't try and contribute to a fight like this. I wasn't even sure I would be in the right state of mind to offer advice. I did want to be with Jamie. "I'm going to see Jamie. Want to join me?"

Irene hesitated for a minute, but eventually, she nodded her head. "Yeah, I guess I need to get out of this trailer before I develop cabin fever. I refuse to see Nik, though."

"Of course," I told her.

When we got halfway to the house, I felt small hands grab and yank me around. It was Shae. She put both hands on my face, scanning it and then my body. Then she grabbed me in a firm embrace. She lifted me off the ground and swung me in a circle. "Nat! Oh my gosh! You're OK!" When she dropped me back on the ground, she swatted my shoulder. "You scared the living crap out of me!"

"Ouch," I said, giving her shoulder a weak shove back. I almost lost my balance, but she grabbed my arm.

"Geez, you are still super weak. You shouldn't be out and about. It's not good for you right now," she lectured.

Now she was telling me I needed to rest. "I'm sick of people telling me to get my rest. I'm fine." I knew she was right, though, and just had concern about my well-being. I took in a deep breath. "We are going to see Jamie. Want to come?"

A somber look fell across her face. "Yes, I will join you."

When we got inside, Shae opened the door to Jamie's room, and I felt a low, involuntary growl escape my throat. I even felt the predator stir. Even it knew by now that Jamie was mine.

My dad was standing by Jamie's bed, looking down at her. "Get away from her," I said in a low, threatening tone.

He looked over his shoulder at me, unphased by my threat. "We need to talk," he said in a commanding monotone.

I didn't acknowledge his words. "I said get away from her." I walked right up to him and stuck my face an inch away from his. I wasn't going to back off. This was my house. I felt Irene behind me, and I knew she would have my back.

"Sit down, Natalia." His face never changed from the stone mask it wore.

"Get out!" I screamed in his face this time, pointing at the door. I felt Irene tense at my back.

"I'm not telling you again. We need to talk… alone." He looked at Shae, who was now by my side, and Irene, silently telling them to leave. "I won't hurt you or the human. I'm just here because I knew you would come back and I could find you."

There was one thing I could always rely on with my father. He always kept his word. I looked back at Irene and Shae and nodded my head. It seemed like he had already dismissed the doctor because he was nowhere to be seen. I didn't like the thought of him being alone in here with Jamie.

As Irene walked by, he reached his hand out and set it on her shoulder. I saw her entire body go rigid. "Irene, I am so sorry about Max. I know he meant a great deal to you. If you need anything, I will always be here for you." His voice was sincere. She didn't look back at him. All she did was storm out of the room. Shae gave one more hesitant look over her shoulder before she shut the door behind them.

We were all alone, except for Jamie. I glared at him and tried to look as strong as I could. I knew I was still weak, but I didn't want him to see that.

"Sit down," he said, scooting a chair to me. I would have refused on a regular day, but not today, not being in the state I was in. I did as he said. He grabbed another chair and faced it toward me, then sat down.

"You know," he started, "being defiant toward me in front of people won't get you very far. You need to grow up, Nat. This isn't child's play anymore. You need to stop acting like a rebellious teenager."

I felt my teeth clench tight. I didn't know how he could get under my skin so easily, but it bothered me. "I'm not defiant. I heard you tried to have Jamie killed. I won't let you do that."

"You bit her without my authorization," he snapped at me.

"I bit her to save her life! I am your heir. I can make my own choices!" I growled back at him.

"Then start acting like it! I still run this house. You will follow my rules." He glared at me.

The next thing he did took me by surprise. He sighed deeply, and I saw his entire body slouch. He closed his eyes and slowly shook his head. His voice sounded tired. "I don't want to fight with you. I came to talk."

When he finally looked up at me, I saw the age in his eyes and written all over his face. I had never in my entire life seen him like this. So tired, so unkempt. "OK. What do you want to talk about"?" I asked, crossing my arms over my chest.

He took in a deep breath. "First and foremost, I need to apologize. I should have believed you when Kyle told me you thought you saw Malcom. I let my own fear control my judgment. I didn't want to believe he was back. I knew if he truly was, he would be powerful.

And I wasn't ready to fight that battle." I felt my mouth hanging open slightly. I couldn't believe he just apologized for that.

I shook my head to regain my focus. "Umm, OK. But it's not just me you need to apologize to."

He was quiet for a few seconds before he replied. "I know. And I will apologize to all parties involved and affected by my choices."

I didn't know how else to reply, so all I said was, "Thank you."

He brought his hand up and rubbed the back of his neck. It looked like the next thing he was trying to say was a bit more complicated. "Shae told me about what happened in the caves and forest."

"There were a lot of things that happened in the caves and forest. What part are you referring to?" I asked, trying to voice how irritated I was with the conversation.

"About the energy you emitted," he said.

I knew this conversation was coming, and I knew he was the only person who would be able to answer any questions I had about it. I had always been aware of the special powers he had, and he always told me power runs in our bloodline. "What about it?" I asked, shrugging my shoulders.

His eyes went wide. "What about it? Nat, have you done that before?"

I exhaled deeply. I guessed I needed to get the conversation out of the way. "No. I don't even know what I did. I got angry, and we were about to get pummeled by an army of oncoming demonic vampires. I felt something kind of snap inside me, and then I felt a strong energy. Somehow I knew to guide it out of my hands."

He stroked his chin after I said that, and his eyes were intense on me. I could see his mind working, trying to figure out what his next words would be. "I have always known you were powerful. More powerful than your brothers and sisters. Even having the potential to be more powerful than me some day."

It was strange hearing him say that because when I was little, he never let me train or work with him or my siblings. He always told me my powers were limited, weaker than everyone else's, and he didn't want me to get hurt. That my abilities were limited to feeling the presence of living things and the energies emitted by living things. That it was too dangerous for me. "What do you mean?" I asked.

He wiped his hand down his face and stood up, his back to me. "When your mother and siblings died, and Irene's family was taken—" He paused. Whatever he was trying to say was taking a lot for him to get out. "I told you I was the one that got to you and Irene. I used my powers to save you." He paused again, running his hands through his hair. He turned to me. I could see sorrow and guilt in his eyes. I had never seen my father so emotional. "I lied. I wasn't close enough to save you. You saved yourself and Irene."

I shook my head. I was sure I remembered that night. I felt energy surround us, block us from the explosions, but not from me. I didn't think so, anyway. "What are you talking about? How could I save us without even knowing about that?"

He took in a deep breath. "Call it self-preservation, if you will. Your body did it to protect itself. I always sensed the power in you, extreme power. Watching the amount of power you had that night verified how strong you really were and could be."

I shook my head. "If that is true, why did you lie to me? Why did you make me think for my entire life that I was a disappointment because I didn't inherit the power everyone else did?" I hated being lied to. Honesty was one of the few things I thought I could rely on when it came to my father.

"To protect you. If people knew how strong you were, I feared they would try to manipulate you. I also feared you would turn more renegade and think you could take on the world. Since you were all I had left, I couldn't allow that, and lose you. You became the most important thing in my life. No one saw what I saw that night—you surviving. How powerful you were capable of being. That's the reason I made you a secret from the world, to protect you." He walked over to me and put his hand on my shoulder. "I don't know what I would do if I lost you, Nat."

I had so many different emotions running through me from what he had just told me. "You say you did it to protect me? Or did you do it to protect yourself?" I shook off his hands and glared at him.

His expression turned to a look of surprise, and his eyes went wide. "To protect me? Of course not! I knew if you found out what you were capable of, you would seek vengeance. You would hunt down everyone that ever had anything to do with Malcom. And I was right. After that, you rebelled at every chance you got."

My father didn't know me at all. "I'm not a vengeful person. Yes, I would have wanted to stop him and to stop evil from happening, but I would never have gone off by myself, destroying things out of control. I rebelled because you treated me like a prisoner, like a secret relic! I lost my entire family that night, dad! Even you! You never comforted me. You never spent time with me after that. It felt like you had erased me from your life, like all I was to you was some tangible object that no one else could have, not your daughter. All I had was Irene." I thought I had gotten over this centuries ago, but I hadn't. I had never told him how I really felt about it. The pain came flooding back.

He bowed his head down. "I'm sorry, Nat. Back then, I didn't know what to do. I lost your mother, my rock, and all I wanted to do was protect you. And I didn't know how to."

He had never apologized to me before. I was sure that was the most sentiment I was going to get out of the old man. "So what is this power I have? Shooting deadly beams of light out of me?"

He shook his head. "No. You have the ability to project your life force energy. What you did in the cave was project your energy, and you used it as a weapon. It was a blast of pure raw energy. It would be like touching the sun for whoever got in its way."

"What good is it, if after a couple of blasts, I'm down for the count?" I asked him, a little frustrated. He had just told me I could be more powerful than him, but if using my power almost killed me, what was the point in using it?

He sat back down in the chair across from me. "Because how you used it isn't its purpose. When you learn to control it, you can use your energy to control the energy around you. What you did was pretty much just blast your life force into space. That's why it almost killed you. Once you can control it, you can manipulate it, control the energy of other things, and gauge how much you are using, learn when you need to stop." He lifted up his hand, and I saw the faintest of glows at his fingertip, and a coffee cup on the table begin to float and then set back down.

"Huh," I said out loud without realizing it. "So, we are like telekinetic?"

He shook his head. "No, it's not our minds that control things. It's our energy that we project."

Controlling energies with our own. I was curious at how powerful my dad was. Could he control another person's energy and make them do his will? Was that how he was so powerful? "How do I learn to control it and use it the right way?"

"I will teach you," he said to me.

I knew that was probably the best way to learn, but I didn't want to learn from him. He had lied to me my entire life. He betrayed my trust, and I didn't know if I could trust him teaching me all I was capable of doing, or if he would shelter me like he had done since my family died.

I shook my head. "Nope. How else?"

I saw his lips purse together, and his eyes squint slightly. I had offended him. He probably thought this could be a way for him to make up for all the years he had been an ass to me. I wasn't going to let him get off that easily. "There are others who might be able to help, but I highly object to it. But when have you ever listened to me?"

I had subconsciously placed my hand on Jamie's and was gently running my thumb over the top of her knuckles. "You can't just expect to gain my trust with one conversation. Just because you opened up and told me the truth doesn't just fix centuries of betrayal. You have to earn it. Yeah, you are the leader of the house, but you lost my trust and respect when you quit treating me like your child, and more like an object, and lied to me." I could hear the dryness in my voice.

I saw his body tense up, and lips purse even harder together. "You are always so difficult. If you want to learn the correct way, find me." His eyes fell on my hand holding Jamie's. He huffed. "She will never be yours, Natalia. Her fate will be determined when she wakes up, but I will never accept her into our house, and you will never see her again." There was poison in his voice. I couldn't tell if it was jealousy or disgust.

My body reacted, and I stood to get in his personal space again. I felt the swell of energy in me. I knew I wouldn't be able to use it, but it gave me just enough to be some kind of threat. "If you hurt her or try to take her out of my life and away from me, I will make yours a living hell, and take everything from you." I tried to pour as much malice into my look as I could.

His glare darkened, and his dark amber eyes burned red. Then I felt a strange sensation come over me. My breath was stuck in my lungs, and I couldn't move. It felt like something was taking over my body. All of a sudden, my legs were moving out of my control. They were being forced to bend. Then my knees crashed to the ground. I found myself kneeling in front of my dad, at his feet. My head started to bow down as well, and I couldn't fight it, no matter how hard I tried.

"I never wanted to do this to you. Force you to be anything but yourself, but you left me no choice. I am still in charge of the house, in charge of you. If you take arms against me instead of learning by my side, I will make you bend the knee to me. You're my daughter and only living heir, I won't let a human ruin everything you are." He turned on his heels and left the room, slamming the door behind him.

After the door shut, I was finally able to breathe and move my body. I felt myself gasping for air that my body had been denied, and then I was on my hands and knees. *Damn*, I thought to myself. *I didn't know he could do that.* Then the door opened again, and Irene and Shae were at my side.

"Oh my gosh!" Irene said, kneeling at my side. "Are you OK?" She helped me into a sitting position on the floor.

Finally, I was able to catch my breath. "Yes, I'm fine. Nik and I just had a disagreement." Both Shae and Irene were kneeling by me. Before I could explain to them what had happened, Jamie's monitor machine started beeping. I stood up and grabbed Jamie's hand. Her heart rate was starting to elevate quickly and was beating fast and hard. I didn't have to look at the monitor to hear it. Her skin was becoming warm again, almost feverish. Color was coming back to her face. She was starting to come out of her sleep state.

The monitor started alarming. "I will go get the doctor," Shae said, turning toward the door.

"No!" I yelled after her. "No. Shut the door and lock it." I unplugged the machine so it would stop making noise. I didn't want anyone else to know she was awake. I wanted to have control over the situation. I wasn't going to let her become some kind of object to be fought over. She was mine.

"Irene," I said, still looking into Jamie's face, watching her breathing get heavier and faster. Irene was at my side in an instant. "Call Lyl. Put her on speakerphone." She dialed the number.

"Hey, what's up?" I heard Lylith ask on the other end.

"Are you alone? Can anyone hear this?"

"I'm alone."

"I need you to come to the house right now. Don't tell anyone, not even your dad. Jamie is waking up, but I want to get in front of the alpha and Nik before they take her away. I just had a very unpleasant talk with my dad, and I don't want either of them turning her into some object to fight over."

"On my way," she said, and then hung up the phone.

Jamie's face started to grimace, and she was whining softly. "Jamie," I whispered. "Jamie, come back to me." I placed my hand on her face and stroked her cheek with my thumb.

Suddenly, I felt Jamie's body tense up. She inhaled sharply, and her eyes shot open wide.

"What the hell?" Irene whispered next to me, flinching backward slightly.

Jamie's eyes were open and glowing a bright light blue. They looked like diamonds glistening in the moonlight, not the normal light brown, golden color I was used to. I felt something different about her, something powerful—not evil, but a benevolent energy. It wasn't frightening, but instead almost an overwhelming calm. "Jamie," I said again. Her heart rate started falling, and her breathing began to even out as she closed her eyes. "Jamie," I whispered to her.

Her eyelids started slowly opening again, and her eyes were back to their former color. I felt her hand tighten around mine. She was awake finally, and alive.

JAMIE

My ears were ringing, and my mouth felt dry as my vision started to clear from a hazy fog. I saw Nat's face looking down at mine, and saw Irene standing next to her. Was I still in that abyss? It didn't feel like it anymore. I felt heavy now, and there was fabric underneath me. I was lying on a bed.

"Jamie! You're awake," Nat said to me. She had a look of worry on her face at first. Then a warm, relieved smile spread across it. She squeezed my hand.

"Am I dead?" My throat felt dry and constricted; my voice sounded hoarse and scratchy. Nat helped me into a sitting position while Irene went over to a desk and grabbed a canteen. When she returned, she held it out for me to take. I knew what they usually kept in those canteens. I looked at the bottle, then at Irene, then at Nat. I remembered the pain I had felt in my neck. I reached my hand up to where I had felt the ache. There was a bandage over it, and I felt a sudden panic cloud my mind. *Did I get bitten? Did one of those evil things bite me? Was I a demon vampire?*

Nat must have seen the sudden distress on my face. "Jamie, Jamie, calm down. It's OK. It's just water. And no, you aren't dead." She reached her hand to my face and stroked it gently, reassuringly.

I reached for the canteen. "Thank you," I told Irene as I started gulping down the water. Once I drank down the contents, I set the canteen down next to me. I felt Nat wrap her arms around me in a firm embrace, and I welcomed it. I clung to her. I didn't want to let her go. She felt so real, and just as I remembered. I still didn't know if I was dreaming or dead, though. "Are you sure this isn't a dream? Or I'm dead?" I asked. I needed verification. My mind still felt hazy.

She pulled away from me with a smile on her face. "I'm sure." She looked tired. I could see it in her face and eyes. She was exhausted.

"Are you OK?" I asked her worriedly.

"I'm fine," she reassured me. "I'm just a little weak right now that's all."

I was still trying to sort through my memories. I wasn't sure if all of what I remembered was real. "What happened? Where are we?"

Before anyone could answer me, there was a light knock on the door. "It's me, Lylith."

Shae was by the door. She quickly opened it, then closed and locked it. Both of them hurried to my side to join Nat and Irene.

Lylith had a toothy grin on her face, and before I could say anything, she wrapped her arms around me in a strong hug. "Welcome back to the land of the living."

After she let go, Shae hugged me as well. "You gave us a scare, girl. I'm glad to see you awake."

"Thanks." I smiled at them.

As much as I was grateful they were there, it was Nat I wanted. I grabbed at her. The last time I saw her, she was being held by those creatures. I started scanning her body and moving my hands over her, making sure she didn't have any injuries. I saw bandages on her arms. Worry clutched my chest, and I looked in her eyes.

She grabbed both my hands in hers. "I'm fine, I promise," she told me. Then she undid the bandages. "See? No big deal." I could still make out faint claw marks, but they almost looked healed.

I let out a sigh of relief. "What happened?" I asked again. "Where are we? Is everyone alright? Where did Malcom and those things go?" I had so many questions running through my head and tried to blurt all of them out at once.

"It's OK. I will answer all your questions, but right now, we need to figure out a plan to keep you safe," Nat told me.

I felt my eyebrows furrow. "A plan to keep me safe? Are we not safe?" I felt another wave of panic wash over me as I scanned the room, wondering if I was being held captive again.

I felt Nat's warm hands on my cheek as she turned my head to face her. "We are in my house right now. There has just been some conflict with my dad and the alpha of Lylith's pack, but we are going to take care of it, I promise." She pulled me into a deep kiss. Her lips were warm, and I welcomed them with urgency. I wanted to get lost in her. Her taste, the way her lips felt as they moved with mine. I clutched at her tighter, trying to get her as close to me as I could. The world around me was fading away. It was just her and me then.

My train of thought and the kiss were interrupted by someone clearing their throat. It was Lylith, "Don't mean to interrupt, but Nat, we need to figure out how to approach the situation."

First, Nat had said something about conflict. Now Lylith had mentioned a situation. "What's going on? Am I in trouble?" Lylith and Shae both looked at Nat. Irene sat in a chair, looking at her feet. Nat looked at the covers laid on top of me. I put my hand on her cheek and made her look me in the eyes. "Nat? What's going on?"

She took a deep breath in. "Well, in the forest, you see, you were dying, and I had no choice." She stopped, but I kept staring at her, trying to urge her on. Whatever she was trying to say was hard for her.

It was Lylith who continued. "You were hurt really bad, bleeding out. The only way we thought to save you was if Nat turned you."

I reached up to the bandage again on my neck. Before I could ask the question I was scared to ask, Nat blurted out, "I bit you." A thousand feelings and thoughts crossed my mind, but I was in such shock that I couldn't figure out what to say at the moment.

"But you didn't turn," Lylith cut in. "We waited, and you just kept getting worse. I wasn't going to let you die, so I bit you." I remembered the pain on my wrist and looked at the bandage there, then at Lylith, who nodded her head.

I didn't know what to make of the situation. "So am I a werewolf?"

Lylith smiled weakly. "No, your body didn't change to either of our bites."

"So I'm human still?" I asked.

Shae was the one who spoke next. "It's unclear and muddy water. They did tests on you. You have both species' DNA in your blood, but it's dormant, nonactive. We have never seen anything like this before. Usually, if a human is bitten and their body rejects a bite, they die. You didn't. You stayed human."

I was perplexed over the entire situation. My brain felt like it was going through information overload and might short circuit.

I felt Nat squeeze my hand, offering comfort. "You went into a kind of hibernation state instead of dying. But because we both bit you and you have both DNA in your blood—" Nat stopped.

Shae spoke. "You have become a controversial issue. Both Nik and the alpha feel like they have the right to figure out what to do with you."

It sounded like they were talking about me like I was property. "The *right* to figure out what to do with me? But I'm still human." Both sides wanted to decide what to do with me. I didn't know how their world worked, but I didn't like what they were saying.

Nat squeezed my hand. "We aren't going to let them touch you. Yes, you are still human. Besides, I bit you and Lylith bit you. That makes you essentially our responsibility, not theirs." I looked at her then at Lylith.

"Don't worry," Lylith said. "My dad isn't interested in keeping you against your will. He will listen to whatever argument I have. He doesn't want a jerk like Nik getting a hold of you, no offense."

"None taken," Nat said.

"That's why he is possessive," Lylith finished.

"How long was I unconscious for?" I wanted to take my mind off the battle that was being fought over me.

"Well, you weren't unconscious," Shae said. "You were in a hibernation state."

Nat had said hibernation earlier, but I just thought it was metaphorical. People couldn't hibernate. Frogs and bears did. "What the hell does that mean?" I asked.

"We don't know," Nat replied. "It's like your body was going through some kind of change. But it wasn't a vampire or werewolf. That's not how creatures like us change. We get aggressive and wild, not sedated."

I looked at my hands, then removed the covers. I started scanning the rest of my body, but nothing seemed different. My brain felt the same—a little fuzzy, but that's it. "I don't feel different," I said to Nat. I inhaled and exhaled deeply. "I still feel the same. Just tired and weak, like I have slept for too long. Always just weak." The last remark I snapped out a bit more angrily than I expected.

I felt frustration start to clutch at my chest. I was so tired of being weak, so tired of being helpless, so tired of being a tool for people to use against other people. I lifted my hands to my head and clenched my eyes shut. Tears of frustration started to burn the corners of my eyes. I hated being the damsel in distress who needed constant saving or protection. I hated not being able to do anything but get carried around and shielded from things. I felt a tightness in my chest and my breathing quicken.

A hand start rubbing my back. "Jamie, you will be OK. We won't let anything happen to you," Nat said to me.

I slammed my hands down on the bed. "I'm sick of being weak! I'm so sick of having to be protected and being helpless all the time!" I felt something surge in my body. All the lights in the room flooded bright and washed out my vision. Then I heard cracking as the lightbulbs burst. My head instantly throbbed.

I clutched my head and groaned, "What the hell was that?" I looked up, but it was dark now. I saw two dark amber eyes looking into my face. They were Nat's. Irene and Shae had backed up away from my bed; Lylith's golden eyes were next to Nat's.

"Jamie?" I heard Nat's voice.

"What?" I replied.

"What did you just do?" Her voice was calm and soothing, but had a hint of tension in it.

I had a temper tantrum. I wouldn't deny it. After all I had been through, I felt like I deserved losing it just once. I guessed vampires weren't used to losing it and needing to scream to get out their frustrations. "I'm sorry I yelled. I'm just a little frustrated."

"No. What did you feel? Your eyes turned bright blue, and whatever you did supercharged the lights," Lylith said.

It was probably just an electrical surge from a faulty transformer. "I didn't do that."

I felt Nat's hand on my face. "Jamie, I felt an immense amount of energy shoot out of you, and your eyes changed. Before you woke up, the same thing happened. I wasn't sure if I was imagining it or not then. What did you feel?"

I didn't know. There was no way I could have done that. Maybe the lights were messing with their eyes. My eyes were light brown, not blue. But they both were supernatural beings. Their eyes were sharp. "I don't know. I felt frustrated. I felt something surge in my chest, but everyone feels that from stress or anxiety. I guess I did have a sharp pain in my head, but that's not completely abnormal either."

My eyes had slightly adjusted to the dark, but not by much. All I could see were their eyes. They looked at each other. "No one is to know about this." Nat's voice sounded commanding. Everyone else nodded their understanding.

"Know about what?" I asked.

I felt her sit down on the bed. "Jamie, something has changed inside you. Some power has either been woken up or gained by you. I don't know if it was the bites that did it or that you almost died. There is a power inside you stronger than I have ever felt."

That couldn't be right. I was just normal. Just a normal human being. Unless... "Did Malcom do something to me? Did he turn me into a monster like those others? Did he do some creepy voodoo on me?" It scared me to even think about it, but that's the only explanation. It scared me, but also made me mad.

"No. I can feel it. It's powerful, but it's tender, light, not evil. Not created by dark magic," Nat replied.

"Some nutjob didn't create it," Lylith chimed in. "It feels old, ancient, like it's been within you for a long time."

"I'm not ancient. I'm twenty-eight years old. I have never had powers. I didn't even know your world existed until a couple of weeks ago, so how could I have something like this in me for a long time?" I felt a deep sigh escape my lips. I was starting to feel frustration growing within me again. None of this made sense.

"Jamie." I heard Nat's voice. "We are going to help you. Whatever it is, we will figure it out. For now, we need to keep it between us. OK?"

"OK," I replied. I took a deep breath in and let it out, trying to exhale all the pent-up frustration and anxiety that was clutching at my heart. "So, what now?" I asked.

Nat was still sitting on my bed. She had one of my hands intertwined with hers. It made me feel like I was safe. "Who can we trust? We need to get as many people here that are on our side as soon as possible."

Lylith spoke up. "My guys are with me no matter what." She sounded confident.

Shae was the next to speak. "Don't be mad, but I have been texting Kyle. He doesn't know all the details, but he will side with us, and I know he has a handful of guys with him. Jessica also came down. She brought some friends with her. We can trust her."

"OK, tell everyone to come here as soon as possible," Nat told everyone. "No one else is allowed in my house, got it? Irene, can you take care of securing the house? Make sure that doctor is gone."

Both Shae and Irene left the room. Lylith stayed behind. "Nat, can I talk to you real quick?"

"No," I said more forcefully than I intended. "No more secrets from me. Stop hiding things from me. If something is happening to me and I'm changing and in danger, I want to know everything. I don't want to be hidden away or kept in the dark."

She looked from Nat to me, then took a breath in. "OK, that's fair. I have this friend. She goes by Raven. She is a mage."

I heard Nat exhale sharply. But then Lylith started again. "I know you aren't keen on mages, but she could help us. She might be able to help teach you how to use your powers. She might be able to help us figure out what is going on with Jamie."

Nat was quiet for a long while. I could tell she was mulling over if she wanted to accept the offer, because I felt her hand clench and unclench like she was having an internal argument with herself.

"Yes," I said. I felt both their eyes fall on me. "I should have a say in it since no one here knows what the hell is happening to me."

I felt Nat's hand relax, and her thumb started rubbing the back of my hand. "OK, yeah. Jamie if you are ok with it and want it let's bring her in."

I heard Lylith exhale. "Good, because I already told her about the situation, and she already agreed to speak to us." She grinned. Her teeth were so white they glowed in the dark.

"What? When?" Nat asked.

"Just now. I texted her," Lylith replied. "I will let you know the details when she can meet up." Then she walked out the door.

Now it was just Nat and me alone. I felt like my world was crashing down around me. Nat wasn't saying anything. She probably was waiting for me to break the silence. I knew a lot was about to change, now that I potentially had powers. A werewolf and vampire bit me. Two supernatural leaders were fighting about who gets to decide my future. It was all weighing heavily on my shoulders. But those weren't the things that were troubling me the most. I didn't want to be taken away from Nat again. I didn't want her to have to sacrifice her well-being to rescue me again. I just wanted to be with her, to be a normal couple. I knew that our relationship had started fast and had grown even quicker, like fire touching gasoline, but in that short time, she had become my everything. I leaned into her, gripping at her.

I felt her put an arm around me. "Is everything alright?" she asked.

"I can't do this anymore, Nat." I felt her body tense at my words. "I can't constantly be taken away from you. I just want our relationship to be normal without having to fight off demons and crazy vampires and now supernatural leaders fighting over what's to become of me. I don't want to be separated from you again. I can't watch you or others get hurt trying to save me. It kills me."

Her arm pulled me even tighter to her. "Jamie, I promise I won't let anyone take you away from me ever again." Her voice was unyielding.

"How can you fight both leaders? Don't they have tons of people fighting for them?"

"Lylith's dad will listen to whatever she has to say. He trusts her. And trust me, she won't let Nik take you. They are possessive creatures, and she bit you, so she most definitely has your well-being as a priority."

"But I'm not a werewolf. And what about the fact I'm with you?"

I heard her let out a low chuckle. "Well, her DNA is in you. Whether it's dormant or not, she still feels like she is responsible. And when it comes to our relationship, she feels you being with me is the best for you, so she welcomes it. Plus, I bit you too. My DNA is in you as well, which makes you my responsibility." I felt her playfully nip at my neck.

It tickled and made me smile. "So, what? Now that you have marked me, you are claiming me?" I teased.

She gently pushed me back, so I was lying on the bed. I felt the pressure of her body on top of me. It was still dark in the room, but her eyes were shining bright and inches away from my face. "Something like that." Her voice was low, possessive, but soft. It sent a shiver through my body. I found the hem of her shirt and worked my hands under it. I slowly moved them up her back, tracing along her solid, defined muscles. She was so strong. When I reached the back of her neck, she let out an approving "Hmm" deep in her throat. I pulled her into me, gently kissing her lips, showing I was hers, entirely hers. I could taste the desire behind her lips. A warm pressure began to build deep within me. One of her hands came to rest on my side. She moved it up further, around my back, lifting me closer to her, deepening the kiss. She had so much strength. I moved my arms so they were wrapped around her neck. I felt her nibble at my lower lip, and it made me grab at her tighter. I was getting pleasantly dizzy from the kiss, and I felt myself becoming overcome by a primitive desire. I wanted her so bad. I wanted to give her everything, but I knew now wasn't the time for this.

I didn't let the kiss last long. As much as I wanted to have her then and there, time was of the essence, I had come to understand from the earlier conversation. I pulled my lips away from hers. Not far, though. When I spoke, I could feel them brush against hers. "What about your dad?" I asked.

I felt her body go tense at the mention of him. "I'm stronger than him, and if I have to, well, I will show everyone that." Her voice was cold and stern. "Jamie, I'm not going to let him touch you. I promise." I knew she wouldn't. Something had changed about her. I couldn't tell what it was. She felt more powerful than before, stern, fixed, commanding. I couldn't place it, but I knew she would keep me safe.

NATALIA

My desire for Jamie was so strong at that point that it took everything within me to keep from taking her and showing her how much she was mine. I had been drinking blood since I woke up and felt so much stronger, especially since Jamie had woken up too. I still wasn't up to my full potential, but I had gained a lot of my strength back, so I was able to control my yearning, but barely.

I was still on top of Jamie when I heard a knock at the door. "Nat, it's Irene. Kyle is here. He needs to talk to you."

I reluctantly pushed myself off Jamie and crawled out of bed. "Come in," I said.

The door opened, and Kyle walked in. He came over to me and reached out his hand like he was going to shake it. When I grabbed it, he pulled me toward him and wrapped his other arm around me. "You are one of the most insane person I have ever met. I'm so glad you are alive."

"Thanks, Kyle," I replied. "So, what do you need to talk to me about?"

He looked over to Jamie. "I'm glad to see you alive and well too, Jamie. I was scared we might lose you." She smiled and nodded her head in response. Then his attention turned back to me. "Shae filled me in a little about what was going on but didn't give me in-depth details. Nik isn't happy, Nat."

"I know he isn't happy. Does he know anything about her waking up yet?" Somehow my dad could find things out even if they were kept very secret.

He slowly shook his head. "I'm not sure. But you know him. He is going to try and get rid of her when he finds out she is awake, regardless of the fact that Lylith bit her too. When it comes to you and your personal life, he loses his composure. He doesn't listen to anyone, and now that Max is gone—"

I heard Jamie inhale sharply. "What do you mean, Max is gone?!" she asked breathlessly, scooting out of bed.

I still hadn't told her what had happened and who we lost. Kyle looked towards me. I could tell he didn't want to be the person to break the bad news. I turned to look at her. She had her legs dangling off the side of the bed and was about to stand up. I placed my hands on her thighs to keep her in the bed. "Jamie, you're still too weak to stand. Take it slow."

She looked in my eyes. I could see sorrow and pain, and it hurt me. "Nat, what does he mean by Max is gone?"

She stopped trying to get off the bed, so I put my hands on her shoulders. I took a deep breath. I wasn't sure I would be able to keep my composure telling her what happened. "Max didn't make it."

I saw tears begin to form in her eyes, and her mouth fell slightly open. "What?" I could feel her shoulders start to rise and fall as her breathing quickened.

"Jamie, breath, take deep breaths," I told her, trying to calm her down.

"I can't!" she said through a sob. I pulled her into me and held her tight. "He was killed because of me!" She was growing hysterical.

"No, Jamie, he wasn't killed because of you. He died because a psychopath was a coward. It's not your fault, Jamie." I rubbed her back to try and soothe her.

Her hands grabbed me tightly. I felt that same energy begin to seep out of her as before. "Jamie." I whispered, but it wasn't helping.

"Nat!" Kyle said behind me, frantically. I looked back and saw everything in the room had a small tremor. "Is this you?" he asked.

I shook my head. "Jamie, baby, it's not your fault. He was protecting you. That's what he did best. He wouldn't have done it if you weren't worth protecting." I pulled her tighter into me.

I felt her clutch tighten, and then she let out a loud cry. Everything in the room lifted up and then came crashing down. Then it was over. Her breathing slowed, but I could still hear the catches when she breathed in. Her grip on me began to loosen.

I heard footsteps out in the hall. Irene came bursting through the door. "What the hell was that?" She looked around the room at all the scattered papers and broken objects.

I didn't answer her. I held Jamie. She had been through so much, and now she had to deal with this. I rocked her back and forth, still holding her tightly to me.

"Could you feel that through the entire house?" I heard Kyle ask Irene.

"Yeah. I don't know if anyone outside felt it, but if they did, you know Nik will be on his way," Irene replied to him.

"Where is Shae?" I asked over my shoulder.

"She is still in the living room," Irene replied.

"Go get her," I said. I needed to get ready to face off with Nik and the alpha. This needed to happen fast, and I needed as many allies with me then. "Kyle, text Lylith."

"I'm already here," Lylith said as she walked through the door. "What happened?"

I didn't want to bring it up right now. Upsetting Jamie more wasn't on my list at the time. I looked at her with a silent "*I will fill you in later.*" Just then, Shae walked in. "You know Nik is going to be heading this way."

I nodded in reply. "Shae, I need you to stay with Jamie while I go sort this out."

"No!" Jamie yelled, pulling out of my grasp and looking at me. "I don't want to be left in here to be protected like a child anymore. I don't want to be separated from you anymore."

I knew how she felt, but I knew if Nik saw her, it would provoke him even more. I reached one of my hands up to her face. "I know you don't. That's not what I'm trying to do. Do you trust me?"

She still was looking into my eyes. I could see she didn't want me to leave her. "Yes, I do," she said quietly.

"Thank you. Everything is going to be OK, I promise." I pulled her into one last, kiss.

Lylith, Kyle, and I headed out of the room to the front door. We all piled onto the porch. Irene was already standing outside at the top of the porch stairs, arms crossed in a defensive posture.

We all walked up next to her. Kyle was standing on my left. "Are you OK with doing this, Kyle? Standing opposite from my father?"

I saw the corner of his lip curl into a small smile. "If I want him to respect me like he did Max, I need to stand up for what's right. His mind is clouded right now, and he isn't thinking clearly."

I placed a hand on his shoulder. "Thank you."

I had my eyes fixed on Nik's trailer. It only took a few seconds before he walked out with a couple of men tailing him. He walked toward my house.

"Lyl, I think it's time to invite your dad," I said.

"Already on it, Nat," she replied, slipping her phone in her pocket.

I could feel my predator getting restless. Irene's was too. Kyle was calm, but Lylith was rigid. I could feel the wolf right under her skin buzzing with anticipation.

We all stood still, waiting for my father to approach. He was taking his time on purpose. It was a gesture showing he had all the time in the world, and he wanted to show he was in control. When he got about twenty feet from us, he stopped and scanned my group. He ran his hand through his hair. "I'm going to take a guess and assume the human is awake. I felt a strange little tremor. Was that you, Nat, or her?"

"Her name is Jamie," Lylith said in a stern tone, not addressing his question.

I saw his eyes squint a glare in her direction. "I take it the doctor is seeing to an examination of the human?" he asked.

"No," I snapped at him. "The doctor is resting comfortably on the couch." I had seen him lying there as we walked out. I'm guessing Irene or Shae had knocked him out.

His stern face fell back on me. He took two steps forward, then stopped. "Let me pass to see what we are dealing with."

"Out of the question," Irene said before I could respond. "You have no interest in her well-being." She practically spat out the last words. "You aren't going near her."

His gaze never left my face. "So, you are defying me then."

I clenched my teeth together. "I wouldn't call it defying you. You aren't thinking clearly. You want to get rid of her just because she is in my life. That is childish and immature."

His lips turned into a sneer. "You spoiled little brat. You are letting this human warp your mind. You are royalty! And you are going to let her ruin your life!" he huffed. "Let me inside to see how I need to handle this situation." He took another step toward the house.

It was pure instinct that made me react. Before I knew it, I was inches away from his face. "You aren't going anywhere near her!" I hissed through my teeth.

I saw his eyes start to burn red amber, like before. I was hoping I had gained enough strength to fight his manipulations this time. I felt the pressure envelop my body. I felt his will trying to bend me, but I was fighting back. I knew what to expect this time. From a distance, it probably looked like we were having an intense stare down when it was actually a power struggle.

His face started to contort as he began pouring more of his energy into trying to move me.

I felt sweat start to gather on my forehead as I fought back. His strength was starting to strain me, and I could feel the slightest tremble form in my legs.

We were so focused on each other that neither of us heard Jackson, the alpha, walk up. "I see the party started without me!" He walked up with his arms spread out wide. He had on a black tank top, baggy jeans, and flip-flops. His thick, brown wavy hair hung almost down to his shoulders. You could see the faintest of grey streaks throughout his scalp. It reminded me of a surfer's hairstyle. He had dark, tan, tough skin, much like Lylith's, but he had far more scars all over his body from battles. He stood a towering six foot ten inches. Where Lylith's body was riddled with strong, lean muscle, he had the frame of a bodybuilder. He shared the same facial structure as Lylith, that primitive wild look. You could tell she was his daughter. His eyes were a deep, shining, molten golden color. "Nik, how could you leave me out of the loop, my old friend, skipping out on the invite?" At his words, both our concentrations were interrupted. We both took a step back from each other, breathing heavily from the energy we had just expelled.

"Jackson, nice of you to join us," my dad replied in a sarcastic tone, never taking his eyes off me.

"I heard the girl is awake. This should be a time of celebration, not a time for quarreling."

"Stay out of this, Jackson. This is between my rebellious daughter and me."

Jackson had taken on a more severe and authoritative tone. "I'm afraid not. Both our heirs bit the girl. If anything, she is their responsibility, not ours."

Nik turned to face Jackson. I saw his body tense up. Jackson hadn't moved, but I could feel his power pouring off of him. He was ready to shift at any advance from Nik.

I didn't want a war to start in my front yard. We had bigger things to deal with, like tracking down Malcom and stopping his crazy plans and not fighting because my father was having a power complex issue right then. Werewolves and vampires haven't had a war for centuries, and I wasn't about to let it start right in front of me.

"Enough," I shouted. "He's right. She is our responsibility. You aren't going to punish her because of what I have done. There are more important things to deal with now, like how Malcom is creating an army of demonic vampires using blood magic."

Nik looked at everyone around him. I could tell he knew I was right. Then his gaze fell on me, and he glared even harsher. He walked right up to me into my personal space. I knew he wouldn't try and hurt me, so I just stood there. He leaned close so no one could hear what he was about to say. "She will never be part of this house or a part of us. I will not let you ruin your life for a human. You will never be allowed to keep her." He hissed, then turned to walk away, but I grabbed his shoulder and turned him back toward me.

It was my turn to make a stand. I got close to his ear. "If you touch her, or try to take her from me, I will show everyone in the house just how powerful I am. You will be bending your knee to me next time."

He jerked away with a look of disgust on his face. I could see his predator dancing behind his eyes. I wasn't sure what his next move would be, so I prepared myself for a fight. I was just about to shift when I saw my dad exhale deeply and slump his shoulders. His head fell, and he started to shake it slowly back and forth. "You were right earlier. Malcom should be our number one priority right now. We can finish this discussion later." He straightened his body posture. He stared back into my eyes. Slowly he turned and started walking to his trailer.

I didn't take my eyes off him till he had gone inside. I exhaled and let my body relax. Then I felt a large arm wrap around my shoulders and slap me hard. "Well, that was exciting, wasn't it?" Jackson boomed with a laugh.

Werewolf hierarchy was different than vampire hierarchy. Very laid back. Jackson was very relaxed and playful, full of life, and all about fun. But I knew he was deadly and dangerous, an outstanding leader, and demanded respect when necessary. I had seen it before.

"Thanks for showing up, dad," Lylith said to him, jumping down the steps and jogging to us.

"Well, it seemed like the two of you had everything under control."

"Kind of. Having your presence here, I think, put a little more weight to our argument."

"So, how is the girl? I have no doubt you two will take full responsibility for her. I felt something earlier coming from your house. I don't know if it had anything to do with her." His tone was sterner, commanding now. He looked at both of us flatly.

"Of course, we will," I replied to him. "She seems fine. Something does seem to have changed within her, but I don't know what yet."

He had an earnest look on his face and was nodding to what I was saying, taking in all the information. "I talked to Raven earlier. She said she would help figure out what was going on with Jamie and help Nat figure out her stuff too," Lylith told Jackson.

"OK, good. Keep me in the loop. I trust you, Lyl, but this is new turf. Be careful with her. And Nat, I know you and your father are butting heads, but keep him informed as well. He is still in charge of your house. There is no need for anyone to be going on a warpath when we have a psychopath like Malcom on the loose. We need to come together to fight this guy." His tone was more fatherly than demanding.

I nodded my understanding. He was right. I know my dad and I weren't getting along, but I didn't want to fight with him right then. We couldn't risk our emotions getting in the way.

"Lyl, when you are done here, stop by and see me. We need to talk about some things." Then he turned and headed toward the forest.

Once he was gone, I felt everyone around me relax. I even let out a long exhale. I was exhausted. I had gotten a lot of my strength back, but the power struggle I just had with Nik must have taken a lot more out of me than I expected. Irene hopped off the porch and walked over to me.

"Are you OK, Nat? What was that, with you and Nik?."

Lylith chuckled. "I'm thinking they were asserting their dominance. I could feel a ton of power-clashing between you two."

I nodded, confirming Lylith's theory. "Yeah, before in Jamie's room, he caught me by surprise and made me kneel to him. He tried to do it again, but I was ready this time. A little longer, though, and I probably wouldn't have been able to stop him."

I felt Irene's shoulder against mine. "I knew he was strong, but using his power to bend his own daughter's will like that is a bit much."

Kyle leaned on the porch, railing. "He's just scared. He doesn't want to lose Nat or be replaced by someone. He thinks if Nat has Jamie, any kind of amends between the two will be lost."

I knew that Kyle was right. Having Jamie in my life threatened him. "But that's not true. I need time. A relationship as strained as ours can't be mended overnight."

Irene intertwined her fingers with mine and set her head on my shoulder. "Maybe you should tell him that. Maybe he needs to hear it from you."

I knew where Irene was coming from, but I also knew at that point, it wouldn't have been a great time to talk to him. I needed to wait until he cooled off from this conflict. I nodded my head. "Yeah, maybe you are right. Later though. Right now, I need to be with Jamie and figure out what has happened to her."

"Of course," Irene replied to me, and we started walking back to the house.

JAMIE

After Shae and I were left alone in the room, I moved back into the bed. Shae came and sat down on the bed beside me. "How are you holding up?" she asked.

I had no idea. There were too many feelings at that point. "I don't know," I replied honestly. "Crappy, I guess. Physically and emotionally. Max is dead." Then an unsettling feeling came over me. "Did anyone else die?"

I saw Shae's brows and lips furrow together. She didn't reply at once. I reached out my hand and placed it on hers. She let out a heavy sigh. "Neither Jason nor Isaac made it. Sasha and a few other werewolves died too."

I felt a heaviness in my chest, sorrow and sadness growing there, like a bottomless black pit. My head involuntarily hung down. Shae shifted on the bed. Her hand wrapped around mine. Then she pulled me into her and wrapped her arm tightly around me. I buried my face into her shoulder.

"It's not your fault, Jamie. Malcom is a psycho. He would have done this evil regardless of whether you would have been in the picture or not. You can't blame yourself for his actions."

I knew she was right. He had no heart. Down in the caves, I had realized whatever magic he was conjuring had taken away any ounce of kindness or goodness inside him and replaced it with pure evil and darkness. I had never met someone as cold as he was. It still hurt, though, that it was me he targeted to destroy Nat, and that people had died trying to rescue me.

I lifted my head and sat up straight. "Thank you, Shae." I was still holding her hand. It didn't feel awkward, though. I guessed when people had gone through situations like we had gone through, it brought everyone closer together. I trusted her. She reassured me I wasn't alone. "My entire world has been turned upside down, and

I don't know how to handle it. It's like one terrible thing after the other. I feel like there is no break or end to it."

She looked in my eyes. Her amber eyes were darker than Nat's. There was an empathy behind them. "I can't imagine what you are going through and what this experience has done to you. But I do know Nat cares deeply for you, Jamie. I have never seen her care so much for someone. She will never let anything happen to you. Especially now that we know what we are dealing with."

I wanted to cling to her words, but it was so hard after everything that had happened. He had gotten to me almost effortlessly twice. He has figured out how to create unstoppable creatures.

Shae must have been able to tell what I was thinking. "Jamie, it won't happen again. She won't let it. She brought everyone together, and now we have the manpower to stop Malcom."

I gave her a small smile. Maybe she was right. Perhaps now they would be ready for whatever Malcom had to throw at them. But there was one more thing that worried me. "What about Nat's dad and the werewolf alpha wanting me? What do they even want me for?"

She squeezed my hand. "Trust me on this one. Nat won't let Nik touch you. And Lylith is one of the most protective people I know. Since she bit you and you are with Nat, she won't let either of the bigwigs get to you either."

I reached out and hugged her. "Thank you, Shae, for being here for me."

"Of course," she replied. "That's what friends are for."

I heard the door open, and Nat entered the room, followed by Lylith, Kyle, and Irene. "How did it go?" Shae asked as she hopped off the bed.

I saw the faintest smile form across Nat's face. "It didn't go too bad. No fighting happened." Nat walked over to the bed and sat down beside me. She wrapped her arms around me. I leaned into her chest and wrapped my arms around her the best I could. I shut my eyes and took in her warmth, took in the rise and fall of her chest when she breathed, the sound of her heartbeat. She was everything I wanted.

"Nik still isn't happy, but he agreed to let it go for now. The alpha had no issue with Jamie. As far as he is concerned, she is Nat's and Lyl's responsibility. He won't let Nik take her, though, so that's good for us," Irene said.

"What's the plan in the meantime to find Malcom?" I felt Nat's chest vibrate as she asked the question.

"Well, surprisingly, both sides have been pulling their resources together to locate the most prospective places he might be. Once we pinpoint likely spots, they want to have a meeting about how to attack him," Lylith replied. "There won't be a fight for a long time. Right now, it's just trying to figure out where he is going and surveillance."

"For now, I think you all need to rest and recover. I will keep everyone updated on what Nik plans to do," Kyle said to all of us. "Jamie, I truly am glad you are with us again." He smiled at me. "If you need anything, don't hesitate to ask. I need to get going though, and make sure Nik doesn't do anything stupid." With that, he turned and left.

"I probably should go too. Dad's expecting me," Lylith said. She looked over at Irene. "Are you still going to crash with me?" For a second, I saw something in her eyes. A sense of longing maybe? I wasn't quite sure.

Irene looked at Nat. There was a questioning look in her eyes as if asking permission. "Yes, I still don't think I can stay here. Is that alright, Nat?"

"Of course it is. I understand," Nat replied.

Irene walked over to the side of the bed. I slid out of Nat's arms so she could hug Irene. It was a long, strong hug. "If you need anything, let me know. I will be here, OK? Anything at all," Nat told her.

"Thank you," Irene said. She pulled out of Nat's arms then wrapped her arms around me. "Thank you for coming back. I don't know what I would have done if we lost you too." She kissed me on the cheek, which brought a smile to my face. She had such a loving spirit. She walked over to Lylith, who put her hand on the small of her back to guide her out.

As they reached the door, Lylith turned back. "Oh Nat, tomorrow we are going to see Raven. I hope you're good with that." They turned, and right before the door shut, I saw Irene's hand slip into Lylith's.

I looked up at Nat with a questioning look. She looked down at me and smiled. She saw it too, but all she did was shrug her shoulders. I guess everyone grieves in different ways. Maybe it was nothing.

"I think I need to get going too, or Jessica will have a fit," Shae said. She gave both of us a hug, then left the room.

It was just Nat and me now. "What about us?" I asked Nat, crawling back into her arms.

She took in a deep breath and kissed the top of my head. "Now I never let you out of my sight again."

"But what about work?" A horror ran through me. I felt my body straighten up. "Oh my gosh! Work! I haven't been to work in a few days and haven't called in!" I felt myself start to panic. I didn't even know where my phone was to call in.

I started to crawl, trying to get out of bed, but Nat grabbed me and placed me back where I was. "Jamie, relax. Kyle already took care of it, with the doctor's help. We called in and said you had been in an accident and had to be flown to a specialty hospital, but had the best of care and that you were recovering. The sheriff gave you all the time you need to recover."

That made me laugh. "Wow, you guys really do have everything covered."

"Well yeah, we have had centuries to perfect things like covering up certain situations. How do you think we have kept secret for so long?"

"I guess you are right. I hope no one tries to visit me in that specialty hospital or that my parents don't find out." I had no idea what time it was. There were no windows in this room, but I was tired. I felt a yawn escape me.

"Are you tired?" Nat asked me.

"I'm exhausted. I guess I haven't quite recovered yet, and all the crying took it out of me." I looked around the room. The bed I was in was only a twin size, and wasn't comfortable at all. "Can we go to your room?"

Her face lit into a significant smile. Then I felt her sweep me up into a bridal carry. It was so fast I let out a high-pitched squeal. Then I started laughing excitedly as she carried me out of the room.

I heard her start to laugh too, probably at the noise I had emitted. "I love your little squeal noises," she said as she carried me down the hall toward her room.

When we got inside, she carried me to my side of the bed and set me down. I stripped down into my underwear and crawled under the soft covers. I felt the bed shift as she crawled in. I scooted closer to her, and then her arms were around me, pulling me into her. There was a pressure on the top of my head where she kissed me. I didn't know how I managed to start falling in love with this woman so fast, but I was. "Nat."

"Hmm." I heard her respond.

"I'm falling in love with you," I whispered.

I felt her pull me into her. "I have already fallen in love with you." I heard her reply as I drifted off into the most relaxing sleep I have had in days.

I woke up to the sun shining through the window. I still felt the pressure of Nat against me. I could feel her breathing was even slower than usual, the slow rise and fall of her chest. She was still asleep. I smiled to myself. I never woke up before her. She must have been exhausted. I lightly kissed her collarbone and heard a soft "Hmm" from deep in her throat in response. Her arms squeezed me tighter.

"Good morning." she whispered through a sleepy voice.

"Good morning," I replied to her, snuggling myself deeper into her. I didn't want to get out of bed. I didn't want to think about everything that was going to take place in the near future. All I wanted to do was stay in bed wrapped in her arms, but I knew we would need to get up. I reached backward for the clock on the nightstand to see what time it was. Before I could, Nat tugged me back into her and grumbled.

I couldn't help the giggle that escaped my mouth. "I'm just checking the time."

"No, stay here. You're comfy."

I obliged her. If she wasn't worried about getting up, I wouldn't be either. We stayed wrapped in each other's arms for a while. I couldn't tell for how long. I had just started to doze back off when I heard a buzzing coming from her nightstand.

In response, she let out a low growl and reached behind her to grab her phone. When she looked at the screen, she let out a disapproving breath. "It's Lylith. She wants us to start getting ready so we can go see Raven."

I idly traced my fingers along her collarbones and neck. "Do you think she will be able to help us?"

I felt her shoulders shrug against me. "I don't know. Maybe, but I think she is our best bet. Lylith seems to think she can help."

The next thing on my agenda was a shower. I couldn't remember the last time I had taken one. "I'm going to go clean up a bit." I pulled out of her arms. She gave a grumbling noise, but let me get up. I grabbed her hand and kissed the top of it before I made my way to the bathroom. I went straight for the shower knobs and turned the water on, adjusting to the perfect temperature. I turned around briefly while I took off my underwear and saw myself in the mirror. I let out a small gasp. I didn't have a scratch on me. My face wasn't swollen or black and blue. There wasn't even pain. I looked down at my stomach, and there were healed scars where I remembered the vampire stabbing through me. I ripped off the bandage on my neck and wrist. The bites had healed too. All that was there were scars as if the injuries had happened years ago.

I threw open the door. Nat was sitting on her side of the bed, intently looking at her phone. When she looked up, her eyes went wide, and her cheeks flushed bright red.

"Uhh," she managed to utter.

I looked down and realized I was completely naked. I had forgotten. "Come on, Nat, this isn't the first time you have seen me naked."

She shook her head, "True, but I wasn't quite expecting it right now."

I walked in front of her. "Look," I said, pointing to my stomach. I saw her mouth slightly hang open as her finger brushed over the scars. "And here," I said, signaling to my neck. Her hand moved to my neck, and I felt her thumb tracing the bite mark. Her eyes were so intense now, scanning my entire body for injuries. "What does this mean?" I asked her.

She slowly started shaking her head. "I have no idea," she whispered. Her gaze fell on Lylith's bite on my wrist. Then I felt her other hand brush the side of my face that had been bashed in. Her gaze fell to mine. There was a look of uncertainty in her eyes.

"Was it the bites that did this?" I asked her.

Her hands fell to my bare hips. I felt her thumbs start tracing small circles. Her gaze fell to the floor, and I could tell she was deep in thought. I reached my hand under her chin and lifted it so she was looking at me. "Nat?"

"I don't know. I don't know if it was from us or if it was caused by whatever is in you. Hopefully Raven can help us figure it out today." Her voice was filled with uncertainty. I couldn't tell if it was a worried uncertainty or curiosity.

I placed my hand on her cheek and gave her a slow kiss. "We'll figure it out." I turned and headed back toward the shower. I could feel her eyes follow me until I shut the door.

I didn't want to get out of the shower. The warm water felt so relaxing against my body. When I finally did get out and went into the bedroom, Nat wasn't there anymore. I found some clothes and threw them on.

I walked down the hall and smelled food cooking. Bacon and eggs. I walked into the kitchen and saw Nat by the stove, tending to a skillet. My stomach growled loudly. Nat slightly turned her head toward me. "Hungry?"

Thinking of it, I couldn't remember the last time I ate anything. Down in the caves, we never got fed. "I'm starving."

I sat down at the table, and she set down a plate full of bacon, eggs, and toast. "Thank you so much!" I said before I started devouring the food.

After we had finished breakfast, I followed her outside. Lylith was sitting on the porch swing with a book in her hand. When she heard us, she set the book down and looked up. "Are you two finally ready?"

"Yeah, we're ready," Nat said. "Look at this, though, Lyl." Nat looked at me to ask permission. I nodded my head, and she pointed to the bite mark on my neck and wrist.

"Wow," Lylith said. "She is completely healed. What about her stomach?"

I lifted my shirt just high enough to reveal the scars there. She was so tall she had to kneel on one knee in front of me. "Incredible," Lylith said, examining the scars. "When did this happen?"

"I don't know. Overnight maybe. Her face was still injured yesterday," Nat replied. "I was out of it as long as she was, and the bandages were covering them. I didn't even think to take them off to examine them."

"How did it happen?" Lylith asked, now looking at Nat.

"I have no idea," Nat replied.

Lylith stood back up. "Raven is waiting for us. Maybe she will have some answers. Did you tell your dad you were going?"

"No," replied Nat. "If he knows, I think it's just going to make things worse."

Lylith shrugged her shoulders. "Whatever you say. Let's get going."

Her SUV was parked right by the house. Lylith hopped in the driver's seat. I got in the back, and Nat took the passenger side.

"It's about a three-hour drive. I hope you guys are up for it," Lylith told us while she drove down Nat's driveway toward the road.

"That's fine," I replied. "Where is it?"

"It's in Jackson. She owns an uppity shop that sells expensive skincare and hair products."

"You said she is a mage," I stated. Lylith replied by nodding her head. "What's the difference between a mage and a witch?" I had seen and read enough books to know that it seemed like they were one and the same, but so much of pop fiction had been proven wrong already. I wanted to make sure I had the correct information.

Lylith's mouth curved into a smile. "To be honest, they are the same thing. Some people get offended by the word witch."

"And what do they prefer to go by?" I didn't want to say something wrong and accidentally offend anyone, especially if they had agreed to help us.

"You can usually never go wrong calling them mages," Lylith replied.

In all honesty, magic kind of scared me. Especially since the only real magic I had seen created demon vampires. I was looking at my shoes now, and Nat must have felt the sudden damper in my mood. I felt her hand grab my thigh. When I looked up, her eyes were locked on mine, and she had a reassuring smile on her face. "We are going to figure this out, Jamie." I looked in the rearview mirror, and Lylith's golden eyes were looking at me. They were soft and reassuring as well.

I felt my chest lighten. I had two powerful supernatural beings protecting me. I knew Malcom had gotten to me with ease before. I had to forget about that and trust these two. I grabbed Nat's hand and squeezed it. "I guess I'm still just a little on edge. Human nature."

The entire drive was pretty much in silence. Nat let me hold on to her hand the whole ride. Lylith pulled into the parking lot of a fancy-looking shop and parked. She pulled on a leather jacket and put a baseball cap on. She fixed her hair so her animal like ears were hidden. Then she put on some classic aviator sunglasses. It made me giggle a little. "This is your incognito look, Charlie from Top Gun?"

Her laugh was loud at my comment, and I could see all her shiny teeth when her mouth opened. "I never thought about it like that, but I guess I do give off the vibe with these on." She whipped her head around and started singing *Danger Zone* while headbanging. I couldn't help but laugh, and Nat joined in as well. Once our playful moment had come and gone, we piled out of the car.

I didn't know why, but I felt nervous about going into the store. Nat came up and placed her hand in mine. The contact helped calm my nerves. When Lylith opened the door, hundreds of smells filled my nose. Everything in this store was so elegant. Momentarily I forgot why we had gone there and walked up to the first display table that had an assortment of lotions and perfumes. I took the top off one, and it smelled amazing.

Nat patiently waited for me to get my fix in. Once I remembered why we were there, I stepped back to her side. There weren't a lot of customers. We followed Lylith to the perimeter of the store, where I saw a woman bent over counting product on a bottom shelf.

"Raven!" Lylith called out to her.

Hearing Lylith's voice, the woman straightened. She looked to be in her forties. She was of average height and build for a woman. Her hair was an auburn color pulled back into a loose messy bun. She had white, flawless skin, but it wasn't a pale color. It was ivory that almost shined. Her eyes were a mossy green color. Her lips were plump and red, and they formed into a smile when she saw Lylith.

"Lylith darling!" she said as they embraced each other in a hug. "It's so nice to see you after all these years."

Nat and I hung back a bit as they caught up with small talk. I had subconsciously scooted more behind Nat.

"This is Natasha," I heard Lylith say as she introduced Raven to Nat.

Nat extended her hand. "It's a pleasure to meet you."

"The pleasure is all mine. Finally, I get to meet the great Nik's daughter. I have heard some incredible things about you, Nat." When their hands met, a look of surprise washed over Raven's face. "Wow," she said, looking from where their hands were meeting to Nat's face, "You do have a lot of power living within you."

After their hands separated, Raven leaned to the side more to look at me. "And who do we have here?" Hearing her say that made me feel like a child, small and puny.

I mustered up my courage and stepped to the side of Nat. I put on the best smile I could form at the time. "My name is Jamie Stone. It's nice to meet you."

A warm, inviting smile fell across her face. "It's nice to meet you too, Jamie." As our hands met, I felt something inside my chest, almost like a candlelight flicker.

The smile that once was on Raven's face was gone. Her eyes were wide, and her mouth hung open slightly. It looked as if she wasn't breathing. Her eyes seemed to be looking at something else—something beyond me—like she was looking at a picture of a memory.

Her hand was still clutching mine, and I felt Nat's body tense next to me, but she didn't intervene. "Raven?" I heard Lylith say as she placed a hand on her shoulder. It was as if she had pulled her out of a dream.

"It can't be," Raven whispered. I started to get scared. I saw her other hand lifting toward my face. As much fear there was inside me, I didn't stop her. Her hand was trembling, but once she set it on my cheek, a warm, bright smile formed on her face. Her hand was tender where it touched, and instantly I had no fear.

"We have been waiting a long time for you to come back," she said. "One of the long, lost Auras."

NATASHA

Before any of us could ask her what she meant by aura, she whisked Jamie through a door in the back to an office. Her office was very extravagant and plush. She had a luxurious couch with a La-Z-Boy chair and a Lovesac. She also had a computer desk with the most exquisite computer chair I had ever seen.

Raven sat Jamie down on the couch. I sat down next to her, instantly reclaiming her hand in mine. Lylith plopped herself down in the Lovesac next to us, and Raven brought her computer chair around so she was in front of Jamie and me.

I had never heard of a person being an "Aura" before. I had no idea what she meant by it. Before I could ask, Lylith spoke up. "Raven, what exactly is an Aura?"

"Well, I'm pretty sure she is an Aura." Before Raven sat down, she unlocked a thick wooden cabinet and pulled out a heavy leather book. She sat down and started to flip through until she got to a page. "Auras were very mighty beings that used to walk among us, some say the most powerful of all. They kept balance and peace among all the different factions on earth. They had power and control over all the elements of the planet and lived with nature in harmony."

She turned the book around so we could look at it. The writing was in a language I had never seen before, and I had seen hundreds of languages in my time. "I don't recognize that language."

She laughed. "I would think not. It's extinct. Only a few people in the entire world can read it. This book has some of their histories. Unfortunately, Auras haven't been among us for so long that they became legend and then became almost completely absent from knowledge. Most texts that had any information about them vanished with time. It's been centuries since one has been seen."

"Wait, wait, hold on," Jamie said. "How can I be an Aura if they haven't been around in centuries."

"Why do you think she is an Aura?" I asked before she could answer Jamie.

"I know because I felt it when I touched her. I have intuition like that as part of my powers," Raven replied, skimming through some of the pages in the book. "A very long time ago, they were around to help keep peace on earth. There were only a handful of them because of how powerful they were. It was a time of great peace among everyone. Then war broke out, brother killing brother, friends betraying friends, mindless destruction of the planet, the harmony and balance was destroyed. They tried to bring peace back, but the harder they tried, the worse things got. They all met in a final gathering and decided that it was time for them to leave and let humanity work itself out. It is said that they would return when they were needed most." She shut the book and smiled at me. "And here we are."

"They would return when they were needed most? What does that mean?" Lylith asked.

"No one knows. One day supposedly, they just disappeared." Raven shrugged her shoulders. "If you are an Aura, they must have somehow hidden their power in their DNA, and it would activate in one of their descendants when the time was right."

"Hold on. We aren't really assuming I am a super-powerful ancient being, right?" Jamie asked.

I didn't know if I could trust that Raven knew Jamie was an Aura just by touching her, but it might explain some of the things that had happened. I gripped Jamie's hand tight. "Maybe it's something to think about, Jamie. The power I felt come off of you was the strongest I have ever felt."

"OK, so let's say hypothetically I am an Aura. How would we for sure know? I mean, is there a test to see?" Jamie asked.

"Well, there isn't a definitive test, but if you train with your powers, we can figure out what you are capable of doing. The powers of an Aura can't be replicated. I would be able to feel and differentiate it and any other type of magic," Raven said. "Have you had any strange dreams or visions recently?"

I could tell Jamie was deep in thought, trying to think back. "I remember after the attack when I was unconscious, I saw a woman's face. She told me I had to wake up, that I had things I needed to do. I thought it was just a dream, though." Jamie became rigid. Her brows were creased together, and her lips were pursed.

I saw Raven reach out her hand and put it on Jamie's leg. "That was probably your ancestor trying to help you."

Jamie stood up swiftly and wrapped her arms around herself. She walked over to a wall and faced it.

"Jamie." I followed her and put my hands on her arms. She was shaking uncontrollably. "Jamie, what's wrong?"

Her breathing was shaky. I turned around, and both Lylith and Raven were standing with worried looks on their faces.

"Jamie? What's going on?" I asked again.

"I don't know. I don't even know how to interpret all this information. I was a normal human being just trying to make it in the world, being the sheriff's deputy a few weeks ago, living a simple, quiet life. Now a mage is telling me I am some sort of ancient being that was in charge of keeping peace in the world. Vampires and werewolves exist. Magic is real."

I couldn't even imagine what this must have felt like for her. I had been born into this world and had lived in it for a very long time, so when new things like this popped up, it didn't bother me. I had learned to roll with it. But Jamie was a human who had just been plunged headfirst into a world she knew nothing about.

She was taking deep breaths then, trying to calm herself down. I wasn't quite sure if she was this Aura that Raven had told us about, but regardless, she did have powers. Something was happening to her that was beyond humanity.

"Jamie, you aren't in this alone. I know it's a lot for you to take in right now, and I'm so sorry you were thrown into my world like this." I wrapped my arms around her, reassuring her she wasn't in this alone.

I held her for a few more moments then turned her to face me. Her eyes were shut, and she was frowning. I hated seeing her like this. "Jamie, nothing is going to happen to you. Lyl and I will protect you."

She let out a long exhale. "I'm not worried about my protection. I never asked for powers. I never asked to be some kind of person that is meant to bring world peace. I just want a normal life, Nat." She rested her head on my shoulder and slid her arms around me. "I don't even know how to use the powers I have."

"We can help you with that, dear," Raven chimed in with an enthusiastic tone. "Specifically, my daughter. She is an elemental. She can control water. Of course, she draws power from herself to control it, and you draw power from the earth itself, but it is the closest kind of teacher you will find. Plus, she can help you, Nat, with your power control."

"What am I obligated to do if I accept being an Aura?" Jamie asked flatly.

"You have absolutely no obligations to anyone or anything whatsoever," I told her. I didn't want her to have to feel like it was her responsibility to make everyone happy or to protect everyone. "All you need right now is to focus on yourself."

I felt Raven's presence by our side. Jamie pulled away from me enough so she could look at her. "Jamie, you can't choose to be or not to be. This gift was given to you for a reason. You are what you are. But it is your choice what you do with the power that has been given to you. Train with your magic. Figure it out. Let it become part of you. Maybe then you will see the possibilities of the future."

I heard the door to her office open, and a young woman entered. She had auburn hair, just like Raven's, pulled back into a ponytail. Her eyes were more of an emerald green. She smiled at us with red lips and pink, rosy cheeks. She had a petite frame and was about Jamie's height.

"Melissa, thank you for coming in," Raven said to the girl. "This is my daughter, Melissa."

"You can just call me Mel," the young girl interrupted.

"You know Lylith already." They both smiled at each other. "This is Natasha and Jamie." I moved my body so I was standing side by side with Jamie. I slipped my arm around Jamie's waist so she could still have a physical connection with me.

"It's nice to meet you both," Mel said from across the room.

"Can you teach me?" Jamie asked in a quiet voice.

Mel looked from Jamie to her mother. "Come here, dear." Raven gestured for Mel to come closer.

Without hesitation, Mel walked up to us. "May I?" Raven asked, gesturing to Jamie's hand. Jamie gave her an approving nod.

Jamie lifted out her hand, and Mel reached for it. When her hand connected to it, Mel's smile grew even more significant. "Is she an Aura, mother?"

At the word Aura, I felt Jamie's body tense up, and she leaned closer into me. "I believe she is," Raven replied.

"That is amazing! I never knew I would live to see the day they came back!" Mel said. "Quite frankly, I always thought that maybe my mom was a crazy old fool full of stories." She winked at Jamie, which made her smile just slightly.

Raven swatted at Mel. "She needs someone to teach her. It would be best if an elemental as strong as you could help her."

"You want me to teach her? I don't know anything about the Aura magic. They pull their power from the earth and elements. I only manipulate it," Mel said.

"Yes, I know how your magic works honey, but yours is the closest to their type of magic," Raven told her.

"Of course, I would be willing to help you learn," Mel stated, turning back to Jamie. "It will be new territory for both of us, but if you're patient with me, I will teach you everything I know." Her smile was so comforting, and I think it was good for Jamie. Then she turned her attention to me. "I can also help you control yours. I heard you nearly drained your life force. That can be very dangerous."

I nodded at her. "Yeah, I didn't even know I had the power in me."

She placed a hand on my shoulder. "Alright, two new students. This is going to be great! How do you want to go about doing this? I'm sure you don't want to travel for three hours to get lessons."

"No, actually. There has been a lot going on with the werewolves and vampires at my house lately. A tyrant vampire by the name of Malcom has figured out how to use blood magic." Her face turned stern when I mentioned that, but she listened intently.

After we had filled both Mel and Raven in on all the details, I made it clear that Jamie wouldn't be leaving my side, and it probably wouldn't be safe to leave my property a lot for long periods. "Well, in that case," Mel said, "I could come and stay on your property if it wasn't an imposition, for the time being."

I was mulling the thought over in my head—vampires, werewolves, and mages all in one setting. I didn't know how it would go. Before I could finish, Lylith answered. "Of course, it wouldn't be an imposition. It would be nice to have someone like you around anyway."

I shot Lylith a look. She shrugged and leaned back into the Lovesac. "Hey, Aura or not, she still has a bite from me, so I get some say-so."

I shook my head and gave a soft laugh. "You can stay at my house."

"Great!" Mel replied. "I just need to square some things away here and make sure mom is well taken care of."

I saw Raven's hand slap her shoulder again. "I do not need taken care of, young lady. I'm perfectly capable of doing things on my own."

"Yeah, OK. It will only take me a couple of days. I can call when I'm ready to head that way," Mel replied.

"Sounds like a plan," I replied to her.

She smiled and said goodbye to us all then left the office. After that, Raven led us back to the storefront and wished us all a farewell.

She tried her best to be delicate with Jamie. She understood it was going to take some getting used to.

When we got to the car, I sat in the back seat with Jamie. She didn't seem like she wanted me to leave her side. I was completely fine with that. We all piled in, but Lylith didn't start the car immediately. She turned around in her seat. Jamie was looking down at where our hands were intertwined.

Lylith lifted Jamie's chin, so she was looking at her. "Jamie, I know this is a lot to take in. Are you going to be OK with this?"

Jamie let out a soft exhale. "Yeah. Maybe if I learn how to control this magic, I can help stop Malcom and make sure he doesn't hurt anyone else."

"Something else is bothering you." Lylith's tone was soft and soothing.

"What if I fail? What if I was born to be this thing, and I can't do it? I'm already so weak." I pulled her into a tight embrace. I had felt hesitation and tension radiating off her, but that was not what I thought was causing it.

"Jamie, you could never be a failure in anyone's eyes. You are one of the strongest people I have ever met. Whether or not you are an Aura, I don't care. You are the most selfless person I know. I promise that whatever obstacles lay ahead, we will meet them head-on together," I told her.

She looked up into my eyes. "You promise you will never leave me?" she asked.

"I promise I will never leave you," I replied to her.

"Alright," she said. "As long as you are with me, I will try."

I looked toward Lylith, who was smiling at us. Then she turned around and drove out of the parking lot and we were on our way back home.

Made in the USA
Monee, IL
11 January 2022